BOOK DIVA

A AMBITION 2

A NATHAN WELCH EPIDEMIC

A Killer'z Ambition II: New World Order

A Nathan Welch Epidemic

ISBN: 978-0-9887621-3-8

Publisher's Note
This is a work of fiction. Any names historical events, real people, living and dead, or the locales are intended only to give the fiction a setting in historic reality. Other names, characters, places, businesses and incidents are either the product of the author's imagination or are used fictiously, and their resemblance, if any, *to real life counterparts is entirely coincidental.*

DC Bookdiva Publications
#245 4401-A Connecticut Ave
NW, Washington, DC 20008
dcbookdiva.com

ACKNOWLEDGEMENTS

Verily all praises belongs to ALLAH, the creator of all the worlds and everything that exists. We praise him and we seek his guidance and we seek his protection and we seek his forgiveness. Verily whomsoever ALLAH guides, then there is no one to misguide them. I bear witness that there is no one worthy of worship except ALLAH, and Muhammad (PBUH) is his slave and final messenger sent to all mankind. Without the Blessings from ALLAH, none of this would be possible!!

I have to say a few words to the woman who gave me life, Ms. Patricia M. Welch - sorry for the misprint in the first book. Everything I am now as a writer, I owe it all to you. You are a wonderful Mother and a true testament to a caring woman. Your strength inspires me to keep on pushing forward though this storm, even when I want to quit sometimes. I LOVE YOU MA AND ALWAYS WILL!

To Ms. Tiah Short, it took a minute but you believed in me enough to publish my work. Only you, the DC BOOKDIVA, saw something in me and took a chance on it. I'll always love you for that and will forever be loyal to you and the company. I know I may get on your nerves at times with all the phone calls, but that's just me. To all the DC BOOKDIVA authors: Eyone Williams, Kwame Teague/Dutch, Pinky Dior, RJ Champ, Frazier Boy, Darrell Debrew, Ben, and the newest authors signed to the team, please keep working hard so we can lock down the Game and have everybody geekin' to read our projects.

To my man, Eyone Williams, author of *Fast Lane*, *Hell Razor Honeys 1&2* and *Lorton Legends*, keep doing your thing, Homez. You epitomize hard work and constant grinding, and I pray that my work ethic reaches that level one day.

To Arthur Pless, aka Plexman of Bedland Publishing, thanks for the look out on publishing *No TURNIN*. You help further my literary career. As we first ventured down that road, our connection was tested more and more, but when the smoke cleared, you still came through. I am eternally grateful, Bruh-Bruh!

To my lady friend, Ms. Tiffany Cherry, thanks for holding me down during this bid. Even though you fall off at times, I am forever grateful for the way you touched my life, and no matter what happens or who we are with, always know that I LOVE YOU!

To my Sahaba, Alton *Ace Capone* Coles. ALLAH allowed us to cross paths for a reason. I want to say thanks for all your advise, wisdom and knowledge of the business you shared with me. I pray that ALLAH return you to society to be with your wife so you can change some lives in a positive way. I know *Go Hard* will do huge numbers, which should open many doors for Capone's Book Gang. Much love, Ock!

To my family: Sidney Pegram Sr. – RIP, Pops, I still made it work, Morticia P. Gray, Henry L. Welch, Sharon Williamson, Ronnie Williamson, Sidney Pegram Jr., Cousin Lil Paul Dessessow, Bunny, Kia, Corzetta, and to the entire Scott/Warner family: Ms. Vernie, Sandy, Lakisha, Torry, Dirk, Leo, Sheeka, Meeka, Tammy, Yogi, Shamea, Jay T. Warner, Angel Warner, April (RIP), Lonny, Putty, Nu-Nu and Ms. Moosha. Thanks to all y'all for being there for me during this dark chapter of my life. All of you have touched my life and I love you all. Now please, spread the word and help me sell some books!!!

To all the good men around the country doing time in the Feds who have crossed my path during this bid and touched my life- thank you and hold ya head! My Big Brah, Michael Lucas, Andre D.C. Lane, Titus Webster, Henry Lil Man James, Applehead ROB and Jay, Cardoza Swol Simms, Harold Stone, Charles Ford, Colie Shaka Long,Eastgate Fats, Reginald Flathead Belle, Big Vernon Boykins (RIP), Raphael Parker, Madd Dogg Jamal, London Ford, Jermaine Baby J Anderson

(RIP), Sugar Shane, Upshur Bey, Jayvan Big Bug Allen, Marvin Jackson, Jo-Jo Green, Gregory DC Wright, Larry Hagins, Bucky Fields: You a real beast with that pen, Moe, loved *Ultimate Sacrifice*! Keep doing your thing! Samuel Chin Carson, Maurice Lil Moe Fells, Timothy Tim-Dog Hairston, Marquette Cheadle, Azariah Head Israel, Handsome Jamaal, Zap-Out, Marcus, Andre Darden, Wayne Taylor, Lance Big Six Applewhite, Rico, Rome, Cee aka Tuchi Faluchi, John Moyr, Nardo Pixley, Darius Nook Coghill, Shauib, Horsey, Nut, Whack, Fatty, Young Arizona Ron form Tucson who push the black Yukon, Juvenile, Doo-Doo, Wee-Wee, Migo Mike, 3-Stacks Dre, Michael MD Davis, Aaron Davis, Chico, the Picture guy (Hey, get the fuck outta here!) Lil Dion from Butler Gardens, Pierre Mercer, Facemob,Yusef Yu-Yu Odemns, Kofi, Jontay Black Magic

Robinson, Vincent Big Head V Henderson, Pickles, Clifford Milhouse, Marky, Big Tiny, Randy Shaw, Pusshead, Cat Eye KK, Penitentiary Juan from Trinidad, Skeet, Big Roy, Lil swerve, Lil Donny, Hollywood, Fat Ray, Larry Manute Convington, Wild Bill, E.T., and Jamaal Grasshopper Guffey - the best jailhouse book critic ever, you geekin' ma'fucka! Now call a meeting on that!

Yusef (Philly), Lil Nut (B-More), Twin (B-More), Jim Bob (B-More), Lil Black Frank White (B-More), Umfa, Day-Day and all the B-More homies in the system, Jay (Detroit), Debo (Detroit), Poodah (Detroit), Fu (Grand Rapids, Michigan), Mike Ho-Driver Larry (Kalamazoo), Antiowan KD Lofton (Nap-Town), Nate (Gary,Ind.), Special (Boston Latin King), Lil Rob (N.Y.), Pistol (Chi-Town), The Good Rev, Bro. Flamer (Philly), Bro Jalil (Philly Representer for Capone's Book Gang!), my man Weezy F. (OH-10---Get Money Records) HP (MY Brick City homie), Lil Wadu (also out of Brick City NJ), Prophet (Rasta), Big Boogie Down (Rasta), Solo (N.Y.C.), Lil Montrell Jit (out the Raw, aka Riviera Beach, Florida) The Good Chef/Sotre Man, ED Lover (Mt. Vernon, N.Y.), Great Thoughts (N.Y.C.), Danny (N.Y.C), RR (Tex.), Tight White (Tex.), and my Barber Sleepy (Texas). To all the Muslims on their Deen, As-Salaamu-Alaikum, and if everybody else that I have met in my travels, if by any chance I have forgotten you, please sign your name here ______________________, so you won't be left out and be mad at me. I got nothing but love for Thugz.

Finally and most importantly to all my fans, especially my first fans, Ms. Sheba D. B from Dallas, Texas. Thanks for the in-depth review and all your support. Ms. Sunshine 123, thanks for the review, love, and support. Ms. Michelle Renee Rawls, thanks for the solid review and support. Mr. Sharod H Bankston, I really appreciate your review the most because you were my first and that means a lot. Thank you for your support.

To all the fans of the urban street lit genre, you really make it possible for me and other writers to keep doing what they do to entertain you. I really appreciate all the love, feedback and support you gave me on *A Killer'z Ambition Part I.* Without you guys, Part 2 wouldn't have been possible! I am eternally grateful to each and every one of y'all. I hope you enjoy the second installment of the Chronicles of Carmelo.

Please let me know what you think.

Post your comments, inquiries, criticism, and reviews on Amazon.com, DC Bookdiva.com, B&N.com, Goodreads.com, and Facebook.

PRELUDE

"What?" I said in disbelief over the telephone. I was talking to my partner N. He was about to come home in a few days. Well, at least I thought he was. Apparently another rat was willing to come to court and testify against him. "Slim, you sure it's him?" I asked again because I was shocked. The person he was accusing of telling on him had me jive messed up in the head, because I would have never thought that he would switch sides like that. Everybody loved the nigga.

"Yeah, homeboy," N said. "Slim, I'm too close to be getting beat down at the finish line. You need to holla at that nigga for me."

"Ay, say no more. I'ma come over the jail and see you in a few days, a'ight."

"A'ight, bet. Oh, and Riff-Raff say good looking out on that thing. He should be getting some play in court any day now."

"A'ight, well look, Moses. I got my lil man with me right now, so I'm gone. Love you, nigga, and I'll see you in a few days," I said.

"Love you too, nigga," N said and ended the call.

I couldn't believe that after close to twenty-eight months of being out of the game, it jumped up and pulled me right back in. I had been lying low after doing a lot of killing in the city because I messed around and got caught on a surveillance tape by the feds while I was kidnapping a rat lover. The tape was weak, but I wasn't taking any chances, so I just lay low all together. Now I was a father of a healthy two-year-old son, co-owner of a nightclub, CEO of Omerta Press (a small publishing company that specialized in urban literature) and engaged to marry my baby Markita, the sister of a rat who I had to kill a few years ago. Hopefully that skeleton never got out of the closet.

We moved out to Alexandria, Virginia into a nice $400,000 Toll Brothers home to be closer to the nightclub. I made Markita quit college after she had the baby. I had enough money to hold us over for the time being, plus the nightclub was jumping, bringing in tons of money on a nightly basis. I even allowed a few go-go bands to play out there, which really got the club notoriety from people in the city. Now I had to jeopardize losing all that to help out a good man who I really felt deserved to be back on the streets.

This time I would definitely be moving with caution. A few years ago I was reckless and just didn't give a fuck, which cost me my best friend, Aaron. He was murdered because he was close to me and the rat that wanted to kill me dogged him out just to get me to come out of hiding. Aaron's death still hurts to this day because he wasn't in the game. He was just an ordinary Moe – a working man. I knew what I was up against now and I had no plans of going back to prison for nobody. I done tied up all my loose ends so I could finally live a peaceful and normal life, but just like an old timer told me one day, "You never get outta dis shit once you in it, young nigga. The only way out is the graveyard or getting an asshole full of time in the penitentiary!"

I been there and done that asshole full of time in the pen, and believe me, it was nothing pretty at all. I got a second chance after getting back on appeal on a technicality. After handling my business, I just finally got around to living a normal life - until I got N's disturbing phone call. My loyalty to the game and rectifying all the wrongs done to it by rats and fake motherfuckers had me ready to jump back into it full throttle. I knew if I let this rat live, I wouldn't be able to sleep well at night. I know it may sound crazy to some, but the way I came up in the game, staying true to it was the only thing that mattered to me.

If you feel where I'm coming from, then buckle up your seat belts and take a ride with me through a city where it goes down at. A couple dudes are real, but for the rest…yeah, they low down rats.

CHAPTER 1

I drove my car into D.C. with one thing on my mind: killing. I pulled up around Montana Avenue to locate the snitch who had been faking all these years like he was a stand-up man, but the whole time he was a rat wrapped in official man's clothing.

I spotted him chilling in front of the Montana Recreation center with Champ, N's partner. For the life of me I didn't understand why Champ was hanging around this joker if he knew about his unforgiveable sin and betrayal to the game we grew up in. After pulling up to the curb, I jumped out and passed out Big Nate's book, No Turning Back, to a few guys loitering out on the strip.

"Hey, Carmelo…Anthony!" Cornell Best greeted me with a smile, shooting an imaginary jumper, which caused a few guys to laugh. Cornell Best still looked the same with his beady small afro, and he had on a multicolored We R One sweat suit with the new Jordans to match.

I chuckled, gave Champ a nod, and pulled Cornell Best to the side. Once I got him alone from the crowd, I pulled out some cash and gave it to him. "Ay, Slim, I need you to go with me real quick on this move."

"Oh yeah?" he said, giving me a funny look.

"Listen, it ain't nothing serious. All I need is you to drive and I'ma handle the rest. And I'ma break down with you fitty-fitty."

"How long it's gon' take? 'Cause I jive got some shit lined up 'round here."

"Like what? You ain't doing shit but hanging out and bullshittin'. You might as well come drive out there, and you just pay attention so you know how to get back, cool?"

"Fitty-fitty?" he asked, and I figured his greed had him ready to go with me.

"Yeah, nigga, what you gon' do?" I said, sounding impatient.

"Let me holler at Champ real quick."

"Whatever, I'll be in the car," I said and stepped off.

Once I got in the car, I eased my gun out, putting it on my lap while I kept my eye on Cornell Best's body language and the way he interacted with Champ. I felt a little bad about what I was about to do to him because this nigga was loved by so many stand-up men in the city. But I wondered how many would love him if they found out he snitched on N back in the day?

Yeah, his fate was sealed and I had to carry it out, I thought as he returned to my car and got inside.

"Let's do this, man," he grinned, sounding just like Chris Tucker off the movie Friday.

I laughed, but the laugh wasn't sincere. It was just a reaction to keep him comfortable. We talked for a while about what was happening in each other's lives, which repulsed me because I was interacting with this rat and answering his questions like we were cool. Once, when he asked me if I still messed with N, he indirectly told on himself that he was still snitching.

I kept my cool and said, "Naw, Moe, I just be doing me, Slim. I got a few things going on and I don't have time to be going backwards, you dig?"

"Yeah, that's what I was tryna tell Champ, but Slim don't want to hear that shit when it comes to his man N. I mean, you know how that shit goes," he said, making me mad as hell.

I hooked a right on New York Avenue and drove towards the Florida Avenue intersection near the Wendy's fast food restaurant. As I drove Cornell Best to the point of no return, I glanced at him a few times, letting my anger boil over.

"Ay, Moe, get some of that sour diesel out the glove compartment and twist up."

"Nigga, I fuck with joint. I don't do that lil boy shit," he cracked, rubbing his nose.

"Oh, I forgot about that," I said, pulling up to a red light at the bottom of New York Avenue. I looked around to make sure the coast was clear. I spotted a Muslim brother pushing Final Calls and bean pies and used that as my opportunity.

"Ay, Moe, look at that geekin'-ass nigga out there hustling hard for Farrakhan who ain't gon' give him shit but a bunch of speeches and dreams," I cracked, causing Moe to look in that direction.

Soon as he turned to look, I raised my gun quickly and shot him three times in the head. Blood and brain fragments flew everywhere as his head banged hard against the passenger side window. I made a quick right turn and then drove up inside the FedEx mailing depot. I sat there in the car with the dead rat for a minute, feeling nothing - no emotion, nothing. I got out of the car, got a towel from the trunk, and cleaned the blood off the window so I wouldn't get pulled over by the feds while I took the rat to his final resting place.

After handling that, I got back in the car and pulled off. Every time I got the urge, I shot Cornell Best's corpse at close range while I was driving just for the fuck of it. By the time I dropped his body off on the ground in front of the emergency room doors at Washington Hospital Center in Northwest, I had put over thirty bullets holes in the rat, leaving him DOA, which I believe he truly deserved.

CHAPTER 2

After dropping off Cornell Best's corpse, I headed over to the post office to see if I had some mail. When I got there and opened the box, I found that I had tons and I needed a wheelbarrow to take everything to my car. This little fine caramel-skinned sister who worked there asked if she could assist me. Her shoulder-length dreads were dyed fire engine red, just like how that R&B singer Rihanna be rocking her mane. I peeped her hard nipples pointing at me through the white button-down U.S. post office shirt she wore. I could tell those succulent melons she possessed didn't need the assistance of a bra to sit upright. Yeah, Shorty was definitely a prize catch and sexy enough to make gay men rethink their sexual orientation.

"Yeah, I can always use a hand," I told her while checking out her body. Even though her soft round face only scored a 6 in the looks department, she had a full set of pouty lips that I wanted to slide my dick between. Now her ass, that was a perfect 10 all day. She looked at me with her soft brown eyes and smiled as we got out to my car. Shorty had to be about 5'4" and she was thick in all the right places. If I wasn't engaged to Markita, I'd –

"Is that blood?" she asked, breaking into my lustful thoughts and startling me.

I looked down at my clothes and saw a few blotches of Cornell Best's DNA. Damn, this nigga's still snitching on a nigga even after he dead and gone. "Naw, that's how they make these clothes, you know, like somebody been painting," I lied smoothly. "Thanks for your help, Shorty," I said, lusting over her curvaceous frame, which was covered with some tight, dark grey slacks that highlighted the swollen mound of her camel toe.

"You know you be having a lot of mail constantly coming to that box. You not doing nothing illegal, are you?" she asked, raising an eyebrow that was dyed red like her mane.

"Whoa, Shorty, where dat come from? Ay, who sent you?" I asked, getting defensive and ready to crush her ass if she didn't explain herself.

"Nobody sent me. I just want to make sure you straight, 'cause the police just busted this guy last week for having drugs and shit sent through the mail at a P.O. Box."

"Oh yeah? Thanks for the heads up, Shorty, but I don't do shit but publish books."

"Oooh, for real?" she said, getting excited. "I be writing poetry and I just finished up my first urban book."

"Oh yeah? What it's about?"

She smacked her lips loudly. "It's about this girl, right, who was fucking with this big drug dealer, but then he went to jail because some guys told on him, so she went around killing all the guys who told on her boo."

"That sounds like something I'd really love to read," I said. "Ay, what's your name, Shorty?"

"Razetta, but my friends call me Zetta."

"Look, Razett - "

"It's Zetta," she blurted, cutting me off.

"Look, Zetta, I think I'd like to put you on the team - that's if you willing to work hard and make sure your book sells."

"I'll do whatever to get out there. I'm tired of doing this 9-to-5 bullshit," she complained with a lot of attitude.

"A'ight, give me your number and shit and we'll talk about getting you down on the team. But you know I have to have a few people read the book to make sure it's official before I fuck with you, 'cause I'm not just putting out no bullshit," I said, trying to convince myself that this was strictly about business even though my mind still hovered in a state of lust. Shorty was definitely a traffic jam waiting to happen. I mean, she had one of those "DAMN! She phat as shit!" bodies.

"I feel you…I feel you, but I think you gon' like it." She smiled. "Give me your cell phone number."

I gave her my phone and she put her name, number, Facebook page, Twitter page, and e-mail address in there. I looked over her contact information and told her I'd call her within the next week.

"Don't just be saying that, 'cause if you don't call me, I'm not going to let you get no more of your mail," she said in a joking manner as I climbed inside my car.

"One thing about me, Shorty, you gon' learn I always keep my word. It's all we got in this world," I told her before pulling off, heading back out to my normal life in Alexandria, Virginia.

During the entire ride, I couldn't get the meeting I just had with Razetta off my mind. She might be just the person I'd been looking for to carry on the legacy of eliminating all the poisons that destroyed the game. I mean, with a little schooling, of course, I knew I could make her into a beast.

I began wondering what the hospital staff would think once they found Cornell Best's bullet-riddled corpse outside the emergency room.

CHAPTER 3

Nu-Nu walked out of the Superior Court Building feeling invincible. He had just beaten a murder beef and wanted to get back to his hustle. After escaping death two years ago for dealing with a rat, Nu-Nu began hanging over Southeast up on 37th around his uncle, Moe-Styles, who was very well respected around D.C.

One night while hanging out on the block, some guys came through the area shooting up the strip. Nu-Nu ran out of the cut shooting a fully-loaded ACP with a drum magazine at the fleeing car and he got off a lucky shot. The guys that did the drive-by shooting ended up telling on Nu-Nu. To Nu-Nu's surprise, a few guys from around 37th decided to eat that cheese also – the same chumps he tried to protect that night.

Moe Styles eventually found out who was snitching on his nephew and he had them eliminated. After being locked down for twenty-six months and enduring a three week murder trial, Nu-Nu walked away a free man.

Nu-Nu began walking home from the court building, enjoying the sweet air of freedom again. He always wondered what happened to the guy named Carmelo who stormed the uptown dope house he was hustling in that night. Nu-Nu wanted to hook up with him and talk to him about that night, but he didn't know where to start.

I wonder if my Uncle Moe-Styles knows about Slim. He just might, 'cause his ass knows everybody, Nu-Nu thought. He walked a few blocks until he reached Chinatown. While standing in front of the Hooter's restaurant, Nu-Nu got on the public pay phone and gave his uncle a call. Moe-Styles answered on the third ring.

"Yeeaah?" Moe-Style answered in his smooth voice.

"'Sup, Unc? Ay, you know I just got out and I'm tryna come holler at you."

"That's what got your lil geekin' ass in there the first time. You still ain't learned, huh?""Go 'head with that, Unc. I just need to get back right so I can make a few moves."

"Well, right now I'm at the hair salon getting my shit done. After that I'm flying out to Vegas for the fights. You know I gotta see my man Floyd knock some shit out."

"Unc, I need you to get me right before you go outta town so I can be straight by the time you get back."

"Listen, why don't you just wait until I get back and we can do whatever you want?"

"Unc, tomorrow is not promised. I been in for two years and need some change for that weak-ass body. I'm tryna get some bread and fuck some bitches. I have to make up for some lost time."

"Oh yeah? Okay, well meet me up on the Avenue in front of Greenway 'round three o'clock. I should be finished in the hair salon by then."

"Okay, Unc, love you."

"Love you too, young nigga," Moe-Styles said as he ended the call.

After Nu-Nu hung up the phone, he decided to go home and see his mother before he met up with his uncle, even though he knew he'd have to hear her mouth. Nu-Nu couldn't ignore the fact that she made the best food he ever had on earth, and he'd just have to endure her nagging so he could get a good home-cooked meal, which was something he hadn't had in over two years.

****

Somewhere on the Southside of Alexandria, Markita and her son, along with her brother's widow, April, stood at Suede's gravesite. The two year anniversary of Suede's unsolved murder had arrived and they had gone to pay their respects to him. Markita cried for a while, telling Suede how much she missed him, having no idea that her fiancé was responsible for his death. After releasing her pain and sorrow over his loss, Markita stepped back to allow April to have some time alone with her deceased husband.

"Baby, I know you're smiling down on us. I wish you could be here to see your nephew. He's so big and he reminds me of you." April sniffled and her voice cracked a little. "I just want you to know that your legacy will never die. I just wish that you never made me have that abortion, because you could have left a part of yourself here with me and for the world to embrace." April paused, trying to keep it together. "I promise you I will never fall in love with another man. Nobody can ever make me feel the way you did or love how you did.

"Markita and her fiancé really have the club doing fine and I'm working on opening up another restaurant and used car lot with what you left me. I miss you so much, baby. I just - " April broke down crying.

"Momma, auntie cry. Why auntie cry?" little Ray-Nathan asked, pointing at April.

"Shhh…be quiet, baby. Let auntie vent. You stand right here, okay? Mommy will be right back." Markita looked at her son and he nodded, giving her a cute smile.

Markita went to April's side and gave her a comforting hug. "It's okay, girl. Everything's going to be okay."

"I don't think so, 'Kita. I tried to hold it in, but this is killing me inside. He was all I had and he's gone…he's gone." She cried even harder.

Markita rocked April in her arms until she calmed down and stopped crying. After April got herself together, they left a dozen roses on Suede's grave and left the cemetery. Once they got inside Markita's 745 Li BMW convertible drop-top and pulled off, April began asking Markita about her fiancé.

"Oh, he's doing fine managing the club and stuff, keeping me and our son very happy."

"Is that right? I'm so happy for you, girl. At least somebody is happy around here."

"You can be happy too if you move on, girl," Markita suggested.

"I can't ever move on until I settle a few things first, and besides, I really don't think Suede would want me to move on."

"April, I know it hurts, really I do, but you're only depriving yourself of living if you don't move on. I know there's a man out there who – "

"I care nothing about a man who cares nothing about me!" she snapped, cutting her off. "Suede was my everything.

Why you can't just accept that, 'Kita. Damn!" Markita sighed.

"C'mon, April. You're not being rational here.

You mean to tell me that you just intend to spend the rest of your life dickless?"

"Oh My God, 'Kita, shut your ass up," April said, mortified.

"I'm just being real, that's all. I mean, you been celibate for close to three years now?"

"And? So what!"

"I'm just saying. That's why your ass so fucking mean and grouchy all the time." Markita grinned. "You need to get you some."

"But what about Suede? I just wouldn't feel right." She sighed and wiped her tear-filled eyes. "I wouldn't know how to approach a man, let alone open up and trust they ass. Me and your brother have been together since I was a virgin, over seventeen years ago, just me and him," she said. She began telling Markita how she had always wanted children, but Suede always kept telling her to wait until he got comfortable financially. Now she regretted obeying his wishes.

"Look, April, you're thirty years old with no kids and have only been with one man. Girl, you don't know what you missing out on. I'm not saying go out there and be no ho, but you need to go explore the deep blue sea and catch you some dick."

"You stupid." April gave her a weak smile, appreciating what Markita was trying to do for her.

"I'm serious! You need a man to unclog that oven of yours. You probably got cobwebs and some more sh-"

"Okay now, watch it." April smiled, sucking her teeth and pointing a warning finger at Markita. "I mean, how will I know when the time's right to give it up? How long was you with Melo before you gave me up the goodies?"

"Girl, you ain't going to believe this, but we met earlier that day, right? I went to McDonald's to get a bite to eat, and…"

As soon as Markita got inside the fast food restaurant, she felt somebody hugging up on her and groping her from behind. She turned quickly, leaping out the disrespectful and unwanted embrace, ready to kick some ass.

"Nnn-unnh, boy! Excuse you!" Markita stated saucily with her hands on her baby-making hip, while popping her chewing gum. "You can't do no shit like that, boy! You almost got stabbed up in here."

"For real?" Carmelo smiled. "It would've been worth it."

"That's what your mouth say." She sighed, swiping a sandy blond microbraid away from her face.

"Well, I'm not going to apologize for my approach. I had to do something to get your attention."

"Now that you have it, what's next?"

"I'm Carmelo. And you are…?"he asked, grabbing her small, manicured hand.

"Does it matter?" she snapped, snatching her hand away quickly. "All you want is one thing. Once you get it, you'll get missing in action, just like you dogs do."

"How will you know that if you keep playing hardball and don't let me in the door?" he retorted, causing her to smile.

"My name's Markita."

"Now see how easy that was? Now that we're on a first name basis, can you join me for lunch at my table and kick the Bo-Bo with your number one fan?"

"Sorry, baby, I'm in a rush. I have class in twenty minutes. Plus I don't think that your girlfriend would approve of you talking to me." She smirked as if she had just exposed him.

Carmelo smiled and replied, "Markita, my girlfriend has been my hands for the last ten years. I just got out of jail two days ago. Shorty, I'm straight up, no games, no chaser." He added that he liked her and wanted to get to know her on a more personal level.

"That depends, Carmelo," she replied, producing the sexiest smile he'd ever seen.

"Depends on what?"

"If you're still on the same b.s. that got you locked up in the first place, because I'm not with having my time wasted."

"I'm tryna do the right thing, Shorty. Maybe you're the woman I need to steer me in the right direction to help me grow. Will you help me, Markita?" he asked, reaching for her hand again.

"That depends," she said, slapping his hand away.

"Aw shit, here we go again." He sighed.

"Depends on what, Sexy?"

"If I can be the first, only, and last female to welcome you back into society," she said with a seductive wink.

He caught on to what she was saying. "You can do whatever your heart desires, boo."

"And later on that same night, Carmelo came out to my apartment and dug deep up in this good-good," Markita said, getting hot flashes from the trip down memory lane.

After completing the story on how she had met her man, Markita felt her juices oozing down her tunnel, creaming her thong. She suddenly got very horny while thinking about the first time Carmelo made love to her, and she made up her mind to make love to her man soon as she laid eyes on him.

"You for real?"

"Yep." Markita smiled, feeling her coochie tingling. "I need to drop your ass off and get home to my baby." Mmmph, damn, I need some of that dick right now! I can just feel it, she thought. She stepped on the gas pedal some more, picking up a little more speed.

"Girl, you didn't know his ass from a can of paint and you just opened up your legs wide for him. You didn't take the time to get to know him? For all you know, he could have been a rapist, child molester, serial killer, anything," April said, still not believing her ears. She had waited close to a year before giving away her virginity to Suede on her thirteenth birthday.

"Well, he's none of the above you just mentioned," Markita said, getting defensive. "Carmelo's a very sweet and caring man, and FYI, we got to know each other very well after that magical night, and the rest is history. When we get married this year, that will be the icing on the cake to cement our love, partnership, friendship, and parenthood." She beamed, glancing back, and saw her son sleeping peacefully in his car seat.

"Mmm-mmph!" April snorted, rolling her eyes. "I hope you get the fairytale ending you're looking for."

What's that s'posed to mean? Markita thought, looking at April like she'd just lost her ever-loving mind. Markita wanted to pull the car over and curse April's ass out. After giving it another thought, Markita figured that the cemetery visit coupled with the anniversary of Suede's death played a major part in April's stank attitude.

Bitch, I'ma let that disrespectful shit slide this time, but you got one more time to pop slick out the mouth, Markita thought, picking up more speed while driving April to where she lived: Park at Potomac, a neighborhood in Delray, somewhere off Jefferson Davis Highway.

CHAPTER 4

By the time I made it out of my executive luxury home on Quaker Lane after leaving the post office in D.C., it was little after 6 p.m. Rush hour traffic was really a headache. It was a good thing that my home was located right across the 14th Street bridge, about a fifteen minute drive from the District of Corruption.

During the ride home, I received a few phone calls from Safire, my old flame before I went to prison. I ran into her one day while visiting a buddy over at D.C. Jail. She was visiting some guy who ultimately embarrassed her in front of everyone in the visiting hall.

I caught up to her at the end of the visit and gave her some words of wisdom and encouragement. She tried to throw the booty on me again, but I politely declined. We talked for a while after that and I told her that we couldn't ever have sex, but we could work on being friends again.

Apparently, she ate that shit all the way up, because she hasn't stop blowing my phone up in the twenty-eight months since my return to society. I sent her ass straight to voicemail because I wasn't in the mood to hear her begging me to come around her and spend some quality time with her. She knew I had a girl and she still tried to give me the puss. I talked with her from time to time on the phone, but I always managed to avoid going around her because I didn't trust the little head in my pants. I wanted to remain faithful to my fiancée Markita, and hanging around Safire's sexy ass would only cause major problems in my life - something that I didn't need right now.

After entering the kitchen and breakfast area of my 3,200 square foot castle, I breathed a sigh of relief. I was home and I still couldn't believe it. I went from living in a 6x9 prison cell to living in this huge Columbia Brougham stunning five-bedroom home. It had multiple turned gables, a spacious octagonal study with vaulted ceilings, oversized Palladian windows, large family room with a fireplace, a living room next to my study, and a huge center hall that opened up to the second floor overlook. I had another staircase that led up to the second floor from the kitchen, which reminded of how the kitchen area was designed on the sitcom A Different Strokes starring Gary Coleman. We had a powder room downstairs on the first floor, four huge walk-in closets, and my master suite with its own bathroom and sitting room. After Markita got done with the interior decorating, I felt like I was living up in one of them MTV Cribs type of joints. That's a helluva accomplishment for a convicted felon who never finished high school, but sometimes I felt bad for doing the things I had to do to live this way.

Once I reached the octagonal study that I had turned into a home office, I took off my shoes, slipped on my slippers, and headed over to my desk with all the mail I had picked up. After taking a seat in the plush wingback office chair, I began reading every letter. Some letters were inquiries from authors about how they could get their books published by Omerta Press. Other letters came from a few good men who were still trapped in the struggle. Some I knew and met during my ten year prison bid. Others were referrals from those good men who knew about my passion for cleaning up the game that had been overrun and infested with rats.

I opened the fourth letter only to see my old friend, Andre "Dre" Darden's jail photo and a greeting card. I opened the greeting card and smiled at his short missive.

What's up?

I see you done went out there and forgot all about a real nigga, Shorty. I ain't mad at cha' though. It's outta sight, outta mind, huh? Ay, Shorty, I just wanted to let you know I been hearing 'bout you all the way up here in the mountains of Kentucky. All I'ma say is move with caution and trust no one. Holla at me when you can, Shorty.

Much love and respect,

Dre

Damn, I forgot all about him all this time I been home, I scolded myself while conjuring up memories of the wild youngster from Congress Park Southeast who was out at Terre Haute Penitentiary with me. He had an asshole full of time because of three snitches that did the crimes with him, but they didn't hold water and sold Slim out. I couldn't understand how those rats could walk the streets with their heads held high, knowing they committed the ultimate betrayal to the game.

I turned on my desktop computer to check my e-mails and Facebook page to see how many orders I got for Big Nate's book, No Turning Back. Once I saw I had 150 regular orders to fill and a few pre-orders from major book stores like Shiptoinmates.com, Amazon.com and Barnes & Noble, I felt good, which urged me to hit up the Western Union website. I wired some money to Big Nate, Marquette Cheadle, Azariah "Head" Israel, Michael Lucas, Dre, Titus Webster, Samuel "Chin" Carson, Fat Bug, Lil Marvin, Jo-Jo Green, Wee-Wee, and a few other good men to help them cope with the expenses of living in the Federal penal system. I looked at it as the more I gave, the more blessings I'd get in return, and I also could write them off in my taxes for Omerta Press.

One huge blessing came in the form of me selling 8,000 copies of Big Nate's book, working him as the flagship author for Omerta Press, which seemed to be doing fairly good for an upstart small business. Even though Big Nate's novel was doing okay numbers, I needed to give the people something new and refreshing to keep the publishing company in the mix with all the others out there who were saturating the game with a bunch of watered-down bullshit. I really think that chick Zetta might be what I needed for Omerta Press.

As soon as the thought crossed my mind, Markita came sashaying into my office naked as the day she was born. Our son had to be asleep, because that's the only time she walked around the house nude, rocking her 6" inch Cesare Paciotti suede knee-high come-fuck-me boots. She got all her $953 worth and more out of those boots.

"Hey, Baby Daddy, it's feeding time," she said while strutting over to my oak desk. Mating signals were dancing in her eyes. She got right up on the desk and opened up her legs wide, putting the swollen mound of her pussy inches away from my face.

"Feeding time, huh?" I asked, watching her finger fuck herself and rub

her juices all over her clitoris.

"Mmm, yesss, boo. Bon appetit," she moaned and then grabbed my head.

Before I could move, she had pulled my face forward to make contact with her juicy nectar. While using my lips lightly to skin her meaty pussy lips, I had my fingers playing in circles on her budding clitoris. She squirmed a bit, moaning loudly, encouraging my probing tongue to dive inside her pulsating slit…

"Mmmm…ssss…" Markita moaned, licking her lips, while watching me go downtown on her. As she felt my snaking tongue slithering inside her, she slightly adjusted her pelvis and began massaging my head, settling on my ears. Then she grabbed my ears and began humping my face. Moving up, I nibbled on her clit gently and quickly returned back to the meaty fold of her pussy lips. I lapped up one liquid spray after another from inside to outside, up to her clitoris and back inside her oozing nectar.

"Oh my gawd, boo…I'm…I'm…I'm cu-cuummmmiiinnggg!" she shrieked, swinging her legs over my shoulders.

As soon as I felt the ooze of her love juices flooding her tunnel, I lapped them up with pleasure, slurping loudly. I got my jeans down as much as I could from my sitting position while opening her up with my tongue. I explored every fold, sucking her clitoris several times like I was nursing on a breast and trying to extract milk. When I had her at my mercy, I finally eased up to slide my rock-hard manhood lightly up and down her hot, pulsating slit.

"Ssss… Melo…C'mon, baby…Stick it in, baby…Hurry up," she moaned, her eyes wild with lust.

Ignoring her request, I stuffed most of her left breast in my mouth, sucking on her nipple, which was harder than a bullet. I moved to her right nipple and back to the left one as my hands caressed her soft flesh.

"Pleeeasse, fuck me, baby." Her breath caught expectantly as she felt my hard pole inching inside the mouth of her moist coochie.

She rose, resting on her elbows, trying to inch forward, so I dipped inside the swollen mound of her pussy lips. I extracted my steely tube, beating it against the crack of her soft butt cheeks. The more I teased her pussy flesh and sucked on her titties, the more she demanded that I penetrate her love oven.

"I kinda like this better," I teased as she wrapped her fingers around my throbbing hard-on and pumped it several times.

"Boy, you better stop playing with me," she moaned, squeezing my joystick, yanking it roughly towards the mouth of her pussy sheath.

I paid attention to her glassy, lust-crazed eyes. They were focused between her legs, staring at my love muscle, which she had aimed at her slit for contact.

"I been thinking about this dick all morning," she revealed, grinning seductively while easing my pipe inside the weeping mouth of her tunnel.

She was so tight and wet, forcing me to stroke her slow, gently and cautiously, out of fear of climaxing too soon. When I got balls deep inside her thrilling twat and our pubic hairs met, I began churning her sugary walls with my boner like one does when they're trying to make butter from scratch.

"Ssss…ooooh…fuck yeah…fuck yes! Gimme that dick…give me all of it!" she cried, wrapping her legs around my hips and digging her spiky heels in my ass cheeks, urging me on to stroke faster and faster.

Her inner muscles squeezed repeatedly, thrilling my pounding piston to a wonderful tension that ached for release.

"Fuck me, Melo! Beat it up! Ssss…beat dis…pussy up, nigga!" she huffed, hugging me to her, raking her nails up and down my back.

Writhing beneath me, Markita began shaking and crying out joyously. Knowing she was climaxing again, I sank my hammer to the balls and came down on her open lips with a passionate kiss at her next attempt at a scream.

"Mmmm…" she moaned, tongue-kissing me back and pumping her hips back to swallow more of my driving meat into her oozing, suctioning love nest.

When I felt her pulsating walls vibrating and contracting all over my jabbing meat, I couldn't hold back the built-up lust and tension consuming me.

"You want me…to fu-fuck…ya-ya-ARRRGGGHHHHH!" I groaned joyously, feeling my hot splashes of semen rocketing into her well-oiled depths.

As soon as I released my babies inside her tunnel, peace washed over me. I held her in my arms and tenderly kissed her face, her nose, and her mouth.

"I love you, baby, 'cause you da best I ever had," I sang, mimicking that hit single by the rapper Drake.

"I love you more, Baby Daddy." She grinned. "Thanks for the compliment, and I'ma really thank you later on tonight with my special treat after you get off work."

I got hyped, knowing that she wanted to make tongue and mouth crawl all around my love muscle. Even though I was totally satisfied with Markita's freaky lovemaking skills, for some strange reason, that little sexy chick Zetta from the post office stayed on my mind the entire time I was making love to my soon-to-to-wife, which frightened me.

I felt my heart beating wildly against my chest as I tried to ignore the guilt I felt - the kind of guilt that a man feels after cheating on the woman he loves. The kind of carnal thought I was having about that woman Zetta urged me on to imagine myself pounding deep inside Zetta instead of Markita with a hungry appetite and repetitive thunder.

Now I felt like some shit. I hurtled down an emotional sliding board and landed in the sands of regret.

CHAPTER 5

When I arrived at work at Chances nightclub later on that night, I discovered the longest line I'd ever seen. Mostly white, Asian, and Latino women made up the crowd. I forgot all about J-Holiday, the R&B heartthrob, and Wale and his crew coming out to perform tonight. Wale was a rising star on the hip hop scene, trying to bring notoriety to D.C., Maryland, and Virginia, which he called the DMV.

Approaching the front door, I attracted several stares from scantily-clad women. They looked extremely pissed off and began complaining once they saw me walk right pass the 6'8", 330 pound bouncer named Tiny and make my way inside the club.

After entering my gold mine, I learned that all of Big Nate's novels were gone off the glass-encased shelves. I went over to the admission fee window to holler at Kisha, who was responsible for taking the money to gain entry inside the club. It cost $60 to get in, $150 for the party. The fellas were sure to follow in hopes of meeting those sexy women.

"What happened to all the novels, Kish?" I asked over the loud music.

She looked at me a second and then went back to counting money and admitting people in the club. "Oh, them joints flew off the shelves after I told them they get a free copy after paying to get in the club." She paused for a second and then added. "Don't trip on nothing. I added the price of the book in the admission fee, so in reality they paying for the book without knowing."

"How you work that?"

"Well, you know we promoted this thing all over town as $60 to get inside and $150 for VIP? Well, if you didn't buy a ticket before tonight, then I charged their ass $85 to get in and $175 for VIP That way, the $15 for the book is covered, plus an extra $10 for me and you to split."

"You's a schemin' little muppet," I said jauntily.

"What?" she asked innocently and then winked at me. "I just put them under the impression that the book was free as a token of our gratitude for coming out to Chances tonight."

"Yeah, okay," I grinned. "I'ma head on to my office, 'cause I got a lot of paperwork to handle."

"Okay, me and Tiny will be heading up there in a minute to bring you everything the club took in tonight."

"Before or after you pay the artist performing tonight?"

"Where the hell you been at, Melo? I been paid them people two weeks prior to tonight. We do have a business account at the bank," she reminded me, which is why I loved her, because she was always on top of business and never slipping.

"Well, holla at me later on then. I'm gone," I said as I left Kisha to handle her business.

Markita takes good care of all of my sexual needs, but I was jive curious about Zetta. Damn, she had a banging body! I got a slight hard-on just thinking about her perky titties and shapely apple bottom. I was so deep in thought, I never saw the collision coming until I felt the impact.

CHAPTER 6

"Oh my God, I am sooo sorry," I heard the woman saying as I felt her drink splashing all over my $350 cardigan sweater. Then I felt her hand trying to rub it off with a napkin.

My eyes widened in shock as I looked down at her hand smearing the alcohol into the fine fabric. This was the first time I wore the dang sweater. "That's a'ight. You don't have to do that." I sighed, looking up, and swallowed hard. "Safire? Fuck is you doing out here? Your man gonna fuck you up…right after I beat dat ass for spilling your drink on my sweater."

"I'm sorry, Melo," she said, hanging her mouth open in apparent surprise. Her eyes became unfocused like she was walking in a dream. "And FYI, I don't have no man. I told your ass before that I been left his ass," she said, sounding like an irritable and cranky child. Then she gave me a seductive grin.

She sported some black leather pants that looked like a second layer of skin suffocating her plump rump shaker and she had on a bebe T-shirt. Although I had been ducking her for a minute, I now knew why. I knew if the opportunity came along trapping us together somewhere behind closed doors, it was going to be a serious challenge for me not to tap that ass again.

"And why have you been avoiding my calls? I told you that I had something very important to tell you."

"You can tell me now."

"Nope, this is not the place or the time, Melo, and you know it."

"I don't know shit," I said, shaking my head in exasperation. "Look, Safire, I done told your ass we can't ever - ever-ever-ever-ever - be no more than friends," I said in joking manner, sounding like Chris Tucker off the movie Friday, but I meant every word I just stressed to her.

"What?" she yelled as Wale began performing his hit single "Pretty Girls", which pumped loudly all around the club.

I pulled her towards the restroom. We discussed our feelings for each other and figured out how best to remain friends without crossing that "engaging in sex together" line. We talked for close to an hour. She was explaining to me how she wanted to open up a hair and nail salon while I pretended to listen. I was busy keeping my eyes roaming the nightclub. In truth, I really wanted to tap dat ass again, but the way she left me for dead in prison while we were a couple had an effect on me that prevented me from going backwards with her. I could forgive her, but never forget what she had done. Once you crossed me one time, that was your fuck up. If you got to cross me again, then that was my stupidity for allowing you to get that close to me again. So I figured the way I was carrying things with her was cool, because I knew she was geekin' to get me back in her bed, which wasn't going to happen. Suffer, bitch…suffer, I thought as she tried to grab at my crotch area.

I slapped fire from her hand. "Safire, fuck is your problem? I just told your ass!" I snapped, my eyes widening in disbelief over her actions.

"My bad," she sighed dreamily. "I guess I have to blame it on the Goose," she joked, as I backed up a little.

"Well I gotta go holla at my men," I lied, trying to get away from her ass. I let her hold me hostage for most of the night, making me miss most of the artists performing tonight. I didn't want to be rude and just walk away, but I was on the verge after she just tried to feel me up.

"Okay, Melo, but I have somebody that I want you to meet."

"Who?" I asked, getting suspicious.

"Don't trip, boo. You going to love her when I show her to you." She smiled, gave me a kiss on the cheek, and walked off into the sea of people near the front stage of the club.

I watched her heart-shaped ass swaying from side-to-side for a moment until J-Holiday's vocals began invading the club, breaking me out of the trance I'd been under. I looked around for a minute, making sure no eyes were watching. When I felt satisfied that I wasn't being watched, I slipped off to my office.

After reaching my office, I pulled off my sweater and threw it in the trash. I went over to the wall locker, opened it, and pulled out a white button-down shirt. I always kept several outfits in the locker for just in case purposes. After I closed the locker, I had a brief flashback of the night I had killed Markita's brother in this very office. He turned out to be an informant who got one of the men I know a hundred years in prison. Being on the mission I was on two years ago, I couldn't let him live no matter how close I was to his sister. Hell, I was so messed up in the head back then, I would've killed anyone in my immediate family if I knew they ate that cheese.

After cleaning up a little, I headed over to my desk to do some paperwork. As I got focused on handling all the bills the nightclub I had, Kisha and Tiny entered my office, snatching my undivided attention.

Kisha had to be about 5'8" and she had a chubby cuteness about her. Even though she was a big girl, she had an arrogant attitude and swagger about herself that appealed to me. If I ever had sex with a big girl, Kisha would be the one. She had been working at the club every since Suede owned the place. She basically showed me the ropes on how to run things around here. I made her co-manager of the place, giving her free reign to run things how she saw fit in my absence. She was the real reason why Chances nightclub was a huge success.

"This is history, baby," Kisha beamed, dropping the duffel bag on my desk. "It's jam-packed - I mean to its full capacity. If we let any more people inside, the fire marshal is going to shut us down."

"Oh yeah?" I smirked, proud behind what she had just told me.

Kisha and Tiny nodded affirmatively while waiting on my next order. I didn't really have to do a thing but show my face in the place from time to time and handle all the bills. Kisha took care of everything else, from paying all of our employees to marketing and promotional events being held at our club. She always managed to give me all the credit and act like she was following my orders whenever other employees were around, which really made me fall in love with her far as business was concerned.

"Tiny, how many people outside right now?"

"About a hundred and fitty mo', Boss Man," he responded in his deep, country drawl.

Tiny was from Americus, Georgia. He left the small town to attend college in Virginia and play football. He tore his ACL during his third year in school after it was projected that he would go to the NFL. When he tried to return to the gridiron, he kept getting injured, and no owner in the NFL wanted to take a chance on his bad knees. Tiny ended up staying in Virginia, doing odd jobs as a bodyguard and bouncer until he ran across Suede. He had been working at Chances every since.

"Ain't no way possible we can get them people up in here?"

"I mean, we can get about fifty more people in here, Melo," Kisha interjected politely. "But we'll be breaking the law, and if anything happens, your butt is going to be getting sued for years after the smoke clears."

"Fuck it then. Greed always kills, so I guess we're cool on the turn out then." I grinned and told them to give everyone outside half-price coupon for the next time they decided to come out and party at my club.

After they left my office, I pulled the duffel bag closer to me and pulled back the zipper. When I saw all that money spilling out of the bag over onto my desk, I couldn't resist.

"I'm rich, bitch!" I yelled joyously, throwing piles of money up in the air just like LeBron James did with talcum powder before an NBA game.

CHAPTER 7

Four hours later, Kisha and I were closing up the nightclub and hopping inside my Range Rover. Most of the traffic around the club was minimal during the early morning hour. Everything in the strip mall across the parking lot from my club was closed.

A lone Alexandria police cruiser sat in a parking spot at the end of the strip mall's parking lot, probably watching the area on the graveyard shift. Kisha put on her seat belt just as I started the engine and put the SUV in gear.

She looked at me and gave me a wink. "That was fun tonight. I need to throw more shows like that." She smiled. "There was hardly any drama and nothing but fun."

"So that means we're going to expand and open up another spot, right? Kish, I can't be losing out on all that bread we passed up tonight because of some fire code violations. We what's happening, and them people tryna get in and see what Chances about," I said as I cruised out of the parking lot.

"Melo, it's bad enough that I'm doing everything right now. It's going to be too much to open up another spot and get the same business we been getting."

"You putting limitations on your mind, Kish. Sounds like you're content to me."

"I'm not, but if I had a little more help around here..."

"So you gon' blame not expanding all on me, huh? I thought you was cool with our arrangement. You getting paid, so what's the problem?"

"There's no problem, Melo. I just feel like it's not the right time to open up another nightclub. But what we can do is renovate and add on to the spot to make more room."

"You see, that why I love your chubby little mind." I smiled, causing her to punch me playfully on the arm.

"Watch it, sucker! I'm not chubby, I'm plus-sized. Don't get it twisted."

"My bad, Shorty." I laughed, making a right turn on King Street. I followed the street for almost a quarter mile, heading out to Kisha's house in Arlington, VA.

This was the first time in close to a year that I had to give Kisha a ride home after closing the club. She claimed that she had to get her car fixed, but Tiny gave me the 411. He told me that some guy had dropped Kisha off earlier at work and left in her car. Tiny was my eyes and ears around the club when I wasn't around. Some things might get past Tiny, but it was very rare. I figured that Kisha probably let some player-player put the moves on her sexually, and in turn, he was using her for material gain.

A quarter mile and five minutes later, I drove into Arlington and pulled up at a red light. A shiny black Chevy Suburban with gleaming chrome rims and dark tinted windows pulled up next to us. I coasted up a little closer to the intersection to create some space. You know, old habits are hard to break. From being in the streets and pulling moves, I was hip to the fact that a lot of guys got smoked while sitting in traffic, most of the time at a traffic light off the early morning or late at night. Plus the fact that I had close to $230,000 of the nightclub's proceeds from tonight's party sitting in my SUV had me a little paranoid. I was on high alert for any drama and would remain that way until I made it home safely.

The Suburban pulled up alongside us again and I could hear the driver revving the engine, making the huge SUV roar to life. I was itching to run the red light, take the Suburban on a high speed chase, and kill the occupant or occupants of the vehicle. Whoever was behind the wheel of the Suburban had been following us at a respected distance since seconds after we left the nightclub parking lot. Since Kisha was with me, I decided to use a more conservative plan of avoiding the drama and getting her home safely.

"You know anybody who owns a Surburban?" I asked, keeping my eyes in the mirror, hoping whoever was in that SUV didn't try nothing crazy.

"No, why?" Kisha asked as the light turned green. When she saw the Suburban, she unbuckled her seatbelt. "You talking about that Suburban that just passed us?"

I sighed in relief as the Suburban pulled off first. "Never mind. I'm jive trippin' tonight and I don't know why," I said, pulling off, reluctantly following behind the Suburban.

The Suburban suddenly sped up a little and ran the next light just as it turned red. I was sweating from struggling to relax. Probably most of the sweat was from fear. I was on the brink of kirkin' out about that Suburban following me and I was worried about Kisha's safety, my safety, and all the money I had with me.

As we reached the next traffic light, which the Suburban had just run, I saw the driver whipping into a turn in the middle of the street and skidding to a stop. Without warning, the Suburban pulled off, heading straight for us, and I wasn't about to play chicken. I threw the Range Rover in reverse quickly and backed up even quicker. I saw a hand coming out the driver's side window and rapid flashes of gunfire came my way.

"Down! Down!" I yelled a second too late.

Kisha had already hit the floor, balling into a fetal position. I didn't know she could move that quick, I thought as my front windshield crumbled in a spiderweb-like design, making me swerve a little.

"Fuck!" I raged, ducking a little in the cockpit while going for my gun in the stash spot and driving, which was a very hard task.

The Suburban zoomed in on us, closing fast, and rapid gunfire flashed constantly at me. I whipped my vehicle into a dangerous U-Turn, dropped it into the drive gear, and—

BOOOOOOM! The Suburban crashed into my SUV.

Pop-Pop-Pop! I heard the shots steady coming.

Pop-Pop-Pop! Those rapid shots had me ducking as bullets pinged into my vehicle.

"I don't want to die! Please God, help us!" I could hear Kisha praying hysterically from her position on the floor as I pulled off again, taking the would-be assassin on a high speed chase through the streets of Arlington, VA.

I hit a few corners and then took several more turns. Once I got ahead of the Suburban a pretty good distance, I made another quick turn and then hit another side street. I sped down a cobblestone alley and took another turn until I lost the Suburban. The vehicle was nowhere in sight as I sped back towards my house.

"They still chasing us?" Kisha asked me while glancing up.

"Naw, but just stay down there just in case."

"What the hell was that all about? That shit sounded like some Iraqi war stuff."

"Kisha, your guess is as good as mines. I don't know what the fuck just happened." I spoke calmly, hoping it would contain the rage burning me up inside.

Thank goodness I was on point, because if not, I'd be hanging out in the cemetery with all the rats and other people I killed. I heard sirens screaming in the distance and I could see the flash of police sirens two blocks up ahead. I parked immediately because I didn't even want to go through the hassles of explaining what we just went through to these racist VA cops.

"Look, Kish, you 'bout to be pissed," I told her while pulling out my iPhone. "I'm not taking your ass home tonight or ever again."

"You ain't said nothing slick, Melo, 'cause I damn sure ain't riding with your ass ever again! Shoot, I'm too pretty and fly to be dying this young!" she cracked, trying to lighten the mood of the near-death experience.

We sat in the parking spot as several police cars sped past us. I waited for a while and then glanced down at Kisha. "You straight?"

"Yeah, I didn't get shot or nothing," she said, easing back up in the passenger seat.

Damn, I guess guys like me will never be safe anywhere in this country. Karma is a bad motherfucker. It's not biased and it doesn't care who it pays back with a vengeance. After getting shot at tonight, I felt like karma was hunting me down. Two years ago and just recently, I put in some work to eliminate a few rats and poisonous players in the game. The choices I made in life linked me up to this night and the attempt on my life.

Now I had someone out here trying to kill me. But who? I felt like a sitting duck as I called a tow truck and a taxi cab for Kisha.

CHAPTER 8

As Razetta completed the last rep on the sleek-looking pull-up bar bolted across her bedroom door, she had to tell herself to be easy so she wouldn't gas out. Having a banging body took a lot of work. She had three sets left, and then she was through with working out for the rest of the week. She thought about how much she was looking forward to meeting up with Carmelo, whom she hadn't seen in two weeks. He had called her last night and wanted to talk to her about her book. Her brother, Nut, and his friend, D.C., along with Carmelo, were the only people who knew about the book and the plot. None of her girlfriends had any idea that she was actually into writing.

Eventually she'd get around to letting them know about the book - once it came out in bookstores. As she worked through her final set, her mind wandered back to the day she met Carmelo. She couldn't get over how attractive he was. She felt he was also a smooth gentleman with major charm, although he didn't show it during their brief conversation.

Her Blackberry rang, breaking her train of thought. She answered on the sixth ring after completing her final set. "Hey," she said, a little winded.

"I just got the scoop on the nigga Duke - you know, the one who ate that cheese as far as your brother is concerned?"

"For real? D.C., stop playing, boy," she said like she didn't believe him.

"You right," he remarked in an argumentative tone. "Anyway, I'm baking a cake for that nigga today. Care to join me?"

"Join you? Now why would I wanna join you to do something like that?"

"Listen, Zetta, I know you. And I know for a fact that you ain't just come up with the concept of that weak-ass book you writing off the dome. You done got your hands dirty to even have a concept like that."

"Psst, boy, you trippin'!" she retorted.

"You think so? Okay, den tell me this: how come all the guys who snitched on your brother mysteriously got crushed out here in the streets and left for dead with slices of cheese in they mouths? And your brother told me you had that shit in your book months ago and way before them hot niggas started taking dirt naps. Ay, you don't have to answer," D.C. added, catching on to why she suddenly got quiet. "Oh, by the way, it's all love from my end. I watched your lil bad and spoiled ass grow up, and I think how you did your thing really deserves a medal of honor, but I think I should warn you. Never do the same shit when you holla at a nigga. It will only bring dem people to your front door."

"I have no idea what you talking about, D.C., but I'll keep that in mind when I write the sequel to my first book," she said, giving her brother's partner a smooth laugh.

"Yeah, a'ight!" D.C. laughed. "Just in case you tryna holla at this bitch-ass, he s'posed to be at The Farms later on at the Goodman League games."

"Bye, D.C.!" She laughed and ended the call.

Minutes after she hung up, Razetta re-activated her Blackberry and called Carmelo to change up their meeting venue.

"I don't understand. Why do you want to talk business at a basketball game in the heart of the ghetto?"

"It's not just some b-ball game in the heart of the ghetto. This is the Goodman League, boy! That joint be jam-packed like shit, which is another way you can get your hustle on and sell some books."

"You got all the answers, huh?" Carmelo remarked.

"Just for today I do," she replied with a slight giggle. "By the way," she added, thinking that it was to her advantage to get the bar understood between them, "I mean, don't take this personal of nothin', boo-boo, but just because you're interested in publishing my book, does not mean we can ever mix business and pleasure. So if we are going to work together…"

"I respects that one hundred percent, Shorty, and I'ma keep that in mind. So I'ma go pick up some books for our meeting. Do you need a ride, or you cool?"

"I'll see you there around four o'clock, 'cause that's when most of the people be out there."

"A'ight."

"Okay, see you soon," she said and ended the call.

I gotta be extra careful on this one, she thought, resting her chin on the knuckles of her balled up fist. D.C.'s old ass could be trouble, acting like he hip to me, and the last thing I need is niggas all up in my business.

CHAPTER 9

Back in the day, Razetta's mother left Southwest seven years after giving birth to her first born, Columbus Daniels, when she got public assistance to move into a house around Trinidad Northeast. Columbus met the original knuckleheads and troublemakers on the block - D.C., Roy, Skeet, Dave, and Juan - at the Trinidad recreation center.

Being the new kid on the block, Columbus wasn't accepted into the fold so easily, but he hung around the rec center so much, fighting many battles over sports and other minor things, that he earned the nickname Nut and their respect in the process. Nut began hanging out on the block with the fellas, but had his sights set beyond just loitering and joyriding in stolen cars. He wanted to escape poverty. Despite his mother living in a big house, they were still dirt broke for years - until the crack explosion in 1986.

In spite of all the hoopla and activity centered on the War on Drugs campaign from the Reagan Administration, D.C. was in the midst of a growing crack epidemic in 1986. The streets were filled with the unemployed and the hungry, and there were massive wars taking place in the inner city for drug turf.

Wanting to get in where he fit in, the fourteen-year-old hooked up with a few guys who sold drugs for Jaybo Redmonds on Orleans Place, getting a job as a look-out. The job lasted for six months with all-expense-paid shopping sprees in Georgetown and Virginia. Being a look-out was a rough, turbulent task in the dead of winter and it was all work and no play in the summer. Nut hated every day of it, but he never lost focus, for every day brought him nearer too his dream of being a boss.

As Orleans Place became popular and flowing with money and drug activity, a lot of people changed. Many of the hustlers began branching off to do their own thing in other parts of the city, miraculously putting Nut into the picture.

When Jaybo Redmonds saw his work force depleting, leaving him stuck with tons of cocaine to move, he began giving it out in plentiful sums to guys who stayed loyal to the block. Nut was one of the beneficiaries of Jaybo's generosity.

Nut returned to his old neighborhood in Trinidad and approached some guys he had grown up with and a few others who were hustling out there. D.C. and Roy were already established in the game, guided Nut through the selling and breakdown process of moving weight. Soaking up the game like a sponge, Nut ran with it until he had a lot of guys hustling for him on Montello Avenue and Oaks Street, aka M&O. While many young men really flourished in the drug trade in 1988, Nut used his money to spoil his newborn sister, Razetta, feed his family, and remodel his mother's home. For several years, Jaybo kept Nut's plate filled with kilo after kilo, sponsoring him as he did his thing in Trinidad. Eventually, the high-grade cocaine quality caught everybody's attention and Nut blew up like the World Trade Center, killing the streets. Nut eventually manipulated his way into controlling a whole city block in Trinidad, becoming a boss before his eighteenth birthday.

Then out of nowhere, Nut's world came crashing down around him. His connect, Jaybo Redmonds, got arrested by the Feds and went away for good. Nut watched, mesmerized that Jaybo's criminal activity and generosity revealed the grand spectacle of a cocaine drought looming heavy over the city. The key ingredients to violence, a lot of backstabbing, double crossing, kidnappings for ransom, and a high murder rate beyond anything Nut's imagination could fathom had arrived.

Adapting to the ways of violence, Nut, Roy, and D.C. began controlling most of the drug trafficking in the Trinidad community, creating a reign of terror around Trinidad as they supplied the younger drug dealers that they liked. But they extorted, robbed, brutalized, and killed drug dealers and residents of Trinidad that they didn't like and who got in the way of their illegal income. By 1992, Nut had already been in and out of jail several times for assault and battery, but those setbacks didn't make him change. In fact, they made him meaner and more violent. One night, Nut went to jail for giving a concussion to a crackhead man, whom he beat about the head with an aluminum bat.

Nut's addiction to violence got him sent to D.C. jail, where violence and murder ran rampant. Nut fit right into that atmosphere. He was as aggressive and mean as any veteran convict, so he meshed well when he teamed up with Titus Webster, another crazy trigger-happy gangster from Uptown. Nut originally met him while doing time in Oak Hill Juvenile Facility, but he could never get the perfect opportunity to hook up with him on the streets.

Once they hit the streets, Roy, Nut, and D.C. began dealing on a large scale. They protected their rackets by bribing some older residents - paying their mortgages, light bills, and water bills. They brutalized the hustlers who didn't work for them, which was Titus's specialty, and the only time he came through Trinidad was to assist D.C. and Nut.

The drug dealers were so scared of Nut, Roy, D.C., and Titus that they began calling the police on them. A vice cop named Mitchell Bimbo, who patrolled the Trinidad area, asked that the crew of four be investigated for murder, extortion, and racketeering. In the weeks following his request, Bimbo was ordered to assemble a task force within the precinct to take down the Trinidad crew, and it would eventually cost Nut his freedom.

In 1996, after four years of investigation, the captain pulled the plug on Bimbo's investigation for the lack of evidence gathered over the course of four years. In 1999 – and, coincidentally on Nut's little sister, Razetta's ninth birthday - an anonymous drug dealer went to the police because he was tired of being extorted by Nut just to hustle on the Montello Avenue and Oaks Street.

Vice cop Bimbo took the informant's complaint and went against everything in protocol in his precinct and decided to take the Trinidad Crew down himself. On strict instructions from Bimbo, the dope boy - later revealed as John Queen - was told to approach Nut wearing a wire and express to him that he wasn't going to pay any more extortion fees.

"Oh yeah, that's how you feel?"

"I'm just saying, Slim, I — AAAAAAHHH!" He screamed like a bitch after Nut shot the informant in the ass, unconsciously taking the bait that Bimbo sent at him.

After violently attacking the informant, Nut threatened to kill him. "And if you think I'm playing, don't have that money in my hand in a few days. I'ma show you what I do to niggas who don't pay their taxes."

The informant agreed to pay under duress. Bimbo went back to his supervisor with the new evidence and another investigation on Nut, minus his Trinidad cronies, had been opened.

Bimbo would give the informant John Queen marked money to pay Nut on a weekly basis. While the cops built their case on Nut via wiretapping and monitored audio and video footage, they caught wind of something deeper. During a phone call with Devin Gray, a reputed drug-trafficking boss, cops heard Nut discussing a murder plot, but they couldn't be sure because of the slang and Ebonics used.

They began following Nut like a shadow. In mid-2004, after an outing to a nightclub, Police watched Nut approach Lendell Hardy from behind as he talked to another unidentified male on the corner at a phone booth. As Lendell Hardy turned around, Nut fired several shots through his face and head, killing him instantly. Nut then killed the unidentified man as well - what prosecutors later said was a need to erase a potential enemy.

After the police confirmed the death of Lendell Hardy, a government informant who was hotter than the bullets that killed 2-Pac, they decided to get an arrest warrant and take Nut down before he killed anyone else.

Police arrested Nut and Devin Gray on crimes ranging from drug conspiracy to conspiracy to commit murder. Surprisingly, nobody testified against Devin Gray, but there was a parade of drug dealers and other guys Nut took for bad in the streets coming into court to testify against him. Devin Gray won his motion to get a separate trial and eventually beat all the charges on the indictment.

Later on in 2006, Nut got his with a superseding indictment by the Federal government accusing him of Obstruction of Justice and killing government witnesses and informants along with extortion, drug conspiracy, racketeering, and murder. D.C., Roy, Devin Gray, Nut's mother, and his eighteen-year-old sister Razetta came every day to view the two-month-long trial and see all the people who were testifying against him. Nut received a double life prison term plus 110 years to be served consecutively.

After Nut's downfall, Razetta's world collapsed. While growing up with a violent brother who gave her everything her little heart desired, Razetta viewed Nut as the nicest guy in the world, and he could do no wrong in her eyes.

Incapable of getting what she wanted after Nut's arrest, young Zetta quickly learned to become an aggressive and smart woman who stood on her feet. She figured that being timid and weak was a surefire way to get swallowed up whole by the cold-hearted world that destroyed her big brother.

As Razetta began venturing out into the streets and going to Go-Go's, many approached her asking stupid questions about how many murders her brother actually committed. Sometime she had difficult life experiences being the sister of a known killer/thug. There were some things that Razetta just knew about and heard about that she felt no need to ask her brother about. When Nut put her on point about the guys who snitched on him out of fear, she understood, which allowed her to decipher the fake cowards from the real thoroughbreds.

Razetta learned that certain actions speak what the mouth always tries to hide. She used that common knowledge in her quest to get revenge against everyone who ever betrayed her brother. With the code of honor and loyalty tattooed over her heart, Zetta believed wholeheartedly that silence was golden. She believed that you never open your mouth to tell on your friends, period.

By the time Zetta turned nineteen years old, she had developed a deep-seated hatred for anyone who cooperated with the police. She wished death on them and prayed to God at night that he'd make her dreams come true.

CHAPTER 10

Street style b-ball has invaded the nation, but the show-stopping, high-flying dunking and ankle-breaking crossover dribbles that World Famous Rucker Park made an infamous Hot Line. D.C. Natives turned it up a few notches, making the Goodman Summer League around Barry Farms a Hot Song!

In town on vacation from the NBA, D.C. natives Kevin Durant, superstar of the Oklahoma City Thunder, Michael Beasley of the Minnesota Timberwolves, and Delonte West of the Cleveland Cavaliers received less than a welcome home as they entered the court rocking black and white "We R One" jerseys, sponsored by Steve Francis – a team many in the home crowd hated.

"Aww, I see somebody done flew the stars in here! Aww shit, now who we got on this mob in the world famous BF Coliseum?" Miles stated in his signature tone that drew laughter amongst the crowd.

"I see you, Durantula! Ah, look at D. West…ay, ay, you still tapping dat ass and playing Lebron's stepdaddy?" Miles laughed, drawing responding laughter from the crowd. "We're all witnesses!" he added, causing Delonte West to shoot him the middle finger before going into his stretches.

I couldn't help but laugh hearing that jokes blaring over the PA system as I tried to get through the entry gates leading to the courts. Security guards were patting down numerous dread-sporting young men and women for weapons as DJ Big John got busy on the 1's and 2's, spinning that love go-go music for the waiting crowd, street ball lovers, and NBA fans.

"Ay, ay…I must remind y'all, man, no gambling today or packing that shit, 'cause I just got word that dem people sliding through and you know they looking for a reason to shut down the Goodman League, so y'all be careful, man," Miles cautioned, basically alerted everyone in attendance that undercover jump-out squads were out in full swing, looking to lock somebody up.

"Aww, shake it like a white girl. Shake it! Shake it!" Miles sang, sounding like Sugar Bear from E.U. as the classic Rare Essence "Get Cha' Freak On" began blaring through the speakers. Several make-up-caked and scantily-clad females sitting in the bleachers rushed to center court and started shaking their money makers. Despite the makeshift strip club demonstration, the crowd stared on, seemingly unfazed. They were primarily here to see the headliners, D.C's adopted sons Gilbert "Agent Zero" Arenas and Caron Butler up close.

Before the spotlight shone on the Goodman League, things were all about The And-1 MixTape tours and world famous Rucker's Park until the late 90's. In 1998, only a year after returning to D.C. from serving in Iraq, Miles began painting the rims and holding pick-up games there every weekend, trying to bring back the fun he used to have while growing up in Southeast. Kirk Smith, a well-known basketball legend, came out every weekend, causing quiet riots and gossip for days until the next game was scheduled on the Southeast court. Miles, along with Kirk Smith's dazzling moves, drew throngs of wild teens to the games every weekend with no radio promotion at all. Miles used to visit high schools and drug-and-crime-infested neighborhoods all over D.C., passing out flyers. With audiences larger than the ones he'd played in front of at the infamous Urban Coalition games and Kenner League games in Georgetown at his disposal, Kirk "Trouble" Smith showed his ass, dropping sixty-five points, earning fans with the Jordanesque performance.

Before long, word spread like wildfire, attracting even more fans and b-ball players from all over the nation. Even the NBA Cares foundation stepped in with the help of Gilbert Arenas and the Washington Wizards, who renovated the court with new asphalt and breakaway rims.

Miles saw the potential in the events and began charging each team $500 to enter the tournament. He'd give the Barry Farms $1,500 for the use of the court and keep the rest to buy trophies for the MVP players of the tournaments and championship trophies for the last team standing victorious. When local disc jockeys from 93.9 came on board, they attracted even more fans. Local go-go bands came out to perform at the halftime shows, raising the level of the Goodman League to the national spotlight and making it an annual must-see event.

I entered the court area just in time to see Agent Zero, Caron Butler, and Sam Cassell take the court along with the Kirk "Trouble" Smith. They led the rest of the Shooters Sports team to the lay-up line under the loud cheers from the positive energy of the frenzied crowd, which looked and dressed like members of BET's 106 and Park studio audience.

I couldn't believe this shit. For years, men from D.C. paved the way with go-go music, creating our own style of fashion only to have it forgotten by all these Lil Wayne wannabes and groupies. It's a shame what happens when weirdo rappers like Lil Wayne start influencing the youth in D.C. I even saw a few guys in my early 30-something age bracket rocking dreads and tight-fitting Ed Hardy T-shirts that showed off their tattoos and ripped up jeans with biker chains hanging from their belts to their front pockets like they were rock stars. I'm glad I came up in an era when snitchin' wasn't what's in. I shrugged off my feeling and took control of this opportunity to sell some books.

Suddenly a random outburst came from the crowd, as if someone was challenging Kevin Durant's thoroughness, but the quiet NBA cooker, who also went by the name Durantula, ignored the hecklers. With little fanfare, the We R One made up of mostly NBA and D-1 college players began doing dunks and pretty reverse lay-ups in the lay-up line.

I walked around the court, marveling at the jam-packed crowd in attendance. You'd think Ricky Rozay, Lil Wayne, or Jay-Z was waiting to perform - not some basketball players.

As soon as I went to try to sell a book, I got put on display by Miles, the master of ceremonies.

"Whoa...whoa...whoa, baby! This ain't Barnes and Noble, but we respect the hustle up here in BF Coliseum. Just make sure Old Miles gets his cut before you leave." he said, causing a bunch of people to look at me and laugh.

When I turned to check his ass, a few young guys began asking to look at the book so they could buy them. Fuck he mean give him his cut? He got me fucked up, I thought as I got my hustle on, selling out the 100 books I brought inside the court area. Other women and men were asking to buy the books and I told them I had a few more copies out in the trunk of my car. I walked around to find a seat and eventually saw Zetta entering the court, rocking damn near next to nothing.

"Dayyum!" I said, biting my fist, loving the bold entrance she made in a hot pink Lycra body suit that looked like stretched latex covering her mouthwatering and traffic-stopping curves.

She crossed the crowded court, heading in my direction. My first thought was that maybe she was the headlining video vixen in a music video being shot, because all eyes were definitely on her, from the smattering of onlookers standing around the court to the b-ball players on the court who stopped warming up to get a good look at her.

I turned a speculative eye on Zetta as she approached me with the most enticing strut ever. When she reached me, we shook hands automatically, exchanging benign pleasantries. With her, I knew there was no point in jumping right into business. Plus she was a cutie I admired, even though our relationship was strictly business.

"So this what you wear to an official business meeting?" I finally said as the basketball got underway.

"I don't see nothing wrong it," she said, catching D.C. engaging in a conversation with Duke. "Plus I never been to an official business meeting before. I'm only twenty years old," she revealed, smiling politely.

I saw her head jerk to the side and I followed her movement as she turned her head in the direction of the court, watching the game. I could feel my manhood start to swell in my cargo shorts. In one of those tingling sensations of lust, my gaze flickered to the bright pink V in the crotch of her body suit, which showed off a bulging camel toe. I focused on the sight with a curious sense of what it would feel like to tap that ass.

"What you looking at?" she asked, snatching me out of my lustful daydream.

"What am I looking at?" I repeated, somewhat stuck at getting caught looking at her.

"Yeah, what are you looking at?" she pressed.

"That tight-ass bodysuit you're wearing, which tells me that you can't possibly have the book on you."

"Nice save," she grinned, causing me to smile.

It felt natural to be around her. I mean, I wanted to tap that ass, but it wasn't no press type thing because I had a woman at home and Shorty probably had a man in her life. I wasn't into chasing women anymore. I got something special in Markita. "Anyway, where's the book at, Shorty?"

"At my house, probably collecting dust," she said in a carefree type of way, puzzling me.

She just stressed to me how she wanted to get her book published. Now, when it came time for her to show and prove, she didn't bring the book with her. Interesting. She might not be as hungry as I thought she was. "Well, what good is that if you don't bring it out to a meeting so I can check out your work," I stated in a sarcastic tone, which caused her to sigh. "I mean, you do want to put the book out, right?"

"Yeah - "

"OOOOOOOOHHH!" The crowd exploded in an uproar as Kevin Durant pulled up from half court, nailing a three-point jumper like he was shooting a lay-up.

"Oh my goodness, baby!" Miles hyped up the players while walking back and forth on the court with his play-by-play broadcast. "Did you just see Durantula pull up for Da swish! Yes, in de face, baby, in de face!" He pointed the microphone at Caron Butler, who was supposed to be guarding him.

From that point on, I decided to ease back from rapping to Zetta and just enjoy the festivities of what would go down as one of the best double overtime classic games played at the Goodman League.

CHAPTER 11

After the first game ended, I left the court to head to my car to grab some more books. Zetta followed close behind me like she was my bodyguard. We began talking on the way to my ride and she came clean with me, admitting that she wanted to come to the game today because she wanted to meet somebody.

"Did they show up?"

"Yeah, but I just wouldn't feel right just leaving you out here all alone just to talk to 'em. That would be rude, don't you think?"

"Damn, Shorty, you could've taken a rain check with me. It ain't that serious," I told her, not really that mad about her using me because I did make some money out of the deal by selling a few novels.

"I know, but I did want to meet you today," she said in an innocent tone, causing my manhood to twitch. What is this little bitch, doing to me, I thought.

Then I noticed this rat exiting the court area, walking with a light brown-skinned older guy who looked like he could be a drug connect. I remember the bitch nigga Duke from www.Ratz.com while reading the website the other day, confirming Cornell Best's ultimate betrayal to the game. While scrolling through the site, I had seen the picture of the guy that was walking towards me right now. He had testified in a 2002 shooting he had witnessed, which eventually got a solid man sixty years in prison. Now he was out here living life without a care in the world like it was all good.

Damn, how can I crush this rat out here in front of all these people and get away? I wondered as the older guy headed towards me and Zetta with the rat by his side.

After they reached us, Zetta gave the older guy a warm hug. "What's up, Uncle D.C.?" she greeted him. "Who's your friend?" Zetta asked as I looked around, trying to see who was actually watching this area of the parking lot.

We were standing over by Gilbert Arenas's ivory white four-door Bentley GT with the factory rims on it. Storman Norman's van was also parked in the vicinity. It was a bad area to kill the rat, so I decided to lay on him and watch his ass until I got the perfect chance to strike.

"Oh, his name's Duke, but we ain't like so. Slim just wanted to come over here and holla at the chick who was shutting shit down in the pink body suit."

"Oh yeah? What he want to holla at me about?" Zetta replied like I wasn't even there.

I was glad, because the less people I knew, the less could identify me for what I was about to do. "Ay, Zetta, I'm 'bout to slide over on the court to pump some more of these books," I said.

"Okay, I'll be over there in a minute."

"Ay, D.C., support Slim's hustle," I heard her saying as I walked away. "You know I can't get my book published by him if his books don't sell."

"I don't be into reading dem weak-ass urban books," I heard the older guy saying as I headed over near the court.

"D.C., stop playing, boy!" I heard Zetta getting loud as I got closer to the fence.

Seconds later, I heard D.C. calling my name, yelling for me to stop. Once he caught up to me, he asked to check out a book. I gave him one, glancing back at Duke's hot ass. He was dying today if I had something to do with it. Even though I didn't deal with the guy, Duke snitched, and I still felt it was my duty to exterminate the rat.

"Ay, I know this fat-ass nigga, Big Nate," D.C. remarked. "He fuck with my man Titus."

Titus? How he your man? I thought, focusing my attention on D.C. "You and T cool?"

"Yeah, me and Slim go way back. He on any day status now. He s'posed to be getting out probably in a few months."

"Yeah, I heard that too," I said nonchalantly, not wanting to reveal too much. I knew the exact date my big homie was coming home, but I wasn't going to tell this nigga. He could be an old enemy or anything. I played it casually, preferring to be safe instead of sorry for having loose lips. That's how my partner Aaron got killed: by fucking with a chick who had loose lips.

"Yeah, next time you talk to Titus, just ask him about me, he'll hip you - "

Boom! Boom! Boom!

The sounds of gunfire cut D.C. off, making me hit the ground instinctively and glance around. I looked over by my ride and saw Zetta lying in a fetal position on the ground near the rat she had just been talking to. His brains were splattered all over the pavement, and he was drenched in the blood oozing from his dome.

Man, let me get the fuck out of here, I told myself, seeing everybody in the area running for safety. I saw D.C. running off with the book he wanted to buy and thought, Fuck it. I'll just have to pay for it out of my pocket. I dashed over to my ride and saw that Zetta wasn't hit. She looked up at me with fear in her eyes as I helped her to her feet.

"What happened, Shorty?" I asked, opening my door.

"I don't know," she stammered. "One minute we was talking, and the next minute somebody knock dude's shit loose," she said, backing away from me.

"Where you going? C'mon!" I told her.

"Go on. I'm fine. I got my motorcycle up here," she said as she took off running towards a flaming red Kawasaki Hyabusa. I got stuck for a second watching her ass jiggle in the body suit as she ran.

As soon as I started my car to pull off, a cop screamed for me to get out of the vehicle. I looked over and saw that he had his gun pointed right at my head. At that moment, I realized the second I spent lusting over Zetta might have gotten me into some bullshit I couldn't get out of.

CHAPTER 12

After easing out of the car, I was shocked to see so many police already on the scene. My adrenaline started pumping and I got nervous with the quickness. The 6'4" husky undercover cop did a quick pat search on me with one hand before walking me in the direction of his car at gunpoint.

"I see you back up to your old tricks, huh?" he said, forcing me inside the backseat of the Cadillac DTS.

"Listen, I can explain, I—"

"I don't want to hear shit from you, you murdering sack of shit! Yeah, I know all about you. You like to play with gasoline water guns," he said and then slammed the back door shut, making me scared as hell.

He got in the driver's cockpit, started the engine, and then pulled off, driving me down Wade Road towards the train tracks around Barry Farms. I quickly scanned the vehicle and noticed his police badge swinging from the rearview mirror. He also had a walkie-talkie and a police radio transmitter inside the car.

"Yeah, I know all about you," the cop kept repeating, making my heart pump even faster in my chest.

I'm about to go down over some bullshit that I didn't even have shit to do with, I thought as the cop pulled me out the back of the car and slammed me against it roughly.

"Fuck is you doing?" I asked, holding my hand up in surrender as he patted me down again, but this time he went inside my pockets and pulled out the wads of cash I had made from selling the hundred and twenty books at the game before the shooting.

"How much money is this?" he asked, shoving it inside his pockets without waiting on a response.

This nigga on some straight up bullshit. Damn, I wish I had my gun on me right now! I'd let his bitch-ass have it, I thought while trying to explain where the money came from. "Listen, I was just sell—"

"Didn't I tell your bitch ass I didn't want to hear shit!" he raged, sending a misty spray of saliva particles into my face. I finally felt like my time in society had truly come to an end.

Surprisingly, the undercover cop opened up to me, telling me his name, which was Gamble, and how much he knew about the gasoline murder I had committed a couple of years back in these same projects. I still denied everything. He'd have to prove it in a court of law. As I continued listening, he dropped the hammer on me.

"I was beginning to leave well enough alone until I saw a photograph of a suspect in the Washington Post who looked just like the description I received on the night of that murder. I even had a composite sketch done. It wasn't the best, but it does bear an uncanny resemblance to you. And you know there's no statue of limitations on murder," he emphasized.

"If you got all this evidence on me, then why am I still standing here with no handcuffs on?"

"You haven't gotten the picture yet?"

I shook my head no.

"Well, let me break it down for you, sleaze bag. I have several descriptions of you from eyewitnesses who were out and about the night of the murder you committed, and three of those witnesses are very reliable informants who owe me favors. Checkmate." He grinned.

Damn, I didn't expect that shit, but I knew karma wanted me badly and had finally caught up to me for all the shit I had done and got away with. "I have no clue what you're talking 'bout, Detective. I was just selling some books at the basketball game when the shooting happened."

"Oh, really?" he remarked like I was lying through my teeth. "Well, that's not what my eyes seen." He smirked and I saw an evil look in his eyes. "I'ma tell you what I seen. I saw you shoot that man at point blank range after some type of argument y'all were having and toss the gun down here on the train tracks in the woods somewhere before I apprehended you. Now you tell me whose testimony is going to hold up in a court of law – mine or yours? You're some two-bit punk who is already a suspect being sought for questioning in connection to an unsolved murder and kidnapping case from over two years ago."

I hated the way his bitch ass had me boxed in with no room to weave away from his blows. This is exactly what I didn't need and had been ducking for the last two years: heat on my ass. All I could do now was hope that I come out on top at court. This altercation really had me fucked up in the head and I couldn't fault anybody but myself for trying to look out for Zetta.

"Man, what you want from me? I'm just out here tryna earn an honest living."

He smacked me with his gun. I dropped to my knees and held the knot that was quickly growing on my left temple.

"And if your ass wants to keep earning a living and being free out here, I think you need to start doing exactly as I say from this day forward."

CHAPTER 13

Nu-Nu stood a few yards away as the coroner pulled up to cart off the body. Nu-Nu had been at the game when the shooting happened, out chick hunting. After the chaos died down a little, Nu-Nu saw a man aiming a gun at Carmelo right before kidnapping him. Nu-Nu couldn't believe his eyes. After he had escaped the crack house of death two years ago in the midst of

Carmelo's murderous rampage. Nu-Nu hung around, lurking in the shadows, wanting to see who survived the shoot-out.

When he saw the albino-looking man creeping out the back door of the crack house, Nu-Nu automatically figured him to be Carmelo, the crazy guy who yelled out Twan's name, alerting everyone in the house that Twan was a rat. Nu-Nu always thought about what he'd say to Carmelo if and when he saw him again. When the day finally arrived, somebody kidnapped him. Nu-Nu spotted a curvaceous woman sitting on a motorcycle and decided to take his shot to see if he could get inside those panties.

Zetta saw the 5'8" tall, skinny, pretty boy approaching her with a swagger like he knew he had a shot. She wasn't thinking about him. She was worried about Carmelo and wondering why the man kidnapped him at gunpoint.

Good thing I didn't go with him, 'cause I'd probably be with his ass right now, or even worse, hanging with the main man in eternal rest over by Carmelo's car, she thought as the skinny, pretty boy spoke to her.

"I'm fine," Zetta said with a stank attitude, letting him know that she didn't want to be bothered.

"Oh yeah? You don't sound like it. I mean, is it me, or is it the heat that's irritating you?"

It's your pressed ass, she wanted to say, but she kept her thoughts in check. "It's neither one. I'm just waiting on my boyfriend, that's all, and I don't want to be arguing with him over no dumb shit like who you is and why I'm talking to you," she lied. Then she added, "He's very jealous, you know."

I can see why, with all that ass you got, Nu-Nu thought, giving Zetta a quick salute. "I can definitely take a hint, Shorty. I'm gone, but you enjoy life," Nu-Nu said politely, then he busted a U-turn.

As soon as Nu-Nu turned on his heels, he spotted Carmelo walking towards his car, rubbing his head. Nu-Nu put some pep in his step, trying to catch up to Carmelo before he left the area.

Nu-Nu had no idea that Zetta was watching his every move.

CHAPTER 14

"Ay, Moe! Ay Moe! Let me holla at you for a second!" I heard somebody yelling as I got closer to my car.

When I turned to see what was happening, a knot formed in my throat and it was hard for me to swallow. Give me a fucking break! What's this, the ghosts from my past day or something? I wondered, looking at the little guy who was hanging out with Twan's hot ass the night I stormed Twan's crack house and murdered everything moving.

Twan was the creep who snitched on me, getting me life in prison. After I got out on a technicality, I went on a hunt for Twan. Before I could eliminate him off the face of the earth, Twan killed my best friend, Aaron. I always wondered what happened to this nigga who was approaching me right now.

I was so fucked up in the head about the undercover cop, thinking about him telling me all the dirt he had on me and how he just got up and let me go. I didn't know what to do. When the detective took my driver's license and logged down my information, I knew I had to get my family out of that house as soon as possible. After returning my license to me, he gave me his cell phone number with strict instructions to call him in three days.

Yeah, right, picture me calling him! I'd be long gone by then on some catch me if you can shit. "Ay, Moe, can I holla at you for a minute?" he asked in a cordial manner.

The police and coroner were inches away from us, still hanging around my car, so I felt pretty safe that this guy wasn't crazy enough to smoke my boots right now. That would be outright stupid on his part. "What's up, Slim?" I asked, a little apprehensive.

"Look, Moe, I waited two years to get this off my chest…" He trailed off, looking around, and I began wondering if he didn't care who was around to see him get his revenge. I didn't know what was going through his head. I might've killed somebody in that house that he was close to or was his kin.

"I just want to thank you," he said, extending his hand to me, gesturing for a handshake. "You know, for putting me on point about that creep-ass nigga Twan."

I reluctantly shook his hand as he went on to tell me how he had waited around the house and saw me right before I made my getaway. Even though he came in peace, I still looked at him as a loose end.

Was he working with that bitch-ass cop who just pressed me out? Why the fuck he showing up now all of a sudden? And why he didn't kill my ass two years ago when he had the jump on me? Yeah, you really making me feel my past sins, huh, Lord? I asked God in my head as the guy ranted on about a bunch of frivolous b.s.

I needed to keep him close to me so I could clean his ass up when the perfect opportunity arrived. I mean, he opened the door on the past - our dark past - and I just felt the need to close it on him for good. I never want to go back to jail, so I vowed to never snitch and by any means to stay in the free world.

Now that I had the po-po and this little guy on my back, it was time to go directly at them until they were sleeping eternally in a cemetery somewhere.

"Yeah, Slim, you know that nigga Twan had me do ten years on a life sentence before I got back in court on a tech," I said, frowning at the memory of all the hardship and suffering I endured in prison.

"You know, I never liked his bitch ass for some reason. I mean, he was getting money and looking out so that's why I was with the nigga," Nu-Nu explained.

But I still had my guards up. Niggas get rocked to sleep every day, and I just didn't want to be one of them. "Yeah, you know when I hit the bricks I had to get his hot ass, you feel me?"

"I feel fucked up that I ever had any dealing with dat hot-ass nigga," Nu-Nu said with a mean mug. "Moe, after I heard you screaming that night about that cheese-eating nigga, I wanted to smash his bitch ass myself, but I figured you'd handle that, feel me? At the time, I had to protect my own ass, you dig? But that's why I waited for a minute to see if Twan made it out the joint, 'cause if he did, I was going to light his ass up right then and there."

"It's good to hear that," I said as we went into another long conversation while standing off to the side.

I think we talked for a good forty minutes while the police conducted their investigation. Nu-Nu slipped me his contact information and pressed me to stay in touch with him.

Oh, I definitely will, I thought, watching the coroner cart off the dead rat in a body bag.

A few minutes later, I heard Nu-Nu say, "Ay, Moe, I'm 'bout to slide on out, but holla at me, Slim. I'm sure we can get some bread together."

I could literally see the difference in Nu-Nu's walk as he stepped off. I was really disturbed about this latest development. Being approached by Nu-Nu wasn't cool at all, especially at a time like this. I knew our connection was based solely on a rat and the fact that Nu-Nu could implicate me in the rat's murder.

CHAPTER 15

Just as things in my life were becoming normal, my dark past returned full throttle, threatening to destroy the joys of life as I knew it. My iPhone began ringing, breaking my train of thought. I answered on the third ring.

"Hello."

"What you doing, boo?" my baby Markita asked.

"In the city, selling a few books. 'Sup with you?" I lied, not wanting to tell Markita what had really happened. Markita would go crazy with her overprotective ass. I still had to come up with a good way to tell her what I was about to publish Zetta's novel and how we'd be working together from time to time. Pray for me, America!

"Nothing, I'm about to cook dinner for you and your bad-ass son. What you want to eat?"

"Make me some spaghetti and some of that banging-ass garlic bread off the butter sauce you be making," I told her.

"What time you coming home?" she asked and then added, "You know you have to go to work tonight. Kisha already called here and said she needs you tonight."

"Why she couldn't call me and tell me that shit?"

"Don't start, Melo…do not start," she said, checking me on a motherly tone. "You know that girl always calls me about you and our club just in case you forgot. We are partners in that." She smacked her lips loudly, getting real ghetto on me.

"Yeah, whatever. I'll be home soon as I can get my car out of this traffic jam," I said, hearing my son in the background raising ruckus about something, but I couldn't make out what he was crying about. "What's wrong with him?"

"He wants his da-da," she said, laughing.

"Tell him I'm on my way right now."

"You tell him when you get here."

"A'ight, smart ass, keep it up, hear?

I'ma punish your ass."

"And how you going to punish me?"

"I ain't gon' give you no dick for a month straight."

"And watch me fuck you up and take it," she retorted in a playful manner.

"Yeah, a'ight, I'm gone. I love you."

"I love you more," she said and then ended the call.

For the next thirty minutes or so, I waited patiently until the police gave me clearance to move my car. I drove straight home, smoking two spliffs on the way, trying to use the exotic herb to help me figure out my next move.

I knew I caught a helluva break already because the detective let me walk. Why didn't he just lock me up and throw away the key? I mean, he had me toe-tagged and body bagged with ease. I sat in my car for a minute pondering that and enjoying the ride the exotic hydro had me on. A voice in my head began screaming, "Fuck the police!"

That's when I knew I couldn't let that cop live after he let me walk away with my freedom. I began plotting out the detective's murder as I walked inside my home and ate dinner with my family.

When we finished eating, I picked up my son, threw him on the couch, and began rough-housing with him.

"Melo, you bet' not hurt my baby!" Markita warned as I tickled Ray-Nathan into a laughing fit.

"Shut up, woman, ain't nobody hurting him!" I grinned, looking down at my giggling son. "Ain't that right, Ray-Ray?" I tickled him some more. "You having fun, ain't you?" I tickled him, making him laugh his little heart out, which brought me peace and made me forget all about the day's drama.

After running around and playing with my son until he fell asleep in my arms, I picked him up and took him to his bedroom. After kissing him on the forehead and tucking him in, I headed to my bedroom and found Markita lying on the bed already naked and waiting on me with her legs wide open with a huge smile on her face.

I ran over and dove on the king-sized bed, making her laugh. I kissed her all over her face as she reached for my crotch, fumbling to pull down my zipper.

"I love you so much, you know that, right?" I said. Markita freed my dick and stroked it a few times until it grew harder and harder in her small hand.

"Actions speak louder than words," she replied, squeezing my rock-hard love pole until it hurt.

I grunted in delight as she slid my boner straight inside her wet pussy and took me on a very enjoyable ride. We reached Heaven on Earth, exploding together in a memorable climax. Markita and my son were my heart and exactly what I needed in life.

I'd be a damn fool to let one cop - or anybody else, for that matter - interfere with our plans of getting married, raising our son, and living happily ever after.

CHAPTER 16

After I finished making love to Markita, I took a nice, long, hot shower. I spent some time just sitting on the marble rock-like shower benches, looking at the water run down the fogged up windows, trying to figure out the whole mess I had suddenly been thrown into.

Part of me just wanted to chill where I was, where it was safe. But too many loose ends were out there, threatening my freedom and my future with Markita and my son. If I had never gone to that dumb-ass basketball game, I wouldn't be going through this shit. But it was not too good to start dwelling on all the what-ifs. That shit makes you crazy. Being paranoid is cool; being crazy is dangerous.

Some people get so paranoid that they go crazy from fear. I saw a lot of that happen in prison. I stayed out of prison for twenty-nine months without so much as a traffic ticket since my release, but now this undercover cop was on my ass. I could just pick up and flee the country, but I really didn't want to leave my home, Markita, and my son.

Before the cop let me go, he told me that I was getting a blessing and stressed the fact that he rarely gave out blessings like the one I received from him. He was a dirty cop, I assumed from the way he robbed me at gunpoint. I hoped he asked me to meet him someplace where there weren't a lot of people around so I could crush his bitch ass and get my life back.

I cut off the shower, got out, and went inside the walk-in closet, found my favorite bone marrow white Lenin suit, a light pastel peach-hued button-up dress shirt, and some crispy white-on-white Air Force 1's that were intended to rock off the no socks. I dressed quietly, kissed Markita on the forehead, and left early for work to help Kisha.

After activating the garage door, I began backing up Markita's 745 Li BMW. I figured that her car meshed better with my linen outfit than the souped-up 1996 bubble Chevy Caprice I had been driving since the accident with my Range Rover. Speaking of which, I checked my iPhone to see if the mechanic who towed my ride had called to let me know it was ready. It'd been like sixteen days already.

As I scrolled through the previous calls, I noticed Zetta's phone number. She had been calling every five minutes on the hour since we got separated at the game earlier that day. Now it was little after 8 p.m. and her last call came in at 7:55 p.m.

I backed down the short driveway, feeling like Zetta was just calling to tell me that she made it home safely. I hadn't realized how transfixed I had become with all of Zetta's previous calls until I looked up and saw the undercover D.C. cop who let me go earlier.

When I saw him aiming a semi-automatic handgun at my head, I hit the brake pedal, stopping dead in my tracks.

CHAPTER 17

After getting no response from Carmelo, Zetta thought about him. She didn't know what made her feel worse, teasing him earlier in her provocative bodysuit or deceiving him to come out to the game where he got kidnapped at gunpoint.

When she saw Carmelo talking to the skinny guy who had tried to talk to her, Zetta eased off her motorcycle. She couldn't deny her attraction for Carmelo, even though she had told him they had a straight business relationship. Carmelo fit every quality she looked for in a man. He possessed a swagger befitting a man with sexy looks. Unlike most men, Carmelo didn't even attempt to crack for the pussy, respecting her wishes. And he worked hard, trying to secure a bright future of financial comfort.

Zetta's brother always taught her to have sex for financial gains, not for love, because she'd get hurt every time. Zetta believed Carmelo was the ideal man to share her body with for financial gain and love. All she had to do now was seduce him and get him under her spell.

As Zetta parked her motorcycle down on Delaware Avenue and N Street, she got off her bike and began heading for an apartment building around the James Creek Dwellings. While walking, Zetta thought about Poobie, a lover she was en route to meet. They had an arrangement that worked out well during the three years after losing her virginity to a cheating dog of a man who crushed her little heart. When Zetta needed maintenance on her coochie, Poobie had always come to her rescue. Zetta loved the way Poobie's horse dick stretched her pussy out of whack. Poobie's good sex game made her keep the weekly sexual therapy appointments, never missing her fix of Poobie's good loving.

As soon as Zetta hit the projects in James Creek, she got bombarded by lustful stares from a group of thugs loitering on the block getting their grind on. Zetta counted eight males and one dyke female, but only one guy caught her attention. Zetta modeled the intricacies of a nasty strut as she sauntered pass them - something she learned by watching several fly-dressing gold diggers from her neighborhood who used to visit her house on her brother's arm.

Zetta saw the dark-skinned guy she was attracted to with huge diamonds in both ears pass off the bottle of Remy he was drinking from and head in her direction. Zetta knew she had him caught in her web when he nearly choked on the drink to check out her jiggling ass while she walked towards the building. Zetta pretended to bend over and tie up her Nike Shock jogging shoes to give him a better view of the size of her ass. As she raised back up, Zetta caught him licking his lips as he approached her, holding his dick through his sweats. Zetta smiled politely at him when he grabbed her arm gently. "What's up, Shorty?" he greeted, biting on a plastic spoon.

"Why you gotta put cho' hands on me to talk to me?"

"I just couldn't resist. I may never get to touch another angel again in this lifetime, so I just had to see if you were real." He smiled.

"I hear you, smooth operator." Zetta liked his come-on line, so she played easy to get and gave him her phone number. She figured if the bling-bling in his ears repped the money he was making on the streets, she couldn't let him get away from her until she made a withdrawal from his bank account.

Zetta could smell his weed and alcohol-scented breath as he stepped closer to her. "Look, I'm tryna take you out tonight, what's up?"

"I don't even know your name. How you gon' take me out somewhere?"

"Shit, you ain't tell me yours, so that makes us even."

"Check your phone, I put it in there along with my number…duh!" Zetta teased, sticking her tongue out at him.

"My name's Sean Bullock. Everybody hip to me. So what's up? Can I take you out or what?"

"I'm kinda busy tonight, boo-boo, but you can call me tomorrow so we can hook up."

"Damn, Shorty, I might not be alive tomorrow. You know that shit ain't promised."

"Well, I suggest you pray real hard tonight then before you go to sleep so you can make it to see another day." Zetta grinned and walked off, switching extra hard, heading inside the building, leaving him with a lustful gaze and his mouth hanging open.

Sean couldn't take his eyes off all that ass walking away from him and he made a mental note to follow up on their meeting as soon as possible. He wanted to tap that ass and he didn't care how long it took him. He would make that dream come true.

I steadied my trembling hands against the steering wheel, wanting to get control of my anger and fear so I wouldn't lose it and kill this bitch-ass nigga for coming to fuck with me at my home. Some things you just don't do, and I could see this son of a bitch didn't care how disrespectful he was being to my way of living.

He waved the gun, beckoning me to shut down the engine and get out of the car. Even though I hesitated for a second, I obeyed out of force and shock. Obeying him caused my body to cringe. I still couldn't believe he didn't have anything better to do than to come to my house. I had to crush this nigga - no ifs, ands, or buts about it.

"You have a really nice home here, killer…real nice. I guess crime really does pay, huh?" he quipped, which I didn't find funny at all.

"Long hours of working legally paid for that house, Detective," I emphasized, leaning back on the Beamer.

I could tell that he didn't take kindly to my response. His face contorted into a mask of rage. He even placed the gun against my chest before placing his cards on the table. "So you's a smart guy, right?"

I didn't understand where his anger came from, considering he held all the trump cards. He knew where I lived and had enough dirt on me to send me back to prison for life and then some. "Never, Detective. I'm just tryna live, that's it, that's all," I replied calmly as I tried to ease the tension beginning to develop.

He laughed belligerently. "Don't give me that bullshit! Motherfucker, you kill people for a living," he said in a sly tone. "You have no regard for life, so why should I care about destroying yours?"

We both exchanged mean mugs while he waited on my response. I was becoming anxious because I had far more pressing business to attend to than going back and forth with this lame excuse of a dirty cop.

"'Cause I can pay you," I stammered, feigning nervousness, all the while imagining that I had a .44 Bulldog aimed at his head and squeezing the trigger until his bitch ass bled.

He lowered the gun. "You're going to pay me regardless. Here's the deal, Mr. Glover. I want $20,000 a month from you, and in return, I'll let you stay on the streets."

"Don't let that house fool you, Detective. I'm up to my ass in bills," I lied, trying to get him to lower his extortion fee. Damn, he's really trying to tax my ass, I thought as he laughed again.

"Tell you what. You do a little favor for me and I'll consider lowering my initial price down to, let's say, $15,000 a month, non-negotiable."

"How long do I have to pay you all that money to stay free?"

"Let me see…" He paused, looking up in the sky, placing the gun on his cheek like he was deep in thought. "Murder carries sixty years easy in D.C., right, so I'm going to let you off with a thirty year payment plan."

"What!" I snapped, unable to keep my cool any longer.

"Don't have a baby on me, Killer," he grinned. "All you have to do is carry out this little job that I need done and I'll look at it as a favor, and I'll reconsider my offer," he said in a sly tone, causing me to wonder what he wanted me to do.

"Listen, if you want me to snitch on anybody or help you build a case on anybody, that's a dead issue. You might as well slap the handcuffs on me right now," I said, looking around my prestigious neighborhood, feeling hot around the collar. I wanted to try his bitch ass so bad and scream self-defense to the first officers on the scene, but I didn't know if I could get the jump on him and take the gun before he got off a few shots. I decided not to risk it.

Detective Gamble shifted his eyes and pursed his lips. "No, it's nothing like that. I just need you to do what you do best!"

It didn't take a rocket scientist to figure out that this crooked bastard, a sworn peace officer who got paid to uphold the law, was asking me to commit murder.

CHAPTER 18

"Even when your hustling days are gone, she'll be by your side, still holding on. And even when those twenties stop spinning and all those gold digging women disappear, she'll still be here!" I sang along with the Lyfe Jennings slow tune as I sped into the District of Corruption.

The level of frustration and tension I felt inside increased by the minute and so did my fear of returning to prison along with the urge to kill. I had never had so many bullets coming my way so fast in my entire life. I had to release this frustration or I'd blow up on the wrong person, which I didn't want to do.

About nine o'clock, I finally made it around Langston Lane in Southeast, looking for Danny Anderson: a piece of shit-ass rat who snitched on a little guy named Pierre Mercer that I knew. Shorty could rap his ass off and didn't deserve to be wasting away in a West Virginia Federal Penitentiary because of a rat.

I wondered, did the guys he hung around with know about his betrayal to the game? And if so, why hadn't they crushed his ass? Was it because they condoned snitching? Could they be on some bullshit where they felt like he didn't snitch on them so he was cool just as long as they didn't fuck with him? All that was bullshit in my eyes, and I was about to straighten this shit.

I been meaning to get around to this shit, but raising my son and trying to stay low hampered my movements for a minute. Plus the fact that my face was on the front page of the Washington Post two years ago as a person of interest being sought for questioning in connection to a kidnapping and a shooting played a major part in my delay from killing all snitches, rats, informants, and lames who ruined the game in D.C.

I pulled up to mingle with the guys out there on the drug strip on the Lane – a.k.a. Da Lenchmob. I viewed how their illegal business was jumping off only a few yards away from the 7th District Police Station, which was right across the street on the other side of Alabama Avenue. This was a bold move, but that crooked cop had me so mad that I was moving recklessly on this one. I spotted Woo, Pierre's little partner who came home a couple years before him. I called him over to Markita's Beamer.

He was all smiles, the type of smile one gives you when they haven't seen you in a while. I shook his hand and gave him a manly hug.

"Fuck is up, Moe?" he greeted with a smile while twisting one of his long dreads. "I ain't seen your ass in years, Moe. Kill…I thought you had an elbow for that body you had?"

"God is good," I replied, making him laugh. "Naw, I got back on appeal."

"Oh yeah? So what brings you across the Anacostia, Moe?"

"I'm tryna see that bitch-ass nigga Danny."

"Oh, Slim up there in Woodland over this little bitch house he be fucking," he told me like everything was kosher.

"Slim, you mean to tell me he snitched on Pierre and he's still walking around here in one piece?"

"Moe, I told everybody 'round here about his hot ass, but the nigga jive-feeding a rack of niggas with that work, so you know how that goes."

"Naw, I don't!" I retorted. "Niggas compromise their principles, morals, and beliefs for some money?"

"Yep," he nodded

"You know where this bitch lives at?"

"Hell yeah!" Woo smiled and I figured he wanted to get down with the get down.

"Let's go," I told him and climbed back in the BMW.

After Woo got inside, I pulled off, heading for Woodland Projects to exterminate another rat and release some pent-up frustration that the crooked detective put on my shoulders.

CHAPTER 19

I scanned the house that Woo pointed out to me. At a little past nine thirty, I spotted Danny leaving out the door. He stood by the door and kissed some redbone. Woo pulled out a Glock-40 and cocked it.

"There his bitch ass go right dere," Woo said. "I always wanted to get the nigga, but I could never catch him slipping."

"Ain't no sense in rushing things, Slim," I said, not wanting Woo to jump out and steal my glory and my avenue to release this pent-up frustration. "We gon' crush him."

I kept glancing at my watch because I knew I had to get to the nightclub and help out Kisha, which would also be my alibi if my name ever came up in what I was about to do. I began getting a little impatient, but I waited to get this rat in the perfect rat trap.

When he pulled off, I waited for a few seconds and then I pulled off behind him. He turned down a few back streets and I followed until we pulled up near 51 Liquor Store. Danny pulled into the apartment complex known as the Marlboro House, which was across the street from 51 Liquor store.

As soon as he parked his Jaguar and got out by the swimming pool, I tapped Woo on the leg, signaling him to get ready. Before I could park, Woo sprang from my ride and ran towards Danny with his gun raised.

"Shit!" I blurted in frustration, throwing the Beamer in park as I rushed from the vehicle.

I saw Danny's eyes growing wide as fifty cent pieces when Woo got the jump on him.

"Naw, Slim, naw!" I called, stopping Woo from doing whatever he had in mind.

I pulled out my .45 compact ACP with the suppressor on it and walked up on Danny. "Listen, Slim, all we want is the bread and you can live," I told him.

"Don't kill me, man, I ain't got nothin' but a stack on me," he said as he started crying. "Please, man, I got four kids and a wife at home." He pled for his life as Woo patted him down and took the money and his keys off of him.

"You ain't got no stash spot nowhere?"

"Naw, man…I swear," he said. I couldn't tell if he was lying or not.

"You Danny, right? Danny the snitch Johnson? You told on Pierre Mercer, right?" I asked, looking him in the eyes. I saw fear registering in his brown eyes.

"How you - "

They were the only words he got out. I shoved my .45 in his mouth with the quickness and fired rapidly until the back of his head exploded. As the rat crumbled to the ground in death, I peeped Woo jumping back, somewhat startled.

"Moe, you just knocked his shit all the way loose! Got-dayyum!" Woo exclaimed like he was fascinated with my work.

"You can get your thing off now. I just had to hit him first, you dig?" I said, slowly walking backwards from the body, which had a crown of blood forming around his head. I'd never forget this killing. The ugly face Danny the rat made swallowing the first bullet in death would forever be sketched into memory.

"Shit, ain't no more I can do to his hot ass," Woo said, looking at me with a goofy smile. "Moe, you slaughtered his anything ass."

"You got to do something. I know you ain't just come along for the ride to spectate?" I remarked, wanting him to put some holes in the rat so I wouldn't have to kill his ass for being a witness to my crime.

"You right," Woo said. He stood over top of the dead rat and pumped his head full of slugs until the chamber jumped back on his Glock-40.

By the time Woo finished putting in work, I had the BMW backed up and ready to pull out of the Marlboro House apartment complex. We drove straight back around Langston Lane, where we split up the $1,600 Danny had on him.

I contemplated crushing Woo only out of fear that he'd snitch on me later if he ever got pinched on another charge and didn't want to do the time. I had seen a lot of guys get jammed up like that. After giving it another thought, I said fuck it. Whatever was going to happen was going to happen and I couldn't stop it no matter how much killing and covering my tracks I did.

"Moe, you jive wicked," Woo said, breaking into my train of thought. "When we was in the Feds together, I didn't see you as the putting in work type."

"You can't judge a book by its cover, Moses." I smirked and peeled off $200 of the money that Woo gave me. He looked at me funny when I gave him back $200. "What's up, Moe?"

"That's you, Champ. I really don't need this money. I'ma just use it to send to Pierre and few other good men I know that are locked up."

"Yeah, I'ma send P some bread too," Woo said and then added, "All courtesy of Danny's hot ass!" We cracked up at that statement for a good minute.

We smoked a few j's of exotic 'dro before I told Woo I had to roll out. "A'ight, Moe," he said, giving me some dap as he got out of the car.

I pulled off and drove back towards the liquor store across the street from where I had just exterminated the rat. When I pulled up to the liquor store, I saw the flashing blue and red lights of the police and the orange lights of the ambulance dancing off the white stones of the building in the Marlboro House apartment complex parking lot.

I nodded in that direction and began nodding my head to the classic Scarface song. "I come around this ma'fucka and do your ass just like Jesse James…Blow out your motherfuckin' brains…" I let the lyrics ease my body and the tension I felt earlier as I kept driving towards the Suitland Parkway, heading back out to my club in VA to help Kisha. During the drive, I began smiling and imagining that the rat I had just smoked was the crooked cop who'd been harassing me.

CHAPTER 20

My adrenaline was still pumping over what Detective Gamble wanted me to do. Even though I had killed a rat to get Detective's Gamble proposal off my mind, the shit he wanted me to do really had me tripping good. Here was a crooked cop who wanted me to kill another cop who worked in Internal Affairs. Apparently, the Internal Affairs cop had opened up an investigation on Detective Gamble, trying to take him down for various complaints of corruption, police brutality, and extortion.

Murdering the cop for Detective Gamble should have been fair exchange, no robbery. But no, Gamble's creep ass wanted his cake and ice cream. He wanted me to kill the cop and still pay him a ransom to remain in society—picture that!

After climbing out of the Beamer, I spotted a small crowd standing outside the club. They were the first people here, trying to beat the crowds who loved visiting my club. I saw Tiny at the front door checking out identification and frisking the partygoers with a small wand-like metal detector.

"What's up, Big Boy?"

"Ain't shit, Melo. You know Kisha's waiting on you. She's been acting like she on her period all day, so be careful." He laughed, making me laugh.

"Thanks for the heads up, Big Guy. Remind me to give you a raise."

"Yeah, I'ma do that so I can start rocking dat all-white everythang like you," he said in a sly tone, referring to my outfit as I stepped into the club.

"Go 'head with dat bullshit, boy!" I waved at him before disappearing inside.

Once I got inside the club, I heard Kisha calling out my name. I ignored her, making a beeline straight for my office. As soon as I entered my office, I flopped down face first on the low plush couch near the door. I growled loudly in the cushions at what the crooked cop wanted me to do just to keep my freedom.

I didn't mind killing, but only when it was for the right cause. I mean, I had killed a cop before, but he was a childhood friend of mine who got in my way while I was trying to gun down a rat. This situation here was too wicked even for my taste. I mean, to kill a cop for a cop, what would that make me? I thought, turning over on the couch to the sound of knocking on my office door.

"It's open!" I called out and Kisha walked in, rocking some wide-legged gray wool slacks over medium-heeled open toe sandals and a pink button up blouse that suffocated her huge DD-sized breasts. She had a pearl necklace hanging down in the cleavage of her huge melons and some matching pearl earrings.

"What's wrong with you? I know you heard me calling you. Why you ain't stop for me?" she asked, leaning over me, putting her big hooters right in my face.

I could see the pale lipstick and too much eyeliner and I smelled the sweet perfume that she wore to hide her natural body scent.

"You wouldn't want to know, Kish." I sighed and motioned for her to take a seat in one of the leather chairs sitting in front of my desk.

Kisha took a seat, crossed her chubby legs, and folded her hands over one knee. One of her fingers had a nice platinum ring with a diamond on it that had a faint canary-yellow hue.

Kisha looked incredible. Everything fit together on her nicely. But I couldn't offer the usual compliments I gave her because I was stressing over how this punk-ass detective was harassing me and coming out to my home.

Kisha sat as calmly as a lioness waiting for dinner to cross her path, and the fact that I didn't compliment her didn't seem to unsettle her. She didn't look like she was waiting on a compliment from me anyway, so I just asked, "Why you call the house instead of me, claiming that you needed my help tonight, when you know you can handle this shit by yourself?"

In her professional, neutral voice, Kisha said, "Because I needed to talk to you." She sighed and then added "I want more than a co-manager position here. Melo, I want to be your partner, fifty-fifty."

"Why, Kish?" I asked, not really caring about her reasons. But this quick question usually provided a good idea of how much money somebody wanted to take from me.

"Is that important?" she asked. "I'm damn near running this place on my own anyway."

"And you getting paid, ain't you? How do I know you ain't making money under the table behind my back?"

"If I did, you wouldn't know, since you're rarely here anyway," she argued.

I didn't need sarcasm from her right now. "Don't say that, Kish. You have no idea what you getting yourself into with your mouth."

"So you can't make me your partner?" she asked, sounding like a spoiled brat.

"Where's all this shit coming from? Shit was good just a week ago."

She obviously didn't understand the complexities of my life. I had at least twenty niggas I was taking care of in prisons all over America from time to time. Even though I loved every minute of it, sometimes it drained me, but it kept me on my toes and was a constant reminder on where I could end up on any given day. Now this crooked cop was trying to get me to kill another cop and push me back into a jail cell if I didn't meet his monetary demands. On top of that, Kisha up and starts demanding a partnership. I figured I'd make out better all the way around the board if I crushed Gamble's cruddy ass before the deadline he gave me to kill the other cop expired. I'd just have to drag him along until I could find a way to kill him and get away with it. Kisha, on the other hand….

"So you just going to ignore me, Melo?" Kisha pressed, breaking into my thoughts.

"Ain't nobody ignoring you, Kish, Damn!" I griped, knowing I'd have to keep her happy for a few more days, at least until I took care of this police business, so that I could focus on my business here at the club and with my publishing company.

Kisha's such a genius at running things around the club that I couldn't risk losing her, and I think she realized that. That's the reason why I thought she was pressing the issue to be my partner all of a sudden.

"Listen, Kish, I understand where you coming from, but I don't have time for this right now. I got a lot of shit on my mind. Just let me handle my business first and then we'll rap about a partnership, okay?"

"Are you sure you going to keep your word to me?" she wanted to know.

I pretended to think that one over, making her suck her teeth loudly in irritation.

"Look, Kish, I didn't keep you around here for nothing, right? But if you can't have some patience and wait 'til I handle a few things and you prefer to do you, just say the word. I'm sure you'll be missed, but life goes on with or without you around."

"All right, Melo, I'm sorry," she sighed. "Maybe that wasn't necessary, but ever since that shooting the other night, I been thinking. I was like, damn, if I die right now, I wouldn't have shit to leave my family."

That's funny. She didn't look like the "planning to help her family in the event of her demise" type. "Kish, I got you. Just hang around for me, okay?"

"Yeah, whatever," she hissed in a nasty tone. "I'ma hang around here for thirty more days. If you ain't ready to talk business and partnership by then, I'm handing in my walking papers." She got out of the chair and sort of shook herself a little, making her outfit settle back on her chunky frame without wrinkling.

As she stepped towards the door like she was a runway model on the stage in Milan somewhere, her wide hips moved in a way to express that she was annoyed, but not ready to sever our business relationship. Somewhat entranced, I raised up on my elbows to watch her angry exit.

Kisha stopped at the door and looked at me long and hard for a moment. "You need to make out a living will just in case something happens to you before the thirty days up, so your wife knows to bring me on board as her partner…just in case!" she emphasized before leaving and slamming the door.

What the fuck? Just in case? Bitch, you probably the one who paid someone to take a shot at me the other night so you could own this club! Then again, she ain't crazy enough to ride with me if she wanted me dead. But she did get low with the quickness, right before the shooting happened, I thought, making a mental note to really keep my eyes on Kisha from here on out.

"Just in case," I repeated, becoming annoyed and even more suspicious by Kisha's sudden suggestion for me to make out a living Will.

CHAPTER 21

Zetta danced on the balcony to the sounds of Ludacris's "Pimpin' All Over the World", totally astounded by the view of the nightclub under her stiletto-covered feet. The balcony hovered over the nightclub's V-shaped bar and faced the C-shaped stage. Chances nightclub was immaculate. Zetta's was enchanted by the lake of people on the dance floor as they grooved to the sounds of DJ Cliff cutting up on the 1's and 2's.

Zetta raised her arms high in the air and began winding her hips like a Hawaiian hula girl as her favorite song came on.

"I was gettin' some head…gettin'-gettin' some head!" Zetta sang along with the chorus of Shawna's DTP Classic.

With her arms still raised, Zetta moved her curvy frame with a stripper-like swagger, causing several pairs of male eyes to zoom in and lock on her dirty dancing routine.

"Go Shorty! Go, go, go, go Shorty, it's your birthday. We gon' party like it's your birthday. We gon' sip Bacardi like it's your birthday. And we don't give a fuck that it's your birthday. You can find me—WHERE?" DJ Cliff screamed, urging loud chanting from the crowd.

"In da club, bottle full of bub, Mami got what you need…" The crowd went wild to the sounds of 50 Cent's classic blaring through the speakers.

Uproarious celebration erupted around the nightclub as everyone got their boogie on and anxiously awaited DJ Cliff's next song selection. DJ Cliff started off so smoothly, and by 11 p.m., he had the crowd buzzing with hype. Zetta concentrated heavily on her dancing technique, trying to entice every man she saw looking her way.

"Ay, Shorty, you can't be dancing all freaky like that up on my balcony."

Hearing the husky, manly baritone invading her ears from behind, Zetta stopped dancing immediately and turned around. Staring at the familiar face in front of her, Zetta's heart began beating wildly in her chest. She had never imagined that she would run into him in a nightclub.

I had been counting different denominations of bills, diligently trying to put away the cash that my club brought in tonight. It was a very slow night. After the drama I had experienced earlier with the crooked cop, the cash going through my hands and into the money counting machine made me feel much, much better.

Right now, I had $8,000 from admissions into the club. I figured with the cash being taken in at the bar, I'd leave tonight about $12,000 to $14,000 richer. This club is definitely a gold mine, I thought, looking up and admiring the thick, curvy sister who was getting her dirty dancing on right outside my office window on the balcony.

I quickly put the bills in $1,000 stacks and wrapped the cake up in rubber bands to keep it organized. I threw the money in the drop safe in the floor directly under my desk, locked it, and rushed from my office to see the chick moving all that ass.

After reaching the balcony and standing behind her for a minute, I recognized her. It was Zetta. She sported a very short single strap skintight mini dress that was backless and I could see the top of her butt crack. I noticed a fresh tattoo on the back of her neck that wrapped around her left side. I got so close to her trying to see the tattoo that I could smell her sweet, tropical perfume. The way she was moving her body played games with my mind and I felt my manhood acknowledging her seductive moves.

"Ay, Shorty, you can't be dancing all freaky like that up on my balcony," I finally said, making her stop dancing instantly.

When she turned on me, I noticed her fresh tattoo was done in fancy cursive letter that spelled OMERTA, which means "silence" in the Italian language.

"Excuse you?" Zetta said, smiling at me, looking surprised.

"I said it looks like you having a ball, Shorty."

"Huh? I can't hear you?" she said, pulling on her right ear.

"I said," I paused and pulled her closer to me until we were face to face, "it looks like you having a ball dancing all freaky up in here."

"Mmmmph!" she sighed, and I could smell her minty breath as she backed up a little. "I was just doing me, releasing some stress. But anyway, how you doing? Are you okay?"

"Yeah, yeah…I'm cool, Shorty," I replied.

"You don't look like it," she said. She told me that she had seen me get kidnapped at gunpoint. She told me that she ran to the police to get help, but when they returned, I was long gone.

"Thanks for your help, but I don't go to the police about shit I can handle myself."

"You probably blame me, don't you?" she asked.

"I don't blame you for anything but looking good," I said, causing her to lower her head for a second to hide her smile.

"Good. So that means I still have a chance to get my book published, right?"

"From what I see on your neck, I think you'll fit in perfectly with what I'm pushing. You know the name of the company is Omerta Press."

After I said that, Zetta couldn't stop smiling. Then she did something that I would never expect from her. She stepped in close to me, gave me a hug, and then gave me a soft, sensual kiss on the lips.

"Thank you for bringing me on board," she said with a smile after disengaging her lips and stepping back from the hug. She wiped the lipstick off my lips with her thumb as she stepped back, letting me get a good look at her curves.

"What ever happened to mixing business with pleasure, Shorty?"

"I think we both know there's some sexual tension between us that needs to be addressed," she said, throwing me off.

"I can't lie, Shorty, you like that and I'd love to put it on you, but I'm engaged and it just wouldn't be right to cheat on my girl. She saved my life, you feel me?"

"I understand." She sighed like she was frustrated. "It won't ever happen again. Just strictly business, deal?" she said, extending her hand for a handshake.

"It's a deal." I shook her hand. "But I still need to see the book so I can go over the joint."

"I'll have it for you the next time you come to the post office to pick up your mail, so you don't hafta be stalking me," she joked.

"I was here first, Shorty. I own the place. So when I saw you, I thought you was stalking me."

"Never that. I just came out here 'cause I heard this was the place to be, you know."

"Whoever told you that know what they know. C'mon, let me show you around," I said, putting my hand on the small of her back and leading her downstairs.

I enjoyed Zetta's company for the rest of the night. We talked, we laughed, and we made fun of the white people who tried to stay in sync with the beat while they danced. Zetta revealed that she had gotten the tattoo as a tribute to her brother, who was in prison behind several guys snitching on him, and she mentioned how she despised rats. I couldn't believe she was related to somebody that played in the streets and hated rats just like me.

Zetta was so articulate and smart. I'd never guessed that she had those type of morals and principles instilled in her. Even though I was having the time of my life hanging out with Zetta, I felt guilty as hell. I knew this wasn't right and that there would be hell to pay if Markita ever found out about my actions tonight.

CHAPTER 22

After closing up the club, I headed to my car, still not over how much fun I had hanging out with Zetta. During the night, I caught Kisha giving me several funny looks like she was jealous or something behind the way I was mingling with Zetta. I hoped she didn't call Markita and start no bullshit. She had never done it before when she saw me chilling with a lady in the club, but after our little disagreement tonight, I wouldn't put it pass her. Women are very unpredictable.

I decided to leave the money in the safe tonight and put it in the bank first thing in the morning. It would be stress on the body getting up so early because I basically became a night owl, living like a vampire. It was a little after 4:00 a.m. and I'd only get about four hours of sleep at the most before heading to the bank. On second thought, I decided I might as well take the money with me so I wouldn't have to do so much driving.

With that in mind, I got back out of the car and headed back to the club. I put the key in the master lock that held down the steel curtain and opened it. After pushing the steel curtain half way up, I opened the front of the club. As soon as I pushed the glass doors open, I heard rapid gunfire.

What the fuck? I thought, instinctively diving into the club and slamming the door. I lay on the ground for a second, heart pounding wildly in my chest. I tried to see the feet of my assassin. I didn't see anything, but I heard more gunshots hitting the steel curtain and then hitting the glass door. A few shards of glass flew in my face when the glass exploded at the bottom.

I bolted up to my office to grab the Mac-90 that I kept there for just-in-case purposes. I kept all the lights out and waited with my back against the wall. If I was going to die, I intend on taking whoever wanted me dead with me.

The suspense was killing me as I waited for the deadly confrontation. I stayed in hiding for a good little while and never heard a peep. When I felt safe enough to move, I eased out of my office onto the balcony of the club. I glanced around and saw no signs of entry. And then I looked over at my right shoulder and saw my white linen suit covered in blood.

I became weak instantly, more out of shock than anything else. I'd been shot and

I didn't even feel it until I saw the blood. I couldn't die like this - not by some lucky shot from a cowardly assassin. I fumbled in my pockets for my iPhone, hating myself for what I was about to do.

"9-1-1, what's your emergency?"

"I need some help. I just been shot while closing up my nightclub," I said hysterically. While she questioned me, all I could think about was Kisha telling me to get a living will.

Just in case, I thought as the emergency operator asked me for the address to the club. I gave her the address and she told me to put a warm towel over the wound and press hard to stop the bleeding.

"Okay, but please send somebody quick before I die," I said and then I hung up the phone.

I rushed to my office to stash my weapon and then rushed to the bar to grab a few towels. By the time I made it outside the club to wait on the cops and ambulance, the whole top right side of my all-white linen suit had changed to a crimson red. I pressed the warm towels over my fresh gunshot wound and retrieved my iPhone again to call Markita. All I got was the answering machine. She usually stays up waiting for me to get home, so I called her again.

She answered on the fourth ring. "Hello?"

"Markita, baby, don't get scared or nothing, but I'm on my way to the hospital." I winced a little, feeling the burn in my shoulder blade.

"For what? Baby, what's wrong?" she asked, and I heard the concern in her tone.

"Somebody was shooting tonight while I was closing up the club and I got shot."

"Oh my God! I'm on my way right now. Where - "

"No, it's not safe for you to come here. I just need you to call my bouncer, Tiny, and Kisha and let them know what happened. Have Kisha get someone down here pronto to watch the club until she can get the glass and shit fixed on the front doors."

"Baby, I want to be with you." She began whining like a baby.

"I'm going to be fine. Besides, you can't leave the baby in the house by himself. I'll call you as soon as I get to the hospital, okay?"

"Okay, baby, I love you and I need you to come home to me."

"I will, soon as I get fixed up."

"Okay, and we need to talk about you working in that club. My brother died in there and I don't want it happening to you. I just don't think I could take it."

"Ain't nobody dying, Kita. I got this."

"I don't care what you got!" she snapped. "We gonna talk, because you not gonna have me worried sick to death about you every night that you go out to work."

"Okay, we'll talk. I have to go 'cause the ambulance is here."

"Okay. I love you, baby," she said, giving me a kiss over the phone.

"Love you more," I said and ended the call. The ambulance was nowhere in sight. I just didn't want to hear all that nagging from Markita.

Looking around the front entrance of the club, I saw several bullets on the ground by the steel curtain. I walked out by Markita's car and noticed several shell casings on the ground. That really scared the hell out of me, because whoever was shooting at me could have just crushed me before I got back out of the car and I'd never see it coming. Maybe this was a warning from that crooked cop, letting me know I could be touché. Or maybe somebody wanted to kill me, and I thought I knew who it was.

Just in case, huh? Damn, I knew she wanted a partnership, but I didn't think she'd go this far to get what she wanted, which was to be the head bitch in charge, I thought. I decided to talk to Kisha the first chance I got.

CHAPTER 23

After I reached the hospital, I had to be rushed into emergency surgery. I found out I had gotten hit in the back also, but nothing was life threatening - well, at least I didn't think so. While the X-rays were being conducted, the nurse informed me that a bullet was lodged in the muscle tissue right next to my vertebral column - the bony column in the back of the vertebrae, basically the backbone. I found out that if I would have kept moving, I would have paralyzed myself bullshittin'.

I came out of surgery feeling way worse than I did going in. My throat was sore as hell and my whole body was sore, especially my back. The nurse and doctors told me that I'd have to stay for at least a week and a half to make sure I didn't have any complications from the surgery.

Damn, I really got caught bullshittin' tonight. Why Kisha wanted to knock me out the box like that? Over a club? It just didn't add up, because she could have smoked my ass anytime. Why now, after all these years? Other questions raced through my mind concerning who and why somebody wanted to kill me.

I had the nurse call up Markita and let her know the latest developments. Before 9 a.m. rolled around the corner I saw Markita rushing into my hospital room. I felt drowsy off the Tylenol-3 medications so I really couldn't talk to Markita as she shot a thousand and one questions at me.

"Baby, I'm here. Me and Lil Ray-Nathan are right here and we're not going anywhere," I heard her say.

I drifted off to la-la land, thinking, Damn somebody out there really trying to kill me and I'm a sitting duck until I found out the 411 and deal with it accordingly.

Zetta woke up and took a long, hot bubble bath. After getting out of the tub and drying off, Zetta called up the guy Sean Bullock that she had met the day before to set up a date for later on that night. He answered on the third ring.

"Yeah, who dis?"

"It's the only angel you have never touched on earth," she quipped, making him remember her instantly. He couldn't forget that big, juicy ass she had even if he wanted to.

"Oh yeah, what's up, Shorty?"

"You forgot what we talked about yesterday?" Zetta asked.

"Oh yeah, so what time you want me to pick you up?" he asked.

"Where we going first of all, 'cause I'm telling you now, I'm not going to no hotel with you or none of that shit, so don't even expect nothing from me so soon."

"Damn, Shorty, what's wrong with letting a nigga hit? I mean, you already know you phat as shit, so why don't you let a nigga sample dat box?"

"'Cause I don't know you like that." Zetta sucked her teeth. "You have to at least get to know me first."

"So how long do we have to play this game before you let a nigga tap dat ass?"

"Depends on how I feel about you after tonight."

"Yeah, whatever. Look, I ain't got no time for no little kiddy games. When you ready to let me fuck, give me a call."

"So you just want to fuck me and have nothing else to do with me, right?"

Basically, he thought before answering. "I ain't say all that, Shorty, you did. I mean, it depends on how I feel after I sample the goods, you feel me? If you got that come back…I'ma come back." He laughed, causing her to giggle.

"You crazy, boy! So are we still hanging out tonight or what?"

"It's on you. I'm not taking your sexy ass out with me and spend up all my bread on you and end up with blue balls at the end of the night. I gots ta get my dick wet some kind of way with the head or something."

"Let me give it some thought, and by the time you do pick me up, I'll have an answer for you. Just make sure your money right too, boo-boo."

Geekin'-ass bitch, just like the rest of these nothing-ass hoes out here. Tryna work a nigga for all they can get before setting out the pussy. Won't get me, he thought and said, "Naw, that ain't working, Shorty. I need an answer now, or I ain't coming to scoop you. And for the record, my money always stay right."

"Well, then I guess you'll never know what an angel's lips will feel like wrapped around your dick. Ta-ta," Zetta said and hung up.

Before she could put her bra and panties on, her cell phone began ringing non-stop. She looked at the cell phone and noticed Sean's number. She sent him straight to voicemail and decided to make him suffer a while before answering his call. That way she'd have him right where she wanted him: geekin' to do anything she asked of him.

CHAPTER 24

Across town in Southeast, Detective Gamble sat at his desk, staring at the naked women engaging in oral sex with each other on his computer screen while Detective Newsome looked on with a smile as he stood behind him. Gamble and Newsome were like two super cops who were dirtier than the porn stars they currently watched.

Like all cops thought in the beginning after leaving the academy, Gamble and Newsome thought they could make a difference by arresting most of the violent criminals terrorizing the Southeast streets of the District. Once they began going undercover in the streets, dealing with mayhem, disorder, and drug dealers who bribed them with more money than they could earn legally in a month, the detectives became weak to the power of money. The bribes they began taking dictated a different result.

In 2002, after being vice cops for three years, Gamble and Newsome organized a massive business of taking bribes, extortion, and protecting drug dealers who could pay their expensive monthly fees. They turned a blind eye to illegal drug transactions going down in the hoods they patrolled until their superiors wanted a bust for political reasons.

Gamble and Newsome shook down the streets throughout the morning, afternoon, and evening. During 2004, Gamble made the most money between him and Newsome, taking in anywhere from $1,000 to $6,000 per day, shaking down dealers and taking their money. Although Newsome made a little less in addition to dealing marijuana, he would help Gamble instill fear in new dealers sprouting up around Southeast and Southwest with threats of arrest for murder charges, or even worse, death itself.

Gamble and Newsome's illegal extortion ring was surrounded by a culture of violence and intimidation that grew stronger each day due to the criminals who paid the taxes the crooked detectives implemented.

"Damn, that lil slut sure knows how to suck that pussy," Newsome remarked, getting a little excited.

"None of these lil bitches can fuck with that bitch Pinky or Jada-Fire," Gamble said as a short, middle-aged black woman appeared holding a manila folder.

She leaned over the desk and dropped the folder, which made Gamble hit the power button, shutting down the hardcore XXX-rated website.

"Here's everything you requested on one Carmelo Glover: his age, fingerprints, aliases, and convictions that go as far back as a possession with intent to distribute a controlled substance in 1989."

"'Preciate you, Tiffany," Gamble said in a playful manner, giving her a wink.

"That's nothing, Detective. I get paid to do this," she said and then turned and began switching away, giving them good view of how her soft rumpshaker jiggled in the tight pencil skirt during each step she took.

"Remind me to pay you back in my own special way!" Gamble called after her in a perverted manner.

"Don't do me any favors!" Tiffany said with a wave of the hand over her shoulder, batting down his advances as she kept it moving.

Gamble diverted his attention to the folder. "Yo, Newsome, this guy right here is our man," he said before passing the folder to Newsome.

Detective Newsome opened the folder, paying attention to Carmelo's old police mug photo. "Whaddya mean? He's a new victim or what?" he asked, quickly glancing over Carmelo's criminal history.

"Think about it, compadre. We get this guy to eliminate the little problem we're having from that hot-ass faggot upstairs in I.A.D."

"How do you know he can pull it off?" Newsome whispered, quickly finding a chair. He pulled it close to Gamble's chair. Newsome wanted to hear him clearly and keep any unwanted ears from eavesdropping on them while they talked about putting a hit on another cop.

Flying under the Internal Affairs Division radar for corruption came to an end for Gamble and Newsome at about 2:00 a.m. in the early morning hours on a day in October 2006. A resident of Congress Park was awakened to the sounds of four individuals outside. When she looked out her window, she saw two undercover cops arguing with Wild Bill and Roscoe, who was in a truck, two guys that she knew who grew up and hustled in the neighborhood. She reported to the police that the cops demanded the men to get out the truck at gunpoint. When Roscoe and Wild Bill complied, the cops began searching them. Wild Bill and Roscoe began to fight the cops and took off running until they were shot twice by Gamble and then kidnapped. The witness knew the identities of the shooter and kidnapper as cops because she'd seen them patrolling her neighborhood on several occasions.

Coincidentally on the same morning in October, a witness living in the Arthur Capers housing complex in Southeast called the police at around 2:30 a.m. after seeing two men pull up in a truck, jump out, and began shooting other individuals in the truck. First District police arrived on the scene and found the truck riddled with bullet holes and two dead black males inside. Both men were reported dead on the scene from being shot thirteen times each, eight of which were shots to the head. A First District homicide detective investigating the crime later learned that the two murdered men were Wild Bill and Roscoe.

When Gamble learned about the investigation via a leak from somebody in I.A.D, Detective Gamble became concerned and told Newsome, "We need to stay on top of this shit, so eliminating whoever gets in our way is top priority and we'll approach this shit like a full time job."

Since that day, Gamble and Newsome had been trying to track down the investigating officer and plot out a way to erase him and get the investigation out of the picture for good.

"Listen to me, partner," Gamble grinned. "The way I got this son of a bitch by the balls, it's not a question of how I know he can pull it off…it's when he'll do it." Gamble began telling Newsome how much dirt he had on the pawn they intend to use to eliminate the Internal Affairs investigation on them.

"This is the smartest and craziest move you've ever made." Newsome laughed. "You're an evil muppet…pure evil, man." Newsome giggled.

"Thanks for the compliment, partner." Gamble grinned.

Later on that day, Zetta met up with Sean Bullock. After his repeated phone calls, Zetta finally answered the phone and let him persuade her to go out on a date.

Zetta hopped out of her car as the guys hanging out in James Creek and the surrounding area watched her in admiration and lust. She smoothed down her black Gucci silk floral bustier dress that flashed a sexy sliver of skin at the waist, stretching down to her left hip. Her sky-high snakeskin Louboutin slingback peep toes revealed the perfect burgundy polish of her pedicure.

Zetta grabbed a huge snakeskin tote bag from the passenger seat before closing the door. As she turned, Zetta saw Sean Bullock walking out of the building wearing a pair of tailor-fit jeans, a leather vest, and a tight-fitting Hally Henson T-shirt along with a goofy smile.

He walked over to her and held out his arms. "So you just gon' make me stand here like this or are you going to give a nigga a hug?"

Zetta stepped into his open arms and gave him a hug. As soon as he wrapped his arms around her, his hands locked in on the soft mounds of her rumpshaker. When he palmed her cheeks and squeezed for a moment, Zetta shoved him away from her.

Zetta was speechless. Just to be disrespected like that by him felt like nightmare coming true for her. "Boy, you don't be doing no shit like that," Zetta griped. "Everything has its place and time."

"Yeah, you're right, Shorty." He licked his lips. "That's my bad, but I just couldn't resist. I promise you that'll never happen again."

Yeah, right! Don't be stupid, girl. You saw his face. He only wants one thing. Now you know he's going to try his hand again, she thought. She said, "Can we just go before I change my mind?"

You know you want this dick or you would've left off the break after I grabbed that big ole' ass you got. "Sure, we outta here. Where you tryna go?"

"Surprise me," she said while thinking, You pervert! Zetta looked into his eyes and saw the lust exuding from them. "Then again, let's go out to eat somewhere and then go to Teddy Carpenter's comedy club out Greenbelt."

A broad with some sense would have just charged me some bread for the pussy right now instead of going through all this romantic bullshit. "You lead the way and I'll follow that soft ass you got, sexy," he said with a smile.

"You stupid! Shut up with your nasty ass."

"Trust me, you ain't seen nasty yet. We gonna do a rack of nasty things together," he said with determination in his eyes as he followed Zetta over to her car.

At the same time, D.C. and his little man, Ugg, were chilling outside around Montello Avenue and Oaks Street, watching several guys and addicts loitering on M&O, doing illegal transactions. D.C. stood by his Mercedes Benz coupe with the hard top missing, engaging in meaningless conversation with Ugg about their plans for today. Just as D.C. got ready to say something, Ugg cut him off.

"Ay, Slim, why you ain't see what's up with Zetta's lil ass? You keep faking like she your niece and shit. I know you fucking the shit outta her lil phat ass," Ugg smirked.

"Naw, Champ." D.C. shook his head quickly, denying the accusation. "Zetta's my man Nut's lil sister. I just be looking out for Shorty on the strength."

"Yeah, whatever, Moe. You can tell that shit to somebody who don't know no better." Ugg grinned. "Shorty is too phat for you not to be hitting that box."

"I'ma call her right now and let you ask her then, since you never believe shit stinks," D.C. said, pulling out his Blackberry.

As D.C. called up Zetta, a cluster of dealers began jumping on a male crackhead, trying to beat him to a pulp. D.C., listened to the Young Jeezy ringtone on Zetta's phone, while watching the second and third generation of Trinidad hustlers put in work. Zetta answered a few moments later.

"Hello."

"'Sup. What your lil ass doing?"

"Oh, hey, Uncle D.C.," Zetta said cheerfully. "I'm just riding around with my friend."

"You gon' bring her round' here so I can fuck?"

"No, boy, ugh! It's not no girl. He's my new boo - if he acts right," she said, glancing over at him. Sean Bullock winked at her, eating up every word he had just heard her say over the phone.

"Who your new boo?" Ugg asked aggressively after taking the phone from D.C. "I thought D.C. was putting dat dick on you?"

"Ugh, shut your bama-ass up, Ugg!" Zetta giggled.

"Zetta, stop playing with me. You throwing me off, chilling with another nigga. You know I'm in love with you, girl."

"Boy, shut up and stop saying anything. Put D.C. back on the phone."

"Nope, not until you tell me who you with."

"You don't know him, boy." Zetta sucked her teeth.

"I know everybody, Shorty. I'm international Ugg, don't get it twisted."

"His name's Sean…Sean Bullock," Zetta said and Ugg heard the phone go dead.

CHAPTER 25

Sean Bullock snatched Zetta's cell phone, and cut it off. He wanted badly to haul off and smack the taste out of her mouth, but he realized he'd only ruin his chances of getting the pussy. He'd been around long enough and heard numerous stories about guys getting set up to be robbed and murdered because they trusted a big butt and a smile. If he could help it, he wasn't going out like that.

"Give me my phone back!" Zetta demanded. "Fuck is your problem, boy?"

Sean Bullock shook his head from side to side. "You the one with the problem, giving out my name and shit to some niggas!"

"Boy, you tripping! That was my uncle." Zetta sucked her teeth, expressing her frustration openly as she sped towards Trinidad

"Ay, D.C., Zetta's phone just went dead, homes," Ugg said while passing the phone back to him.

D.C. took the phone and called her back. "What the fuck happened?"

"She told me that she was riding around with some bama named Sean Bullock."

"Sean Bullock…Sean Bullock?" D.C. repeated with a frown. "Dat bitch-ass nigga hot as shit!" D.C. riffed off so fast he made Ugg laugh. "Man, they got the paperwork and everything on that hot-ass nigga on how he was telling on niggas in the Feds out Terre Haute."

"Oh yeah?" Ugg remarked in disgust. "You think Zetta know he ate that cheese?"

"I don't know, but I'm sure 'bout to find out," D.C. said as Zetta answered the phone.

Sean Bullock waited until Zetta began ignoring him before he gave her cell phone back. He felt like their date was a complete wreck now. His hopes of getting her in bed had dropped to an all-time low.

"So you still going to ignore a nigga like a lil baby even though you was dead wrong for giving up my name and shit?"

Zetta was shocked to hear the words coming out of his mouth. She gave him an evil look as they reached Montello Avenue. As soon as the light turned green, Zetta pulled off and her phone began ringing.

"Hello?"

"Ay, Zetta, you know that nigga you got in the car with you is hot."

"For real?" she asked, glancing at him as she pulled up near Neal Street.

"Fuck yeah! The nigga's so dangerous, Zetta, he'll snitch on his own mother. Where y'all at?"

"I'm about to stop by my mother's house to drop off her money."

"Say no more. How long you gon' be?"

"About twenty minutes."

"Yeah, a'ight," D.C. said and hung up.

"Who the fuck was that?" Sean asked as he whipped out a seventeen shot Ruger 9mm.

"Listen, Sean." She sighed while pulling over on Montello Avenue and Oaks Street. "You tripping like shit, boo. I'ma take this money to my mother real quick and then I'm taking you back down the West, cause you lunchin' too good for me right now."

"I ain't lunchin'. You the one…" Sean trailed off after seeing all the guys hanging out on the corner. He felt like a gazelle sitting off to the side from a pack of lions. He wanted to curse Zetta's ass out for putting him in this type of situation. He clutched his gun, just watching the guys get their hustle on.

"Zetta, you on some fucked up time. Why you ain't handle this shit before we hooked up?"

Just as she began to respond, Zetta saw D.C. and Ugg approaching her car. Sean cocked his weapon, preparing to shoot first and ask questions later.

"Boy, put that shit away. You tripping like shit, for real." Zetta sucked her teeth and got out of the car.

"Trippin' my ass!" he yelled as she slammed the door. "You better hurry the fuck up too!" he bellowed as Zetta walked over to her mother's house.

Sean watched Zetta's every move as she walked up on the porch and handed an older-looking woman some money. He began having second doubts that she was trying to set him up, because why would she show him where her mother lived at if she was up to no good? Then Zetta hugged one of the guys who had walked past her car, making him suspicious all over again. He began honking the horn repeatedly.

Up on the porch, D.C. and Ugg looked back at the rat with pure hatred in their eyes. D.C. pulled Zetta off the porch with Ugg in tow, which really made Sean zoom in on their actions and body language.

"Why you fucking with that hot-ass nigga?" Ugg asked her.

"I ain't know he was hot. Y'all acting like I knew that shit!" she retorted, hating the position she was in. Zetta despised rats with a passion, and to think she was chilling with one and was thinking of going the extra mile with him made her sick to her stomach.

"Yeah, Lil Juan was out the Haute with dat punk-ass nigga," D.C. spoke up. "Juan said they got paperwork and everything on his hot ass."

"Well, I'm 'bout to take - "

Baaa-Baaa-Bubba-Baaaa-Baaaaaaaa! Sean hit the car horn again, cutting Zetta off.

"Ay, Zetta! Bring your ass on! Fuck!" he yelled out the window.

"Ay, main man, you better watch how the fuck you talk to my niece! Fuck is your problem?" D.C. said in an aggressive tone, hoping the rat responded so he'd have an excuse to smoke his boots.

Sean Bullock just stared at D.C. and Ugg, who both returned the glare with mean mugs. Sean smiled and hit the car horn again.

"Zetta, can we go please, before your uncle and his lil man get bent all outta shape! Damn!" He sighed in frustration.

"Sucker-ass nigga, fuck you!" Ugg barked, trying to provoke him to get out of the car.

"Yeah, you right, Moe…you got that!" Sean laughed, which infuriated Ugg and D.C.

"I got what? I got what, you bitch-ass nigga?" Ugg snapped, walking forward. But D.C. held him back.

"Calm down, y'all. Y'all leave my friend alone. Y'all wrong as shit. That's why I don't like bringing nobody 'round here. Y'all always starting stuff," Zetta said, pushing Ugg in the chest.

"Where dat bitch-ass bitch be at?" D.C. asked while backing up, making Ugg laugh.

"Down Southwest in James Creek," Zetta informed them before going back up on the front porch to give her mother a kiss on the cheek.

"Baby, you be careful and don't bring that boy back 'round here. I don't like him," her mother told her.

"Okay, Ma," Zetta agreed. She left the porch, making her way back to the car.

By them time Zetta reached the car, she saw D.C. and Ugg hopping in D.C.'s Benz coupe. She waved to her mother before getting back in her car. As soon as she closed the door, Zetta saw D.C. pull off, speeding like a Nascar driver.

"Just take me back 'round the way, Shorty, 'cause you on some bullshit," Sean said in a nasty tone.

"Yeah, okay," Zetta said, starting the engine. "It's too bad things turned out this way. I was really feeling your crazy ass." Before I found out you was a snitch, she thought, putting the car in gear.

"Whatever, Shorty. Just roll out," he demanded, ready to get back on his end of town.

Zetta pulled off, driving up Montello Avenue. After driving several blocks, she reached Mount Olive Road. Zetta took a right turn on Mount Olive Road and then drove down to the intersection of Bladensburg Road. Taking another right, Zetta drove back down Bladensburg Road, heading back to Southwest without saying another word to Sean.

Sean didn't care. He was too busy looking in the mirrors to see if any cars were following them - mainly the black-on-black Benz coupe he saw speed away from Zetta's hood carrying two guys who he had a minor tiff with.

Ten minutes or so later, Zetta pulled up down Southwest and parked her car on Delaware Avenue. Sean Bullock put his gun in his waistband, feeling more comfortable that he made it back to his hood in one piece. He opened the passenger door and shrugged.

"Maybe we can do this again, Shorty, off the late night or something?" he said with a grin.

Not in a million lifetimes, you hot-ass nigga. "I don't know, boy, you be tripping about nothing," she said, shaking her head.

He turned his body, placing his foot outside the car. "Don't let your first impression throw you off."

You already did that, she thought and said, "I don't know. We'll see."

Fake-ass bitch! Bitch probably did try to set me up anyway, but I gated all that shit, he thought before turning to get out of the car.

As Sean Bullock moved to get out of the car, his eyes ballooned in shock and fear when he saw two guys hopping out of a Benz coupe several feet away - the same two guys he'd just had words with around Zetta's neighborhood.

Aw, this bitch did set me up, he thought, going for his weapon. When Sean went to draw his gun, the two guys moving quickly towards him would be the last faces he'd ever see before he heard and felt the loud gunshots that annihilated his life.

CHAPTER 26

Ten minutes later, Zetta stood in the living room of Poobie's apartment in James Creek, looking out the window. She stared at all the police activity happening on Delaware Avenue. The white sheet covering her date's body gave her an eerie feeling.

That's the second guy that was around me and ended up dying for being a rat, she thought while standing there. She felt Poobie's hand grab her from behind. Poobie pulled her close, hiked up her dress, and began grinding away while palming her pussy from behind.

"This is a surprise. I thought that you only wanted me once a week," she whispered in Zetta's ear, slightly kissing on her earlobe.

As much as she wanted to watch the police finish up their routine and take away the rat's body, Zetta couldn't. She needed an alibi for what had just happened. Thinking on the fly, Zetta knew Poobie would be the perfect alibi.

After the shooting, Zetta managed to pull off while everybody was running for cover. D.C. and Ugg gave her conspiratorial nods as she drove past them and made a quick U-turn, speeding inside the James Creek dwelling's parking lot.

"I'm here now, ain't I, so that should answer your question," Zetta mumbled as Poobie pulled her down on the love seat.

Zetta turned on Poobie's lap, throwing her arms around Poobie's high yellow neck. Poobie began playing with Zetta's clitoris as she kissed her. As her fingers probed tenderly, Zetta melted, forgetting about the evil she'd partaken in just outside Poobie's living room window.

Poobie ground her juicy lips against Zetta's, her nose to the left of Zetta's nose and then to the right, holding Zetta captive on her lap. She licked Zetta's lips, then shoved her tongue inside while they shared a passionate and very sloppy tongue-kiss.

Feeling a hot surge, Zetta could no longer sit still and she began moving on Poobie like she was giving her a lap dance. Then she tore herself from Poobie's lips and her embrace. "How you always get me so hot so quick?" Zetta asked after catching her breath and standing up.

"'Cause I'ma woman who knows how I like to be touched, so I explore your body the same way," Poobie whispered as Zetta leaned over, pinning her to the back of the love seat. Zetta began working her knee between Poobie's thick legs and into her crotch. She kissed her hotly.

Imprisoned in her boy shorts, Poobie's pussy pulsated against Zetta's grinding knee. She humped into Zetta's knee, expressing her urgent need. Poobie pulled down her boy shorts and pulled off her tank top.

Zetta closed her fingers around Poobie's huge titties, one in each hand. She caressed and squeezed, snaking her tongue down her neck. Poobie leaned up and kissed Zetta, raising her dress up to her waist. She tore her lips from Zetta's and slid her thong to the side, exposing her meaty pussy. Zetta backed up and pulled off the dress like a T-shirt. Her titties tumbled out, falling on Poobie's upturned face.

"Mmmmmm……sssssss…" Zetta moaned as Poobie's lips and flicking tongue moved from one titty to the other. She took one titty between both hands and guided the dark brownish nipple to her mouth. Her tongue shot out, crawling all around the areola and then teasing the nipple.

Zetta massaged Poobie's head, playing in her auburn-hued wavy hair as she took her nipple between her lips and sucked it, Zetta's back arched, loving the feeling Poobie gave her.

"Aaaaah….Sssss!" she cried out with pleasure when Poobie began biting gently on her nipple.

Poobie's oral titty play sent ripples of pleasure through her body. Every electrifying charge jolted her coochie. Her juices were flowing, dampening her thong. When Poobie eased her finger there, she smiled inside, knowing that she had Zetta primed and ready for penetration. She rubbed her meaty pussy lips with her fingertips. Then she reached down into her thong and slid it down.

When Zetta stepped out of her thong, Poobie massaged the soft mounds of her ass cheeks. Sliding down the love seat, Poobie got her face right up against Zetta's love nest. She snaked her tongue in her slick slit, probing deeper each time she moved up and down.

"Sssss…Poooooobiiiiiieeeee!" she cried joyously, squeezing her thighs together and gyrating her hips as Poobie's tongue licked upward again and again. She gripped Poobie's shoulders and hung on for the fantastic voyage.

Poobie zeroed in on the top of her pussy, using her tongue in a circular motion - slowly, then lapping harder like a dog extracting water from a bowl. Being a woman, Poobie knew the workings of a girl's pussy and needed no instructions to make it climax. She jacked her clitoris the way she loved hers to be jacked.

"Ssss…ahh! No, Poobie! Nooo!" Zetta panted. "No more!" She pushed herself away from her.

"You came over here for it, so I'ma give it to you," Poobie beamed, catapulting out of the love seat.

Poobie bolted in her bedroom and returned quickly with several sex toys. The only toy Zetta had her eyes on was the huge, thick, double horse-shaped rubber penis. Her heart jumped even faster when Poobie slid one end of the curvy dildo deep inside her love cave. The other end of the big brown rubber schlong leaped out of her spread pussy lips, standing up at an angle.

Zetta went to her, pressing herself to her, mashing her hard nipples against hers. Both their nipples burned as they rubbed against each other skin, generating a passionate heat. While embracing, Zetta rubbed Poobie's upthrusting toy with her belly. She moved from side to side, up and down. Poobie answered with a rhythmic motion, feeling every nerve end in her body tingle.

Wrapping her fingers around the rubber shaft, Zetta wedged it between their bodies at the mouth of her pulsating love tunnel. She saw that Poobie's eyes were fixed down on her pussy. She sank to the carpet, making Poobie follow. When Poobie landed on top of her, Zetta opened her thighs wider, readying herself for Poobie's penetration.

Using the thick double-headed pipe, Poobie parted the edges of Zetta's pussy lips, sliding the shaft up and down, making contact on her aroused clitoris.

No man had ever been more gentle or more thrilling for her. Poobie humped the edges of Zetta's slit and clitoris until she writhed and fucked her pelvis up and down. Poobie's hands feathered all over Zetta's body, moving from her highly-charged nipples to the place where the rubber dick touched the silken hair of her pussy.

"Fuck me, baby," she begged in a throaty whisper while reaching for the shaft imbedded in the aroused depths of Poobie's love nest.

Poobie's love juices coated the shaft as Zetta pulled it forward. Zetta's center was so wet with sex juices that the hulking love toy easily penetrated her gaping twat.

"Mmm, shit…you don't know how much I needed this dick," Zetta moaned, adjusting her position to steer the double-penetrating dildo through her inner mouth and up into her sugary walls.

Poobie stroked her with skill and control, timing her plunges with precision. Every time she impaled her, Poobie twisted her hips, grinding her pelvis against hers until their pussy lips kissed.

"Aaaah…aah…fuck me…fuck me, Poooobieee!" Zetta soared, loving the thrill Poobie put on her clitoris and love tunnel at the same time.

Poobie buried the sex pumper to the hilt, quickening her aggressive strokes. Poobie began climaxing so hard that she felt the explosion in her pussy rushing electrical current to her curling toes, making her pound inside Zetta's juicy twat harder and harder.

Wrapping her legs around Poobie's waist, Zetta began humping back to meet the marvelous pounding. She loved it! The sex tool was thrilling both women to the core. Hugging her close and raking her nails up and down Poobie's soft behind, Zetta cried out, "Oooh, bitch, I'm cumming. I'm cuuummiiiinnngg!"

Zetta's climax had barely ebbed, and then she came again as Poobie fucked her at an alarming rate. A minute later, Poobie climaxed again and her lust for Zetta grew, consuming her. Pounding in and out of her, Poobie came until she lost count. Suddenly Zetta squeezed Poobie's ass cheeks, urging her on. She humped upward and locked her lips onto Poobie's with a kiss at the very peak of her passion.

Poobie stroked faster and faster to encourage the rapid release of another mind-blowing orgasm and she felt Zetta shaking and writhing underneath her.

"Oh my goodness!" Zetta screamed, feeling her body sailing through another orgasm as if in a freaky dream.

Poobie was marvelous in bringing her pleasure. Though she'd been on something totally different earlier, that moment Poobie's tender love took her to heaven on earth, Zetta forgot all about the dead rat she left bleeding in the streets right outside, several feet away from Poobie's living room window.

CHAPTER 27

Even with the way I'd been doped up off the medication and had been sleeping since last night, something inside made my eyes open. My body could feel a threat hovering nearby. Markita sat on my hospital bed, waiting and staring at me with an evil look.

I didn't go through the dreaded routine of asking her what troubled her. I just stared at her, becoming acutely aware of the cell phone she held in her hand - my iPhone. I heard her singing the faint frustrating sound she made, blowing hot air my way.

"Who the fuck is Zetta?" Markita asked, and there was something about her question that scared me.

"Zetta?" I mentioned, acting as if I didn't know who she was talking about.

"Yeah, Zetta, the same bitch who has been calling you ever since last night. Forty-six times, to be exact. And she's the same bitch who texted you." She paused looking at the message. "Here, let me read it to you. It says, 'I hope you not one of those guys who ducks a girl after a good kiss, 'cause you're a very good kisser with those soft-ass lips you have?'" Markita glared at me after reading the text message.

My eyes ballooned in shock, roaming curiously around the hospital room. No nurses or doctors were around to save my ass if Markita decided to go crazy and kick my ass. I was at her mercy right now from my bed rest position My attention was everywhere, my body on alert. What the hell made Zetta text me some bullshit like that for?

Markita's tight demeanor loosened a bit. Her main interest at the moment was Zetta and why she had texted me, talking about a kiss. I wouldn't have heard the incoming calls because my clothes had been cut off me last night after I entered the hospital. Markita must have gotten my personal belongings and went snooping through my phone. I never had a problem with her going through my phone before, so I wasn't surprised by her actions. I was more surprised by Zetta's incriminating text message.

"Answer me, motherfucker!" she snapped, punching me hard in the chest.

"Oooh!" I gasped, sitting upright in bed, trying to catch my breath. Coughing violently, I studied her evil look a little more. Pure hatred covered her face as she vigorously chewed on a piece of gum, looking at me like I had committed a capital crime, which sent my heart fluttering with nervousness. I hadn't had any peace in life ever since I got back in the killing game. Now all these phone calls and text messages from Zetta only made matters worse.

Markita eased off the bed and slammed my iPhone on the floor, shattering it into tiny pieces. She looked at me with tears in her eyes. You know the type of look a woman

gives you when she's hurting inside and has no other way of showing that pain? Yeah, that would be Markita right now!

"You know what? You ain't shit!" she cried. "Nothing but a low down, good for nothing, cheating-ass dog! All I ever wanted was to love you and make you happy and this is how you carry me? You do some shit like this to me?" she said, backing up towards the hospital door.

"Markita, wait, just wait," I said as humbly as I could. "Please?" I begged. "You tripping about nothing. Somebody just tried to kill me and all you can think about is who is calling me? What the fuck is wrong with you?"

"Don't even try to flip this shit around, motherfucker!" she went off, letting me know I couldn't reserve the angry game on her. Usually, I'd go off on her and she'd pipe down, but not today!

"Two and half years, Melo. Twenty-eight months, sixteen days, and eighteen hours, I have done nothing but been faithful to you, and you…" She paused with a sigh, looking deep into my eyes. Tears fell from her eyes and she looked away from me, wiping her eyes. "You took my love for granted and cheated on me," she accused, totally wrong about everything. But you can never stop women when they think they're right about something. Right now, she was on a roll, and it would literally take an act of Congress to get her to listen to me. I was in too much pain to be going back and forth with her over something I knew I didn't do.

"Kita, I did not che—"

"Don't lie, motherfucker! Don't you dare lie to me!" she snapped, making my heart drop into the pit of my stomach.

I couldn't believe she was taking the phone calls and damaging text message to the extreme. I know it looked messed up, but if she'd just listen and let me explain, she'd realize that I'd never hurt her intentionally.

"Kita, baby, I love you. Fuck I look like cheating on you and be dumb enough to give out my cell phone number when I know you check my shit every night? That woman is a new author for the publishing company. I swear on everything I love!"

"That's the weakest bullshit I've heard." She laughed furiously. "I don't believe that shit. What the fuck you doing kissing the bitch for if she's just some author?" she raged, opening the door.

"Kita, you tripping over nothing! Don't leave this room mad like this over some bullshit!"

"I'm tripping over nothing? Over nothing?" she repeated, wiping away her tears. "You call kissing some other bitch nothing, someone who just so happens to be blowing up your motherfuckin' phone every day? I had to press ignore and send the groupie bitch to voicemail cause she kept calling you so much. Ain't nobody in the world that pressed for a motherfuckin' job. Naw, naw, you did something with that bitch. I ain't dumb by a long shot, motherfucker!" she hissed, and then she kept going, not giving me a chance to defend myself. "I tell you what, since you like kissing the bitch, you can have her, 'cause I'm done with your trifling, lying, no good cheating ass! I hate you!" she said and then she stormed out of the hospital room.

"Kita! Kita!" I yelled, watching the love of my life walk out on me and disappear as the hospital door closed.

All the machines I was hooked up to made it very hard for me to leap from the bed and chase behind her. I closed my eyes slowly, feeling the tears well up in them. The only thing on my mind was, Why me, Lord? Why you ruining my life by taking my wife from me right now, when you know I need her more than ever?

CHAPTER 28

Nu-Nu chilled inside his used box-shaped Chevy Caprice that sat on 100 spoke shiny rims, listening to his favorite Scarface song and smoking that good exotic skunk with Antione Evans, a.k.a. Twan from Uptown in Clifton Terrace Projects. He was a known rat who pleaded guilty back in 1997 to two counts of second degree murder while armed and conspiracy to kill and assault with a dangerous weapon. In exchange for his guilty plea and light prison sentence, Twan snitched on Tim Dog, a real nigga that did nothing but show Twan love.

Tim Dog was still locked away in the Feds somewhere and Twan was out in society, up to his same bullshit. He'd been hanging over in Northeast, trying to hide from his wicked past in Northwest. But whatever you do in the dark will always come to light. Twan had no idea that Tim Dog was cool with Moe Styles.

During a phone call from the Feds, Moe Styles commented on Twan and how he liked how the little guy always wanted to put in some work. When Tim Dog gave him the 411 on the Twan's bitch-made pedigree, Moe Styles made up his mind to deal with the situation. Moe Styles embraced the rat and let him get all the way comfortable around the hood. When he was sure the rat was rocked all the way to sleep, Moe Styles turned his nephew loose on him.

Nu-Nu got paid a half of kilo of coke and $3,500 from his uncle Moe Styles to crush the rat. Moe Styles told Nu-Nu it was a coming-home gift, but after he told Nu-Nu about the favor he needed done, Nu-Nu knew it was full payment for the hit.

"I'm as real as they come, as hard as they get
They go to talkin' off the wall, I put a
par in they shit.......
I'm the original gangsta, I tell ya' how I do it,
I check niggas from the jump when they
step to me with that bullshit.
I am a fool bitch, an eighty-eight shiner
from the Southside of Houston,
You tuned to the sounds of a nigga
Who don't give a fuck, that's one way or the other
I'ma still get mines—play the game ma'fuckers..
The truth is in the building, it done came to light
And I done sold so many records,
change my name to Life.
If I can breathe in the hood, nigga, feel my pain
And even though they tried to change me,
I remain the same.
And even if I did that chrome-plated grill on my shit
I come from out the ma'fuckin' Bricks
And I'll never forget where I come from, Son
I'm respected in these ma'fuckin' streets I run—
I'm face!

Nu-Nu heard Scarface's voice in a different light. He actually was in tune with the sounds of a lyricist who painted the street life so vividly. As he nodded his head back and forth, Nu-Nu hyped himself up to eliminate the rat who his uncle hated with a passion. It was ironic how the rat's name was identical to that of the rat he'd almost lost his life for over two years ago. That alone made the deal even sweeter for him, giving him extra motivation to do what he wanted to do to the other Twan over two years ago.

"Moe, that nigga Face be going in like shit," Twan said in a hyped-up tone. "These niggas out here faking off all that Lil Wayne and Young Jeezy shit, but none of them niggas can fuck with Brad Joyner, for real."

"Yeah, Slim jive be going all the way—" Nu-Nu stopped talking, pulled out his Glock-40, and shot Twan three time in the head. Twan never saw it coming.

Twan's head slammed violently on the dashboard and slumped over the glove compartment. Nu-Nu looked around to see if anybody was looking at his car. When he saw his uncle giving him conspiratorial head nod, Nu-Nu knew everything was cool.

Nu-Nu began searching Twan's body and he found a .45 caliber semi-automatic on him, $1,200, and a small sandwich bag full of "E" pills. Nu-Nu put the car in gear and sped off with his adrenaline racing. He had never shot anybody at point blank range before. After doing the evil deed, he felt invincible and he wanted to do it again and again. When his adrenaline settled down a little, Nu-Nu looked up and saw that he was at the intersection Minnesota Avenue and Nannie Helen Burroughs Avenue. He drove straight on through over to 48th and Jay Street, past the Chevron Gas Station, and kept driving until he reached Eastern Avenue. After the light turned green, Nu-Nu drove over to the Maryland side of Addison Road and sped to a secluded little spot in the Fairmont Heights high school parking lot.

Knowing the place would be empty because of the summer vacation, Nu-Nu got out of the car and wiped down everything he had touched. Gaining knowledge in forensic science and DNA testing from watching TV shows like CSI and Another 48 Hours, Nu-Nu still wasn't satisfied with just wiping off traces of himself in the vehicle. He thought for a second and then took off running. He didn't stop until he reached the gas station on Sheriff Road and bought a container of gasoline. Nu-Nu lit a book of matches and tossed them inside of the car. He walked over in the cut by the school, lit himself a skunk-laced Backwood, and watched the car slowly become engulfed in flames.

When a small explosion ripped through the car, Nu-Nu jumped back and took off running back towards the gas station on Sheriff Road with killing a rat now attached to his ghetto resume.

CHAPTER 29

As soon as Markita left, I sank into a state of depression. Getting shot at by some ghost who wanted me dead was stressful enough, but to have my wife leave me over some bullshit on top of that took the stress level to astronomical heights.

I couldn't believe that she had walked out on me like that. I replayed Markita's angry faces, teary eyes, and venomous words in my head over and over again. I can't lose her. She's my baby; she's my everything. The answers to solving this puzzle would be very hard to figure out. To add insult to injury, she broke my phone, taking away my avenue to call her ass until she picked up her phone. The only good thing that came out of the deal is that I didn't have to worry about that crooked cop sweating me or putting a trace on my cell phone to locate me.

Lying back on the soft hospital bed, I stared up at the florescent lights and began counting all the black dots in the tiled ceiling. I shook my head from side to side, trying to get rid of the thoughts that danced around in my head - thoughts of me never being with Markita again, thoughts of not being around for my son's next birthday, thoughts of going back to prison, or even worse, thoughts of me being gunned down in cold blood like I'd done countless times to so many others.

I was doing a great deal of thinking when a 6'1" tall stockily-built light-brown-skinned baldheaded guy entered my room with a broom, dust pan, and trash can. At the sight of the janitor, I sat up in bed, not believing my eyes.

He kept nodding his head to some tune playing in his head as he began sweeping up my phone into the dust pan, looking like he enjoyed what he was doing. I paid close attention to his thick Muslim-style beard and the way he chewed on the plastic spoon.

"Hold up, Swol up!" I said cheerfully, causing the janitor to swivel his head in my direction with the quickness.

"Aww shit…aww shit…you better watch it, sucker!" Swol grinned and began doing the Happy Feet dance with joy. "What's up, Melly-Mel, my main apple-scrapple?" he greeted, rushing to my bedside to give me a hug.

The last time I saw Cardoza "Swol" Simms was back in 1999 after Lorton closed down and we got shipped out to the Feds like cattle. We ended up on the same prison yard in Leavenworth Federal Penitentiary somewhere in Kansas.

Being from Uptown, Northwest, Swol and I knew a lot of the same people and ended up becoming something tight like blood brothers in prison while serving time. Swol's prison currency was always longer than a javelin, courtesy of his wicked shot on the dice. Swol would always break the crap games around the yard and he'd always break bread with the homies he was close to. He really showed me love because of the Uptown thing and he looked at me like his little brother. He helped me get a pretty girl while we were on lock, but I fumbled that money by asking her for some money too early in the game, which ran her off.

"Fuck is up, Slim?" I laughed at his outfit. He was dressed just like one of the nurses that worked in the hospital, rocking burgundy scrubs and tan Timberland construction boots. "I see you done really put that pistol play down, huh?"

"Jive," he smirked. "I'm tryna stay out here with all these lovely ladies. I just got home from doing sixteen years straight off a weak-ass ten-to-thirty."

"Shiiid, at least you made it out. It's a rack of good men still stuck in them joints with all of it."

"Yeah, Slim, I know," he said solemnly. "I heard about you getting back Slim, but I thought niggas was wailin' 'cause you ain't write me or none of that shit."

"Wailin' my ass," I laughed, trying to avoid his question of why I didn't get back at him. I had no excuse for it. I just was moving so fast, trying to get at so many guys in prison that I fuck with, that he slipped through the cracks, which made me feel bad, 'cause this nigga jive took care of me for a minute when I was down and out in the struggle. "I told you I was going to get back and I did it, Champ. I did that ma'fucka. But enough about me. What's up, Slim, what's happening wit'cha?"

Swol shook his head in despair. "Staying all the way out the way and working, Melly-Mel."

"Working? I thought you wasn't ever going to work for the white man when you got out?"

"Yeah, I thought I wasn't, but shit hard out here on the boulevard. Shit just ain't the same no more, Slim."

"Fuck you mean?" I asked, somewhat confused. "Slim, don't give me dat joint dere! You raised too much hell Uptown to return to the streets to work a 9-to-5 gig. Say it ain't so, Bob?"

Swol chuckled. "That cowboy shit over for me, Champ. I'm just loving life as a free man. Too many anything-ass niggas and gangbangers running 'round the city now."

"Let me find out them young niggas got you all the way shook?"

"Never that, Slim. I'm just staying out they way so I don't end up in here with no gunshot wounds like your ass. It's they time to shine, Slim. We lost our time to all them years of being locked up," he pointed out.

"Yeah, I hear you, but I ain't get shot for fucking with no niggas. In fact, I was getting off work when I got hit."

"That's fucked up, Slim."

"How long you been working out here?"

"'Bout four months now. It's okay. I get paid a nice little check and get to meet a rack of lil broads."

"That's good to hear," I smiled, still not believing Swol was talking to me right now. I thought I was dreaming, so I had to pinch him to make sure.

"Ouch, Mother - " He jerked his arm away from me. "Fuck you do that for?" he asked and pinched me back even harder.

"Sssss…ahhh, Slim!" I winced and laughed at the same time. "Naw, naw, I just wanted to make sure I wasn't dreaming, that's all."

"You's a geekin'-ass nigga, Young." He laughed.

"Yeah, I know, just like I know this gig ain't you, Slim. What if I could offer you something way better than this. Would you ride?"

"Depends on what you offering?"

"I just need for you to watch my back full time. The pay is like that and you can quit this geekin'-ass job you got."

"No can do, Bob! I can't fuck with them streets no more. I'm jive too old for that shit. I'll be thirty-seven years old next month."

"That's all?" I asked. "Nigga, I thought you was 'bout to say forty-seven or some shit older than that."

"Yeah, I see…I see you still on joke time, Slim."

"No I'm not, especially when it comes to putting some cake in your pockets. All I need for you to do is hold me down."

"You saying like a bodyguard?"

"Fuck no, none of that shit at all, Slim. I just need for you to be on point and keep me on point, just like we use to carry shit out in the Feds. Me and my woman own a nightclub and everybody plays the spot. Once you get down on my team, you guaranteed a job at the club and you won't ever hafta go to work until I go to work. Once we get used to hanging out together again, we can step it up a hundred times more than how we did it in the Feds."

Swol began rubbing his big beard, looking like he was entertaining the thought of accepting my offer. "So you saying, all we doing is hanging out and chilling and you gonna pay me to do that?"

"Yeah, but you might hafta kill a snitch from time to time, or just watch my back while I put in that work."

"Oh hell no!" he interrupted me. "Killing niggas got me ten to thirty years last time, 'cause niggas came to court and wanted to snitch on me, forcing me to take that cop. I'm not stupid enough to go back down that road."

"Swol, it's very profitable road. I been doing this shit since I came home. I been home twenty-eight months now and I live in a big-ass house, own two cars, and I'm a half owner of a popular nightclub. Cleaning up a nigga who fucks with that cheese from time to time ain't bad at all. In fact, it's jive therapeutic, Slim."

"Yeah, until a nigga get caught and face a million years."

"Slim, you can keep being 'noid all you want. I just need a solid man on my team to watch my back," I said, looking at him. "I can guarantee you at least $5,000 to $7,000 every two weeks after taxes, which I know you ain't making up in here sweeping and mopping floors and shit."

Swol looked at me for a long moment, and I figured those figures made him seriously think about my offer. "You making it sound too good, baby. I might have to jump back out there, Slim."

"You stalling, homes. You s'posed to been had your swimming trunks back on the moment I ask you to dive back in the game with me." I sighed. "I need you, Swol-Up, for real."

"Let me think about it, Slim."

"Yeah, a'ight, write down your number and shit so I can get at you while you thinking it over."

Swol reached over on the nightstand to grab a pen and hospital memo pad. As he wrote down his contact information, he kept glancing at me and smiling. "Slim, don't be stalking a nigga, Slim. Hit me once a week.

I shouldn't take too long in to give you an answer," he said, placing the information back on the nightstand by the hospital telephone.

"Hopefully it'll be the right answer," I said, slapping Swol playfully on his back.

"Slim, I'ma tell you now, loyalty means everything in the world to me. After that prison bid I just did, I ran into so much petty, backstabbing, snake shit that I'm real hesitant to extend that loyalty to anybody."

"I'm not just anybody, Swol. Nigga, we ate out the same hook-up bowl in the Feds. You took care of me when I was fucked up in the game. It's only proper that I return the favor, right? Now you just keep that in mind when you weighing out your options," I told him as he rose up off my bed.

"You know I will, Slim," he said, giving me another hug.

Moments later, after sweeping up the room and emptying the trash can, Swol gave me a farewell salute on his way out the door. As soon as he left, I grabbed his information and called him from the hospital room phone.

"Hello?" he said after picking up on the second ring.

"Just making sure you ain't give me no demo," I laughed.

Seconds later, Swol came back in the hospital room, hung up his cell phone in my face, and gave me a funny look. "Are you serious?" He shook his head and laughed at me before leaving the room again.

I got a kick out of seeing Swol again. He made me forget all about my issues with Markita. They say laughter is good for the soul, and all the laughing I just did should re-energize my soul for what I have to do when I get out of here.

Swol and I were similar in many ways. That's why we always had a tight bond in the Feds. I could only imagine how things would be chilling with him on the free side of the prison walls - if he swallowed his pride and accepted my offer.

CHAPTER 30

Markita felt like a total wreck. Her spirits were at an all-time low. She hadn't spoken to or seen Carmelo in the last five days. The last time they spoke they had the biggest argument over some woman calling him over forty times within a two day span. Even after Carmelo explained that the woman calling him was a new author he had signed to his publishing company, Markita called him every lying, no-good, cheating dog in the book before she got fed up and threw his phone on the floor, shattering it into tiny pieces. Carmelo couldn't do anything but look on in shock and disgust as he lay in the hospital bed.

Markita couldn't believe that Carmelo would cheat on her after all she'd done for him. She had opened her home, legs, and heart up to him when he was fresh out of jail, given him a son and half of her business that her brother left to her in his will. Markita felt like she had made Carmelo into the success and everything else he was right now.

The fact that he never told me about the bitch, Zetta, and that I had to learn about that bitch on my own makes his ass look guilty, like he's trying to hide something from me, but he's busted. I caught his ass, she told herself while sitting by the telephone in her house.

Markita prayed that Carmelo wasn't cheating on her just so she wouldn't have to cut off his dick. Even though the text about the kiss really hurt her, Markita felt like she could get past that after he stayed in the dog house with her for a while, but if he cheated on her, there would be no more talking. She'd just leave him and be on to the next one. She was going to confront him when he came home from the hospital. He had a few more days left in the hospital before he came home, which should give her enough time to calm down, call up her sister-in-law, April, and just vent.

April made it over to Markita's house in no time with her cousin, Poobie. Markita noticed the high yellow attractive female who dressed kind of boyishly and wore baggy clothes to hide her femininity. Just imagine a high yellow version of the female rapper Nicki Minaj wearing baggy clothes. Yeah, that be Poobie all day, body and all.

"Poobie, this Markita...Kita, this my cousin Poobie," April introduced them as they stood at the front door.

Markita gave April a funny look as if to say, I only called you to come over here? Carmelo's going to have a fit if he knows I'm having strangers in our house. Then again, fuck him! He had strangers kissing him all in the mouth and shit! She smiled before shaking Poobie's hand and inviting them into her home.

As Poobie took a seat on the plush sofa, Markita pulled April to the side. "Um, Poobie, we'll only be a second. If you want, there's food and drinks in the fridge," Markita said with a smile. "You family, so don't be shy."

Poobie nodded at her, looking like a high yellow pretty boy straight off the dope strip somewhere in D.C. Markita nodded back. "Well, okay, see you in a few," Markita said and left the living room. She took April up to her bedroom to talk in private.

"I thought I asked you to come over here?"

"I did. I'm here now, ain't I?" April said in a nasty tone.

"Yeah, but you brought the entire world with you," Markita fussed.

"Girl, that's my family. I do have a life outside of being your sister-in-law. We was about to go hang out for the day when you called," April explained as she sat down on the loveseat in the sitting room in the bedroom.

"Oh, okay," Markita mumbled, taking a seat in Carmelo's recliner directly across from where April sat.

Markita could smell faint traces of Carmelo's cologne, which made her miss him even more, but she refused to go back to the hospital and apologize. She didn't feel like she was wrong in any shape, form, or fashion.

"So, what's up that I had to stop what I was doing to come over here?" April asked.

Markita looked at April and began crying and spilling her heart out to her. April sat there listening intently as Markita told her everything, from Carmelo getting shot to the point where they had a huge argument after she went through his cell phone and found the text message.

April wanted to say, I told you so! But she kept her thoughts to herself. April felt good to actually be a person Markita could call on at a time like this.

"Girl, I heard everything," April said slowly. "Don't get mad about what I'm about to say." April sighed. "Men are going to be men, Kita, regardless of how much we love them and all we do for them. They are dogs by nature and can't help themselves when they see another bitch in heat."

"No, no, no…not my Melo. He's different!" Markita cried.

"I know you want to believe that he is different, but no, baby, he's not different at all, 'cause if he was, he wouldn't have had that text message on his phone. Now I'm not the smartest bitch in the world, but it don't take no rocket scientist to figure out what went down between him and that other woman. What's the bitch's name anyway?"

"Some chick named Zetta," Markita sniffled.

Zetta? Zetta? Poobie replayed in her head over and over again, getting a little upset while eavesdropping on their conversation from the other side of the door. Poobie had given them a few moments to get upstairs and get comfortable before trailing behind them to ear hustle. Sitting around looking stupid bored her. She got more excitement from doing stuff like this - stuff that could lead to confrontation if she got caught.

After she heard Markita mention Zetta's name as the woman responsible for the text about a kiss, Poobie became hot with anger and rushed back downstairs. She couldn't wait to see Zetta again and confront her about the news she learned today.

While Markita sat upstairs discussing her love life with April, Poobie sat downstairs angry at Zetta, Poobie's ego was bruised. She felt like she wasn't handling her business good enough with Zetta in the bedroom. 'Cause if I was, she wouldn't have to be out in the streets kissing all up on some man, the same motherfuckers she told me that she never wanted to have sexual relations with again. I know it's her ass too, 'cause ain't too many Zetta's in the metropolitan area. Yeah, it's her ass…that lying bitch! Poobie thought, tapping her sneaker on the floor with frustration.

"Ooooh, I can't wait to see her fake ass again!" Poobie barked while mean mugging the huge poster-sized family photo of Carmelo, Markita, and their son that hung on the wall directly over the huge flat screen TV in the corner. "Yeah, soon as I see you, bitch, you getting a piece of my mind and no more dick from me again…ever!" Poobie said, feeling tears of anger and pain well up in the corner of her eyes.

CHAPTER 31

Welcome to the good life…
I go for mines—I gots'ta shine…
Now throw your hands up in the sky!
Homie, tell me what's good
Why I only got a problem when you in the hood?

Welcome to the Good life…
Like I'm new in the hood
The only thing I wish is
I wish a nigga would!

A group of ten young men nodded their heads in sync to the Kanye West featuring T-Pain's classic while hanging out on the block on First and U Streets near an abandoned house - the same house that Carmelo stormed over two years ago to eliminate Twan. Bottles of Remy Martin 1738 and Moet Rose sat up on the grass. Brand new SUVs, old school box Chevys, a few Camaros, one big body Benz, and several motorcycles lined the streets in front of the house. Most of the youngsters loitering in the area, rocking "Stop Snitching" T-shirts and baggy jeans, were getting their smoke and drink on, enjoying the fruits of their labor.

For over the last year and some change, the youngsters had pumped life back into the deserted block. After Carmelo handled his business in the crack house, the police played hot defense on the whole area, virtually shutting down all the illegal income that flowed through the hood.

Now they were owners of the flashy vehicles parked on the street. The drugs being sold on the Uptown strip had fiends lined up, and all the dealers working the block were armed up with tre-pounds and semi-automatics.

The drug traffic that flowed through the area was courtesy of Wee-Wee's son, Lil Wee. He had pumped life back into the forgotten block by selling some bomb PCP water - the popular drug of choice for most of the inner city young citizens between the ages of thirteen and thirty. Lil Wee got the PCP connect from his pops, who was doing time somewhere in the Feds. Lil Wee was getting enough work to front it out on consignment to all the guys around the Le'Droit Park area that he fucked with.

As the PCP strip grew, generating truckloads of cash, second and third generation youngsters from the Le'Droit Park area came out with a variety of other drugs to get their hustle on. Before long, any unattainable drug one wanted could be found on First and U streets.

Small piles of money were stacked on the ground in the center of a huge circle of dread-headed young men and a few baldheaded teenage thugs in training who were engaged in a high stakes crap game. They usually blew the money they earned on the block on the crap games, chasing more money, trying to achieve the phony image of the American Dream.

"Damn, Moe Jenkins, this joint jive all the way back live like Twan use to have this joint rocking back in the day," Leo said, glancing at a Lincoln Town car full of young women pulling and parking in front of the house, blasting the cranking Go-Go music of TCB.

"Fuck Twan's hot ass!" Lil Wee said with a vicious mug on his face. "That hot bitch-ass nigga was probably getting his yak from the Feds anyway."

Lil Wee's pops, Wee Wee, had sent the paperwork on Twan out into the streets to him and told him to spread the word about Twan eating that cheese. By the time Lil Wee could put the word out, Twan got slaughtered off the late night.

After breathing life back into the block, Lil Wee vowed to never have any informants and snitches hustling on that block around him. Whenever a new dealer popped up trying to hustle, Lil Wee made them read the paperwork on Twan and began using Twan's paperwork as a screening tool for the new guys with hustler ambitions.

"On everything I love, Moe, if it ever comes out that you fucking with that cheese or helping the Feds to give a nigga a case, I'm marking you for death, plus your mothers, grandmothers, and kids!" Lil Wee always stressed to whoever came around wanting to hustle on the block.

Most of the guys kept it moving after that warning. Only ten solid young thoroughbreds were willing to step up and hold down the block, accepting the terms of Lil Wee's warning.

The 5'8" tall dark-skinned thug they called Leo laughed loudly at Lil Wee's comment. "Moe, kill my man, you wild as shit!" he said, twisting one of his short dreads. "Naw, I was just saying how shit was back in the days. That hot-ass nigga fed a lot of niggas 'round here."

"Fuck that hot-ass nigga and whoever still on his dead dick!" Lil Wee said wide-eyed getting hyped, sounding like the rapper DMX. "I come up outta a nigga's nut sack who was crushing shit out here in broad daylight during rush hour traffic, nigga, and I'ma carry on the torch 'til a nigga knock my noggin loose or I get a million years in the Feds," he declared, watching a few of his men entertain the females in the parked Lincoln Town car.

Leo watched him for a moment. From the way Lil Wee's bubble eyes and closed lips jumped, Leo knew Lil Wee was pushing his own brand of hustling and willing to kill to enforce it - the kind of hustling that engrossed everybody in the hood with the "don't snitch" mentality.

Suddenly the sound of a car speeding down the block could be heard, drawing everybody's attention. As the Charger with the Hemi engine slammed on the brakes, the young guys on the block began gripping their weapons.

Moments later, the passenger window of the Charger lowered and three arms, clutching guns, extended outward.

"WORK CALL!" Lil Wee yelled, putting everybody on point before ducking low and going for the Tommy gun they kept underneath his big body Benz.

Guys in the crap game circle took off running a second too late. The men in the Charger Hemi fired recklessly. The rapid shots split the sir like repetitive thunder as the men fell just inches from the spots they had attempted to flee, hitting the ground with loud thuds. Glass shattered on several cars. The girls in the rental Lincoln Town car screamed and ducked as low as they could as the gunshots lit up the block like the 4th of July. As the wounded youngsters tried to crawl to safety, some of them took on more heavy fire, collecting more slugs in their bodies while lying on the ground.

When Lil Wee got his hands on the Tommy gun, he knew the next few moments would define him forever. For the first time, he was on the receiving end of a deadly ambush. He wrestled with his conscience for seconds that seemed like an eternity. As he looked at several men who had just been chilling with him lying on their faces in widening pools of blood that oozed from their head, Lil Wee cast his eyes down in grief and he made his decision to strike back right away.

Anger burning his heart, Lil Wee raised up from behind his Benz, clutching the Tommy gun, only thinking REDRUM. He aimed the gun at the Charger Hemi as his sweaty finger began squeezing the trigger. He shot recklessly, cutting the deadly ambush short as the head of one of the shooters in the Charger slammed forward into the dashboard.

Lil Wee continued shooting as Leo rose up shooting at the Charger as well. The Charger sped down the block, fleeing the scene, Leo and Lil Wee ran out into the street, shooting and chasing the car. When the car hit the corner and turned up First Street, Lil Wee and Leo stopped in their tracks and went back up the block to see the damage that had been done. When they looked around and saw all the bloodshed, Lil Wee began trembling with a desire to kill.

The block resembled a bullet-riddled neighborhood in the streets of Iraq after a deadly firefight between US Armed Forces and insurgents. Several young men lay prone on the sidewalks, bleeding badly from gunshot wounds. Four young men died from catching slugs in the head and other main arteries. A few of the guys managed to escape the drive-by shooting.

As the female driving the Lincoln Town car attempted to flee the scene, Lil Wee and Leo ran up on the car, aiming their guns at them. The girls inside screamed for help.

"Bitch, shut the fuck up!" Lil Wee barked, forcing the driver's side door open and literally snatching the driver out of the car by her short hair.

"Aaahhh! Let me go, puh-leeeeeasse!" She screamed and began crying as Lil Wee gripped her hair, yanking her neck back so he could look down into her tear-filled eyes.

"Bitch, you ain't going nowhere 'til you tell me who them niggas was!" he demanded from the shaken young woman.

At the same time, the Charger Hemi zoomed up First Street and didn't stop until the driver reached the Washington Hospital Center several blocks away. Both men inside the car quickly looked over at the passenger seat several times at their unconscious friend. Their hearts pumped with fear. After the driver parked in front of the emergency room, both men hopped out and quickly pulled the bleeding, unconscious man from the passenger seat. Their adrenaline was still racing at an all-time high. They dragged the stickily-built man's body inside the emergency room.

"Help!" the driver yelled soon as the emergency room doors slid open.

The backseat shooter and mastermind behind the drive-by shooting pulled down a black bandana from his face, letting it hang loosely around his neck, and yelled, "Get us some motherfuckin' help! This man's dying!"

Both men dropped their friend gently on the hospital floor and quickly ran out into the night, having no idea that he was already dead on arrival. After jumping in the Charger Hemi and speeding away, both men felt like their mission was a failure. The random act of violence stemmed from thirty months of waiting in frustration from not being able to get revenge.

The drive-by shooting had been carried out by Twan's nephew, Little James, from Congress Park - a neighborhood in Southeast. The act of revenge had been in the makings for thirty months while he waited to get released from residential somewhere out in Pennsylvania. Little James didn't particularly care about the honor code of the street game. In fact, he'd just turned seventeen years old and worshipped the ground his Uncle Twan walked on.

Twan had been taking care of Little James ever since the day his father got killed execution style in an alley near Blaine Street over in Northeast. When he got old enough, Twan brainwashed Little James until Twan had him under the impression that if a person didn't snitch on you personally or the guys you had genuine love for, then it didn't concern you.

"If you worry about other niggas' business all the time and who told on so and so, you ain't never going to be able to handle your own business. Self-preservation is the number one rule of the land," Twan always used to tell him before he got arrested for an attempted murder during a botched armed robbery at the age of twelve.

While being locked away in a juvenile institution, Little James learned about his uncle's death from his grandmother. When she told him that Twan got killed around U Street, several blocks away from her house on Bryant Street, Little James vowed to shut down the block as soon as he hit the streets. He told himself that he wouldn't ever stop shooting up the block until he got the people responsible for his uncle's murder. Knowing that his uncle was a rat made no difference to him. Little James wanted blood: twenty-eight lives for his uncle's single life, which was equal to each year that his uncle lived on earth.

Knowing that tonight was only the beginning, Little James vowed to never let up. He would go through there shooting every day and night until he quenched his bloodthirst for revenge or made the block hot enough to bring in the National Guard patrol, which would make it virtually impossible for the hustlers in the area to get any money. Little James felt that since his uncle Twan lost his life on the block, then nobody else should be allowed to have control of it - period!

CHAPTER 32

The six days after my argument with Markita were the longest days of my life. I barely slept in the past several days. Unfortunately, my luck turned out to be the worse in the world. Each morning came and I willed myself to watch the door, expecting Markita's arrival. Unfortunately, she never showed. Over the long stay in the hospital, recuperating was exactly what I needed. It gave me time to get my thoughts and future plans together.

The anxiety of getting released from the hospital had me wide awake like I had been drinking Red Bull energy drinks all day. I was counting down the last three days of my hospital stay and time moved slower than a turtle race. I worked out hard, paced around the room for hours, and took plenty of showers, trying to rush the time away, but those activities still didn't help the time to pass like I needed it to. The days seemed long and the nights were twice as long.

Now that I was six hours away from being released, I felt happy, but I also feared the unknown. I didn't know what would happen once I returned home. Would the locks be changed? Would Markita let me in the house once I arrived? Would she still be angry about the text Zetta sent me? Those thoughts and many more danced around in my head as Swol entered my room with his janitor tools and a white plastic shopping bag. When I saw him I was reminded about what we had talked about a few days ago. Every day he came to work, he would check in on me and make sure I was cool while I was on bed rest, but he never gave me an answer to the offer I gave him.

He moved over to the bed and I got up to embrace him with a manly hug. "'Sup wit'cha?" I greeted him with a smile after breaking the hug.

Swol gave me the shopping bag. "You, me, and that $5,000 to $7,000 every two weeks you was talking about. The legal nine to five hustle is over for me. I just finished up my time in the halfway house and my parole officer told me to just give her a clean urine once a month and valid check stubs from my job and I'm good. After six months of that, I'll only have to check in with her once every ninety days."

I emptied the contents of the shopping bag out onto the bed, noticing the clothes, my car and house keys, and a brand new AT&T Smartphone. I looked at Swol, demanding an explanation with my eyes.

"Oh, some chick left these clothes and shit for you at the nurse's station," he informed and I felt a little relieved, knowing my baby Markita still cared enough to make sure that I didn't leave the hospital wearing a hospital gown.

I figured she wasn't that mad at me anymore, 'cause if she was, I wouldn't have these clothes, new cell phone, and fresh New Balance track shoes. "Thanks, Champ," I said, pulling off my gown. I put on the Ed Hardy T-shirt and then slipped on the dark blue True Religion jeans and the 1500 New Balance sneakers. "Ay, the check stubs ain't no problem. I can get them joints made up for you at the club," I told him, getting hyped. Now that I had my baby Markita back in my life and a solid man riding with me, I felt a little bit more invincible. Swol gave me the camaraderie and security I'd been seeking every since my best friend Aaron passed away.

Swol and I talked for hours, reminiscing about old times spent on lockdown, until I got discharged from the hospital with a whopping $18,635.46 bill. I gave Swol the hospital bill on our way to his car: a two-door 1978 Monte Carlo Landau. Swol had the car looking sweet sitting on some shiny chrome rims off the sparkling silver bullet paint job with glitter flakes mixed in the paint job.

"I'ma pay that though!" I said sarcastically as we reached his ride.

"Damn, it jive cost like a ma'fucka to heal up in them joints, huh?" Swol grinned, handing the bill back to me.

"Shiid! They need to pay me for holding a nigga hostage that long!" I capped as Swol got in and opened the passenger door for me.

After getting inside, Swol started the engine and the sounds of Maze featuring Frankie Beverly came on singing "Back In Stride Again!" Swol pulled off and I gave him the directions to my house. As he drove me home, I began mentally kicking myself in the ass for being so open and trusting with him. Under no circumstances did anybody know where I rest my head. You couldn't trust too many niggas as far as you could see them in this game. For some reason, I didn't feel like Swol had them cutthroat, snake-like cruddy tendencies. We'd done time together and he'd never showed me that side of him when it came to me. Now for the other guys Swol met at the water fountain, that was a different story.

After I got home, I jumped out of his car and ran to the front door. Swol got out and followed me. Man, I hope her ass ain't in here waiting on me butt naked, I thought while sticking my key into the lock and opening the door.

I could barely erase the scene from my head as we entered the empty house. All the furniture was missing. The house looked just like a vacant house you view when you trying to buy the joint. I ran upstairs quickly, more concerned with the whereabouts of my son and Markita. Checking my son's bedroom, I saw it was completely empty. I hung my head low, checking each of the bedroom upstairs and found them empty as well.

CHAPTER 33

When I entered my master bedroom, tears of anger welled up in my eyes. I clasped my hands together, cracked my knuckles, and slammed my fist against the wall in frustration. I thought about Markita sitting alone with tears streaming down her face while reading that text on my phone. I could only imagine the hurt she felt after discovering another woman had kissed me.

She definitely made me know what it felt like to have everything taken away from me. Markita's sudden abandonment was a sore sight to behold. Our home was empty, just like the first time we came to tour it in hopes of buying it. I sank down to the floor with a hardened expression, letting Markita's disrespectful act occupy my thoughts.

When Swol knocked lightly on my bedroom door, I wiped my tears away and got to my feet. I couldn't believe she just took off like this without telling me or giving me a chance to plead my case.

"Everything cool, Slim?"

"Hell naw," I said in a weak voice as I walked over to my walk-in closet. Once I stepped inside, I saw that all my clothes and shoes were still there, untouched.

"My woman just up and left me, Slim."

"Damn, Slim, fuck you do to make her roll out on you like that?"

As his question invaded my ears, I thought about Zetta and the first day we met. I thought about the opportunity her book offered to my company. Then I thought about Zetta giving me a kiss of gratitude, which caused the current drama in my life.

I couldn't bear losing Markita and my son over a weak-ass kiss. I wondered at that moment if that kiss had dug a grave for my relationship with Markita? It wasn't like Markita to just up and leave and take everything with her no matter how mad she was with me. I wish I could turn back the hands of time to the day when we made passionate love in my home office.

"I can see this is a bad time for you, Slim, so I'ma go sit in the car and wait for you." Swol's voice rang in my ears.

I remained silent because I wasn't used to the empty house around me. The thought turned me into an emotional wreck while I just stared at my clothes and shoes in the closet. I wanted to see Markita so badly right now. If the love we shared couldn't get past a weak-ass kiss, then I needed for her to tell me face to face that she didn't want me anymore.

I pulled out my new AT&T Smartphone and called Markita. She answered on the first ring like she'd been expecting my call.

"What, Melo?"

"What? That's all you can say after leaving and taking my son and shit! Where you at?" I demanded.

She got quiet on me. I went off, cursing like a sailor, and asked her a million and one questions about why she left me and took all the furniture.

"Ask you little girlfriend Zetta why I left your cheating ass!" she fired back with an attitude.

"Fuck that shit! You saying anything! I need to see you and my son right now!"

Once again she got quiet on me. Her silence wrapped around my heart as if to suffocate me.

"So you just gon' act like that, huh?"

"Act like what?" She sucked her teeth like I was irritating her. "Motherfucker, you the one who started this shit!" she snapped.

I nearly choked on the lump in throat after the stinging response. "Started what, Kita? Why the fuck you gotta be so dramatic about this shit? Don't you know I'd kill myself before I cheated on you? That kiss wasn't but - "

"A major fuck-up on your part, Melo." She cut me off and then hung up on me.

After she did that, I called her back immediately and got her voicemail. I looked around the empty bedroom, conjuring up memories of us making love together in my mind, and I wondered if Markita would ever let me make love to her again.

After sucking up my sorrow, I decided to check for my secret stash in my home office. Surprisingly, everything was still in tact, including the furniture, computer, phone, printer, manuscripts and letters piled up on my desk. I walked over to the bookshelf and slid it out a little, leading to my secret bat cave. I always wanted one since I was a kid and I had it installed in this house for a cool million. I'm still paying for it right now.

As I slipped through the crack and closed the door to my private room in the house, I felt like something was wrong with me. I began to see everything through a watery haze, including the piles of money and guns stacked neatly in the corner. I couldn't feel my legs and my chest began to feel tight. I was scared.

I lay down on the twin-sized bed and broke down, crying all alone inside a room nobody in the world new about but me and the contractors who built it. Everything in my life was no longer peaches and cream. There was no way I could stay in this house without Markita and my son.

With Markita mad at me, a killer out there who wanted me dead, and a crooked cop pressing me to kill another cop, I had to get out of the city for a while. No telling what my emotionally unstable mind would lead me to do if I hung around.

Why would Markita leave me like this and take my son? She just wants me to suffer for a little while. She's going to come back to me, I thought, not knowing if my wishful thinking would ever come true.

CHAPTER 34

I gathered up my money, took off my clothes, and put on the bulletproof Spandex suit that I bought from Blade, my weapons connect. He always called me up whenever he grabbed something new from his connect in the military. I felt a little better after donning the safety garment that could stop AK-47 bullets at close range. I should have been wearing the suit after the first attempt on my life, but you know what they say: a hard head makes a soft ass, or in my case, a shot-up dummy laid up in the hospital for over a week and a half.

After stuffing a few weapons in a small Nike duffel bag, I left my bat cave and proceeded towards Swol's car. I told him to drive over Northeast on 46th and Brooks Streets, a little quiet street behind the Shrimp Boat restaurant near Kelly Miller Junior High School - a street where Markita's mother lived.

Swol made it over there in ten minutes flat. I jumped out of the car and proceeded towards Markita's mother's house in hopes of catching Markita over here, but I wasn't so lucky.

After banging on the door like the police, Markita's mom, Ms. Annabell, opened the door. I noticed she wore an evil scowl on her face. Ms. Annabell resembled Angela Basset, but a plus-sized, heavyset version. She wore a sky blue floral housecoat with a silk scarf covering her hair and dome along with worn house slippers.

"What do you want, boy? And where's my daughter and grandbaby?" she asked, her eyes cold and hard.

"That's why I'm here," I said, knowing full well she knew more about Markita's and my son's whereabouts than she were letting on.

She rolled her eyes while scanning my body up and down. "Look, she's not here, and even if she was, I don't think I'd tell you she was in here," she said, and her evil look turned into an intense smirk.

I don't know why, but Markita's mother never really liked me. Ms. Annabell blamed me for keeping her daughter away from her while she got older and grumpier. Even though I always stressed to Markita that she should spend more time with her mother, she still hated me. Every time she looked at me, I could tell Ms. Annabell saw nothing more than a mistake her daughter had made by choosing to be with me.

"Please, Ma - "

I am not your mother, boy!" she cut me off in a nasty tone. Her face contorted into that of a madwoman.

"Nonsense! You mean the world to me, Ms. Annabell, even though I know you can't stand me," I said, arching my eyebrow.

Her eyes widened after my statement. She gave me a funny look like she was surprised. To my surprise, she stepped aside and said, "C'mon in here."

I obeyed her request and stepped inside her house. I watched her lock the door and turn on me. I noticed her raising her hand, but I wasn't fast enough to avoid the swift slap she administered to my left cheek. I massaged my stinging cheek as she cursed me out for cheating on her daughter. She had no right to put her hands on me. Like any concerned mother, she felt the need to defend and protect her child, so I gave her a pass. Maybe Zetta's text hurt Markita more than I imagined.

"You might as well move on with your life, 'cause my baby don't want to have nothing to do with your cheating hindparts." She looked in my eyes to gauge my reaction.

"Ms. Annabell, I swear on my life, I didn't cheat on Markita."

"Well, why in the hell did that girl call you all those times and write you about some kissy thing y'all did on the phone?" she asked, sounding impatient.

"Like I tried telling Kita before, the kiss was harmless." I sighed and began telling my side of the story that led up to this drama. She nodded while listening to me plead my case. "Ms. Annabell, she took my son away from me. I've done nothing to deserve this but try to help somebody out like Markita done for me when I first came home. Being with your daughter makes me happy. I love her, I love coming home to her, and I love how she takes care of me and our son - your grandbaby." I sighed, looking at her, feeling my heart beating wildly in my chest. "Anything you can do to help me get her back will be appreciated. I can't live without her, so I want you to know that I'd never do something to jeopardize losing her."

"Sure you won't. Anyhow, I'll talk to her when she calls me," she said, staring absently into space.

"Thank you…thank you so much. When you think she'll call you again?"

"It don't matter. When she calls, I'll give her your message!" she fired back with attitude.

"Ms. Annabell, this is my family, my life. I'll take a lie detector test and anything else to get you to believe me and so you tell her I'm not what she thinks I am."

"You made your point, boy, and I will talk to her. Now get outta here before I change my mind."

"Thanks," I said and I kissed her on the cheek, causing her to flinch.

I got up out of her house feeling a little better. I had hopes of getting my woman and son back, depending on how Ms. Annabell relayed my message to Markita. I wasn't ignorant to Ms. Annabell's dislike for me, but spilling my heart out to her was as close as I could get to spilling my heart out to Markita.

CHAPTER 35

The moment after I left Ms. Annabell's house and hopped in Swol's car, he passed me a burning spliff of that exotic 'dro. As he pulled off, I took several tokes and felt myself somewhat returning to normal. I got Swol to swing past the post office Uptown so I could grab the mail out of my P.O. box.

As Swol pulled up and parked, I got out and headed inside. As I headed over to my box, I spotted Zetta's sexy ass walking my way.

"Hey, stranger," she greeted with a pretty smile. "You don't know how to return my phone calls?"

I glanced at her and saw a look of admiration and sparkle in her eyes. I wanted to tell her to leave me the hell alone, but right now my lust over powered my brain. "I was in the hospital," I said, opening up my box.

"Oh my God, what happened?" she asked, sounding concerned.

You happened, with that dumb-ass text you sent me! I wanted to yell at her, but simply said, "I got shot."

A deep frown covered her face. "Why would somebody want to hurt you?" she asked as I pulled several envelopes from the box.

"I don't know," I said while glancing at the mail. I spotted a letter from Samuel "Chin" Carson and figured it was important. I think I heard from him about five times since Big Nate introduced him to me. I sent him back a visiting form and got approved, but he never asked me to come visit him.

"I don't want to press the issue, but I want to know when you gonna get at me about putting my book out?"

"How can I put out your book when you sweating my phone and shit, sending dumb-ass text messages and shit!" I exploded, trembling with quiet rage.

"What!" she fired back with fire in her eyes.

"You heard me, Shorty! Because of your text message, my wife left me, Shorty."

Zetta shook her head and rolled her eyes. "Don't blame me for nothing, boy! I seen how your ass be looking at me like you want to fuck the shit outta me, but you too scared to go after what you want, so don't blame me for shit!" she stated with a deadly calm, wearing a sickening scowl on her wide, round face.

"Yeah, you right. Look, I'm gone, Shorty."

"So it's like that? You just gon' say fuck my book, huh?"

"You said fuck my personal life with my girl with that weak-ass text message you sent to my phone!"

"First of all, you need to watch how you talking to me spacing," she said with flashing anger in her eyes while pointing a finger in my face.

"You got me fucked up, Shorty!" I snapped and began walking away from her.

"Naw, I got you right!" she said, raising her voice higher and higher as she continued. "Matter of fact, fuck you, then! I ain't got to kiss your ass for no book deal!" I heard her yelling as I exited the post office.

It wasn't smart for her to be coming out her face at me like that. Not right now, especially when I wanted to kill something to ease the pain over my woman abandoning me and taking my son. Even though Zetta was playing with death, disrespecting me, I couldn't get over the fact that she didn't back down from my angry outburst. Shorty had spunk, pure and simple - the kind of spunk that one shows when they don't have fear of nothing or nobody but God Almighty. She just didn't know how close she was to making me send her off to meet him.

CHAPTER 36

The moment I hopped in Swol's car, he gave me a funny look and pulled off. As he drove down Florida Avenue, he kept glancing at me.

"What's up, Cannon?"

"Why Shorty was yelling at you like that?"

"She trippin' 'cause I won't jump when she say so."

"You always been anything when it came to the broads with your sucker for love ass."

"Man, fuck you!" I grinned as he reached Ben's Chili Bowl, kept driving, and hooked a right turn on 13th Street.

As he drove up 13th Street's steep hill, we talked about my situation concerning Markita and how Zetta had started a whole bunch of bullshit with her text message. I also threw in the problems I'd been having with the crooked cop, plus my suspicions about Kisha having something to do with me getting shot.

"Slim, you going through it out this ma'fucka," he said, making another turn on 13th and Fairmont Streets. "So what you wanna do with the chick Kisha?"

"I need to holla at her and see what's goin' on."

"See what's going on?" he repeated in a disgusted tone. "Slim, you need to clean that bitch up. How she just gon' tell you to get a living will and right after that, somebody hit off at you and send you to the hospital?"

"You right, but Shorty been rocking with a nigga for a minute. She basically runs everything at the club, so why she want to knock me out the box now?"

"Greed, homes. You can never have enough. Once that broad saw how you was cleaning up the bucks in that spot, she probably felt like she deserved that money, not you, 'cause you don't do shit anyway."

Swol had a helluva way of putting things in perspective, but I couldn't go all the way with his insight on the situation. Even though you can't sleep on anybody, I just couldn't believe in my heart that Kisha wanted me dead so that she could have the nightclub. Even if that was the case, she'd still have to go through Makita to get what she wanted, and Markita wasn't letting that gold mine go under any circumstances.

"Ay, I'ma get to the bottom of things. It's like playing chess."

"Yeah, and your enemy already took a vicious shot at you! You can't afford to keep bullshittin'. You need to attack and keep attacking until you clear the board and mate them ma'fuckas," he said, while driving across 14th Street and making a quick left on 14th and Girard Street.

As soon as he pulled onto the block, I spotted a few young guys wearing red bandanas and red Chuck Taylors like they were gangbanging. I didn't want to believe the rumors that gangs had invaded the District until seeing it with my own eyes.

"What's up, Slim?" I asked as he parked and pulled out a big-ass gun. For a second, fear consumed me and the paranoia from getting shot had me thinking that he was about to crush my ass.

"I gotta go handle something real quick," he said, cocking the weapon.

"Fuck all that! You ain't having all the fun by yourself." I grinned, reaching down under the seat to get the duffle bag. I pulled out a gun with a silencer attached to it and gave it to him.

"Naw, Slim, this some personal shit," he said, handing my gun back to me. He told me about wanting to avenge his little brother's murder. Some big shot gangbanger ordered his brother's execution because he didn't want to be a Blood or pay the Bloods some tax to hustle on the block he grew up on all his life.

"Slim, you can't go up in there making all that noise with that big geekin'-ass joint. You have to use your head. You use that joint, you gon' put everybody in our business and we going back to jail," I reasoned.

He sighed and snatched the gun back from me. "You right, but look, I'ma crush my man. I just need you to have my back."

"That goes without saying, Champ," I assured him while pulling out the compact .45 ACP with the built-in compressor that worked like a silencer. The compressor made the loud explosions sound like snap pops: you know, them little white things wrapped in paper that you throw on the ground and they explode on contact, sounding like a weak version of firecrackers. Dealing with Blade on the gun tip had me playing with all kinds of deadly toys.

Swol cut the car off and got out. Before he made it around to my side, I was out of the car, already gripping the gun inside my front jeans pocket. He gave me a nod and headed inside a brown apartment building. As soon as we entered the lobby, the awful stench of old urine mixed in with feces and stale alcohol smacked me in the nose. I spotted several young guys dressed in red like they were battling for supremacy or bragging rights in that department while the others just hung around, smoking and drinking, urging the contest on.

"'Sup, Blood?" one of them asked, turning on us as we headed towards the elevator.

Swol kept it moving and so did I. When the little gangbanger came closer to us, he asked us in a more aggressive manner. "I said, what the fuck is up, Blood?"

"Listen, Slim, we just - " That's all I got out before I saw his chest exploding with three shots in the heart.

"Oh shit!" another gang member screamed, going for his gun. His three cronies did the same.

I whipped out my gun like we were in the old Wild West and began firing at them until they fell. I hit two of them in the face and chest and Swol plugged the other two with deadly shots. As Swol walked over to the young dying gangbangers and stood over top of them, I began searching the first dead man's pockets. I found some cash and a sandwich bag of pills. I glanced up and saw Swol shooting each gangbanger twice in the head.

"Now scream Su-Wuuu bitch and Dadda-Doh!" I laughed while mimicking a famous verse from Lil Wayne.

"Let's go, Slim," Swol urged with wide eyes.

"Man, check them niggas' pockets first so we can make it look like a robbery or something," I told him.

"You do that shit and I'ma watch the front door to make sure nobody else comes up in here."

I moved like lightning. I checked all four youngsters and found enough money and drugs on them to pay Swol for a month's worth of work. I took the guns they had on them with me and decided to sell them the first chance I got. By the time I stuffed everything in my pockets and got to my feet, Swol was exiting the building.

I lowered my head as I walked to his car. Once inside, Swol looked at me, gave me a nod, and started the car. I put all five guns in the duffel bag and just looked down at them. Damn, them little ma'fuckas had some serious shit, I thought while looking at one semi-automatic that had a round drum magazine attached to the bottom of it.

"You's a geekin' nigga, Slim," I said as he pulled of, creating space between us and the recent quintuple homicide. "How you just gon' hit the nigga and not give me no eye signals or nothing?"

"Shiid, you knew what it was hitting for before we even got out the car. Now we married by blood, nigga."

"You felt like you had to test me out, Slim? I am appalled," I joked, causing him to laugh as he made another right onto 15th Street, drove over one block, and turned down Harvard Street.

"Shiid, test you? You look like you don't need any testing to me. You smoked dem other two niggas before I could even turn on them," he said, recapping the work we just put in on five guys at one time.

"Ay, if you gon' keep going like that, then I need to get you the hook up from my mans and 'em, Blade."

"What hook up?" he asked, cruising down Harvard Street.

I showed him my bulletproof Spandex body suit and told him how it could stop AK-47 bullets. He began nodding his head up and down like he was listening to a hitting beat of a rap song.

"Yeah, Slim, you gots'ta get me one of those joints ASAP," he remarked.

"Shiid, I'ma just call the nigga up and pay for it with this bread we just got off them fake Blood niggas back there, 'cause they ain't gon' need it no more," I joked as I began counting the money.

"You ain't never lied on that one." He laughed as I told him to drive over on the Southside so I could handle a little business of my own.

CHAPTER 37

By the time we reached Barry Farms projects, it looked like everybody and their mama in the city had showed up at the Goodman League Games today. Swol parked and got out quickly to get some attractive woman's attention. While he talked to her, I looked around, hoping to spot Pusshead or Cat-Eye KK. I wanted to get some information on this crooked cop who was harassing me.

After Swol came back cheesing like the Cheshire cat, I figured he got the young woman's phone number. "What's up with her, Slim?" I asked as we headed over to the jam-packed basketball court.

"I'ma find out when I call her, but she looks like she tryna go, and she had this phat-ass little broad with her. I was mad as shit, I picked the wrong one," he said as we entered the court area.

"Awww shit! Watch out dere now! The Bookman is back, ladies and gentleman…the Bookman is back!" I heard the MC saying over the microphone, and everybody began looking at me and laughing. "Ay, make sure you leave old Miles a good Bucky Fields urban joint so I can read it on my day off!" he said, drawing laughter at my expense from a few people in attendance.

"You got that!" I gave him a nod and kept it moving.

I spotted the guy D.C. who ran off with the book the last time I was on this end with Zetta trying to hustle. He stood on the sidelines like he was coaching the team in the warm up lines. As we moved over to the bleachers, he waved me over to him. Usually I'd take that as a sign of disrespect, but I figured he probably wanted to pay me for that book he grabbed.

"Wait right here, Slim, I'll be back," I told Swol, who began following me.

"Nope, I'm your shadow, just like you asked me to be," he said.

I just shook my head and began heading over in D.C's direction. When I reached him, he went in his pocket and pulled out a big-ass knot of money. He gave me a twenty dollar bill. "Here go your money for that weak-ass urban book," he said, giving me a funny look.

"Damn, you ain't like it, huh?" I asked.

"Naw, that joint was a'ight, but I just don't be fucking with all dem weak-ass urban joints 'cause all of them say the same shit."

"Oh yeah?"

"Yeah, but what you need to do is fuck with my niece, Zetta. You ain't talk to her yet about her book?"

Yeah, and it ain't working out, I thought before answering him. "I just seen her. Shorty, jive be lunchin'."

"What you mean?" he quizzed, looking over my shoulder.

I turned and looked over my shoulder as a precaution and saw that he was watching his team in the warm-up line. "Naw, we just had some words a few minutes ago, 'cause I told her she jive fucked up a happy home."

"What she do?"

"Nothing serious, but she sent me a text message and my woman seen the joint and went off. You know how that shit go."

"Yeah, them broads be lunchin' like shit. I'm in the doghouse right now with my wife, but fuck it, she'll come around one day. While she's being mad at me, I'ma stay out here and try to get all the pussy I can," he said, making me giggle.

"So what, you coach this team or something?"

"Yeah, this the Trinidad Mob. We playing Miles Great-Eight to get to the championship - Miles, the nigga on the mic."

"Oh, a'ight," I said and an uncomfortable silence passed between us.

"Yeah, Zetta be lunchin', but she's official, Slim, and I'm just not saying that 'cause she's family. I think you should fuck with her. She really has a tight-ass book that everybody in the city needs to read."

"I got you, Slim," I said and turned around to leave.

As soon as I turned, the ferocious blow that slammed into my mid-section made me go down on one knee trying to regain my breath at the same time as I instinctively reached for my gun.

CHAPTER 38

After getting my hand on the gun and gripping it tightly, my desire to kill became full-blown elation as I looked up in Pusshead's face. He smiled down at me before helping me back up to my feet. When I looked at him, I saw all the memories we shared in prison and a few times on the street. Those memories put a great deal of mental restraint on what I really wanted to do to him for the stunt he had just pulled.

"Yeah, you out here bullshittin', huh?" He smirked and pulled me into a manly hug.

I looked around and saw Swol shrugging at me. We had all done time together, so I guess Swol didn't feel a threat when Pusshead snuck up on me. I turned back on Pusshead, scanning his outfit. He wore a tank top, showing off his prison tattoos, some blue denim cargo shorts and a pair of 1300 New Balance jogging shoes. With the temperatures outside feeling like it reached the high nineties, I understood why he wore the garments that would literally keep him from becoming drenched in sweat as the heat waves warmed the District of Corruption.

"Naw, I'm always on point, Moe," I said, flashing my chunky .45 compact ACP on him.

He squinted as the sun reflected off the chrome death toy, causing a bright glint to invade his eyes. "Man, I don't see none of that shit! I'm the King of the South!" Pusshead declared openly before pulling me away from D.C.

"Ay, D.C., I'ma holla at you, Slim," I told him as Pusshead put his short, stocky arm around my shoulder and began stepping off.

Looking over my shoulder, I saw D.C. give me a head nod and go back to focusing on his team as Swol walked behind us, looking back and forth like a trained bodyguard. Moments later, Pusshead led me over to the bleachers where a group of men was gambling. I spotted Cat-Eye KK, Lil Woo from Langston Lane, my co-defendant on a recent unsolved homicide, and G-Love from down Cappers Projects. G-Love had a vicious gambling habit and was known for going all around the city, breaking up the crap games. He stayed gone off that water-water and always kept that hammer on him at all times, which made everybody second-guess themselves about jumping out there with him.

"'Sup, KK?" I spoke and acknowledged Lil Woo with a nod. He returned the gesture and went back to chasing the almighty dollars being wagered in the crap game.

"Not right now, Soldier, I'm jive losing," he said as if in a trance while looking down at the rolling dice.

I detected the warning in his tone, but I didn't care about none of that. We went too far back for him to be talking crazy to me like that. "Fuck you mean, not right now?" I said aggressively, making him look up with the quickness.

KK had that angry screw face look on his mug until he laid his cat-like hazel eyes on me. His frown quickly turned into a smile. "Damn, wassup, Moses?" he greeted me with a huge smile.

"Shit, 'bout to fuck your man Pusshead around for playing with me out here." I spoke directly to KK, knowing Pusshead would fire back with something slick out of his mouth.

"Nigga, we murder for fun 'round here! This dat real side of the city!" he said, causing laughter to erupt from the circle of gamblers.

"Yeah, sounds good. Nigga, it's killers all over the city, so don't get that fucked up!" I retorted with a playful smile while glancing at Swol.

"I can't beat you in a Rap-A-Lot battle," Pusshead joked, causing more laughter.

"Ay, let me holla at you on real shit, though," I said and then pulled him aside to inquire about the crooked cop Gamble.

"Yeah, I'm hip to his hot bitch ass!" he said with a mixture of frustration and grave sincerity.

After Pusshead told me that Gamble had a partner and explained how they got down, I took on a faraway look. My anger at being pressed by the crooked cop outstripped my fear of being arrested by him and charged with murder. "Listen, Puss-Puss, that hot ma'fucka, brought up that gasoline body that I handled 'round here your way back in the day. He told me that he got a reliable snitch who told him I did the shit. It had to be a ma'fucka who was out there that night."

Pusshead's angry expression took on a distant look. He looked like he was someplace else, which made me nervous. "Moe, the only nigga that was out there that night who be fucking with that cheese was the nigga Curt Carter," he said, craning his neck in the direction of the crap game. "The nigga wearing acid-washed jeans and black T-shirt that says "Make Your Children The Right Thing!"

As his direction rang in my ears, I craned my neck to get a good look at the rat for my mental rolodex. I shot an angry look in the man's direction as a violent rage stirred inside me.

"Yeah, Slim, that nigga snitched on Aaron and Michael Davis back in the day. Ain't nobody fuck with him since then," Pusshead added, speaking some degree of satisfaction as if the streets justified his sins after putting him on time out.

The world we come from and the Game we play is fucked all the way up! I thought as he continued talking.

"But you know as time went by, niggas said fuck it and started back fucking with the nigga for their own selfish reasons. I stay far away as possible from that hot-ass nigga."

"Y'all know niggas be snitching and y'all basically condoning the shit 'cause y'all ain't slaughtering their ass," I remarked, keeping my eyes glued on the rat who was scooping up a pile of money.

"Moe, if you try to crush every hot nigga in the world, you gon' wash yourself up," he pointed out, which I felt was a crock of bullshit.

"Not if you do it and get away with it," I said as I walked off to holla at Swol.

Before I could reach him, the guy Nu-Nu appeared out of nowhere, scaring the shit out of me. "What's happening, Slim? I thought that was you. I just had to come over and holla at you," he said, extending his hand for a handshake.

I shook his hand, studying him for a second. Nu-Nu sported an all-white vintage Polo shirt with the Polo bear playing golf on the front and an Onyx dog tag chain with a red Washington Nationals cap and some light green camouflage pants off the high top Prada sneakers, looking sweet. I looked at his attire, thug nature, and mannerisms and saw something wonderful in Nu-Nu's potential - something aggressive, hungry, and coachable, something that needed to be molded. I began wondering how much street schooling he'd already soaked up from others and wondered how much more knowledge in the killing game I'd have to give him.

"What's up wit'cha?" I asked as I pulled him over to the side.

Once I got Nu-Nu in private, I began laying down my spiel, implanting an offer that he couldn't refuse even if he wanted to. By the time the game reached halftime, showing the Trinidad team down by fifteen points against the Miles Great Eight team, I had loaded up enough batteries in Nu-Nu's back that had him begging me to point out the rat, Curt Carter, so he could exterminate him.

CHAPTER 39

The second half of the game was more exciting than I expected. Players were shining and Miles the MC provided the perfect play-by-play calls on the mic, making the crowd cheer and laugh. There were so many people on the bleachers and around the court that it was hard to move. People were cheering for the players, dancing to the go-go music somebody had playing, and just enjoying the spectacular event put together down at the Goodman League.

I felt good about putting Nu-Nu on the job. The only thing that bothered me was the constant questions he had. He wanted to know who Curt Carter told on and why. After I explained to him that it didn't matter and that he had to be eliminated on GP, Nu-Nu nodded in agreement. I guess he was trying to impress me. I really didn't care just as long as the long overdue job got done.

"Aw, look at that nigga. I believe I can fly!" Miles began singing as his star player, Kirk Smith, took flight from the baseline and didn't land until after he put down a crowd-pleasing one-handed windmill dunk.

"What you gon' do about that, D.C.? Trinidad! Trina-Trina-Trinidad!" Miles sounded like somebody rapping on the mic at go-go, teasing the coach of the Trinidad basketball team as his star point guard walked the ball back up the court, trying to hold onto their small lead.

I watched as the Trinidad team worked hard and came roaring back in the second half to take a three point lead with a little bit of time left on the clock. I didn't want to miss this game, but Nu-Nu tapped me on the shoulder. I looked at him and he nodded in the rat's direction. I saw him moving and got up and put Swol on point.

"Don't lose him, Nu-Nu," I said before getting up and heading out of the court in front of the rat.

Swol and I waited outside the court area to see what type of ride Curt Carter was driving. When he began walking towards the train tracks, I couldn't believe it. He was begging to get crushed in broad daylight. Swol and I jumped in his car and pulled off. We sped down Stevens Road and waited, watching the rat walk towards us. I also saw Nu-Nu trailing him with a slow bop.

Right when we were about to get out of the car and cut off his path, the rat took a detour and began walking up the back concrete steps leading to Parkchester Projects. The way the rat walked freely like he didn't have a care in the world angered me. It wasn't so much the way that he walked, but because he was walking around alive after helping the government send two good men to prison for the rest of their lives - taking them away from their mothers, wives, friends, and other loved ones. Curt Carter's outright betrayal and disrespect for the game should have been addressed a long time ago, but everything happens at an appointed time, and right now, the time for this hot faggot bitch had run out. I saw Nu-Nu take off running. I began jogging towards the same steps to back him up just in case he froze up. As soon as I reached the bottom of the concrete staircase with my gun drawn, I heard the rapid sounds of exploding gunfire.

When Nu-Nu saw his target turn and take the concrete stairs, he took off running to catch up with him. This is the moment of truth, he thought while glancing at Carmelo and his buddy jogging towards him. Wanting to make a good impression on Carmelo, Nu-Nu pulled out his Glock-40 and bolted up the steps behind Curt Carter, aiming the Glock-40 at the rat's back.

Curt Carter got a funny feeling that he was being followed and didn't really trip as he eased his gun out of his waistband. If anybody try any funny shit, I'ma light they ass up on these steps, he thought and he turned suddenly with his gun in hand.

When Curt Carter suddenly turned around with his gun drawn, Nu-Nu flinched a little and began shooting rapidly spraying Curt Carter's chest and lower body with hot lead. Curt Carter let off a few rounds after he got blasted in the chest. His finger tapped the trigger a few times, sending slugs flying aimlessly in the air.

As Curt Carter slid down the concrete stairs, he hit the back of his head and began gasping for air. Nu-Nu ran up the steps cautiously and kicked the gun from his downed victim's side.

"This what happens when you eat that cheese," Nu-Nu said. He shot the rat six times in the face and forehead.

Without hesitating, Nu-Nu jumped over the dead body and ran up the steps leading to Parkchester Projects.

I looked on in awe as Nu-Nu handled his business, firing the gun with two hands, looking wicked like one of them action heroes in a blockbuster action film. He was young, agile, and cold-hearted. The way he stood over top of the rat and pumped his face full of hot lead made me gush with pride and love every second of it. Suddenly I felt happy that I didn't go with my little brother. There was nothing else for me to do but pledge my undying love and loyalty to Nu-Nu in hopes of passing on the torch.

"Let's go up Parkchester real quick and scoop up Shorty," I told Swol before looking around to see if anybody was looking.

"He handle that?" Swol asked, pointing towards the steps.

"You can hang around here and wait for all the blood to come running down steps and get bagged by the Feds or we can get up outta here."

Luckily, there wasn't anybody in the vicinity when we hopped in the Monte Carlo and pulled off. We made it up Parkchester Projects a few moments later and saw Nu-Nu walking calmly out of the courtyard. I lowered the window and waved him over to the car. He came walking over with a slight smirk on his face as I got out the car and tried to get in the backseat.

"Whoa, I'm riding in the back, Champ, I don't mind," he said, making me laugh inside.

At that moment, I knew Nu-Nu wasn't green to the backseat rider move. In fact, he was on point, which led me to believe that he had all the potential to be a helluva killer. If he would have gotten in the passenger seat and let me get in the backseat, I probably would have killed him for slipping, but the young nigga was definitely on point.

"You sure? I don't mind," I tested him.

"Naw, I'm cool, Slim," he replied, arching his left eyebrow. "I been riding in the backseat all my life. Ain't no sense in switching things up now, you know?" he said before easing past me and climbing in the backseat.

After I got inside the car and closed the door, Swol and I gave Nu-Nu nods of approval for the stand-up act he had just committed.

"So, what now?" Nu-Nu asked, exuding confidence.

"We ride together and for each other always, no matter what, until death do us part!" I said, and everybody nodded quickly. "I'm serious, y'all. What I'm on is way more serious than just hustling and fucking these little anything bitches out here. I'm into crushing all hot niggas and ma'fuckas who fucked up the game. All that fake-ass shit about claiming death before dishonor, Nigga I'm 'bout that shit for real and I'm willing to kill anybody to enforce it. Even if my mother and father were hot, God rest their souls…if they was living and I found out they was fucking with that cheese, I'd crush they asses without blinking or thinking twice about it," I said and heard nothing but silence. "So I'm saying, if you ain't with this shit I'm on, then you can roll out right now and won't no love be lost," I added looking at Swol and Nu-Nu, I got more silence from them, but they made no attempts to leave the car.

"Once you take this ride, young nigga, ain't no turning back." I looked back at Nu-Nu, who gave me a serious look and didn't say a word. As the uncomfortable silence hung in the air between us, I heard Nu-Nu sigh.

"I can't stand rats and nearly lost my life over the one you had beef with, so with that being said, if you with crushing them, them I'm with it too," Nu-Nu told me, which earned himself some major points in my eyes.

"What about you, Swol-Up?"

"We already talked about this shit, Slim, so you ain't got to test me," he said in a serious tone. Without saying another word, Swol put the car in gear and pulled off, solidifying our pact and beginning our new lives together.

CHAPTER 40

Markita sat in the living room of April's house, playing with her son. April's spacious house was very neat and pleasing to the eye. After she put all the furniture and everything else in storage, Markita went to stay with her sister-in-law. She knew she couldn't go to her mother's house because that would be the first place Carmelo would come to look for her, and she was right. After her mother called her and explained how he came over there pleading his case, Markita became weak and wanted to go back to him.

"Ma-Ma! I make a stinky!" Ray-Nathan said, putting up his arms, beckoning her to pick him up.

"Mmph, you sure did, baby," she said, trying to ignore the putrid odor coming from his diaper as she picked him up.

She walked into April's room and found April's exposed nude body lying on the bed on her tummy watching TV. Markita sighed and walked over and flopped on the bed. April pulled a sheet over her nakedness quickly and looked at her and then the baby, smelling the stench in the air that made her cover her nose. Sensing something was wrong with her, April kissed the baby and sat up. Although the smell was stomach-turning, April ignored it to find out what Markita was going through.

"What's wrong with you now, girl?" she asked, seeing the pout on Markita's face.

"Melo went over my mother's house looking for me and the baby." She sighed. "I don't think I should be here. I should be at home working things out with him."

"Girl, you bet' not break now. It's too early to give in to his ass. Make his ass suffer a little while longer and the next time he'll really think twice before he put his lips on another bitch," April said, and the force of her statement broke Markita's moment of weakness.

She's right. Why should I have to go back to his ass when he's the one that cheated on me? Fuck him, she thought and began smiling. "You right, girl. He needs to recognize who he's fucking with."

"That's right, and once you trained his ass not to fuck up anymore, then you can go home and give him some make up sex, but not a second before then."

"I might not go back to his ass," Markita said, knowing she was lying to herself. She loved Carmelo with every fiber in her being, but she wasn't going to just let him cheat on her like she was some ordinary hoodrat in the street. After learning that he came looking for her, Markita wanted to go to him and make up. Then she had a quick talk with April. Suddenly a wave of sadness mixed with anger overcame her from being so naïve to Carmelo's infidelities. She told herself that he would feel her pain, which would help their relationship in the long run. She wanted a real love that stood the test of time.

"No, you have to go back, 'cause I need my space, girl," April said in a joking tone, invading her thoughts. "Men are dogs, but some of them are good dogs. They go off track for a minute, but that's when you have to put your foot down and train their ass to be what you want them to be."

"You ever have that problem with my brother?'

"Did I! Only on two occasions though. In fact, we was just getting back together when he passed," April said tensely. Her face was filled with a rage unlike anything Markita had ever seen before.

Markita knew asking anything more about April's relationship with her brother would be difficult. Markita sat back and thought about April's words. A tear formed in the corner of her eyes as she let the words marinate in her head. She spent the next few moments in deep thought and then realization.

"It was your idea for me to come here and stay in the first place, so I'm going to stay here for as long as I need to in order to get things straight with Melo and my life, so don't talk that shit now," Markita said, shaking with rage.

"Whoa, whoa, whoa! You can stay for as long as you want to, girl. I was only joking with you," April said timidly, watching the angry look sweeping across Markita's face along with something else, something infinitely deeper.

Markita wasn't in the mood to talk anymore so she simply said, "I'ma go give him a bath." She gave April a stiff smile.

Nodding in agreement, April reached for the remote with her small hands and began changing the channel. "Just come holla at me after you put little man to bed."

"I will, and thanks again for everything, girl," Markita said, looking at her, grateful that April could take her and her son into her home, embracing her and her problems so easily.

"Don't mention it. We family, right? And family helps each other out." April said as Markita left her bedroom.

CHAPTER 41

After cruising around the city for a minute, I told Swol to swing back around my old neighborhood. I wanted to drop off some cash to Wee-Wee's son. I usually did this once a month just to show Lil Wee how to be loyal to his peeps on lockdown.

When Swol pulled up on the block around First and U Streets, I noticed a lot of police activity in the area. I glanced over at the crack house that I had run up in to crush Twan's rat ass. I looked back and noticed Nu-Nu looking at the house with a strange look on his face.

"You remember that joint, Slim?" I asked him from the front seat.

"Do I? I'm just glad I got up outta that bitch when I did. You was a man on a mission," he said in a joking tone.

"I wonder why all the Feds 'round here?" I remarked as Swol kept on driving. I told him to hook a left on First Street to hit the corner store.

Once he pulled up and made a right on Rhode Island Avenue, I spotted Rico, Damian, Leo, and Lil Wee chilling in front of the Chinese Dragon carry-out restaurant. I jumped out of the car and rushed over to give them all some daps and one arm hugs.

"Damn, Habib, what you been up to?" I asked Rico, who was rocking a Kufi and big Muslim beard off the Afghan scarf splayed nicely around his head and neck to go with his colorful T-shirt, blue jeans, and tan Timberlands.

"Shit, I just got out from up Allenwood. I'm tryna get these young niggas to go to the mosque with me," he said with a smile.

Rico was the first guy I ever heard of from my end who was getting niggas' cases thrown out from putting in work on the streets of Northwest.

At the time, I didn't know what he was doing until I heard he got arrested and convicted for obstruction of justice for snaking a government witness. The government was so mad at Rico that they made his defense lawyer testify against him in the case, which eventually got him back on appeal and eliminated an eighty year prison sentence he'd received.

"That's what's up. You cool though? I mean, you don't need anything?"

"Allah is my provider, Habib. I put my faith in him to give me all that I want."

"How long you been home?"

"About a good four months now, and it's lovely, Habib…real lovely." He smiled and passed me a little pamphlet.

I looked at it and read the words. All you need to know about Allah and Islam—the world's fastest growing religion! "What am I s'posed to do with this, Ock? I love swine and everything," I joked. "I don't think I can ever stop eating them good chitlings and bacon, pussy, and all that other shit," I commented and heard Lil Wee and Damian laughing.

"Astaghfirullah!" Rico shook his head in disgust. "Just read the damn pamphlet, you fake joker!"

"I got you, Slim." I grinned and then went to holla at Lil Wee in private inside the carry-out. Once we got inside, I gave him $300 and told him to wire that to his father the first chance he got.

"He already straight. You know I be getting him."

"A nigga never straight in them joints. It cost to live up there, and niggas love playing big when they go to the store and shit. You know how that shit go, so just send him the loot."

"Yeah, a'ight."

"Ay, why all the Feds on the block?"

"Some li'llil bitch-ass niggas came through the other night on some drive-by shit and a few of my men got crushed. Them peoples jive sweating the spot real heavy."

"You know who did it?"

"Nope." He shook his head, looking mad as hell.

"Was you out there?"

"Yeah, I got to working on everything, but the niggas got away while I was hitting off at 'em."

"Ay, be careful out here, Slim. I don't want to be the one explaining to your father that you got caught slippin'"

"Never that, Unc. I'm on point twenty-four seven."

"I told your ass about that Unc shit. It makes me feel old."

"Nigga, you is old!" Lil Wee laughed, making me take a swing at him.

He ducked quickly and jumped into a boxing stance. I backed up and raised my hands in surrender, 'cause I knew he'd whip my ass if I took it any further. Shorty was raised in boxing gym before he started playing in the streets.

"You got that one all day. Just holla at Pops for me and tell him I send my love and regards."

"I gotcha, Unc!" he said just to fuck with me as we exited the carry-out.

"Yeah, a'ight. Keep on bullshittin'," I retorted playfully while backing up to Swol's car.

"Okay, Habib!" Rico called out. "And make sure you read that pamphlet, 'cause I'ma ask you about it the next time I see you."

"I'ma do that for you, Ock, but if it was anybody else, this joint woulda went in the trash soon as I left they ass."

"Which one of the blessings of your lord will you deny?" he asked, which made me stop and look at him for a moment.

What did he mean by that? I hope he ain't go to jail and get brainwashed on that Louis Farrakhan shit? Naw, Rico was a Muslim before he left the streets. I guess doing time in the Feds probably helped tighten up his faith and now he's trying to do the right thing spiritually, I thought as I got back in Swol's ride.

"Ay, Lil Wee, hit me on the hip if you need me to help you cook that little beef you got going on." I laughed as Swol began pulling off.

"I got this, Unc, and if I hafta call your old ass, then it's time for me to get out the game!" I heard him yelling as Swol cruised down Rhode Island Avenue.

We still had about four more hours before the nightclub opened, so I told Swol to hit the mall so we could get fresh.

"What mall?" he asked.

"You make the call," I said as he reached the intersection of Rhode Island Avenue and Florida Avenue.

"Ay, Slim, hit Pentagon City," Nu-Nu blurted. "I know this lil bitch who works out there."

"Pentagon City it is then," I said, leaning down in the passenger seat as the light changed green.

Nu-Nu rolled us a few spliffs of the exotic 'dro and lit all four of them at the same time. He began passing them around and saying, "Puff puff pass, nigga! Whoever fucks the rotation up gotta smoke all them joints to the head!" He threw out the challenge, which made me sit up with the quickness.

"You ain't said shit, young nigga. I smokes for a living," Swol said and I just nodded in agreement.

"We gon' see." Nu-Nu smirked and then lit a Newport and added that into the rotation.

Fuck! I can't stand no cigarettes, I thought, but I didn't want to back down from Nu-Nu's challenges, fearing that he might think less of me or try to tease me. Don't ask why, but when it comes to challenges, guys always accept them, even when they know they have no chance of winning. Maybe it's just pride and male ego.

While we got our puff-puff-pass on, I began thinking about a diplomatic way to approach Kisha so she wouldn't feel suspicious or too disrespected when I addressed her about why she wanted me to get a living will and why somebody tried to kill me right after she made the suggestion.

CHAPTER 42

At a little after 6 p.m., Little James pulled off East Capitol Street in Southeast and parked over on Texas Avenue in front of Tiah's hair salon and barbershop - a little popular spot not too far from Simple City Projects. All the barbers and beauticians inside the shop stopped what they were doing to check out the shiny, charcoal-grey Lexus LS sitting on gleaming chrome rims.

Little James had been laying low after committing a drive-by shooting Uptown, which backfired and ended up claiming the life of his main man, Chew. Little James saw the guy he'd been trying to catch up with every since he got out of residential. When he learned that the man relocated on this end of town, Little James decided to pay the man a visit the first chance he got. He jumped out the car, rocking all-black everything: black Orioles fitted cap, black Armani X-change T-shirt, and all-black Hugo Boss denims off the black-on-black Nike Air Foamposite joints. Little James kept his head lowered as he walked up, catching the man off guard.

When Little James looked in the man's eyes, he saw an ashen look cover his brown-skinned face. Yeah, this nigga never thought he'd see me again, he thought, remembering how he used to take his money and got the bomb head from the guy who stood before him - the same man who used to be terrified of him and literally did anything Little James wanted to keep him off his ass.

"'Sup, Marty?" Little James said, watching everybody out on the crowded drug strip. A few people looked his way, but the majority kept it moving, trying to handle their business.

"Shit, wassup wit'chu, LJ?" Marty said with a mean mug.

When he saw Little James walking up on him, Marty was immediately reminded of all the fear, pain, and homosexual acts he went through to avoid getting on Little James's bad side. Some guys just know how to get money in the hood and just weren't cut out to be hard in any shape, form, or fashion. Marty was one of those guys, and Little James preyed on his weakness.

Little James saw straight through Marty's hard façade. "Ay, let me holla at you right quick, Moe."

Marty sucked his teeth like a girl, sounding like someone had slashed some car tires as he reluctantly walked off behind Little James. Once they got around the corner, a good distance from the crowded drug strip, Little James's calm demeanor turned into outright aggression. "You still sucking dick or what?"

"Naw, Slim, I…I don't do that shit no more. I only did that for you," he said timidly.

"Oh yeah?" Little James replied and swung wildly at Marty's jaw.

"Aaaah!" Marty gasped like a girl after his head snapped sideways from the sneaky blow.

Little James quickly followed up, throwing a hard left hook and right cross to Marty's mid-section. When Marty doubled over, Little James brought up his knee, crashing into Marty's chin. Falling backwards with blood spurting from his mouth, Marty laid down, curling into a fetal position, trying to fend off the ferocious assault.

"Bitch-ass nigga! That's for not sending me no hank while I was out rezzy," he snapped, using the slang term for residential.

Panting and glaring down at his defeated victim, Little James spat in Marty's face and pulled out a big-ass Desert Eagle. "Now let me get all that shit your pockets before I fill your ma'fuckin face up right here with this joint!"

There was a moment of silence between them while Marty looked up inside the dark, pyramid-shaped barrel of the gun and reflected on his threat. He didn't want to die, not when he just got a major connect from Philly. His will to live overcame all thoughts of the loss and embarrassment he currently suffered at the hands of Little James.

Marty's face was filled with sadness unlike anything Little James had ever seen before. Little James knew killing him now would be difficult.

"Hurry up, bitch nigga! I ain't got all day!" Little James demanded, looking around, making sure nobody walked up on the robbery in progress.

Marty pulled several wads of cash and threw them over to Little James's feet. Tears of anger stung his eyes while watching Little James scoop up his earnings for the day. Little James shoved the money in his pockets and began looking around nervously. Marty peeped the way Little James was looking around and just knew he was going to kill him.

"Please, LJ, don't do it, Slim. Whatever you thinking, don't do it. I'll pay you whatever!" Marty begged, spitting out the flow of blood flooding his mouth.

"What if I want you to suck my dick again. You gon' do it?" Little James grilled, getting a kick out of the power he held over the man's life.

Marty closed his eyes. Tears streamed down his face as he fought back everything he believed in as a man and nodded affirmatively.

"I can't hear you, bitch nigga, speak up!" Little James pressed.

"Yes, okay. I'll suck your dick."

"Wrong answer. Sometimes, you have to stand up and be a man or lie down and die like a bitch. You ain't learn shit since I been away, huh? They say you can't teach an old faggot new tricks!" Little James said, aimed the Desert Eagle at Marty's head.

"No! Nooo!" Marty's screams for his life got cut short as Little James squeezed the trigger. The two hollow points erupting from the Desert Eagle tore Marty's head into mincemeat. Little James didn't hang around to see all the blood and brain fragments splattered on the pavement underneath him.

As Marty's lifeless corpse laid out on the ground, Little James took off running in the opposite direction. When he made it back to his car minutes later, Little James saw the once-crowded drug strip deserted like a ghost town in the old wild West.

They must've got ghost soon when I let that big shit go, he thought with a smile before jumping in his Lexus LS. After pulling off, Little James knew that he could no longer worry about who got hurt and what was right or wrong. What had to be just had to be, he told himself as he began mentally planning out another attack on the Uptown Streets where his Uncle Twan perished.

CHAPTER 43

Zetta sat in traffic, still fuming over the argument she had with Carmelo. In fact, he messed up her entire day. She couldn't think straight while working and she decided to leave early. When her supervisor questioned her, Zetta lied, claiming she had cramps and felt like she was about to come on her period. She contemplated calling Carmelo and cursing his ass out some more, but she decided against it. The ringing of her cell phone snatched her away from her thought. She put the Bluetooth adapter in her phone and answered it on the fifth ring.

"Hello?" Zetta said in a frustrated tone while looking over all the traffic on Florida Avenue. She realized that getting over to her mother's house would literally take all day.

"Bitch, why the fuck you out here cheating on me?"

"What!" Zetta snapped, growing hot with anger. "First of all, don't be calling me with no bullshit like that. Secondly, we ain't even like that, Poobie. I mean, we just fuck buddies, and FYI, I haven't fucked nobody else but your freak ass."

"Bitch, that ain't what I heard!" Poobie stated angrily over the phone.

"You can't go around believing everything you hear."

"Where I heard this from, I hafta believe it, 'cause this chick don't live in the city, and it's not that many Zetta's who know about that nigga I told your ass about."

"What the fuck is you talking about?" Zetta asked, getting fed up with the he said/she said game.

"Did you fuck that nigga?" Poobie yelled over the phone.

"What nigga, Poobie?" Zetta asked, sucking her teeth in frustration. Zetta hated when Poobie called her up, acting like a jealous lover. They had already established that they were sex partners, nothing more, nothing less. I guess somewhere along the way, this bitch done really caught feelings, Zetta thought as Poobie dropped a bombshell on her.

"That nigga Carmelo! The same ma'fucka who killed my cousin!" Poobie snapped.

Samuel Chin Carson sat at the computer in the United States Federal Penitentiary in Terre Haute, Indiana reading over the e-mail he'd just received from Carmelo.

I got the message, big homie, and I'm headed out that way this weekend. You got my word on that! Hold your head and always know it's still some real niggas out here to carry on the torch!

P.S. I sent you off some change. It ain't much, but it's the thought that counts, right? (LOL) Oh, give Titus my regards and tell him I'll see him when he gets home!

One Love,

Melo

A week prior to receiving the message from Carmelo, Chin had been walking around Terre Haute's prison track with a boss from Detroit that he had met during Jumuah prayer over a year ago. The man convicted of over a dozen witness homicides in Southwest D.C. got transferred from Lewisburg Federal Penitentiary after it closed down and got turned into a Super Max facility. After talking to the boss from Detroit for quite some time, Chin learned that the man had plenty of money - enough money to pay to get people touched on the streets.

When the man began hanging with Chin and opening up to him about the witnesses on his case that sent him away for life and how he wish he had somebody to dispose of them, Chin's devious mind got to thinking.

Sometimes old habits are hard to break! After giving the idea that he had formulated some careful thought for quite some time, Chin realized that he could raise some money for his legal fees on his upcoming appeal. With that in mind, Chin asked the boss how much the witness' lives were worth.

"Listen, Ock, I'm willing to pay whatever to see them bitches in the ground, real talk!"

"Listen up, Champ, you sure you willing to pay whatever? 'Cause I know some people who know some people, and for the right price, the people you hate can become a distant memory."

The chubby boss looked at Chin seriously and still couldn't get over the fact of how much he resembled the black version of the terrorist Osama Bin Laden. For a long moment he looked at Chin as if he was deep in thought after reading between the lines, catching the real meaning of Chin's words.

"Hassan, you name the price and it's done. Wherever you want the money sent, just give me the information and it's done."

"Whoa, I ain't say nothing about no money, Ock. Slow down, you moving too fast. Let me run the idea by my folks first and I'll get back at you."

"That's what's up then. You do that and let me know something."

Later on that night, Chin put together a serious distress letter for Carmelo and mailed it off, stressing the importance of wanting to see him face to face. Chin figured if he could get Carmelo to put the work in for the boss, then he could get the money he desperately needed to hire an appeal attorney.

Now a slight smile spread across Chin's face after reading the message. He typed in a reply e-mail that said:

I'm looking forward to seeing you, Slim. I got a big idea to get us a rack of loot.

Much respect, Slim,
Chinchilla

Chin's co-defendant, Draper, walked out his cell and called him. Chin looked around and saw his buddy from the streets holding up a couple of plastic Tupperware bowls full of food.

"Sodas on you today, Champ!" Draper said, giving Chin a smile that made him shake his head and smile.

"Yeah, okay," Chin said, feeling a whole lot better after reading Carmelo's e-Mail.

Now that the first phase of his plan had been set in motion, Chin began thinking of a vicious spiel to give Carmelo during the prison visit so they could get all the money the ex-Detroit boss was willing to pay to have the witnesses in his closed case eliminated.

CHAPTER 44

On the back steps leading up to Parkchester Projects, Detective Gamble and Newsome looked over the crime scene after getting confirmation that one of their top informants had met a violent end. Detective Gamble suspected foul play. He told Newsome that he thought Carmelo Glover had something to do with the murder.

"Why you think that, partner?" Newsome asked as a lab technician walked up the steps past him to gather the physical evidence on the scene.

"Something in my gut keeps telling me that. What I want to know is how Glover knew Carter was working for us?"

"You know the streets talk all the time. Carter may have slipped up one day and let the wrong person know about his activity."

"Naw, naw, that would be like committing suicide. Naw, somebody had to put Glover onto Carter," Gamble said, rubbing his chin as if he was deep in thought. "Since he wants to play it that way, I got something for his bad ass. I'm going to get a warrant for his arrest," Gamble said and he began walking down the steps.

"Whoa, whoa, whoa. partner," Newsome said, grabbing his arm. "Let's really think this over first. I mean, if you do that, then how are you going to get him to eliminate our little problem with I.A.D?"

"That's why I need the arrest warrant: to give his ass some motivation." Gamble smirked, causing Newsome to shake his head and laugh.

"You're one evil muppet, I swear." Newsome laughed. "For a minute there, I thought you really was going to lock his ass up."

"Listen, partner, I don't give a fuck if these assholes kill each other out here. Just as long as they out of my way and pay us when it's time to pay, I can give two rat's asses what they do to each other, you feel me?"

"Loud and clear, partner…loud and clear," Newsome said as they headed towards their respective unmarked sedans, hopped in, and pulled off.

Gamble really wanted to get the arrest warrant so he could also get clearance to put a tracking device on Carmelo Glover's cell phone so he'd always know his whereabouts. After their last meeting, Carmelo had gone into hiding, which rubbed Gamble the wrong way. He felt like Carmelo Glover was trying to duck him so he wouldn't have to pull off the murder.

You got another thing coming if you think I'm going to let you off the hook so easily, you slick, murdering bastard. You fucking with the right one now! I own you for the rest of your life Mr. Glover, Gamble thought with a smile as he drove back to 7th District Police Precinct to start the paperwork process on getting the arrest warrant for Carmelo Glover and search warrant for his place of residence in Virginia.

Zetta had managed to calm Poobie down and get her off the phone. She couldn't go on the rest of the day feeling upset, so she called up Carmelo to try and smooth things over with him.

When she got his voicemail after the fifth ring, Zetta began talking fast, "Listen Melo, I don't know why in the hell you went off on me about some weak-ass thank you kiss. I was only showing my appreciation to you for hooking me up with the book publishing thing. You wrong as hell, talking about I fucked up a happy home. Nigga, when I first tried to throw this pussy on your faithful ass, you batted me down, so I don't know why you coming at me with that bullshit all of a sudden. You really need to check yourself, boy, if you want this book. I can take a hint. You should have just told me that you ain't want to publish my book…fake ma'fucka! No, I'm sorry…I ain't mean that. You not fake, it's just that you got me so heated, blaming me for your wife leaving you and shit! It ain't my fault. You need to call me soon so you can apologize to me like the gentleman I know you are. Bye!" Zetta said and hung up. She turned on West Virginia Avenue and sped towards her mother's house.

Meanwhile out in Alexandria, Virginia, Markita sat in the guest bedroom of April's house, pressing a few numbers to check Carmelo's voicemail messages. She listened to a few frivolous messages and then got a very shocking message. She sat there listening to every syllable.

The female message Markita heard shocked her, making her feel bad about accusing Carmelo of cheating on her. Now she believed every word Carmelo was trying to tell her—the same words her mother relayed to her over the phone. Markita learned enough from the message to know that the kiss was harmless and that Carmelo loved her enough to turn down the woman's sexual advances. Markita knew she had to go back home to her man soon and replace everything she took out of the house.

Markita lay back on the bed smiling at the revelation that her man wasn't a dog. She jumped up to go tell April the good news, having no idea that sharing the good news with April would change her life forever.

CHAPTER 45

The moment Swol, Nu-Nu, and I walked inside the dimly-lit nightclub, I spotted Kisha busying herself with counting money in the admittance booth and it made my stomach rumble. As always, she had everything in order and running smoothly, but something about seeing her tonight was different. Not once did she come to the hospital and check on me to see how I was doing, which really made her look suspect in my eyes. Even my security guard Big Tiny showed up to see how I was doing.

I felt like she owed me an explanation. A week and a half ago, she put the press on me about becoming my 50/50 partner. After I told her to give me some time to think about it, she asked me to get a living will and requested that I make her the beneficiary of the club just in case something happened. Then later on that night, I got shot and had to lie up in the hospital for twelve days to recover. That was too much of a coincidence there if you asked me.

"Ay, Bob, I'ma go see what's up with all these chicks in the spot," Nu-Nu said, invading my thoughts as I made eye contact with Kisha.

She looked at me and gave me a warm smile and then went back to counting up the money as if I wasn't even there after my long hiatus.

"Ay, Nu, don't go too far, 'cause we ain't gon' be in here long. I just came to check on something real quick," I told him.

"I gotcha, Champ," he said and began heading into the sea of people on the dance floor. As Nu-Nu stepped off to enjoy himself, I told Swol to keep an eye on him.

"What for? I'm s'posed to be your shadow!" he retorted.

"Just keep an eye on the boy. He knows too much to be slipping out of our sight."

"But you said we made a pact, the Three Henchmen. 'Til death do us part," he reminded me.

"You right, but if he decides to roll out and violate the pact, then where will that leave us?"

"Fuck 'em, we ain't do shit with his little ass anyway."

But order the death of a confidential informant, I thought. Aloud, I said, "Listen Swol, it's always better to be safe then sorry. Just keep an eye on 'im while I go holla at this broad."

"Yeah, a'ight, but hurry up, Slim, 'cause I got some shit I need to do too," he said, then he walked off like he had an attitude.

I studied Kisha's movements and body language for a long moment before walking over to her. When I reached the booth, she looked up and smiled.

"Hey, Melo, it's good to finally have your ass back. Now maybe I can get some rest," she said.

"Listen, Kish, I need to talk to you in private for a moment. Get somebody else to handle this real quick."

"No can do, Melo. You know I never let anybody handle that cash. They may get sticky fingers," she said.

"It's real important, so as soon as you get finished, I need to see you inside my office ASAP."

"Okay." She nodded and went back to handling business.

I walked away and began heading to my office. On my way, I looked over in a dark corner and saw Nu-Nu pushing a blond woman down on her knees. I paused for a second to make sure what I was seeing was true. When the blond woman's head began moving back and forth in front of the crotch area of his black chinos, I figured that Nu-Nu was enjoying the power of the blond woman's brains.

Damn, that young nigga move fast as hell, I thought, looking around for Swol, who was nowhere in sight.

I proceeded to my office. Once inside, I closed the door and took a seat in my chair behind my desk. I opened the drop safe to check on the money that I left there on the night I got shot. It looked to be all there. I pulled it out and began counting it just to make sure. By the time I finished, Kisha still hadn't showed up.

I began looking around my office, thinking of how I should question her. I mean, I have killed people for far less suspicions than the ones I had concerning Kisha, but I didn't want to jump the gun too quickly. She could be innocent, but all the damaging evidence and coincidences was pointing at her.

Suddenly my thoughts shifted as I zeroed in on a quarter-sized hole in the wall directly under the clock sitting over top of the office entrance. I never paid attention to the hole before because it was so small, you'd miss it in passing. I jumped up immediately to investigate the small hole in the wall. Looking up at it, I saw a little camera lens the size of the face on a watch sitting inside, flashing a red light. My heart dropped immediately. This shit had been there before I took over the place, which meant it had to be there when I killed Suede.

I began trying to find where the camera feed led to. I snatched open my office door and looked up. I saw what appeared to be a covered telephone wire painted in gold and black trimming. I began following the long paint lines, feeling sick to my stomach. The closer I got to the finish line, the more anxious I got. You know that feeling you get when you're afraid of heights and you're up somewhere very high and take look over the edge? Yeah, that's the feeling I had consuming me right now, only a hundred times worse. My eyes and body followed the painted telephone lines until they stopped at a custodial closet and ran inside it. My heart pumped wildly in my chest as I went to open the door, but it was locked.

Why didn't I ever check on this shit before? I thought as I rushed back downstairs to locate Tiny.

After spotting Tiny flirting with some pretty Asian sensation with fake boobs that were a little too big to fit her 5'2" small frame, I called him over.

"What's good, Bossman?"

"Why is that custodian closet upstairs by my office locked?"

"I don't know, Bossman. I thought you wanted it that way. Every time I ask about it, Kisha tells me not to worry about it.

Fuck she mean don't worry about it? "You sure she told you that?"

"Yeah, I been meaning to ask you about it, but the shit been slipping my mind."

"For two years, it's been slipping your mind? Come on, Big Guy, you can come better than that," I said, feeling myself getting hot with anger and suspicion. If this nigga is in cahoots with Kisha, I'ma slaughter both they asses tonight, I thought as he gave me a funny look.

"Hey, gang." Kisha appeared suddenly, scaring the shit out of me. "What's up?" she asked with a smile, making me turn on her abruptly.

"That's what I need to find out," I said. I began pulling her upstairs to see what secrets she'd been keeping behind door number one.

CHAPTER 46

The moment we reached the custodial closet, I whipped out my gun and aimed it at Kisha. She looked like she was about to cry and piss her panties. I didn't give a fuck about her feelings at the moment. I needed some answers and I needed them now.

"Whoa, Bossman!" Tiny blurted, trying to intervene.

"Whoa what!" I snapped, aiming the gun at him. "If you don't want to die, I suggest you get the fuck back downstairs and do your fucking job."

"I'm going, man, I'm going but you need to think about what you're doing, Bossman," he said, backing up with his hands held up in surrender.

After Tiny disappeared, Kisha lips began trembling as she looked at me. "Melo, what's wrong?"

"Bitch, you know what the fuck is up!" I snapped. "First you ask me to be a partner in the club, and then when I tell you gimme a minute to think about the shit, you ask me to get a living will and then a ma'fucka tries to kill me that same night. That's too much of a fucking coincidence."

"Melo, I'd never even think about doing what you're insinuating right now," she said, shaking her head.

"Well, why after you ask to be my partner and shit, somebody tries to kill me?"

"Fuck you, ma'fucka!" she raged. "You forgot I was in the car with your ass the first time somebody took a shot at you? You forgot you put my life in danger, ma'fucka, so don't even go there."

"Kisha, I ain't going to go back and forth with your ass. You looking too suspect right now, which is throwing me off."

"Ma'fucka, if I wanted you dead, I could've killed your ass all them times I caught you sleeping inside your office," she revealed, and then lowered her head like she regretted the words soon as they left her mouth. "But I'm not like that, Melo. You kept me around here after Suede died and I am eternally grateful to you for that. But now you coming at me with this bullshit like I want to kill you, which has me thinking that you trying to use that as an excuse to deny my partnership request."

"Why is this fucking door locked then and why you didn't tell me about the cameras in the fucking office and shit?"

"That's some shit Suede had installed when the place first opened. I didn't know you ain't know about the shit. I thought you had the keys to the closet, 'cause Suede was the only one kept the keys to that room. Nobody ever goes in there but him. I just thought you was on the same secret squirrel shit."

"Kisha, right now I don't know what to think. I mean, ma'fuckas want me dead for some type of reason and everybody is suspect, including you."

"Fuck you, Melo!" she snapped. "I don't hafta take this shit. I ran this club for your ass while you was laid up in the hospital and not once did I complain 'cause I knew you was in recovery. I made sure the whole $665,000 for all those days made it to the bank safely. And you come back and accuse me of some bullshit? Fuck you!" she said and began walking away.

"Kisha, don't walk away from me!" I said. But she kept walking.

I took a shot at the wall directly in front of her, which stopped her in her tracks. The loud music downstairs drowned out the mild exploding sounds of my .45 ACP compressor. Kisha turned on me and began walking briskly in my direction. When she got in my face, I felt a little intimidated by the evil look she gave me.

"I know you just didn't do what I think you did?"

"Your ass ain't want to sto - "

WHAP! She slapped the taste out of my mouth, silencing me. I backed up quickly and aimed my gun at her face, fingering the trigger.

"Go 'head, bitch, kill me!" she screamed, rushing at me, forcing her head on the barrel of the gun. "You think I'm trying to kill you, then go ahead and get it over with and kill me!" she challenged, making me second guess her.

Damn, she really going all out. If she was acting, she just won the Oscar for best performance in a sneaky plot to take me out the game, I thought and lowered my pistol. "Just get the fuck out my face, Kisha." I said softly, backing up from her.

"That's all you gon' say after trying to kill me is get the fuck out your face?" she said, looking at me like I sickened her.

"I ain't try to kill you. I just wanted your stubborn ass to stop so I could get my point across."

"Get your point across? Get your point across," she repeated and then added. "Boy, you know what - " She paused, and held up her finger at me before sighing. "Hmph, Lord give me strength," she said and then walked off, switching hard, expressing her anger to me.

"Kisha!" I called.

"Not right now, Melo. Not right now!" she said without looking back, keeping it moving.

Damn, I just fucked up. Maybe Shorty is genuine. She turned in all that money without cuffing one cent. I mean, she probably cuffed some short shit like $5,000 or $10,000, but would I miss it? I thought, knowing I couldn't lose Kisha. I had to come up with a way to apologize and keep her happy before she left me.

I turned on the custodial closet and began shooting at the lock. After opening the door, I got the shock of my life.

CHAPTER 47

The moment the blond woman got Nu-Nu's nature hard as a rock, he pulled her inside the bathroom. When she tried to pull away playfully, Nu-Nu squeezed her B-cup-sized breasts.

"C'mon, Shorty, I know you ain't just gon' tease me like that?" he asked, feeling his dick throbbing with anticipation.

"Someone is going to see us." The blond played hard to get. She was a little tipsy and wanted to get her freak on, but she didn't want him to view her as the freak she actually was.

"Ain't nobody gon' see shit, Kill," Nu-Nu assured her, pulling her inside the male restroom.

When they got inside, he ushered her inside a bathroom stall and began kissing her passionately. She began stroking his hardness as he played with her erect nipples.

"Mmm…you have protection on you?" she asked in a throaty whisper while kissing all over his neck and earlobes.

"Naw, Shorty," Nu-Nu said, hiking up her sundress. He quickly found out that she wore no panties. He inserted two fingers inside her wet twat quickly and began digging for gold.

"Mmmmmmmm. Sssssss….I have some in my purse." She moaned, grinding her pelvis on his probing fingers. In one swift motion, the blond woman pulled a pack of condoms from her purse and ripped one with her teeth. When she dropped to her knees, forcing him to extract his fingers, she rolled the condom on his rock-hard manhood. She had a look of excitement on her face.

"You really big. I may not be able to handle all of that stuff."

"You're a big girl, so I know you up for the challenge," Nu-Nu said as he pulled her back up to her feet and turned her around quickly.

While she bent over the toilet and pulled her dress up over her creamy ass, Nu-Nu wedged his chocolate dick between her rosy cheeks. Feeling his manhood sliding up and down her ass crack made her turn on like a heat lamp. His hot shaft began to poke against her flesh. The blond couldn't resist. She reached down and coiled her fingers around his thickness. Squeezing lightly, she began to stroke, moving the skin back and forth along the lengthening muscle.

Nu-Nu's hands cupped both her titties as she gradually worked his pipe inside the entrance of her small, tight pussy. Nu-Nu teased the entrance for a minute before pushing further inside her slick channel. He began stroking gently in and out, in and out, making her match his rhythm. He eased his hand down to massage her budding clitoris, which made her cry out joyously.

"Awww, fuck me, you black motherfucker! Awww yes!" she screamed out in delight as he began pounding out the inner pink walls of her sucking pussy.

After drilling her in that position for about five minutes, Nu-Nu pulled his dick from her pussy. She wagged her behind at him, urging him to penetrate her again. When he slid his dick inside her anal cavity, the blond screamed like someone was killing her.

"Nooo! Take it out, it's too big!"

Nu-Nu stabbed her a few times and then extracted his love pump and quickly inserted it back inside her tight pussy.

"Mmmm…that feels so much better," she moaned as she began humping back into his stabbing pole until he was plunging to the very root of his dick, making his balls slap violently against her ass cheeks.

"Oh, Gawd, you black motherfucker!" the blond cried. "You're making me cum, dammit!"

Nu-nu stiffened. His body arched, making his pelvis come under the blond's pussy and fuck harder and harder. As she climaxed all over his sawing manhood, Nu-Nu began shaking. In spite of the latex barrier between them, he still felt oozing warm spurts of her love juices. She collapsed on top of the toilet and held on for dear life as he drilled in and out of the depths of her contracting pussy.

"Damn, you got some good muh'fucking pussy!" He groaned and exploded hard inside the condom.

As he basked in the afterglow of their carnal act, the blond said, "If I made you half as happy as you made me, all I can say is wow! This should never end."

When they got themselves together, the blond pulled out her cell phone from her purse and began punching in a few words.

"What you doing, Shorty?" Nu-Nu asked.

"Just logging in the best night of my freaking life." She giggled. "You need to punch my number in your phone so we can do this again very soon."

Nu-Nu laughed and asked for her number. When she gave it to him and began leaving the bathroom, Nu-Nu suddenly remembered that he didn't catch her name. He walked behind her quickly to get that information, not believing how easy she gave up the nappy dug-out.

After opening the closet door, all I thought was, What the fuck? Looking at all the video equipment inside the room, I could see every spot of the nightclub on the ten video monitors inside the room. It looked like the inside cabin of a huge 18-wheeler semi-truck. I began looking at everything going on inside the club. I even caught Nu-Nu having sex with some blond in the male restroom. Suede had this whole club under his watchful eye and I had no idea until now. With that thought in mind, I began searching for the disc that dated as far back to the night I killed him. Nobody had been in this room since that night, so it shouldn't be hard to find. When I looked over and pressed the ejection button for the disc, it slid out with nothing inside.

This can't be happening to me! Where's the fucking disc? And what other person has access to this shit other than Suede? I wondered, feeling like I was going to lose it if I didn't find out the location of the disc. It was the only evidence tying my to the murder of Suede - evidence that could destroy my relationship with Markita forever and basically send me to the electric chair. Virginia didn't play and gave out the death penalty for committing murder just like public assistance gave out food stamps for the needy.

I had to get to the bottom of this shit, quick, fast, and in a hurry. Then it hit me. What if the disc fell into the hands of the wrong person who was taking shots at me? Now it was all coming together. I left the closet worried to death that the person who had that incriminating disc had control over my life as I knew it.

CHAPTER 48

When Kisha bolted down the stairs, still upset from her altercation with Carmelo, she didn't pay attention to what she was doing until she ran directly into Swol. She tried to keep it moving, but he blocked her path.

"Hi, beautiful. You need to watch where you going."

"I'm sorry, really I am," Kisha said, attempting to step around him again.

"See there, you still keep getting in my way," Swol said, stepping in front of her and doing a little two-step dance.

Frustrated with him, Kisha tried to shove him aside.

"Hold up, please don't hurt me, beautiful!" He smiled, liking her instantly. Swol always had a thing for cute plus-sized women. "I'm just tryna make sure you smile before you go out there and kill somebody," he said, pointing over his shoulder at the crowded dance floor.

"I see you ain't going to move, huh?" she asked, a little flattered by the attention he threw her way. In fact, his warm smile cooled her burning anger. Looking up for the first time, Kisha's heart skipped a beat when she saw the handsome, baldheaded man with his beard groomed nicely, smelling like some exotic oils, and she liked the way he wore his white button down shirt, dark grey slacks, and fly up Oxfords. After giving him a look over, Kisha's eyes aimed down at the dangling print of his crotch.

"Please, just one dance?" he asked as the DJ threw on the Jaheim classic "Just in Case."

Just in case I don't make it home tonight...
Let me make love to you for the last time, baby...
I wanna change each moment from the last...
'Cause baby, you're all I have, so just in case...

Kisha's thoughts immediately dove into the gutter after seeing his dick print. She could tell from just looking at the bulge that he definitely was working with a monster. She imagined how pleasurable it would be to have his monster going skinny dipping in and out of her wet love tunnel. If she wasn't so angry with Carmelo, she would have allowed her fantasy to come true. "Boy, you need to move outta my way before I have security remove your ass from the club altogether," she said in a nasty tone.

Thinking she was bluffing, Swol moved in closer to her and began dancing. He dropped down into a quick squat and began humping her thick leg gently like a dog in heat, which made her jump back, slightly startled.

"Boy, stop!" she yelled over the music, trying her best to keep the laughter erupting inside her from flowing out of her mouth. Something in his eyes told her that he wanted her. She secretly thought of all the things she wanted to do with him.

"Stop for what? You need this, so stop being mean and come and get your boogie on," he pressed and moved up on her again.

"You don't even know my name or nothing about me, boy." She pushed him back, keeping him at arm's length and trying her best not to break down under his aggressive charm.

"You absolutely right, beautiful, but I didn't think that I had to know your name just to get one simple dance from you," he remarked as he quickly turned his booty on her and began backing his thang up on her.

Kisha smacked his tight behind and couldn't help but laugh. After hearing her laughing, Swol turned back on her as the Jodeci classic, "Come and Talk To Me", began blaring through the speakers.

"I been watching you for so very long…trying to get my nerve up here for it to be so strong," Swol began singing, butchering the lyrics. "I really want to meet you, but I'm kinda' scared…'cause something…something…something….I forget what to say…." he harmonized, making her laugh until the chorus came on.

"Come and talk to me! I really wanna meet you," he sang with passion. "Can I talk to you, Oooooh yeahhhh…I really wanna know you!" he sang. He decided to pull her chunky frame into his embrace and rock slowly with her.

As they slow danced for the rest of the song, Swol harmonized the lyrics in her ear, using them as come-on lines. "There you are again with the same smile and unique face. I wanna know what it is to make you feel this way - yeeeaah!"

"You look sooo good to me…yes you do! You look sooo fine! Please tell me your name…let me play your game!" he crooned, doing his best to imitate the lead singer, KC.

"Kisha," she whispered in his ear, tingling inside from just the smell of his Somali Rose fragrance and deep baritone. She figured that she'd let him dance with her for a few more songs to take her mind off the confrontation she just had with Carmelo. As fine as he was, Kisha knew that he could have his choice of any woman in the club tonight, but for some reason he chose her. Once the song ended, Swol backed up and took a slight bow. "Thanks, beautiful. Now see, that wasn't so bad was it?"

For some reason, Kisha felt at ease around him and Carmelo shooting at her became a distant memory. "No, it really wasn't," she replied in the best sexy tone she could muster while studying his handsome face. Initially, Kisha had been hot with anger while coming down the stairs, but after running into the sexy stranger, Kisha became enchanted and wanted to spend more time with him.

"I'm Swol, by the way," he said, breaking into her thoughts.

You sure is, she thought and said, "Thanks for the dance, Swol." She smiled, feeling something magnetic in his brown eyes pulling her into his embrace again.

"So I guess you want more than one dance with ole Swol, huh?" he asked, belting out a sexy laugh.

"You the one who stopped me and started this, so I'm going to finish it," She said as Carmelo bent the corner and saw them.

When I rushed down the stairs to locate Kisha, I saw her all hugged up in Swol's arms. I studied their body language for a moment and could tell that they'd be hooking up later on to continue their mating dance behind a closed bedroom door. I didn't really care that Swol was dancing with the same woman who he suggested that I should kill earlier when I told him about her. For now, Kisha looked happy and content in his arms and that's all that mattered.

Swol could possibly be the pawn I needed to keep Kisha's mind distracted from being my 50/50 partner and he could watch her every move. The idea made me smile for the first time since discovering that somebody had me on video committing murder.

CHAPTER 49

When Kisha spotted me watching her, she cleared her throat and pushed Swol away from her. She had to know that he was with me, unless she didn't see him with me when we first entered the club. I decided to keep it moving so she wouldn't bat Swol down out of spite that he was my partner.

Swol tried to call me, but I pretended like I didn't hear him. I walked around the club in search of Nu-Nu. During my search, I ran across somebody that I thought I'd never see. Now this rat was one of the reasons that Chin was serving time. What a surprise this would be to be able to tell Chin that I crushed one of the rats in his case.

The rat's name was Hard Rock. From what I gathered, he had to be in his mid-to-late forties. Rumors in the street had it that he still hung around

Southwest because he figured all the head bustas was in prison. Hard Rock felt safe enough to the point where he didn't think anybody would do anything to him.

Wait until he got a load of me!

I bolted back upstairs to my office to get the Ruger with the attached silencer on it. By the time I made it back down on the dance floor, Swol stopped me.

"Not right now, Swol. I'm on one," I said wide-eyed and he backed up.

"Wassup, Champ?" he asked.

"Nothing, just make sure you stay with Kisha. Take her home and fuck her brains out."

"How you know about her?"

"'Cause she's the same chick that you told me I should kill," I said as I stepped off.

"Naw, Slim, not her. She's too cute to be a snake!" I heard him saying over the music as I weaved through the dance floor in search of the rat.

I spotted Nu-Nu walking towards me and I ducked behind a fat Spanish chick to avoid him. I didn't need any more distractions from what I intended to do. When I spotted Hard Rock again, he was sitting in a corner booth with three women, enjoying some bubbly and their conversation.

I walked over to his table and greeted him and the women. "I'm the owner of this spot and I'm just doing a survey on how I can make it better for your entertainment?"

"Shiid, you need to have a stripper's night up in this bitch so I won't hafta spend all my money buying drinks for all these gold-digging broads," Hard Rock said, which made the ladies sitting with him erupt with uncontrollable laughter. This stupid-ass nigga didn't even know how much he was prolonging his own death by keeping the women with him. It was the only thing that made me hold back from slaughtering him. Now I had to wait and watch him for the rest of the night until the perfect chance arrived for me to do what I wanted to do with him.

"Mmph, boy, you so silly. Ain't he, y'all? We ain't got to take this shit. He probably broke anyway," a little cute redbone said while producing a phony laugh - you know the type of laugh someone gives you when they're trying to kiss your ass or get something out of you.

As she flashed her pretty smile, I watched as her two thick-to-death friends got up from the booth. By the looks on their faces, I figured that they didn't find his joke funny at all. After easing out of the booth, they had to pull their skimpy skirts down over their huge bubble butts. Damn, what the hell they putting in the food these days? I thought, staring at them in lust as they made their exit.

When I was sure they was gone, I took a seat in the booth beside the rat, making him look at me funny. See, Hard Rock's full testimony in Chin's trial was posted on www.Ratz.com. I remember reading something to the effect that Hard Rock testified that he was approached by Chin and another guy about where they could go and buy seven pounds of weed. Hard Rock took Chin and the guy along with another informant named Ronald Horns to an apartment to see Jamaican Stark and a Jamaican named Bliss. Bliss informed the group of men that he didn't have all the weed they needed in the apartment and offered to get it from another location. Hard Rock said that Chin gave the Jamaican Bliss $500 and left with Bliss to get the weed. According to his other testimony at trial. Hard Rock claimed they stayed behind and started playing with firearms with the residents in the apartment. Hard Rock then said that when he received a call from Chin, Chin told him that he was sitting in front of another apartment building waiting on Jamaican Bliss to return, but he was nowhere to be found. Hard Rock told the jury in court that Chin later returned with another man and Jamaican Stark asked Chin and the guy to come back the next day.

"Fuck you mean come back tomorrow? Your man got our shit."

Hard Rock lied on Chin and then told the jury that Jamaican Stark told Chin that he didn't know what was up with Jamaican Bliss because he had never done that before. Hard Rock told the jury that as they were leaving the apartment, Chin pulled out a gun when the group fled the building, but the guy with Chin continued to chase Jamaican Stark outside and then shot him.

Growing heated by the memory of his outright betrayal to the game, I looked directly in the rat's eyes and said, "I seen you jive digging the spot, right? So have a few more bottles on the house!" I smiled, trying to rock his ass all the way to sleep.

"Why, what's up?" he asked, getting defensive.

"Naw, I just wanted to make sure that you remember partying at Chances, that's all." I said, baiting him all the way in while caressing the Ruger in my pocket. I had the weapon aimed directly at him under the table and he didn't even peep it. Neither did his female companion.

"You doing it big like that, huh?" he smiled. "I guess you just reeled in a loyal customer, Soldier," he said and made a quick move to kiss the woman sitting to the left of him.

When he lifted his head to kiss her, I shot him a venomous look, killing him ten times over in my head. The only thing that really stopped me from killing him right now was the fact that I didn't want to make my establishment hot with the police. As his lips slammed into the cute redbone's lips, I leaned over and slid out of the booth.

Bitch-ass nigga! I'ma deal with you, watch, I thought before easing out on to the dance floor. Smoothly doing a two step dance, I began glancing around the club to see if Swol or Nu-Nu were anywhere close by. Damn, where the fuck are these niggas at when you need them? I thought after noticing everyone caught up in their own little worlds. I stepped off to tell Swol and Nu-Nu that it was time to go.

Walking briskly to find Nu-Nu and Swol, I couldn't believe how easily I had been snatched back into the killing game - the same game that had a crooked cop trying to blackmail me into killing another cop and somebody trying to kill me for a murder I committed over two years ago.

CHAPTER 50

About forty-five minutes passed before the little waitress broad, Angel, came and told me that the rat and his female friend were getting ready to leave. By that time, I had already put Nu-Nu and Swol on point, returned to the video room, and erased all the earlier footage of the club's activity. If it ever came out, I didn't want any information to be leaked out that the rat was last seen anywhere inside my nightclub.

"Thanks, Angel, you the best," I said, slipping her a big face $100 bill.

"I'll be even better when you let me see what that dick hitting on," she flirted openly.

"C'mon, Angel, you know wifey ain't going for that shit. I'm already in the dog house. What you think she gon' do if she finds out about us doing the nasty," I joked, keeping my eyes on the front door.

"What she don't know won't hurt her."

"I hear you, but let me get back to you on that, okay?" I told her, brushing past her. I located Swol who was chilling with Kisha and told him to give me his car keys.

"Why you need my keys?"

"'Cause I need them," I said and then looked at Kisha, who was giving me the evil eye. "Kisha, you ain't gotta problem with giving my homie a ride home, do you?"

"He's your friend?" she gasped. "I find that very hard to believe ,'cause he's nothing like your ass!" she snapped.

"You gon' give him a ride or what?" I asked, holding my hands out, beckoning Swol to give me the keys.

"Yeah, boy, stop asking me already, damn!" She argued just to be arguing.

After hearing that, Swol passed me his car keys. After getting them, I gave him a hug and went to holla at Nu-Nu. Nu-Nu was at the bar chilling with the blond who he had just had sex with in the bathroom. When I walked up on him, I could tell that he wanted to chill with her for the rest of the night.

"Ay, Nu-Nu, let me holla at you,'" I said.

He sighed and eased off the bar stool. "Excuse me, beautiful," he said to the blond and then walked over to me. "What's up, Big Dog?"

"Look, you can stay with that bitch. I don't really care at all. I just thought we agreed to…you know what? Never mind, fuck it." I sighed. "I'ma see you later on. You got a way to get home, right?" I asked and he looked over his shoulder at the blond.

"Yeah, Shorty want me to go home with her and finish crushing that joint." He smiled, and I knew he didn't have the gift to do what I did. He thought with his little head, which could lead to his destruction. You can never trust a big butt and a smile.

"Okay, I'ma see you later or then." I gave him a hug, knowing that it would be the last time that I hung out with him.

Nu-Nu's actions tonight showed that he was more concerned about getting his dick wet instead of making a snitch wet. Besides, I had too much on my plate to be babysitting a grown-ass man. On another note, I didn't really know Nu-Nu's pedigree. He could flip on a nigga at any given moment or signs of pressure, so it was better for me to cut all ties with him right now.

At that moment, I realized that I couldn't be hanging around Swol either because I was really a loner with a troubled past - a past that needed to be cleaned up before I could move forward with Swol and Nu-Nu. I would call Kisha and make sure she hired him with the agreed-upon payroll I had told Swol about. I didn't know how that would pan out between them since they had some type of chemistry, but I couldn't worry about that now. I had to focus and switch my mind over into murder mode and do something that I felt needed to be done for a good man stuck in the belly of the beast.

In New Carrolton, MD, Little James leaned on the wall in the La Fontaine Bleu Lounge, nodding his head to the cranking go-go sounds of TCB. He attended the Go-Go for two reasons: to scope out who was getting money in the streets and reel in some pussy for the night. He sported some 1996 retro black and white patent leather Air Jordans, a thin silk Versace Medusa face T-shirt, and some True Religion jeans. The money he robbed Marty for paid for the expensive outfit. A few female heads turned when Little James walked up in the dimly-lit nightclub.

"We got that bounce....bounce with us. Grrraaaaaah!" Little James heard the man on the mic singing as the band broke down into an infectious beat that sent the young crowd into a dancing frenzy.

Little James wasn't used to the newest band taking over the go-go scene in the Metropolitan Area. He was used to the old bands like Rare Essence and Backyard. Even though he was young, he had an old soul.

Searching the crowd for prey, Little James spotted some potential food almost immediately. He kept his slanted eyes zoomed in on the 6'3" brown-skinned guy with dreads pulled into a ponytail posted up by the bar with two bottles of Ace of Spades champagne in his hand. Little James paid extra attention to the iced-out big face watch on his arm and the huge diamond earrings in his ears.

Little James nodded to the go-go sounds, subtly trying to make himself incognito while eyeing his prey like a hawk. He was about to move in a little closer to his prey when he heard somebody calling him, trying to get his attention. Little James turned and saw Smurf from Garfield Terrace, AKA Purple City. As Smurf approached him, Little James's whole face lit up with excitement. He remembered the guy his uncle used to be hanging around when he was getting money.

"What's ha-ha-happening Ma-Ma-Moses?" Smurf stammered, giving him a one arm hug.

Little James returned the greeting with a smile and said, "Out here tryna make these bitch-ass niggas feel me."

"I ha-ha-heard that. You good though? Ya-ya-you know…ah-ah-ah your uncle Twan ta-ta-told me to look out fa-fa-for you…whaaa-when you ca-ca-come home."

Little James had to do everything in his power to keep from laughing in his face. The way he stuttered made him look like his face and throat were hurting from the struggle to get the words out.

"Oh yeah? You saying that shit like he knew he was going to die or some shit."

"Whaaa-w-we all gon' die, young nigga. He was j-just preparing ta-ta-ta-to make sure that ya-you was taken care of," Smurf said, leaving out the part about his uncle being a rat.

Smurf had found out about Twan's murder and messed up ways, which messed up his mental. He didn't know how Twan's nephew would react to the news, so Smurf just kept the conversation at the bare minimum.

"Oh yeah?"

"Yeah, but ha-ha-he did had ba-beef with the nigga Carmelo before ha-ha-he died."

"Oh yeah?" Little James asked, his face contorting into a mask of rage. "Carmelo still be round Twan's old way?"

"I da-don't know. I j-just heard about his ba-beef in th-tha-the streets."

"You said Carmelo, huh? It ain't too many Carmelos from 'round there." Little James rubbed his chin, like he was deep in thought.

Little James made a mental note to go through the First Street area, locate Carmelo's closest relatives, and kill them all. Unbeknownst to Little James, Carmelo's parents were dead and he didn't have any close ties with his brothers who lived in Yonkers, New York, some kids his father made before moving to D.C.

"It ain't. That's a r-rare name Ba-Bob," Smurf said, digging inside his pocket.

He pulled out a huge knot of bills and counted out $2,000. Once he looked at Little James and saw a wicked look in his eyes, Smurf reconsidered giving him the $2,000. Smurf put the $2,000 in his pocket and gave Little James the leftover money on his bankroll, which was a little over $12,000 that he had won at the gambling spot last night.

Little James's whole face lit up with joy soon as Smurf put the bankroll in his hands. "Damn, Moe, what's all this for?"

"A start up kitty ta-ta-to keep ya-your bad ass ah-ah-ah-outta trouble. Here's my number. Maybe I ca-ca-ca-can keep you outta trouble if you come Uptown and fuck with me."

Little James took Smurf's business card and smiled. "I'ma keep you in mind, Scrap."

Smurf had no idea that by blessing Little James with that large bankroll he'd just saved the man's life who was balling out of control in the iced-out big face watch that attracted Little James to him.

After leaving the nightclub, I sat in Swol's car and waited for the rat to emerge. I had Tiny hold them up with some frivolous bullshit before releasing them, which gave me enough time to peep the ride he was driving.

When the rat emerged with his girl, I figured that Tiny couldn't get her to stay. I didn't want her to be with him when I worked his ass because I didn't have mask, and she'd have to go also, because I couldn't leave any witnesses.

Maybe I can hit his ass and spare her? It wasn't her fault that she was hanging out with a rat. Maybe she didn't know about his betrayal to the game, so that gave me no right to kill her. Now if she knows, that's a totally different story, but I don't know if she knows or not, so I'm forced to give her pass, I thought, watching him jump in a classy-looking Jaguar. Yeah, he's definitely from the old school, I told myself and started Swol's car.

As soon as he pulled off, I did the same, keeping a close distance between us. He swerved a little, which led me to believe that he was a little tipsy and not alert to his surroundings. He drove for a good three to five minutes until he found a hotel. Perfect, I thought, watching the woman get out of the car to head inside the hotel. She was probably going inside to book a room.

When she walked inside the hotel, I was out of the car with the quickness with the silenced Ruger drawn. I ran up on the driver's side of the car and tapped on the glass. When the rat made a quick move to look my way, I began squeezing the trigger. When his body fell over on the passenger seat, I opened the door with my shirt covering my hand. I leaned in the car, placed the warm silencer barrel on his temple, and shot his ass four more times in the head, leaving his brains and thoughts splattered all over the passenger side seat and door panel.

I jogged back to Swol's car, got inside, and pulled off. By the time I left the parking lot and got out on the street, I could hear the young, cute redbone screaming at the top of her lungs for help, which made me feel a whole lot better than I was feeling just a few minutes ago. There's no better way to release anger and frustration in my book.

CHAPTER 51

During the second half of the go-go, Little James met a thick 5'6" tall caramel brickhouse who wore a thin black Gucci dress and six inch heels. She carried a Gucci tote bag and had huge D&G shades planted on top of her sandy blond mane. She looked too good for Little James to pass up. After eyeing her like a hawk for a long moment and seeing her shoot every guy down who tried to talk to her, Little James stepped to her smoothly and groped her soft ass from behind.

When the woman turned on him, she pushed him roughly. He gave her an alluring smile and pulled her into a tight bear hug. "Bitch, don't get fucked up in here! I just wanted to squeeze the Charmin to make sure it was real before I offered you this bread to fuck."

"I'm not no bitch, boy," she hissed, punching on his chest. "Get the fuck offa me!" she snapped, trying to break free of his tight hold.

"Well, how much it's going cost me for you to be my bitch for tonight?" he asked, releasing her so suddenly that she almost fell on her soft behind.

"$2,000. Can you afford to make me your bitch now?" she said in a sassy tone.

"I sure can, you sexy bitch, you. You ready to go now or what?" he asked, pulling out the money he had just gotten from Smurf. He counted out $1,000 and gave it to her.

"You get half now and the other half after I beat that box up," he said.

Her face lit up after the cash touched her hands. She looked him in the eyes and licked her lips. "You can try to beat it up."

They left quickly. Little James had her follow him to the Ramada Inn down the street from the nightclub. After paying $200 for the suite, Little James got the credit card-shaped key and pulled her towards the elevator.

After entering the 6th floor hotel suite, Little James wasted no time in undressing, making sure to keep his pistol in plain view for her to see to stop any fishy ideas she might have brewing inside her head.

The young woman slowly undressed, staring at his dangling love muscle hungrily. The money he threw her way like it meant nothing to him made her eager to please him in hopes of getting some more of his bankroll. She crawled up to him on the bed, looking like a stalking lioness cornering her prey. After straddling his hips, she let him kiss her and shove his tongue in her mouth. He squeezed her soft butt cheeks, pulling them apart.

"Damn, you phat as shit, Shorty." He groaned before moving his lips to her hard nipples.

"Thank you," she said softly before pushing him back on the bed and kissing on his neck, running her tongue up to his earlobe and then back down to his chest. She began stroking his manhood like she was cocking a pump shotgun as she sucked on his chest.

"Spin that ass around here, bitch!" he said, making her flinch with anger.

Damn, he's ruining the mood, she thought. She said, "I'm not no, bitch!"

"Shiiid, for that two stacks I just paid your ass, you gon' be whatever the fuck I want you to be, bitch! Now turn that ass 'round here."

She reluctantly did as he ordered and began kissing the head of his dick as he ate her pussy in the 69 position. He began fingering her wet pussy in and out while sucking on her clitoris. While sucking her clitoris, he moved his mouth back until it kissed the tiny dark ring of her anal chute.

"Aaaah.....Mmmmmm...Ssss, boy!" she huffed over the boner wedged between her juicy lips as his tongue began penetrating her anal ring.

She began grinding her hips in circular motions, making her wet pussy move all over his chin and face, coating his lips and nose with her sweet nectar. He focused on her tight asshole, stabbing his tongue inside her backdoor, making her squirm and release his dick with a loud POP!

"Aaah! Boy, stop!" she cried joyously, moving her head from side to side as he locked her ass in place over his face. She squeezed his throbbing erection and began stroking him in rhythm to the way he tried to suck a fart out of her asshole.

"Sssss. Oh my Gawd....puh-leasssse, stop! Stop, boy and just fuck me! Hurry up!" she begged, rubbing his dick all over her face and lips while he buried his tongue deeper and deeper inside her back door.

"You got some rubbers?" he asked, kissing on the crack between her soft butt cheeks.

"Yeah," she gasped, leaping off his face.

She rushed from the bed, looking back at him wildly. She couldn't keep her eyes off him as he looked at her stroking himself. She frantically searched her purse for the condoms, keeping her eyes glued to his upstanding shaft. After finding the condoms, she ripped open two of them and returned to the bed. She put both condoms on his throbbing muscle and then moved over top of him to squat down on his rigid love organ.

Looking down at him, she grabbed his boner and slowly sat down, impaling herself. She began riding him fast and hard, making her juicy pussy muscles squeeze his deep, churning pole as her soft ass cheeks smacked loudly down on his thighs.

"Ssssss....Mmmmm...give me that dick, boy....don't stop...you bet' not stop!" she urged, licking her lips and playing with her hard nipples as he banged away at her insides faster and faster.

Riding him forcefully, she pinched his chest nipples and continued fucking him until an intense climax ripped through her body. "Aaaahhh, aah, aah....ah my Gawd...oooooohhh......Godammnnnnn!" she shrieked, clenching her inner walls tightly around his impaled shaft until she made him shoot his load into the condom.

"Damn, Shorty, you jive fucked the shit outta me!" He set her props before getting up and grabbing his jeans and gun.

He went inside the bathroom and began washing off the traces of their intense sexcapade. While washing off his manhood, he contemplated on robbing her for the money he just gave her. Naw, she jive put it on a nigga. I can't carry her ass like that. I should teach the bitch a lesson about acting all smart and shit, he thought while grabbing a towel and drying his groin area.

After cleaning up, Little James returned to the bed area wearing his jeans. She looked up and asked him what was wrong.

"Ain't nothing wrong, bitch," he grinned. "I just need to roll out, that's all. I got shit to do," he said before reaching inside his pocket and pulling out his money. He counted out $1,000 and made it rain down on her body on the bed while she gave him a warm smile.

"Thank you, uh…" She trailed off, waiting for him to give her his name.

"LJ…Call me LJ, the bitch handler." He grinned.

"Boy, shut up!" She smiled. "Well, you gon' leave me your number or what?" she asked.

"Why? I thought you don't like to be called a bitch?" he asked, just to fuck with her as he pulled on his T-shirt. He knew that money he threw her way would make her change her religion if he asked her to.

"I don't, but the way you just ate out my ass and fucked me, I'll be whatever you want me to be, for real," she grinned.

"Just give me your number, Shorty, 'cause I just came home and I'm not really with ma'fuckas blowing up my phone and shit."

"Okay, give me your phone then."

After Little James gave it to her, she put her phone number and name in it. LJ looked at her name and said, "Jennifer? You don't look like no Jennifer, so I'ma keep calling you bitch."

"It's Ms. J-Bitch, thank you," she retorted playfully.

"Yeah, okay," he said and gave her a passionate kiss before he left.

Once he got to his car, he called her number. When she answered on the second ring, he said, "I'm just checking to make sure that Charmin's phone number is real, that's all."

"Boy, you need to stop!" She laughed. "I really wish you didn't leave so soon, 'cause I wanted to put it on your ass, for real."

"It's gon' be other times, right?"

"Yes."

"I ain't hear you?"

"I said yes."

"And free of charge, right?"

"Yeah, boy, dang."

"That's all I need to hear then, Ms. J-Bitch. I'll holla at you later, Shorty," he said and then hung up, knowing that he had her hooked on his Thug Passion.

CHAPTER 52

During the drive back to my house, I pulled out my phone to call Swol and check on him. When I noticed it was turned off, I couldn't believe it. This new AT&T Smartphone apparently had a mind of its own. I turned it back on and saw that I had a million and one calls from Markita and one call from Zetta. Looking at my watch, I realized that it was too late to return any of their calls. I checked the voicemail and listened to Zetta's message.

She really don't care how she talks to me, huh? I thought, pulling into my driveway.

I locked up Swol's ride, headed inside, and rushed straight to my closet. I grabbed a carry-on bag and threw a few outfits inside for my out of town trip. Since it was early Friday morning, I figured I could book the first flight heading out of Ronald Reagan International Airport and be in Indianapolis by noon. I walked inside my home office, and grabbed my iPad and a couple of urban novels for the long flight. As badly as I wanted to take my guns with me, I had to leave them. After 911, the security in the airports was tighter than fish pussy. I shouldn't need them out of town.

I stashed my weapons in my secret bat cave and made sure everything was in order before leaving the house. Once I got back in the car, I pulled off and called Swol. He didn't answer and I got the voicemail. I figured he probably was doing his thing with Kisha. Needing something to do during the ride out to the airport, I checked the voicemail again to listen to Zetta's message.

Her voice sounded so good over the phone. I couldn't believe I froze up on tapping that ass and I still got in trouble with Markita.

For all the bullshit I'm going through right now with Markita, I should have went all the way, I thought, wondering what made Markita call me all those times? Could her mother have gotten through to her about me? Maybe she missed a nigga and wanted to come back home? Whatever the case was, I'd just find out in the morning during my flight.

At the same time, Markita sat up in the dark, staring at her cell phone. She couldn't stop crying. She thought calling Carmelo a few times would be enough to get him to come racing back to her. Apparently he had more important things to attend to than his relationship with me, she thought, feeling neglected by him. She wanted to beef with him, but his honesty and love for her settled in her mind like tiny seeds sprouting shots of doubt. She began to waver on her decision to carry on the feud. After hearing the estranged woman's message on his phone, it was clear to Markita that his love for her couldn't be denied. She wanted to be with him now and express how she really felt about him. She wanted to be back in their home, making love to him and whispering sweet nothings in his ear, but he was nowhere to be found, which worried her.

What puzzled Markita the most was how April still tried to keep her away from him after she told her about the message. April went on claiming that Carmelo probably paid some chick to leave the message, trying to put all sorts of doubts in her head about her man. Markita remained quiet, really seeing April for what she'd become: a bitter woman without love in her life who wanted to inflict her misery on everyone else around her. Markita wasn't falling for her crock of bullshit and the way she tried to salt her man down. After her talk with April, Markita began calling Carmelo non-stop, and she couldn't believe that he didn't return any of her calls.

He's never avoided my calls before. Something has to be wrong, she thought, looking at the alarm clock on the nightstand that read 3:45am.

Markita decided to lay back and try to get some sleep so she could try to reach him again in the morning.

CHAPTER 53

Bright and early the following morning, Little James cruised down First Street with only one thing his mind: finding Carmelo and his closest relatives. It had been a long time coming, but learning about the person who killed his uncle seemed to be coming together. He dreamed of being back on the streets and avenging his uncle's murder and he still couldn't believe the day had finally arrived.

Once he called Jennifer and hung up on her. She had been calling him all night. He got a rush out of the way she was sweating him. He'd been tempted to go back to the hotel and tap that ass some more, but he had more pressing business. Making a left turn on Bryant Street, Little James drove over onto Flagler Street and parked in front of his grandmother's house.

He got out of the car and walked up the steps to her home. When he knocked on the door, it opened instantly. He couldn't believe his grandmother still left the door wide open like everything was safe. Fear and worry consumed him as he stepped inside the big three story house. The aroma of fried bacon invaded his nostrils. His stomach began grumbling. He rubbed his stomach and walked further inside the house.

"Grandma! Mama!" he called out, looking around her spacious front room with plastic-covered furniture everywhere. He saw his baby pictures sitting up on the mantle over the fireplace and walked over to take a closer look at them.

A single tear slid from his eyes while looking at his mother's pretty smile. He couldn't believe it'd been five years since her death. She had been riding with some guys after leaving the Go-Go and somebody shot up the car she was in, gunning for the driver. His mother caught two stray bullets in the chest and died two days later in the hospital. Little James cried for the entire forty-five day stretch he had to do. When they released him back into population, he got a single tattoo tear under his left eye and vowed never to cry again.

"Boy, what the hell you yelling for?" Little James jumped after hearing his grandmother's sweet voice.

Wiping away his fugitive tear quickly, Little James turned on the 5'8" portly brown-skinned woman and smiled. "'Cause you left the door open, Grandma. I didn't know what was up."

"If you bring your tail around here more often and check on your grandma, you'll know what's up. Besides, I been living around here for thirty-seven years. Ain't nobody gon' mess with me. Everybody loves themselves some Mama Vernie. I make plates and feed all these children round here."

"But still, Grandma, a crackhead or anything can come up in here and try to rob you," he said, sounding like a baby instead of the cold-hearted individual he was in the streets.

"That's why your butt needs to come back home and live with me. Now, I done told your tail about running them damn streets trying to be like your uncle. You see where it got him. It's two options you have when running them streets, boy." She paused, giving him the evil eye.

Aw shit, here we go again, he thought, hoping she didn't lecture him about staying out of the street life.

"The prison yard or the graveyard - just two choices," she emphasized in a motherly tone.

"I ain't doing nothing in the streets, Ma," he lied. "I just need my privacy when I need to take my little girlfriends somewhere. I don't want to disrespect your house like that - plus I just wouldn't feel right."

"I know you grown and hot in the pants, baby." She grinned. "I'm just glad you like girls and didn't grow up in the jail liking them boys. You know God hates that, I tell you what. You come back here and live with your Nana and I'll fix up the basement for you and you can come and go as you please. But I have one stipulation."

"What's that?" He arched his eyebrow, looking at her.

"You have to pay me some rent and eat and go to church with your Grandmama every Sunday."

"C'mon, Grandma, that's three stipulations," he whined.

"So what? You know I'm old and senile." She laughed. "Bear with your Nana, boy, before I beat your hindparts."

"I'ma think it over, okay?"

"Okay, baby, now come give your Grandmama a hug and some sugar." She opened her arms and he rushed over into her embrace.

Little James chilled with her for the rest of the morning, getting a good home-cooked meal and learning bits and pieces of information from her about Twan's enemy Carmelo. She told him that at one time or another Carmelo used to be real tight with his uncle.

"Once that Glover boy went to prison, your uncle didn't seem the same anymore, like he lost his best friend or something. Then one day, that Glover boy wrote me a letter from jail and told me that my baby was the reason for him being in jail, but he'd never hold that against me, 'cause he loves me just like his mama. I never heard from him again until your uncle told me that boy was out of jail, and a few months later, Twan passed away."

He was murdered in cold blood by that bitch-ass nigga. He ain't pass away shit, so stop trying to clean the shit up! That bitch-ass nigga Carmelo is the reason you're all alone right now, but you can't see that. You always see the good in everybody no matter what they do! He wanted to yell at her, but he remained quiet, keeping his anger in check.

Once he found out Carmelo's last name and that he didn't have any living relatives around the hood, he felt a little disappointed. He wanted to hurt Carmelo just like he'd hurt his grandmother when he killed his Uncle Twan.

Since I can't crush your family. I'm going to come after you and crush your bitch ass! It's on sight wherever I see you! he thought as his grandmother pulled him up from the kitchen table to show him around the basement in which she wanted him to live.

After looking over the spacious and dusty basement, Little James figured it would be the perfect place to live in once he fixed the place up. Plus the living arrangements would give him better access to ambush all the guys hustling on the drug strip down the street that his uncle built from the ground up.

CHAPTER 54

The plane ride from Virginia to Indianapolis had been longer that I expected. I got some much-needed rest with my urban book resting over my face. When the Airbus taxied down the runway in Indianapolis Airport, I gasped at the sight of so many black people. When I was locked up inside Terre Haute prison, I thought Indiana was mainly populated with Caucasians.

After getting off the plane, I went through the crowded terminal to the baggage claim to retrieve my luggage. I immediately headed over to the Avis car rental booth to get some transportation. I zoned out looking at the catalog of expensive cars they had for rent at the cheapest prices ever. I picked out a champagne-colored Cadillac Escalade and slid the pretty white lady my credit card. After processing my paperwork, she gave me the keys with a friendly smile.

"Thank you for riding with Avis, Sir," she said, looking sexy in her pinstriped green and white uniform.

I ain't into white women, but you can definitely get it, you Jennifer Love Hewitt-looking ma'fucka, I thought before responding. "Thank you," I said and then paused. "Um, can you refer me to a hotel here in town? I'm here on a surprise visit to a friend."

"Oh, sure," she said with a smile as she began punching some keys on her computer. "Ah yes, the Embassy Suite Hotel located here on Washington Street is a very good choice," she offered with a Colgate smile, easing my dislike for white people a little. When I was incarcerated, the Caucasian officers and inmates hated me so much, I just thought it was natural to hate them in return. Seeing how nice the brunette was being to me let me know that prison is another world within itself.

"Thanks."

"Uh huh." She smiled as I walked away and headed out to the car depot to pick up my rental.

Once I got situated in the cockpit of the Escalade, I looked at my watch and saw the time had just reached noon. I called Markita up and she answered on the first ring.

"Hey baby, I love you sooo much and I'm sorry for beefing with you. Where you at? Come home right now. I need to see you. I need to make love to you so bad it's killing me." She said it all so quickly that I couldn't catch all her words.

"Damn, why the change of heart all of a sudden?"

"I just realized that I can't live without you, plus my mother called me and told me about your little visit over to her house."

"So you'd rather take your mother's word over mine, huh?"

"No, well, I mean, Mom always know best. Plus I was just mad, baby. You know how I get over the dick. I don't want you giving it away to nobody else."

"I been told your ass. I'm only down for you and nobody else, so I don't know why you be so insecure all the time."

"I know, baby, I'm just in love with you so much, I don't want to lose you."

"You really know how to show me you don't want to lose me by taking all the shit out the house and my son from me and shit. You jive carried me like I'm some anything-ass nigga!"

"Baby, I'm sorry!" she whined, breaking me down little by little.

Even though I was mad at her for pulling that stunt, I couldn't stay mad at her when she was trying to reconcile. Even though she had some trust issues that she needed to work on, Markita had no other flaws in her character and she was the perfect woman for me. She kept me grounded and reminded me of that old school love.

"I ain't going for that little whining shit. I'm jive fucked up at you for real," I lied, knowing that would put her at my mercy and make her do anything to try and get back in my good graces.

"Boo, I'm sorry. Please come back home. Let me make it up to you…puhlease!" she begged, turning me on. There's nothing like having your woman beg for you to come home and serve her up with some make-up sex.

"I can't do it right now."

"Why not?" she said, sounding angry.

"'Cause I'm out of town."

"What? Who you fucking, Melo? You can tell me, 'cause I - "

"See," I blurted, cutting her off. "There you go with that bullshit again. I'm gone, man."

"No, no, don't hang up. Baby, I'm sorry. I just don't understand why you went out of town without me?"

"Are you serious?" I said looking at the phone like she could see the expression on my face. "When you sit back and replay all the things you've done, I think you can pretty much answer your own questions on why I went out of town without you. But naw, I had to visit my man in the Feds to go over a few things that I couldn't talk to him about on the phone or in a letter.

"Where you at?"

"Out Indiana."

"Indiana? When you coming home, boo? I miss you."

Yeah right, sure you do. You just want to get me back because you think I'ma fuck something while I'm out here, I thought and said, "I'll be back in a few days."

"You forgive me for doing what I did, right?" she said in a baby-like whiny voice.

"We'll talk when I come home. I have to go before I get a ticket for talking on the phone and driving."

"Okay, I love you," she said, sounding sexy as hell.

"I love you more. Oh, before I forget, did you know about that video room in the nightclub? I mean, did your brother ever tell you about it?"

Silence hovered over the phone for a moment before she replied. "No, but he did have a partner who might know about that room."

A partner? What, this nigga hunting me from the grave now. Now I got to find out who this nigga's partner is and crush his ass now, I thought, realizing Markita's news just eliminated her and Suede's wife, April, as being potential suspects who wanted me dead for killing Suede.

"You know his name?"

"Some dude named Tank, but right before my brother died, Tank went on the run from the police for something he did. I remember Suede crying about it and cursing Tank out for leaving him high and dry with all the bills of the club."

"Tank...Tank..." I repeated, trying to see if I knew him. "You don't know his real name or nothing?"

"Naw, why?"

"Nothing. I just wanted to return something to him that I found in the video room, that's all," I lied quickly.

"What is it?"

"None of your business, nosy, damn!" I said and heard her giggle. "It's good to hear you laugh again," I added.

"I love you sooooo much," she replied, making my nature rise.

"Yeah, I hear you."

"I'm for real, Melo, don't be that way. I said I'm sorry now, shoot."

"I know you are, but we'll talk more on it when I get home."

"Okay, call me tonight before you go to bed so we can have some phone sex."

Man, she's trying hard. Yeah, she knows she fucked up, I thought before saying. "You nasty. I'll think about it though."

"Boy, don't make me come through this phone on your ass!" she fired back, making me smile at her sassy tone.

"I love you, I gotta go, the police pulling up right now," I lied and hung up her.

I knew if I didn't get her off the phone, we'd be talking all day. I made a few turns and ended up on Washington Street. When I saw the hotel, I pulled up and parked. I got out with my bag and headed inside to book a room. My phone began ringing. I looked at the call, saw Markita's name, and pressed the ignore button, sending her to voicemail.

After reserving the suite for the weekend, I paid the $500 debt with my credit card. I had to use plastic so I could keep the little $15,000 in cash on me for emergency purposes. I went up to my suite and took a long, hot shower, trying to think of what I was going to do about Suede's phantom partner Tank pursing me with deadly intent. All I could do was hope that he didn't ambush me again before I could get some information on him and deal with him for trying to kill me.

CHAPTER 55

Back in Virginia, Detective Gamble and Newsome along with the several cops from Alexandria warrant squad were walking around Carmelo's empty house looking angry and frustrated. They had raided the beautiful house a little after 8 a.m. only to find it empty like somebody had put the place up for sale.

After giving the house a thorough search from top to bottom, the warrant squad cop from VA looked at Detectives Gamble and Newsome like they were some idiots. Seeing the looks on their faces, Detective Gamble pulled his partner Newsome to the side, trying to ignore the chuckles and whispers from the Virginia police.

"You know how this makes us look, right?" Newsome whispered, looking over his shoulder at the other cops who searched the vacant house.

"I don't give a fuck!" Gamble snapped. "That son of a bitch isn't getting off the hook that easy. He can run, but he can't hide." Gamble smiled, holding up a piece of paper.

"What's that?"

"Authorization for a cell phone tracking - Mr. Glover's

cell phone."

"Sweet." Newsome smiled. "So you never intended to have him arrested, huh?"

"Now you thinking like a real cop, my friend." Gamble smiled. "I just had to get the warrant so I could get this warrant right here, which is the most important. Carmelo can be anywhere in the world and I can locate him just as long as he keeps his cell phone on him."

"What we gon' do about these creeps here?"

"Fuck 'em, let 'em think we some bumbling idiots. We know what we after," Gamble said before stepping towards the front door.

"Hey, hey!" one of the warrant squad cops called out, stopping Gamble and Newsome in their tracks at the front door.

"Yeah, what's up?" Gamble said as the white man with the military crew haircut walked up on him.

"So what's going on here? I mean, you get a warrant to search this place and to arrest the occupants of the house, and there's nobody here. It looks like someone left in a hurry, Bub," he said, giving Gamble one of those "you stupid motherfucker" looks.

"So I guess you just answered your own question as to what's going on here - nothing," Gamble said, sarcasm oozing from his tone.

With that said, Gamble gave his partner Newsome a nod and they exited the house without looking back, which really left a sour taste in the Virginia warrant squad cops' mouths, making them feel like they had just been slapped in the face. As Gamble and Newsome headed to their cars, jumped in, and pulled off, they had no idea that they had just became responsible for those Virginia cops developing a serious grudge against all D.C. cops.

CHAPTER 56

After the reinvigorating shower, I got fresh dressed, feeling like a million bucks, but I kept my swagger simple and relaxed by rocking a white tee, blue jeans, and some 1500 New Balance jogging joints.

I called up a little fly guy I knew named KD from Indianapolis, a.k.a. Nap Town. We did some time together while I was locked up in the Feds. We used to trade urban novels and we had our own little book club. I took a liking to him because he had a cool laid-back demeanor and didn't roll with a gang.

I don't knock any man for what he does, but I just feel like if you're in a gang, then you're weak-minded and more content with being a follower instead of a leader. Some places like the Midwest and California have a different culture, and growing up to be in a gang and gangbang is just a normal way of life for some. After seeing KD and other guys like him from other parts of the country where gang affiliation is heavy in their cities, I felt different about the cultural aspect of it. Guys like KD came from that area and made a choice to be a leader instead of a follower, and I tip my hat to guys like him.

KD answered the phone on the third ring. "Yeah, what it do?"

"What's up, nigga? You know who this is?"

"Nawl, can't say that I do," he said smoothly.

"It's me, Carmelo, nigga, your old book club partner in the Feds."

"Oh, what's up, nigga?" he said, sounding more excited then when he first answered the phone.

"Shit, just out in your neck of the woods. I came out to visit my partner out in the Haute, but that ain't until tomorrow. I was hoping you can show me what Nap Town hitting on tonight."

"Fo' sho'. Where you at? I'm finna come scoop you up right now."

"I'm at the Embassy Suites on Washington Street, somewhere downtown."

"Cool, cool. I know exactly where you at. Only bosses like me stay up in that spot," he bragged.

"Oh yeah? I see you ain't change, huh?"

"Only thing change on me is the skin when it's hot outside, you dig?" he said and cracked up laughing.

"I feel you, Champ. Ay, how long you gon' be, 'cause, I can go outside and wait for you."

"Give me about fifteen to twenty minutes. I'll be right down there."

"See you then."

"That's a bet," he said and hung up.

I ended the call on my Smartphone and headed out my suite to go outside and wait on KD. I couldn't believe I was actually in society hooking up with a guy I'd done time with from another city. After doing time in the

Federal prison system, I learned that there were some real genuine and solid men all over the country who don't be set tripping on that geographical time.

D.C. guys are public enemy number one in the Federal system for some strange reason. I guess it's because of our aggressive natures and no-nonsense attitude when it comes to violence and putting in work, or maybe it's the fact that the older guys from D.C. had laid the law down so viciously in the Feds before I was even born that the tag still hung over the later generations of D.C. inmates who were currently doing time in the Feds. Whatever the case may be, I was glad there were men like KD who could see past the b.s. and respect a man for a man and not feel a certain kind of way towards you solely based on where you come from.

When I reached the lobby of the hotel, I saw a fine redbone sistah wearing a sexy and cool skintight striped dress and nude-colored high heels. I gave her a wink just to mess with her, and to my surprise, she winked back.

"Don't start none, won't be none," I said on my way out the door as she walked past me.

"Your room or mines, big boy, 'cause I ain't down with Rap-A-Lot," she said, and the deep huskiness of her tone made her sound like R&B soul legend Barry White, which scared the shit out of me. I immediately began looking and checking for signs to see if she was really a he.

"I'm cool, sweetheart," I said politely and kept it moving, looking back over my shoulder again at the fine woman who could possibly be a man.

If she is a man, his ass needs to go on the Maury Povich show so he can trick a million people about his sexual orientation, I thought as I stepped into the Mid-wicked heat that had me sweating instantly.

Damn, I put on all that dumb-ass lotion, I thought as I bolted for the rental Escalade to chill under the air conditioner while waiting for KD to show up.

CHAPTER 57

Thirty minutes later, I spotted KD pulling up in a sky blue 1965 Buick Skylark sitting on some big-ass shiny chrome rims. Climbing out of the Escalade, I smiled as he parked and jumped out rocking a sky blue outfit to match his ride. When he got closer, I noticed the Pelle-Pelle button up shirt, Pelle-Pelle denim shorts, and the Carolina Blue retro Air Jordan sneakers he wore with the ankle socks.

"What the business, Mel?" he greeted me with a one-armed hug.

"Shit, fuck kind of rims you got on that joint?"

"Oh, you know I had to put the fo's on her fine ass. What you think about that bitch, she fly or what?"

"Yeah, I can see you doing it."

"I'm a boss, I can't have it no other way." He smiled, flashing the single gold tooth situated close to his fourth top front side tooth.

"So, I'm riding with you or should I bring out the Escalade?" I asked, nodding in the direction of the rental.

"Naw, leave the rental. I would stunt in that bitch, but it ain't got no shoes on it," he said, and I figured he was referring to rims.

"A'ight, give me a second," I told him. I went over to the Escalade and locked it.

When I returned to KD's car and got inside, he already had a Swisher Sweet of that sticky-icky-icky burning and the sounds of Rick Ross blaring so loud I thought I'd go deaf. He gave me a nod after I closed the door.

"I'm the biggest boss that you seen thus far…I'm…I'm the biggest boss that you seen thus far…'Cause it's just another day in the life of a gotdamn boss!" he sang along with the chorus as he pulled off, heading to God knows where.

At the same time, Markita walked up to her house carrying her son. April, Poobie, and Zetta had come over to help her get her house back in order. Markita asked April to help her fix the house back up. April in turn called up her cousin Poobie and asked her to come and help.

"Damn, Cuzzo, I'm in here having make up sex with my boo," Poobie said.

"A'ight, stay your ass right there, but when you need me, don't expect me to come running to your aid with your selfish ass!" April told her off.

"Okay, damn, you ain't got to be so nasty. I'll be out there in thirty minutes."

After Poobie showed up to April's house with Zetta, she introduced her to Markita. Zetta and April met months ago and were cool on the strength of Poobie.

"You said her name's Zetta?" Markita stepped back, feeling her heart drop into her stomach. I know this ain't the same…no, it can't be, she thought as Poobie gave her an affirmative nod.

"Can I talk to you in private for a second?" Markita asked, cutting straight to the chase. She wanted to know if she was the same woman who had been flirting with her man.

"What about?" Zetta asked, getting suspicious.

"Just step in the room and find out."

April looked back and forth at them like she was watching a tennis match, not having any clue as to what was going on. Poobie laughed inside, knowing some shit was about to hit the fan. Ever since Zetta cursed her out on the phone, Poobie had been planning a way to put Zetta in Markita's face and let Markita do what she really wanted to do to Zetta.

Poobie was so far gone over Zetta that she didn't want to do anything to lose her. She figured by doing this, she could see Zetta get her ass whooped for a second and then jump in and play the hero, which would earn her more brownie points with Zetta.

Zetta walked off first with Markita following her. April tried to stop Markita to find out what was going on, but Markita waved her off and kept it moving.

Once behind closed doors, Markita got right to the point. "Do you know my man, Carmelo?"

"Carmelo? Yeah I know him."

"So you the same Zetta who left this message, huh?" Markita said, quickly punching in a few numbers and letting the message play.

What kind of stalking bitch is this? Zetta thought, listening to her own voice vent her anger at Carmelo and reveal how she tried to throw the pussy on him.

"You got me, but honestly, your man's too fine for me not to go after," Zetta confessed.

Bitch, I should beat your ass! she thought, trying her best to contain her temper. "I know he's fine, that's why I have him and not you. Get the point?" she said, laying claim to Carmelo like he was a piece of meat.

"Loud and clear, boo boo. Don't kill me. It was a simple mistake. I didn't know he was tied down until he told me he was. I just met him at the post office and was trying to get my book published, that's all. I guess in the process, I fell weak in the knees for him. You know just as well as I do that nigga fine." Zetta smirked, making Markita's ego swell over having something that the young woman wanted.

"Listen, Zetta, from now on, you do business with me and only me. Give me your book and I'll read it and then I'll have my husband read it. If he wants to publish it, then I'll contact you and we'll go from there okay."

"Yeah, I feel you, and again, I apologize for stepping to your man."

"Don't trip. Just don't let it happen again," she said, making the warning clear. "And to make sure that it don't, just lose his number, okay?"

"I got ya, girl." Zetta smiled and held open her arms for a hug.

"Uh uh, I don't get down like that. I'm nobody's sloppy seconds. First you try to book my man and now you trying to book me," she joked, making Zetta laugh. "Hell no!"

"Girl you is wild!" Zetta chuckled. "So, we cool?"

"Yeah, everything's cool." Markita and Zetta caught Poobie and April making sudden movements like they were trying not to get caught eavesdropping at the door. "Y'all nosy asses ready to go or what?" Markita asked, letting it be known they were busted.

"I don't know what you talking about," April said quickly.

"The first one to respond is always the guilty party," Zetta commented, making Markita smile.

"Ay, Poobie, I like your girlfriend here. She reminds me of me." Markita smiled, making Poobie boil with anger.

Shut the fuck up, you weak-ass bitch! I know if that was my man, I'd be all over this bitch's ass! With your weak, scaredy ass… Don't worry though, I still got another trick up my sleeve for your bitch-ass man killing my cousin. Yeah, he's going to pay. He's definitely going get everything he got coming to him, Poobie thought, knowing her initial plan had backfired and brought the two women closer together.

After the moving truck arrived, Markita took her son inside the house and began directing traffic. Once everything was returned to the home, Markita, April, Zetta, and Poobie began cleaning up the house and redecorating the place. While they worked, Zetta and Markita talked and laughed with each other like they'd known each other for years, which lit a fuse, making Poobie explode with jealousy and anger.

Back in D.C., Little James sat in his grandmother's house playing on the computer. After putting Carmelo Glover's name into the Google search engine, he began smiling like a Cheshire cat. He looked at the screen as a satellite picture zoomed into the place of residence of the man who had killed his uncle

This Internet shit is some dangerous shit, he thought, watching all the activity going on outside the house. He stayed glued to the computer monitor, checking out the four women, little boy, and the four guys on the moving truck to make sure that they weren't moving out of the house. After making sure they were moving into the house, he became happy like a kid in the candy store.

"I got your bad ass now, Carmelo," Little James mumbled while staring at the images on the computer. "You never thought your yesterday would come back to haunt you. Believe me it comes back to haunt you," he repeated, quoting a memorable line from a Geto boys song. He began devising a devious plot to destroy Carmelo Glover's world before destroying the man himself.

CHAPTER 58

After KD parked, I spotted so many thick women heading inside the mall. I asked him where we was at, but he just smiled and got out. I followed suit. We headed inside the mall and walked into the foot court.

"This Lafayette Mall. All the hoes be out here." KD smiled and then winked at a cute Indian-looking broad, who walked over to him with a smile on her face. I watched them talk for a minute before KD sent her on her merry way with a light tap on her butt.

"What's up with Shorty?" I asked, watching her walk away, blowing him a kiss.

"She recognized a real boss when she saw one. I'ma fuck her later on, probably tomorrow or something while you go on your visit."

"I see you jive working."

We chilled at the mall for about two hours, messing with the females and shopping. I couldn't believe how many young ladies wanted to chill with me when KD told them I was his cousin from D.C. I couldn't keep them off of me after that. I felt like a real rap star with groupies. After collecting several numbers that I'd never use, KD got me to go in some popular clothing store with him.

When we entered the store, the sounds of Pastor Troy's classic "Vice Versa" invaded my ears. This clothing store looked more like mini version of a nightclub. It had a bar and DJ booth in the corner with a few young ladies dancing in the aisles to the music. KD took off, nodding his head to the hypnotic beats and lyrics of Pastor Troy, and began throwing clothes in a shopping bag without looking at the price tags. He offered to buy me something, but I declined. I just got a kick out of watching him ball out of control.

After we left the mall, KD drove over to the Southside of Nap Town and I could smell the difference in the air. Yeah, we definitely had arrived in the hood. I saw several guys standing around in front of clean, old school cars with shiny chrome rims. Scantily-clad women were out and about, trying to catch themselves a hustler out on the block to take care of their needs. Little kids ran around in the street playing tag and football. Crackheads walked up and down the block, looking like zombies. Several men were engaging in a craps game. At that moment, I realized hood life was the same all over America, but each hood in every city had their own little twist and style with them.

After we got out KD's ride, three guys walked up to him and gave him brown paper bags. He threw the bags in his car. Apparently he didn't care about somebody robbing him of the dope money he had just collected.

Damn, young nigga jive doing himself something, I thought as one of the guys began complaining to KD that some guy came around trying to rob them.

"That bitch, gon' get his. He should have been dead with all those people he told on," KD griped. "He ain't get none of y'all, did he?"

"Nawl, but he said he'll be back to get up wit' you."

"With who? That rat-ass nigga don't want it with me. I'm a boss. I'll fuck around and have his ass dumped in the Wabash County River."

"Ay, KD, let me holla at you for a second," I told him and pulled him over to the side.

Once we got out of earshot of his crew of workers, I asked him what the problem was. Usually, I wouldn't interfere in another man's business, but when I heard that the guy trying to rob him was a rat, that piqued my interest.

"This lame-ass nigga named Michael Salley from Grand Rapids, Michigan. Them niggas ran him outta town 'cause he snitched on some boss up there. Now he relocated down here with his cousin and he's trying to take over. Nigga don't want to do him none, 'cause everybody love his cousin's fine ass. I hit the bitch a few times and moved on with life, but now I guess the bitch salty about something and put the nigga on me."

"I know you ain't going for that shit."

"I mean, what can I say? I ain't give a fuck about the nigga until today. Acting like he gon' come rob me. Oh, it's on!" he said and I saw his upbeat demeanor switch to something darker and more dangerous.

"You know where the nigga be at?"

"Hell yeah."

"So what you gon do?" I asked.

"I don't know. I'm trying to get this money. You know when you beefin' and shit you can't get money out here, and that's what I'm all about."

"Listen, you got some hammers around here?"

"Hammers? What the fuck you talking about?"

"Heat, guns, gotdamn, Moe! I know you ain't that slow." I grinned.

"Oh yeah, yeah. They in the trap house. Why, what's up?"

"Here's what we gon' do. I need for you to go inside the trap house and get them hammers and bring them to me."

"Nawl, I can't have you getting in no shit out here, dog. This ain't fo' you, man."

"Yeah, it is. I can't stand hot niggas. So I feel it's my duty to take out as many rats as I can."

"The nigga be in a public place at all times, which means a lot of witnesses, dog."

"So what? You got a costume store around here?"

"Yeah, why?"

"Good. After you get the guns, take me to the store. Here's what we gon' do..."

CHAPTER 59

It took about an hour and some change for me to get the costume and get fully prepared to go out and kill another rat. I followed KD's car in the rental Escalade, feeling very awkward in the fat suit I wore, which really made me feel like a fat person. I got the idea after watching the Nutty Professor movie. I figured I could kill freely in the suit and all the witnesses would report to the authorities that an obese man committed the crime.

Today was my first time trying out my idea, but I went all the way out and bought a short platinum blond bob wig and threw on some fire-engine red lipstick. From a distance, you would think I looked like big girl with a bad outfit. The hot pink flight suit made me look like a big, fat-ass balloon. When I came back out of the hotel in my costume, KD began laughing so hard that he started crying.

"Quit playing, Slim. You on joke time and shit when I'm tryna help your ass."

"I know, dog, I know, but you look funny as hell." He giggled.

"Just get in the car and drive over to the spot."

I worked out the plan with KD for him to drive over to the rat's hood and call him out like he wanted to pay him to leave him alone. Once we got close up on the car, I'd leave his hot ass right there in the street. I checked the two Glock 40's he gave me and loved how they felt in my hand.

I couldn't believe I was out here doing this shit when I initially came to Indiana to see a good man. I couldn't resist the urge. I felt addicted to killing rats like a fiend was addicted to drugs. We made it around to the rat's hood ten minutes later. As KD pulled up in front of an abandoned-looking house, I noticed people everywhere as I pulled up right behind him. This hood looked lucrative enough for everybody to get money, so I didn't understand why the rat wanted to take over KD's block.

"Yo, Mike Salley!" I heard KD yelling after he parked.

By that time, I had already exited the SUV and began caressing the Glock 40 inside the tote bag I carried. When I saw a sexy woman calling out the rat's name, I watched the 5'8" tall dark-skinned guy with platinum chains and iced-out watch look out into the street before leaving the porch of the abandoned house. As he began easing towards the car, I moved in to cut him off.

Before the rat could reach KD's car, I stepped in front of him and smiled.

"Move, you big bitch!" the rat said in a nasty tone. "All up in my face with that big dumb-ass mustache."

"Don't hate, honey, big girls need love too."

"Love, I wouldn't fuck your fat, nasty ass with a full-blown AIDS dick, fat bitch!" he countered as he began laughing loudly.

"But I'd love to fuck over your black, hot ass," I said as I let the Glock 40 loose.

The sounds of death exploded from my tote bag and penetrated the rat's torso at point blank range. While everybody scattered from the sudden sounds of rapid gunfire, I stood over the rat and aimed the smoking tote bag at his head. He held up his hands over his face as if that would stop the bullets I was about to put in his head.

"You s'posed to been dead, you hot ma'fucka!" I said. I began pulling the trigger, pumping the rat's face and head full of slugs until the Glock 40 snatched back, alerting me that the gun was empty. I pulled out the extra Glock 40 and held it out for all the witnesses to see. "Anybody see anything? Huh!" I yelled, looking at everybody trying to get ghost. "I said, did anybody see what the fuck went down right here!" I bellowed as everybody tried to get the hell away from me and the bloody homicide.

"Yeah, that's what the fuck I thought," I said before quickly jumping back in the SUV and pulling off.

KD pulled off behind me and then sped past me. I followed him back to his hood on the Southeast of Nap Town, feeling good.

One less snitch I gotta worry about. He's outta here and that's how it turns out, I thought, knowing that the underworld of Nap Town would be an entirely better place without Michael Salley's hot ass lurking around in the streets.

CHAPTER 60

Markita had just finished getting her master bedroom suite in order when Zetta walked in on her, carrying her son. Little Ray-Nathan seemed at peace and looked like he loved being in Zetta's arms. Markita looked at the way Zetta handled her son and could tell that she'd be an excellent mother.

"I was trying to fix up this room, but he wouldn't let me do a thing until I picked him up and gave him a kiss," Zetta said while lowering him to the ground and tousling his curly hair.

"Back uppy, now!" he demanded, holding his arms out.

"No, boy!" Markita said sternly. "Now get before I get my belt."

Ray-Nathan looked at Zetta and then at his mother before taking off running for the bedroom door. Before he made it to the door, he tripped and slid across the carpet like he was sliding headfirst into home plate on the baseball field. Looking back and laughing, Ray-Nathan got up and bolted out of the bedroom.

"You have a wonderful son. I bet you he's spoiled to death," Zetta said, walking around the huge suite, admiring everything about Markita's home and bedroom.

"Girl, you don't know the half of it. I try to keep him grounded, but his father gives him everything he wants even when I say no."

"Mmmph," she grunted. "So basically you saying that you spoiling your man, 'cause he seems like he gets his way around here."

"I don't look at it that way, but we do agree on a lot of things. It's not all about him, trust me on that. When it comes to his firstborn, Melo don't want to hear nothing about what he can and can't do for little man." Markita beamed while making the statement, which made her miss Carmelo even more.

"I wish I had somebody like that. I'm sick and tired of this girl's shit," Zetta confessed with a sigh before sitting on the sofa in front of the bed and turning on the huge flat screen TV.

Markita and Zetta watched as a white male news reporter stood in a parking lot, explaining the gory details of man being shot down in cold blood last night.

"Details are sketchy at this moment, but Alexandria police spokesperson said they have no suspects or motives in this brutal killing. If you know anything about this heinous crime, please call the number at the bottom of the screen for Crime Solvers. The number is - "

Markita cut off the TV and took a seat beside Zetta, trying to be nosy. "What you was saying, girl? I didn't catch everything you was saying before you turned on the TV."

"It's nothing, I'm just fed up with being lied to by that fake-ass bitch in the other room."

It's two bitches in the other room, hello, be more specific here, Markita wanted to say, but instead she simply said, "What are you talking about, Zetta?" Markita took a seat beside her, trying to be nosy.

"That bitch Poobie think she got all the sense. At first I didn't put it all together until a few minutes ago. She brought me way over here so we could get into a fight over your man."

"No, Poobie wouldn't do a thing like that," Markita said, unable to see through Poobie's true colors.

"Yes she would! I mean, she goes out and does her thing all the time and I don't ever say shit. I'm not even tripping about her and April's ass."

"Hold up, dear, you moving way too fast for me. So you saying you and Poobie are together, like in a relationship together?"

"Yeah, we sex buddies."

"Wow, I didn't know all that," Markita said and then swallowed hard. "You want to explain to me what you mean by knowing about her and April? April's her cousin."

"No, she's not. Them bitches faking. Cousins don't be sneaking around corners and shit, tongue-kissing each other like lovers do," she said and then told Markita how she had just caught them in the guest room, kissing passionately.

Fake-ass bitch, talking about she hasn't done shit with a man since my brother died. Well, technically she hasn't, Markita thought before exclaiming, "Shut up! You for real?"

"Yeah, they got me too with all that cousin shit until they exposed their hand today. Them bitches bumping pussies, but I ain't tripping 'cause I'm about to go back to the city and find some real dick. Fuck her."

"No, no, no Zetta. You can't react off of emotions like that. Just act like you don't know a thing and continue to get all you can outta Poobie. When you get fed up, use what you found today as reason to give the bitch her walking papers."

"Hell yeah, that's exactly what I'm going to do." Zetta smiled weakly and Markita could tell she was hurting over the recent discovery of her sexual partner's cheating ways.

"Yeah, don't ever let nobody get over on you. Make sure you always get the last laugh - always."

"Thanks, girl. You know you pretty cool and easy to talk to."

"Keep that in mind the next time you think about making a pass at my man," Markita playfully said, but she meant every word.

"I told you that's over with and his number has already been forgotten," Zetta said before getting off the bed. She walked over towards the bedroom door, and glanced back at Markita. "Thanks for the talk and advice. It really means a lot to me."

"No problem. That's what friends are for."

"Friends? So you saying we friends now?"

"Yep. I can sense the genuine honesty and realness in you, so if you want, we can hang like sistahs and shit," Markita said with a smile, making Zetta feel a whole lot better than she'd been feeling after discovering the truth about Poobie and April.

CHAPTER 61

Little James decided to take Smurf up on his offer while he was on his side of town. He stood at the back stairs on Florida Avenue that led into the backside of Garfield Terrace Projects. Staring towards the top of the concrete jungle, alarm bells rang across his mind.

The move to get money was underway. He held his hand clenched to the gun inside his pocket, anticipating drama. Walking up the stairs, he heard the noises of life going on in the projects around him: the screaming a newborn baby, the blaring sounds of a stereo, and people talking and yelling. Little James pulled his skully down lower, closing in on his unsuspecting prey. He wanted to conceal his identity, but he was also alert enough not to draw attention to himself. Little James eased up another flight of stairs.

Just ahead, off in the cut smoking on that loud pack, two men rested their butts on plastic milk crates, apparently unaware of who was stalking them.

Time to get this money, he thought as his finger pulled down the skully ski mask, covering his face completely. He whipped out his gun with his right hand.

"You know what's happening! Strip, niggas!" Little James ordered, aiming the gun back and forth between the men after catching them completely by surprise.

They got caught slipping, their defenses breached. Flurries of demands erupted from the masked gunman's mouth, echoing hollowly in their ears. They were being robbed in broad daylight and they couldn't do a damn thing to stop it. If they made any attempts to yell or tried to make a run for it, they were sure to get shot in the back or head.

The light-skinned, lanky baldheaded guy dropped the burning spliff, stepped to the side, and began stripping, throwing his clothes, shoes, and other valuables at Little James feet. The remaining short, dark-skinned guy with long dreads stood ready to follow orders, half facing forward, half backwards, looking wary of all the gunman's movements.

"You, pick up that shit and check all the pockets and shoes…make any sudden moves, kill my motha, I'ma smoke yo' ass!" Little James warned, keeping his gun trained on the half-naked man who stood there with his hands in the air, wearing only his boxer underwear, white tube socks, and a white tank top.

After checking the man's pockets, the short guy with the dreads handed over everything to Little James.

"Now you, strip the same way and pass that shit over to main man," Little James ordered while stuffing the valuables and cash in his pocket. "And you, put your shit back on and act like everything cool." He told the skinny guy.

After making the skinny guy search through the pockets of the short guy with the dreads, Little James snatched the money from his hands and made them lay on the ground.

"C'mon, Slim, you ain't got to do this. We ain't even did that!" the skinny man began whining, thinking the masked gunman was about to kill them.

"Ma'fucka, lay the fuck down before I crush your bitch ass!"

After doing as they were told, Little James looked off to the side a few times, making sure there was nobody out and about to see him do the evil that men do. As he got ready to pull the trigger, he spotted an old woman with a cane exiting the building.

Fuck! he yelled inside, feeling messed up that he couldn't kill them. "You bitch-ass niggas bet' not move," he hissed while backing up.

Both men felt their hearts beating in their ears as they laid down at the mercy of the masked gunman. Their bellies shook violently with nervousness as they hugged the ground, expecting to taste the promise of death before their appointed time. After a long moment, they looked up, only to find the masked gunman gone in the wind.

"Go get the joints! Hurry up!" the short guy rocking the dreads hollered while racing to put his clothes back on.

By the time the skinny man ran in some young woman's house to get the guns and return to the scene, Little James was riding around in his car, making his way up the 11th Street's hill. He threw his ski mask under the passenger seat and pulled off his T-shirt, deciding to rock the wife beater to throw off the two guys he'd just robbed in the event they showed up around him after he pulled in the front of Garfield Terrace to go meet up with Smurf.

Over in Southeast, inside the 7th District police precinct, Detective Gamble couldn't believe his eyes while looking at the computer screen that told him the coordinates of Carmelo Glover's cell phone. He called Newsome over to his desk. Newsome damn near broke his neck trying to see what was so important that Gamble had interrupted his delicious lunch from Hogs on the Hills Restaurant.

"Hurry up and look at this shit," Gamble said, growing angrier as he watched the blinking red dot the GPS monitor flashed. He wouldn't abandon the plan he had laid out for Carmelo to complete. Before he did that, he would make matters more difficult for Carmelo, who sought suddenly to take flight.

"What's up, partner?"

"Our little killing machine has flown the coop. He's currently somewhere in Indianapolis, Indiana. Can you believe this son of a bitch?"

"Wow, that's not good," Newsome said, taking a step back.

"Tell me about it. Motherfucker!" Gamble fumed. The knuckles of his fingers ached as he punched the heavy duty computer monitor screen.

Getting Carmelo to do his dirty work was becoming harder than he'd expected.

CHAPTER 62

Somewhere inside the D.C. Superior Court, Ian "N" Foreman sat down in the seat at the oak defense table, awaiting the judge's appearance. He felt a little nervous and he didn't know what to expect. After getting Carmelo to eliminate all the possible witnesses who were willing to come back to court and testify against him, N felt like noting stood between him and freedom.

He learned from his lawyer that the government's attorney was trying to bring up Obstruction of Justice charges on him because all the witnesses mysteriously turned up dead right before his evidentiary hearing for a re-trial. Once N explained that it was virtually impossible for him to kill them or have someone kill them from prison after being gone for so many years, his lawyer fought tooth and nail in several motions hearings to get the charges dropped. Now all he had to do was go through the formality of his hearing and wait for the judge to turn him loose.

"All rise for the Honorable Judge Rankin," the clerk of the court announced as a nerdy old white man walked in the court and took a seat on the high bench overlooking the oval courtroom.

N and his sexy brunette lawyer stood up along with the gray haired District Attorney, who wore a cheap tan suit, until the judge gave them the go ahead to take their seats.

"I understand this is a hearing to determine whether the State's Attorney wants to retry Mr. Foreman?"

"That's correct, Your Honor," N's lawyer spoke up. "But if it's okay with the court, my client would like to plead guilty to the charge of second degree murder and ask the court for time served. He has been incarcerated for nineteen and a half years and has tons of rehabilitation certificates that show he has changed. He just needs a second chance, Your Honor."

"All right, Counsel, do you have any objections to Mr. Foreman's eagerness to plead out to the charges of second degree murder? Because he was charged with first degree premeditated murder while armed."

Look at this racist, faggy bitch here, N thought, looking at the judge with hate in his eyes.

"That is correct, Your Honor, but the appeals court reversed Mr. Foreman's convictions and remanded the case back to the trial court to start the indictment process all over again. I think this will cost the taxpayers unnecessary monies and manpower, which I feel is really not worth it. By Mr. Foreman's plea agreement, the government still wins in this case."

"I see," Judge Rankin said. He looked down at N. "Mr. Foreman, do you understand what is going on here today?"

"Yes sir."

"Has anybody forced you or promised you anything to plead guilty?"

"No sir."

"And you do understand that by pleading guilty, you waive your Constitutional right to trial with a jury of your peers sitting in?"

"Yes sir."

"Before I pass sentencing, is there anything you would like to say Mr. Foreman?"

N stood up, looked at his lawyer, took a deep breath, and then looked at the judge and began speaking from the heart. "Your Honor, I'ma be straight up with you. I'm tired. I'm so tired of being in prison and having to look over my shoulder every day, wondering if somebody is going to stab me in my back or kill me based solely on the color of my skin and what city I'm from." He sighed before continuing.

"The prisons I have been housed in are segregated and the prison officials promote the shit, excuse my French. I think I paid my debt to society and have learned the necessary tools to be a productive citizen in society, if given the chance. I made a terrible mistake when I was younger, but at the time, I was under intoxicants everyday, not caring about whether I lived or died. The nineteen years I been locked up have really helped me grow into a man and appreciate freedom. I'd like to be able to go home and take care of my mom and build a relationship with my daughter and grandson and just live life, man. I think I'm entitled to a second chance. Even God is a very forgiving God, so there should be no reason why you can't be the same way, Your Honor. If you look at me rehabilitation package, you can see for yourself that I didn't go in there and be a jerk and say fuck it, which I could have easily done, but I wanted more for myself. I wanted to be able to come before you or the parole board one day and show them I have changed for the better. I have changed, Your Honor, and now I am asking you to change my life for the better. Thank you." He took a seat.

Judge Rankin adjusted the glasses sitting on the bridge of his pointy nose and began reading a few papers. "I see you took a few college courses here...CDL License certificate, very impressive, Mr. Foreman," he said and looked down at N. "You do understand that murder is a very serious crime, son, the worse crime of all?"

This bitch-ass cracker just can't let me walk. He about to smoke my ass again, N thought before answering, "Yes sir, and I truly regret what I have done."

"Taking into account that you have showed that prison can rehabilitate, I'm going to sentence you to twenty years, all but one year time served. You'll be released into the custody of supervised probation for a period of two years. God be with you, young man, and don't ever let me see you back in my courtroom again. This court is adjourned." Judge Rankin banged the gavel, making N a free man.

N looked at his attorney confused, thinking he had to return to prison for two more years. Even though it was a slap on the wrist, he felt like the judge could have let him walk today. While waiting for the marshal to come and escort him to the back of the courtroom to a holding cell, his lawyer shook his head.

"Congratulations, Mr. Foreman, you're a free man."

"What? You wanna run that by me again?" N asked, feeling his heart thumping with excitement.

"You are free to go. All you have to is report to the probation and parole office before you leave the court building."

"Stop playing, Nikki. You playing, right?" he asked again just to make sure.

"No, I'm not. You are free man to do as you please. Try to stay out of trouble, okay? I believe in you." Attorney Nikki Locks gave N a warm smile before packing up her briefcase and leaving him standing at the defense table.

N looked around waiting for the marshal to come get him. When he realized that he was actually free, he ran out of the courtroom and jumped for joy.

"Aaaaaaahhhhhhhh! Woooooo-hoooooo!" N yelled excitedly, causing several people in the corridor to look at him strangely.

N began asking for directions to the parole and probation office. As he walked to his next destination, he made a mental note to call Carmelo the first chance he got and thank him for all that he had done to help him escape the belly of the beast.

Yeah, ma'fuckas, I'm back! N thought with a smile. He began thinking about all the pussy he was about to get and all the people he wanted to get revenge on.

CHAPTER 63

Later on that night, KD and I along with three guys from his crew arrived in a rental stretch Hummer limo in front of Cloud Nine, a popular nightclub in Indianapolis. While picking up the stretch limo, KD told me that celebrities and professional athletes played the spot on the regular. That gave me motivation to change into a black and gold Louis Vuitton button-up shirt, black Armani slacks, and some black Kenneth Cole Reaction ankle-high leather joints that could pass for boots and casual shoes. KD rocked a grayish-blue Gucci print denim outfit with matching Timberland boots. The three men in his crew dressed fly as well, wanting to impress the crowd.

I thought KD was over-exaggerating about the celebrities earlier until the limo pulled up. From inside the stretch Hummer, I could see the long line of women, men, and several celebrities mingling outside, waiting to get inside the city's hottest and most talked about night spot. The area near the front door had a red velvet rope that was packed with Nap Town's finest and groupies who were out on the prowl trying to hook a baller and hit the ghetto lottery.

Tonight seemed like all the heavy hitters in the city came out to party at Cloud Nine, backing up KD's words. I spotted Roy Hubbert, Danny Granger, and a few more Indiana Pacers NBA players heading inside the nightclub with a large entourage. Dwight Freeney, the Pro Bowl defensive end of the Indianapolis Colts, posed for the camera with a few ladies on the red carpet and Gary, Indiana's beloved street rapper Freddy Gibbs posted up in front of the club passing out mix tapes and CD's . Then I saw R&B

singers Bobby Valentino, Keri "Ms. Keri Baby" Hilson, and Ciara signing autographs in front of the club.

I grinned from ear to ear, slightly star struck as we exited the stretch limo like we were stars in our own right. We headed directly for the front door. My eyes stayed glued to Ciara's sexy, tall frame as KD tapped my shoulder.

"What's up, Slim? You see who that is?" I remarked, nodding at Ciara. She glanced at me, smiled, and went back to signing autographs.

"Man, c'mon, that hoe ain't no different from the rest of the hoes who gon' be up in here choosing us!" he said loud enough for everybody in the vicinity to hear.

Damn, he just played big as these ma'fuckas, I thought, catching Keri Hilson and Ciara along with several other sexy women staring at us with pure hatred in their eyes. I just shrugged in response to the evil looks and followed KD and his men inside the club.

After making our way inside the nightclub, we navigated through the shoulder-to-shoulder packed crowd of people and entered the VIP section five deep. The VIP held close to two hundred people. The table booth we got sat next to a table booth reserved for Ciara. Un-fucking-believable!

"Yeah, money ain't a thang, for real!" KD bellowed over the DJ Khaled "Welcome to my Hood" remix.

KD began ordering expensive bottles of bubbly, which kicked off our night of stuntin'! KD's crew began ordering bottle after bottle of bubbly, Remy, Patron, and Hennessy. You name it, they had it at the table. Every time they ordered something to drink, they threw stacks of money at the female waitress, making her pick it up. I can't fake, KD's team sure kept the bottles poppin', making it rain money continuously at their table, and all the nightclub's baddest bitches kept jockin'.

"Who run dis town?" KD yelled as that new Young Jeezy came blaring out of the speakers:

"You think you ballin' 'cause you got a block---WHAT!
He think he ballin 'cause he got a block---WHAT!
You know the hoes love to see me ball---UNH!
You know these hoes came to see me ball---HA-HA!

"I'm poppin bottles in the club 'cause dat's what winners do! Yeeahh!" KD sang with Young Jeezy's verse, stuntin' hard for anyone who looked his way.

Apparently KD felt like he belonged in this element, because he greeted every celebrity he saw like someone beneath him in the hood. I mean, I knew KD was a little arrogant, but to see him performing like this took the cake for me.

Ciara and a small entourage of sexy dime pieces entered VIP and went to their table. When they walked past us, they began shaking their heads, Ciara rolled her pretty eyes and switched that petite ass of hers extra hard over to the table and flopped down in the booth.

I fell out laughing loud as the women with Ciara took their seats. I couldn't believe a star of her caliber had let some hood niggas get up under her skin. I guess stars are just ordinary people with feelings. Seeing them on TV all the time, I felt like they had tough skin and were used to people ogling over them and hating on them. Tonight, Ciara proved me wrong. Once the Fabulous joint came on, I began nodding my head, enjoying the atmosphere. The VIP became packed quickly, resembling a New Year's Eve after party in the Big Apple.

We were just on our second hour of partying and I was having the time of my life. KD and his team mingled with some single ladies, while I stayed in the booth getting my sip on, praying that the Feds never get me for the shit I'd been doing in the streets.

I just couldn't see myself ever going back to prison after experiencing partying on this level with the stars. I hadn't expected to have so much fun while trying to fight off all the female groupies who kept mistaking me for the Killa-Cali rapper Nipsy Hustle. I could get accustomed to this lifestyle. Tonight just gave the motivation needed to get on a serious grind and push Omerta Press into cities all over America. Even though KD was spending drug money, he did it looking like he belonged in the upscale crowd of stars.

Out of nowhere, a pretty high yellow broad with bluish hair and matching liquid blue contact lenses appeared and began dancing in front of me. The tight-form fitting blue mini dress she wore held my full attention as I zeroed in on her titties bouncing up and down with each move she made. I tried to move and give her room to do her thing, but she jumped in front of me, penning me in the booth with no room to escape. She moved in closer to me and sat on my lap.

Either I wanted her to do this or the alcohol wanted me to do it, because I didn't put up a fight at all. Yeah, Blame it on the Goose, got me feeling loose!

After sitting on my lap, she licked her finger and began sucking on her thumb like she was giving a nigga some head. As her soft apple bottom gyrated slowly on my dick, I looked away, then I felt her hand grabbing my face forcefully to make sure I looked into her eyes.

This bitch, tripping like shit, I thought as she spoke to me and did the unthinkable.

CHAPTER 64

"I really like this song. Do you like it?" She asked, easing a Trojan lifestyle condom out of the pocket of her bra.

I couldn't even focus in on the song. I was in a trance, watching her tracing the condom along the slit of her cleavage and up to her juicy blue lipstick-coated lips. Her question and actions had my dick hard as a rock, making me nod vigorously. Feeling a good buzz off the drink, I just went with the flow, uncertain, but surely willing to journey further and learn all about the stranger giving me a lap dance.

"I always wanted to get fucked to this song," she said, grinding harder on my dick, making it jump in anticipation. "Are you tying to help me out?"

I swallowed hard and began sweating. This chick actually wanted to have sex right now in VIP in front of everybody.

"Damn, Shorty, I don't even know your name," I muttered, feeling slightly intimidated by her aggressiveness.

"Don't even trip; it's better that way, no strings attached." When she said that, she ripped open the condom and freed my stiff boner.

The DJ began doing some mixing to the record, taking it back to the beginning. She rolled the condom on my dick so smoothly, nobody would've ever suspected that we were engaging in carnal activity around all these people. When she eased her dress up a little, she moved her thong to the side and eased the mouth of her wet pussy down on my shaft towards my balls. While KD and his men were stuntin' hard for the ladies, probably setting up a freaky rendezvous at the hotel, I was in the booth digging balls deep all up in this strange woman's guts.

It was so hard for me to believe that a woman could fuck a total stranger in a crowded nightclub until tonight. I still couldn't believe it until she really got into it, riding me hard, making my lust mixed with the alcohol take over. She nibbled on my earlobes as I palmed her soft butt cheeks and fucked upward. She gyrated her hips in slow, circular motions as we got our spontaneous sexcapade on.

"Ssss, damn, boy! Mmm, shit…sssss…I'm cuuuuummmmiinnnnggg s-soooo hard right now," she huffed in my ear before making her pussy contract on my impaling love muscle.

She climaxed on the dick two more times before I picked up speed, slamming her down on my lap repeatedly until I exploded inside the condom, feeling her inner walls milking all the warm semen from my Magic Stick. I hugged her tightly and gave her a passionate kiss.

We kissed for a minute and then began laughing at what we just done. When she eased off my limpness, I looked down and saw her love juices had soaked the front of my slacks, ruining them for any future wear. She smiled as she removed the condom.

"That was good, but I bet you this will be even better," she said, raising the condom up to her mouth. She began sucking the semen out through the condom like she had a milkshake in a latex straw.

"Damn, Shorty! Check, please!" I joked, making her giggle while she handled her business, swallowing every drop of my DNA.

After getting her protein drink for the night, she eased off my lap, got up, and walked away like nothing ever happened between us. I got up and went after her. By the time I caught up to her, we stood in the small waiting area leading to the male and female restrooms.

"At least give me your name, Shorty, so I can add it to the memory."

"Cloud Nine, you sexy stud you." She smiled, gave me a hug, and headed inside the female restroom, leaving me jive messed up in the head - in a good way.

I rushed inside the men's restroom to wash myself off. When I got inside the restroom, I slapped myself twice in the face and even pinched myself as hard as I could to make sure that I wasn't dreaming. "I know I didn't just fuck that bitch in VIP in front of all them people?" I asked myself, looking in the mirror over the sink before looking down.

The leftover white stains of her DNA painted all over my crotch negated any doubts I had about what just happened. After freshening up, I returned to the VIP to the sounds of Ace Hood's banging single "Hustle":

"Hustle—hustle—hustle, hard!
hustle—hustle—hustle, hard!
hustle—hustle—hustle, hard!
Closed mouths don't get fed on this boulevard!"

I thought about calling it a night, but that would make me look weak in KD's and his team's eyes. I was already all in, so fuck it! I decided to hang tough until they were ready to roll. It took a minute, but KD and his team wrapped up their night of stuntin', took several women with them, and loaded up the stretch limo. This is no bullshit, we came to the club five deep, but we left the club with enough sexy women on our arms who seemed to be D.T.F., it was a 2-to-1 ratio and way more than I could handle in one night.

Watching three females strip butt naked and make out in front of us in the limo made the fifteen minute trip back to the hotel pass with ease. When the driver pulled up at the Embassy Suites, I had never been so happy to see a hotel before. Beyond tired, I ducked out on KD and his team and the ladies who wanted to screw my brains out. I made it back to my room and crashed out on the bed with all my clothes on, giving my body a chance to get some rest before being consumed by a two hour drive out to USP Terre Haute in the morning to visit Chin.

CHAPTER 65

I wondered every day when I'd finally lose it and see my entire life explode all around me. I didn't enjoy killing, never would. Yet I couldn't bring myself to stop seeking retribution for the forgotten ones on lockdown and the unwritten street code of Death Before Dishonor. That's why I enjoyed making the drive out here to visit Chin.

While getting processed to gain entry inside the prison's visiting room, I spotted a racist C.O. that I wanted to kill. He made my life a living hell out here while I was locked down like an animal. Now the animal was free and he didn't even know it. He gave me a nod and kept it moving down the hallway.

I'ma deal with your bitch ass one day, I thought as I entered the visiting room and awaited Chin's arrival. While waiting, I began mentally replaying all the things outside of the prison, like the cameras and guard towers. They were the only things keeping me from killing the racist C.O. on the premises.

When Chin showed, he took my mind off wanting to kill the racist C.O. and I enjoyed the visit. He had a rack of time, but he still remained upbeat and strong. The visit even provided me the opportunity to exterminate more street vermin and help Chin pay for an appeal lawyer. An hour into the visit, Chin threw the assassin-for-hire idea at me. When he reminded me that I was killing hot niggas for free anyway and on the strength, he suggested that I might as well get paid for all the work I'd been putting in. My stubborn ego caused me to give Chin a funny look.

"Slim, I don't really give a fuck about getting paid for crushing them hot niggas. My blessings come from knowing I got back for somebody suffering through jail time over a rat. You jive throwing me off, talking 'bout I might as well get paid to uphold the morals, principles, and codes of the streets that we came up under."

"Look, Slim, I'm not telling you nothing wrong. It's beaucoup bread in this shit for you and me if you can pull the shit off," Chin said and then came clean, revealing that the Detroit boss was willing to pay $50,000 a head.

"Slim, that's $200,000 easy for us if you crush all four of them niggas. I could have gave you any figure, but I wanted to play all the way fair with you, 'cause I ain't doing shit but negotiating the deal."

Unlike most men in his situation, Chin didn't even let the greed make him attempt to skim some money off the top, which I really respected. After working out the intricacies of the arrangement, I felt obligated to assist a good man in the struggle. Even though I didn't really need the money, I could always use it to put up for my son's future - pay for his college tuition and buy him a new car for his sixteenth birthday.

"I got you, Slim. This is a fifty-fifty deal, right?"

"Shiid, you the one putting in all the work, so it's basically your call."

"I know you need the loot, so make it fifty-fifty," I said and we shook on it, sealing the upcoming deaths of four rats who roamed the streets of Detroit.

"Ay, make sure you holla at main man when you get back, 'cause after I leave you, I'm shooting straight out there. Tell him to have his peoples on point and ready with them hammers and expecting my visit."

"I got you, Slim. I'll never forget this, Champ." He smiled, making me feel good about helping him out.

I could have just given Chin the money for legal fees and headed back home to Markita and my son, but the work call waiting to be handled in Detroit was calling me just like the crack rock did to that rat Pooky in that New Jack City movie.

"It ain't nothing. I'm just doing what's right for a solid man," I said, hoping my fate didn't turn out bad like Pooky the rat.

CHAPTER 66

Sometime after my visit with Chin, I waited in the Federal prison parking lot for a while with the look of a tourist in a foreign land. The landscape of the area had changed dramatically over the last eight years since I'd served time in that particular prison. Maybe it had always been this way and I couldn't tell by being an inmate. I just saw things from the inside out, not outside in. It's a shame how immaculate the prison grounds and manicured lawns look from this side when the inside resembles a dark dungeon full of cells, lost souls, and brothers doing time because of a snitch. No matter how much different the prison looked, the prison officials who worked there rarely changed. As I sat in the rental SUV, taking in the familiar sights of the prison, the racist C.O. Gregg emerged from the lobby dressed in his prison guard uniform. They had stopped wearing the grey uniforms and now wore blue and white or blue-on-blue.

After the way he and his crew of Klansmen tortured me in retaliation for the ass-whipping I put on Gregg, I just couldn't let that shit go without getting some get back. That's why I pieced together a quick note this morning before coming out here. I cut up the local newspaper, using different letters, until I crafted a short note that read:

Let This be A LesSon AnD Warning to aLL whO AbuSe ThEir AuthoRity BeHiNd PriSon WALS!

KARMA'S A BITCH AnD C.O. GREGg felt EvErY

Bullet of What GoeS Around ComEs AROUND!

-KILLA-

I figured that if I ambushed him in traffic and left the note on his body, it should give the police all the knowledge they needed to understand why the C.O. had such a violent send-off from the land of the living. I could have just said fuck it and moved on with life, but sometimes a very clear message needed to be sent to the racist crackers doing dirt behind the Federal prison walls. C.O. Gregg had been doing dirt to various inmates, including myself, for a number of years in the S.H.U. - Special Housing Unit, or to those that know, the Hole - where nobody can hear you scream for help or see the evil that C.O's like Gregg do on a regular. I was just fortunate enough to be apart of karma's plan to punish his racist ass.

As the racist C.O. talked to a few of his colleagues for what would be the last time, my hand caressed the Glock 40 laying on my lap as if it were a big booty female. After killing the rat yesterday, I had destroyed the Glock 40 used in that murder. I decided to keep the other weapon I got from KD for protection until I left the state of Indiana.

Seeing the amused look on the white C.O's face made me angry, and I couldn't wait to wipe that look off his face and see one of alarm and fear plastered all over his mug before I sent him off to meet his maker and answer for his sins.

I watched him for a few moments longer before pulling off with the memory of the model and color of the Chevy pickup truck he climbed into embedded in my mind. After getting past the final checkpoint on the grounds, I pulled off and then parked on the side of the road like I had a little car trouble. I knew he had to come this way because there was only one road in and one road out.

Minutes later, C.O. Gregg's pickup truck cruised past my rental, totally oblivious to karma stalking him. I pulled off, following him onto the long stretch of road. When he turned on a two lane highway, I sped up on his ass and rammed hard into his rear bumper. The impact of the crash pushed his truck a few feet forward. He slammed on the brakes and jumped out of the car holding his neck. By that time I had already exited the SUV, clutching the gun behind my back, hidden from his view.

"You stupid son of a bitch!" he gritted, rubbing his neck and spitting a wad of chewing tobacco onto the pavement by my foot. "What the hell wrong with you, boy?"

Boy? "My brakes went out on me," I lied, easing closer to him. "I'm totally at fault here. I'm sorry, man."

"Your brakes went out? Your brakes – hey, wait a minute!" He paused, looking hard at me, and I winked at him just like he'd do to me after they beat the black off my ass and made me say, "yes sir" and "no sir" like Toby did on the movie Roots.

It only took him a few seconds to recognize me, but it only took that funny look he gave me to make me draw on him.

"Did you wait a minute when you tortured me, ma'fucka? Huh?" I snapped.

"W-wait a minute, Bub, I ca-can explain - "

I cut him off with a quick burst of two shots. The back of his noggin, blood, and brains blew all over the window of his pickup truck. His eyes stayed open as he slid down the ground. I heard car tires screeching and engines revving full throttle as I dropped the note on his chest. Then I pumped six more rounds into his white face and head. I looked around and saw several cars full of witnesses pointing their cell phone at me as I rushed back to the rental. Since the trip back to Nap Town was 2 hours, and knowing the witnesses were probably taking pictures of me and the rental with their camera phones, I made a quick U-turn, wasting no time disappearing from the scene of the crime.

After reaching the hotel in Nap Town, I jumped in the shower and scrubbed away my sins. I just hoped that I could make it out of town before getting arrested for what I had just done. After the long shower, I came out sat down on the bed and dried off. I turned on the TV and a "Breaking News" bulletin began flashing across the screen. I turned up the TV to listen on the news.

"Today a man was brutally gunned down during a traffic accident." The petite white woman reporter began her coverage of my latest victim. "It has been confirmed that the man, who has been pronounced dead on the scene, was a Federal Correctional Officer who worked at the Federal penitentiary just a half-mile from the sight of the gruesome homicide."

A picture of C.O. Gregg's smiling face suddenly appeared on the screen. Then the screen cut to the highway where the murder occupied. A bunch of police stood around directing traffic. The swirling lights of the police cruisers could be seen on the camera.

"Police say they're looking for a dark-colored SUV and an obese African American man that was seen by numerous witnesses fleeing the scene of the murder."

Several pictures showing me in the pink flight suit covering the fat suit jumping back in the Escalade rental appeared on the screen. I paced the hotel suite floor, shocked. I had to admit that although committing murder in the fat suit had been ingenious, I was fucked up over the pictures of the rental being shown on the screen. It made me feel like I was slipping, being sloppy by acting impulsively off pure emotion. I couldn't report the vehicle stolen because I figured that would ultimately tie me to the scene of the crime. I decided to take the Escalade back at night and get my ass on the first plane leaving Indiana bound for the Motor City of Detroit.

CHAPTER 67

After catching a late flight, I made it safely to Detroit two hours later. I disembarked at Metro Airport and then moved swiftly through the terminal. I felt naked after leaving the other weapon in the Wabash County River along with the fat suit, but it had to be done. If somebody found the disguise, all traces of my DNA would be washed from the suit and all fingerprints on the gun would have vanished as well.

I went to the Avis Rent-A-Car counter and decided to pay for the car in cash this time. After making my selection and going through the processing time, I got escorted to a car depot. Seconds later, a driver pulled up in a silver bullet Volvo station wagon. I wanted to be able to stay under the radar while tracking down these four rats who had violated the wrong man. I mean, to be willing to pay $50,000 a head, they must have really made main man salty. During my flight, I received a ton of phone calls from Markita that I ignored. I received a few calls from Kisha and Swol and two calls from a private number. I wonder who would be trying to reach me?

Then I got an e-mail from Chin. He sent me the contact info: some guy named Jay from Detroit. When I read that he'd be my eyes and man in Detroit, I prepared myself to handle business swiftly as possible and try to get back home before anybody in the streets of Detroit found about the rat's deaths and started spreading rumors.

When I read on further and found out that they were going on lockdown because of C.O. Gregg's sudden death, I released a triumphant smile, but immediately felt a little bad that I put the prison on lockdown. I didn't understand why the prisoners had to suffer a lockdown. I killed the racist bastard a half mile away from the prison.

After hopping in the Volvo, I called up Jay and he answered on the second ring.

"Whuddup, Dough?"

"What's up, Slim? I'm s'posed to be meeting you. A friend from the Haute sent me out here to holler at some of his old friends."

"Yeah, yeah, I been waiting on you all day dog. Where you at?"

"At Metro Airport."

"Damn, that's way out in the suburbs, my nigga. Listen, why don't you meet me downtown at the Motor City Casino and Hotel?" he suggested. He quickly gave me directions to get from the airport to downtown Detroit. I put all his directions into the GPS system in the Volvo's dashboard and pulled off.

"Now please turn here on Highway 94-East," the computer generated voice blared from the GPS system.

I drove until the car told me to get on 75-North. I did that and continued driving until I spotted the Grand River/Motor City Casino exit. As soon as I came off the exit ramp, I saw the huge hotel and casino. I figured this would be a good spot to stay while waiting on Jay's arrival.

I registered a room and went upstairs. Once I got inside the suite, I felt the effects of jet lag. I laid down and decided to take a quick nap that eventually turned into ten hours of much needed sleep.

CHAPTER 68

After catching a victim slipping at the Go-Go, Little James took all that man's valuables and left him buck naked in the trunk of his car in the parking lot. He decided not to kill the man because he wanted to save all that rage for Carmelo Glover. Plus, PG police were out on the prowl in the area all around the perimeter of the CFE nightclub. He couldn't believe he got away with robbery without getting caught. Once he slid up on the man and shoved his gun in his back, the victim begged him not to shoot and did everything commanded of him to keep his life intact. He had been getting himself prepared to put his plan in motion and he figured he needed a little more money so he could chill after putting phase one of his plan into motion.

After the petty robbery, which only netted him $2,300 and some fake jewelry, Little James called up Jennifer. She answered on the first ring. He told her to meet him at the Super 8 Motel on New York Avenue in Northeast. Before he arrived, Jennifer had beaten him there and already had the room ready for them

Slightly suspicious of her – he saw a lot of guys get tricked out of their lives for trusting a big butt and smile. Little James told her to turn the key back in and get another room. When she complied without showing any signs of betrayal, he followed her inside the office to make sure she didn't call anybody on the cell phone and give them the switch-up plan. Even though he'd fucked her on a few occasions, Little James lived by the motto "Never trust anybody under any circumstances!"

Moments later, Little James and Jennifer entered the room and began undressing. No words were needed. They knew why they'd come to the hotel. As soon as they got naked, he took her in his arms and covered her mouth in a passionate kiss. Her whole body came alive from his lips and touch. She molded her thick, soft body to his stocky frame, her titties mashing against his chest. Her nipples were hard and they tingled and burned when she pressed closer.

"Damn, I'ma tear this ass up," he huffed, rubbing all over her soft ass as his dick sprang up to attention.

"Mmm....actions speak louder than words, boo," she whispered as she rubbed his granite pole against her thigh while their tongues whipped back and forth. He inched his hand down and found that her juices were flowing. He could tell that she missed being with him.

She's geekin' for the dick, he thought, feeling her reaching down to grab hold of his manhood.

She began moving her hand between her thick legs and over his love pump. She rubbed his hardness with the back of her fingers, trying to ease him. Then she turned her hand around and began stroking his hard-on like she was cocking a shotgun back and forth. While she did that, he kissed all over her neck until his tongue lingered over her left nipple. Feeling the enlightening pleasures her hand job gave him, he began massaging her nipple with his wet tongue and lips, turning her on like he never had before.

"Aaaaaah....ssss..." She gasped, feeling the electrifying thrills his lips sent all the way to her pussy. She was wet, pulsating, primed, and ready for penetration. "Fuck me...fuck me now," she said in a throaty whisper, pushing him back until they both fell on the bed.

"Damn, bitch, you geekin like a ma'fucka for the dick, huh?" he said excitedly, making her squeeze his pipe.

She had an overwhelming desire to take his dick in her mouth and suck it until he begged her to stop. It looked so adorable to her the way it stood up like the leaning tower of Pisa against her hairless belly and he was harder than a broomstick.

"It's Ms. J-Bitch," she corrected him before easing her head down to lick the underside of his throbbing boner from his balls to the tip of the head and back down to his balls again. Then she forced his stiffness downward until the head was in line with the parted O of her lips. She leaned forward and engulfed a few inches of his hard dick inside her warm, wet mouth. She began sawing her lips back and forth over his pipe.

"Damn, bitch," he moaned. "You sucking this ma'fucka like you tryna make a nigga fall in love with your ass or something. Damn, you like that?" he asked, palming her head as it bobbed up and down on his thick love rod.

To heighten his pleasure, Jennifer fondled his balls with her free hand. At times, she stroked his smooth thighs. Then suddenly she released his shaft with a loud POP!

"I need for you to beat this pussy up like you ain't never gon' get it again!"

"Anything you say, bitch!" he said, watching her crawl over top of him and get in a doggy position, face down, ass up.

He crawled behind her, feeling hot rushes while looking at her wagging her soft ass back and forth at him in an inviting manner. The look in his lustful eyes came straight from the depths of hell. He got up and spread her soft cheeks. His hands seemed to sink inside the soft mounds of her ass as he guided his dick to the mouth of her swollen pussy lips.

She grabbed his pole and began moving it all around, up and down the opening of her slit. Her clit responded with tiny pulsations from the semi-hard friction.

"Stop playing and get the rubber," he said.

She ignored him, taking hold of the stiffness and guiding his raw tool inside her wet love tunnel. That stretched her pussy lips apart, thrilling the inside of her honey pot. As he drove deeper and deeper inside her inner sanctum, she bit down on her bottom lip, making the ugliest sex face ever. His bareback love muscle was thrilling her in a way no other latex-covered dick had.

He gripped her tiny waist, driving to the core of squishy sex, making her inhale sharply. "Dis dick hurtin' you, ain't it?" he asked, feeling his ego swell while twisting his boner in and out of her glazed inner walls.

"Boy, please," she lied, wanting him to go faster. She looked at him over her shoulder with devious smile on her face. Her chin, mouth, and facial cheeks were glazed with pre-cum juices from his dick mixed with sweat.

"Oh yeah?"

"Yeah," she moaned and he began moving faster.

As he sped up, she began screaming out his name, urging him to go faster and faster. When he got to full speed, she felt her clit vibrating from his jackhammer-like thrust. At the same time, he eased his ring finger into her anal sheath. It slid in and out with ease and sent boiling blood racing through her veins. She began humping back and forth, fucking onto his probing finger and spearing herself on his thrusting dick.

"Aaahh shit…aah shit…aaaah… I'm about to cum…I'm about to…." She gasped with pleasure, barreling over the top. "I said I'm about toooo….cuuuuuuummmmm, bitch!" she shrieked, climaxing all over his stabbing love muscle.

When she began climaxing, she thought she would never stop. The climax swept through her body like a twister destroying a small country down in the South. Little James extracted his finger from her tight anal cavity and then pulled his dick from her oozing pussy.

"Put it back…put it back in…" she said breathlessly.

"Say please, bitch," he taunted her, rubbing his dick up and down the crack of her ass cheeks.

"Please stick it back in," she gasped.

"Tell me how you want the stick to slide back up in you, fast or slow?"

"Just like this." She worked her finger around his steely shaft and shoved him back inside her neglected honey pot. She threw one knee forward, collapsing on it, making him follow her and move astride her hips. Taking hold of his dick with her inner muscles, she gyrated her hips in circular motions until his dick slid inside her oily pussy sheath down to the balls. She started moving back and forth slowly, feeling her juices flowing down his stiff love muscle.

"Ahhh fuck!" A half-strangled grunt burst from his throat as his back arched, lifting her back up on all fours. "You nasty bitch! You nasty little bit—arrrggggh!!" He groaned and thick, warm semen shot out of his dick, flooding the inside of her love nest.

While strings of his milky semen lashed against her inner sugary walls, Jennifer fell forward, causing his dick to jump out of her and spray her ass cheeks and the small of her back with the leftover semen gushing from his boner. When Jennifer got herself together, she eased her hand around his slowly deflating shaft and moved in closer to him. She kissed him passionately and squeezed his dick hard as she could, making him jump in pure pleasure.

"LJ, I want you to be all mines, for real," she said, still dazed in the afterglow of their mind-boggling sex.

"I'm jive married to the street right now, bitch," he said jokingly, making her suck her teeth and pout.

"I don't care," she said dreamily. "I want you and I'll take whatever I can get until you leave that bitch in the street alone. She can't ever do you like I can."

"What if I go in and do a bid, how you gon' feel then?"

"I like you better out here in this pussy, but if it comes to that, then I'ma ride for you, nigga."

Little James looked deep in her eyes, trying to determine if she had really just told the truth or if she was just consumed by the lustful moment. He knew one thing: he'd never, ever fuck her raw again unless they were a couple. Little James didn't want to catch AIDS for a few minutes of pleasure.

He told himself that he couldn't let Jennifer be too much of a distraction to him because he had some serious business to attend to concerning his uncle's killer, Carmelo Glover.

CHAPTER 69

The next morning, the contact guy Jay called me and told me to meet him in the lobby in twenty minutes. I woke up a little groggy and looked at my watch. It was a little after 10 a.m.

"Why so early, Moe?"

"We have to be at the spot so you can see them niggas. I know you ain't tryna miss, right?"

"Naw, naw. I'll be ready," I said and hung up. I took a quick shower and got ready to embark on my new journey as a hired hitman.

Twenty minutes later, I met the six foot tall dark-skinned brother. He was dressed in some blue baggy basketball shorts, Air Jordans sneakers, a cut-off white tee with the Jordan Brand in the center, and the matching headband and arm sleeve. As he walked up to me, gave me a one-armed hug and introduced himself, the only give-away that he played in the wicked streets was the blinding forty-inch platinum and multicolored diamond-encrusted chain swinging around his neck with a huge 7 Mile pendant. The canary yellow diamond earring he wore could go for $15,000 with ease.

"I'm Jay, dog. My man told me about the business. Consider me your official chaperone around the D, nigga!" He smiled and told me that his old friend called him up and told him about the guys he wanted pointed out. Jay would get an easy $20,000 for just pointing out the rats.

"I'm trying to be in and out quick as possible," I said as we headed outside.

Once inside, Jay walked over to his ride, a 2009 bone white Camaro with the black racing stripes on the hood and some shiny chrome rims. He looked back at me, I guess waiting for a nod of approval for his choice in wheels.

"I call that bitch piano keys, my nigga, 'cause she looks just like one," he said in a slick, proud tone. "Go 'head and hop in. Got that bitch straight out the factory for the lo-lo!"

"I jive wanted to take my rental so I could follow you around and learn about the streets and shit, if you don't mind."

"That's cool too. I just hope you can keep up. I got a heavy foot." He smirked and jumped in his flashy ride.

I got in the Volvo, pulled up beside him, and honked the horn. When he lowered his window, I could hear the classic Biggie Smalls Life After Death CD blaring "Sky's the Limit". I gave him the signal to lower the sounds before inquiring about the guns. He got out quickly and headed to the trunk of his car. After fumbling around for a few seconds, he returned to his cockpit and then re-emerged with two Philly blunt cigar boxes. He passed them to me and I put them on my lap. "I had them in the stash spot,'cause ain't no telling when them rollers will stop a nigga 'cause of the way I be speeding 'round the town. But you cool with this nerdy-ass white boy car. They'll never think about fucking with you." He laughed and returned to his ride.

I looked inside one box and saw a .45 caliber with a silencer laying beside it. Both tools were wrapped in clear plastic. The silencer could get a nigga life in prison alone, but getting the chance to eliminate some rats was worth the risk I took by having it in my possession. Then I looked inside the second box and saw a a Glock 40 caliber with another silencer. Both of those tools were also wrapped in clear plastic, giving me the impression that they were brand new. Whoever Chin had criminal ties with was on some big boy shit for real. I began liking this already. I felt like a real hitman going on a mission. Placing the boxes under the driver's seat, I looked over at Jay and nodded.

"We out, my nigga. If I so happen to lose you in traffic, I'll hit you up on your cell and tell you where I'm at and you just come out there, a'ight."

Why the fuck would you want to lose me in traffic when you s'posed to be showing me around the city? I thought, but I just nodded.

When Jay pulled off, he wasn't lying. He definitely had a heavy foot. As I pushed the Volvo station wagon through the streets of Detroit trying to keep up with him, I thought his ass was auditioning to be in the next Fast and Furious film. All I could hope for was that he didn't crash and kill himself before he got the chance to point out the rats to me.

CHAPTER 70

The ringing telephone interrupted Markita while she tried to get lunch prepared for her son and herself. She sighed in frustration before picking up the phone on the fifth ring. "Hello?"

"Yeah, I'm trying holla at Melo."

"He's not home. Can I take a message?"

"Please, this N. We was locked up together and I wanted to get in touch with him and thank him for getting me out."

"Got you out? I mean, how he do that?" she asked, being nosy.

"Oh naw, he just paid for all my lawyer fees, that's all, and I wanted to thank him," N said, withholding the other facts about Carmelo killing people to ensure that he regained his freedom.

"That's why I love that man so much." Markita beamed and gave N Carmelo's cell phone number.

"I called this number, but he ain't answer. That's why I called you, thinking he changed number. He told me to call this number because it'll never change."

"The number's the same, hon. He's just not answering his phone right now. I don't know why," Markita said, wondering why Carmelo wasn't answering his cell phone.

After speeding behind my contact guy through Detroit like we were in a high speed chase, he slowed down and parked on 8 Mile Road and Woodward Street. I paid close attention to everything as I got out of the rental and saw hundreds of people. The people in attendance on the basketball courts reminded me of the Goodman League back home. Jay walked over to me and gave me the 411 on why we were there.

"This the Joe-D, my nigga. We be hooping out here every Sunday," he said, nodding his neatly French braided head. "Niggas be betting heavy on the games too."

I was trying to figure out why he wore all that expensive jewelry just to come out and play basketball as he continued talking.

"The niggas you looking fo' is Gy and Red. Both of 'em are some lame-ass niggas, but they can hoop. I didn't know they was working with the Feds until now."

"Just point 'em out to me and I'll handle the rest."

"You can't tear 'em off right here. The rollers and all these ma'fuckas out here will be on your back before you make it back to the hotel. You gon' hafta follow 'em and do your thing," Jay said, putting me on point about my surroundings.

Damn, that's gon' take more time to follow these bitch-ass niggas, which is more time that I'll have to be away from my son and Markita. I know she's going to kill me now.

"I'ma go over and do my thing. The niggas on the court right now. So when I get on the court, I'ma run into both of them a few times and pull their T-shirts."

"You scared to point them out to me straight up?"

"Hell naw. Nigga, you stupid?" He smirked. "I didn't know if you wanted to be recognized by anybody round' here."

"Why should I care? I'm not gon' be hanging in your city after I finish doing what I came to do. Just introduce me to the niggas like I'm your cousin from D.C. who looking for a connect or some shit."

"Fo' sho'." He nodded and told me to follow him over to the court.

"Ay, Gy!" Jay began yelling. When the brown-skinned man looked over at the crowd, he looked scared, like he'd tell something soon as the police caught him.

"Whuddup, Dough?" he greeted Jay, holding up both hands over his head.

"I got winners!"

"Well, get ready to play us then," the rat said. He dashed around and began yelling for the ball. As soon as the ball touched his hands, he shot a pure jumper that hit nothing but net, ending the game.

While everybody cheered, Jay took me on the court to meet the infamous rat named Gary "Gy" Young, a member of the 952 Boys. Jay told me that the rat's mother lived on Archdale Street.

"Yo, this my cousin from D.C. He came out here to get that work on his face," Jay said, quoting a line from the chorus of Rick Ross's latest single.

"Oh yeah?" the rat said, looking me up and down.

I laughed inside at the way this bitch-made tramp was looking me over like I was suspect. I gave him a steely expression the whole time, which made him look away and call somebody. As the light-skinned pretty boy walked over, Jay tapped my leg.

"Red, whuddup, Dough?" Jay greeted, putting me on point about the second rat I had to eliminate.

I wanted to crush their asses right there and get on about my business. After Jay told me how things would turn out, I had to play it smart and use a little patience about this matter.

"Whuddup, Jay. How much you betting on the game today?" Red asked, flashing a platinum grill smile.

"I only got $5,000 on me right now, 'cause I don't want to rob you niggas no more. I damn near bought a Maybach off you niggas the last time I cooked y'all asses out here." Jay laughed, rubbing his last win in their faces.

"Oh, I see whuddup," Gy blurted. "This nigga's tryna show off fo' his cousin, Red. You know this cat's looking fo' a connect."

"I may can do something fo' him. I hafta get up with Lucky first," he said, and I couldn't believe my ears.

Damien "Lucky" Hawkins was the name of one of the rats I got paid to come out here to take care of. Jay pulled off his chain and passed it to me." Hold that fo' me, Cuz."

"I got $20,000 more to put with it to say you ain't gon' win shit!" Red added.

"If you sure you can beat em', Cuzzo, then I'ma back your play with re-up money. Even if you lose, I'll still have enough to get a brick and a half," I lied, hoping that this guy Jay had game. If not, then I'd have to shoot my way out of there and probably be on the run from the law for backing Jay's play.

Back in D.C., Detective Gamble and Newsome sat inside the 7th District Precinct, looking at the computer screen that showed Carmelo's cell phone whereabouts. Ever since getting the first read on Carmelo's phone, Gamble never shut off the computer.

"Now this son of a bitch is in Detroit, Michigan?" Gamble said in frustration. "What the hell is doing out there? I mean, he goes from Indiana to Detroit in two days. This guy is definitely up to no good. I can feel it."

"You think so? I mean, he could be out there visiting friends and family," Newsome said, causing Gamble to give him an "are you kidding me?" look.

"Fuck! Well, he needs to hurry back so he can handle our little problem. How long you think it's going to be before they come with those warrants for our arrest?" Gamble wondered before turning back to the video monitor to look at the flashing red sign that signaled the solution to all their problems.

CHAPTER 71

Over the next ten to fifteen minutes, my stomach felt funny, like a swarm of angry wasps were flying around in there as I watched the basketball game. The rats' team went up quickly by six points. I watched as Jay walked the ball down the court and passed it off to a lanky white guy who shot a brick. As everybody went up for the rebound, I saw Jay flying out of nowhere, catching the ball and throwing down a windmill dunk.

"Aaaaaahhhhhhh!" Jay yelled out loudly as everybody watching the game ran on the court, interrupting the play.

After the crowd settled down and went back to their seats and places where they stood, the rats' team brought the ball up the court. When Gy got his hands on the basketball, he shot another pure jumper that hit all net and then he held up his hands, shrugging like Jordan did when had hit all those three-pointers in an NBA game.

This nigga gon' fuck around and make me have to kill everybody, I thought, caressing the Glock 40 in my pocket and glancing over at the score. Jay's team was still down by six points.

Jay came down, ran around, two screened, got freed up, and got the ball. As soon as the ball touched his hands, he fired a three-pointer and got fouled. It seemed like an eternity, watching the ball sail through the air. When it dropped through the nets I breathed a sigh of relief.

"Fo' point play, nigga! Fuck outta here!" Jay said, talking trash as he walked to the free throw line. He shot a hard brick and went after the rebound. Catching the ball in the air, Jay did a reverse slam dunk, sending the crowd into a frenzy and running on the court again.

"You niggas can't fuck with me!" he yelled back up through the sea of people, running around on the court. "Let's go!" he yelled, clapping his hands.

Damn, this nigga really got game, I thought, watching the crowd leave the court. The things he was doing were something you'd see happening in a NBA All-Star game. Over the next few minutes, Gy and Red got their points here and there, trying to maintain their lead. Then Jay went on a tear, a one man wrecking team. Some of his points were harder to get than others, but overall, Jay kept true to his part and saved my ass by winning the game by a three-pointer.

After the game left the two rats $40,000 poorer, Jay decided to throw me $20,000, I guess for backing his play.

"I can't take that, Moe. That's all you."

"Shiid, if it wasn't fo' you, I wouldn't have the shit in the first place. Go 'head and get that work on your face from them niggas wit dey' own money," Jay teased Gy and Red after they paid him right on the court.

"Next time, bring you're A-game, niggas!" Jay laughed, put his chain back on, and stood over on the sideline, soaking up all the female groupies and little boys with basketball dreams who ran over to congratulate him.

While Jay got his fifteen minutes of fame, that rat named Red began talking to me, inquiring about how many kilos of cocaine I wanted to buy

"How much they going for?"

"Since I just took a loss, I'ma hafta charge you $18,500."

"What you gon' gimme for $85,000?" I asked, throwing a bogus number out there. I only had the $10,000 left on me after staying in Indiana, and the $20,000 that Jay just donated gave me a grand total of $30,000.

The rat's eyes widened and he smiled. "We gon' talk. Let me get up with my partner first. You got a number where I can reach you?'

I gave him my cell phone number and walked off. As I began taking a few steps, I stopped, turned around, and caught him staring at me.

"Ay. Slim, just so you know, I ain't sweet at all, so if you thinking about trying to rob me or bring me any type of move, I'ma be on point," I told him as I walked off.

CHAPTER 72

A day after having sex with Jennifer, Little James found himself walking the streets of the Le'Droit park neighborhood. He headed to the corner store to get some things for his grandmother. He used that time as a way to learn all about the different cuts, alleys, and hangouts of the guys in the hood. His intended target was whoever he caught hustling on First and U streets - his Uncle Twan's old strip. He wanted to stop all the currency flowing through the area. He felt like they didn't deserve to be capitalizing off all the blood, sweat, and tears that his uncle sacrificed.

Little James walked past First and U Streets and saw two guys standing out there. After five minutes of watching them, Little James knew they were out and about trying to get their hustle on. When he decided to step on them, a black Chevy Tahoe pulled up and parked until one of the men sold them something and walked away.

Little James smiled and headed up the street before the Tahoe could pull off. The driver of the Chevy Tahoe pulled off, never noticing Little James walking up the street and pulling out a gun. Both young men were arguing over the last drug sale, just as little James aimed the gun at them.

"You know what time it is! Where dat shit at?" he demanded.

The young men, named Tricky Rick and Man-Man, had never been in a situation like this before in all their years of hustling on the streets. They had heard about plenty of guys getting robbed and always said they'd do this and do that if somebody tried to rob them. Now that they were looking down the barrel of a chunky automatic, they froze.

"Both you niggas strip!" Little James said. He made them go through the same procedures as he did during the robbery in Garfield Terrace.

Little James kept the gun trained on both of them until he eventually had all the money and other valuables they made during their time working the strip. After putting their clothes back on, Tricky Rick began giving Little James a mean mug and tried to save face about getting robbed. Little James looked at him and felt offended.

"Something wrong with your face, bitch nigga?" Little James demanded.

"Gotdamn, I'm just saying, Slim… You come 'round here taking shit from a nigga when a nigga out here grinding all day for this little bit of shit." He went off after getting over the initial shock of being robbed. "You making it hard as shit for niggas like me who already ducking the Feds and shit to get this bread."

"It's how the game goes. Deal with it." Little James laughed.

"Yeah, a'ight," Tricky Rick said as he began walking away.

"A'ight what?" Little James retorted, unleashing four bullets into his back.

When Tricky Rick fell on the ground, Man-Man tried to make a run for it, but he got caught with three bullets to the back of his legs and hindparts. Tricky Rick took a few breaths and died right there where he fell.

Fearing for his life, Man-Man tried to crawl to safety as blood pumped from his fresh gunshot wounds. When Little James walked up to him, Man-Man turned over and began begging for his life to be spared.

"How long you been hustlin' round here?" Little James asked in a calm tone.

Man-Man swallowed hard before looking up and seeing the barrel of the chunky automatic aimed at his head. "Ahhh…'bout a year and some change," he answered nervously. "C'mon, Slim, I got two kids to feed, that's the only reason I'm out here."

Little James looked around nervously, knowing somebody heard the gunshots and would be alerting the cops at any minute. Little James thought about sparing the man's life so he could be a message to all who wanted to continue hustling on the block, but remembered what his uncle told him. "Remember, young nigga, dead niggas tell no tales. Whenever you make a move with somebody, the only way to keep that secret is if one of y'all dies with it!"

"You think that's a good enough reason for me not to kill you?"

Man-Man nodded. "Let me live, Slim, please. You got all my money and it's gon' take me forever to get back from this loss."

"No it's not, 'cause ain't no coming back on this one," Little James said and began firing at point-blank range at Man-Man's head.

For a split second, Little James looked up at the crack house his uncle built from the ground up and took off running down the block. Once he got on First Street, Little James began walking to the corner store like nothing had happened. He got everything his grandmother wanted and walked straight back to her house. By the time he made it back home, Little James heard the sirens wailing in the distance, which became music to his ears.

Back in Virginia, Markita jumped out of her seat as she finished reading Zetta's novel, realizing that the story she told was a winner. Ever since Zetta gave her the manuscript two days ago, she couldn't put it down. She made her way into Carmelo's home office and put the manuscript on his desk. Then she picked it up again and decided to re-read it. Even though the manuscript had a few misspelled words and minor typos, Markita knew that with the right editor, the book had potential to be a bestseller.

Markita picked up her cell phone and tried to call Carmelo to give him the good news about the manuscript. After several rings, she got his voicemail. She tried calling him two more times only to get the same results. She closed her phone slowly before looking at the family photograph of them on the desk. She remembered the day like yesterday, because they almost got caught having sex in the photo studio's bathroom by their son and the professional photographer. Markita touched the picture, rubbing her fingers over Carmelo's face before kissing his paper lips, wanting the real thing.

Why you avoiding me, baby? What did I do wrong? I told you I was sorry for leaving you. Why are you doing this to me? I miss you so much. When are you coming home to me, I'm going to give you the surprise of your life, baby, and make sure you never leave me again, she thought as a sea of tears streamed down her face.

Inside Chance Nightclub, Kisha just got finished giving Swol a tour of the club. She had received a text message from Carmelo telling her to put Swol on the payroll as the head of security. Kisha knew Tiny would be upset about Swol's new position, but she didn't care. She really liked Swol, who only wanted to be around her ever since the night they met at the club. She wanted to have sex with him that night, but he avoided her and said he'd call her. She thought he was gay when he turned her down. When he met her today at the club, rocking a wife beater and some blue denim cut-off shorts and Gucci sneakers, her pussy began pulsating instantly. She couldn't figure out why he always made her juices flow down to her womb so quickly.

"So how did you like the tour?" she asked, smoothing down her business skirt.

"It was a'ight," he said walking closer to her. "But it could've been better," he said trapping her in between the bar.

"What are you talking about, Swol?" she asked in a throaty whisper as he began feeling all over her body and rubbing on her big booty.

"You know what I'm about. Take that shit off."

"No, boy!" She gasped, getting so turned on that she thought an orgasm would rip through her at any time.

"Fuck you mean no? I'm the head of security, and whatever I say goes," he said as he roughed her up a little, twisting her around so that her big booty faced him. "Now bend over and spread 'em," he demanded, pushing her forward onto the bar.

Kisha gripped the top of the bar as he roughly pulled up her skirt and began frisking her like a cop doing a pat search. "Sssss…Swol, we can't be doing this," she moaned, out of breath as he ripped her thong off and spread her big butt cheeks.

"Did I tell your ass to talk, huh!" he yelled. He quickly penetrated her wetness, taking her breath away.

"Nooo…ssss…get a condom, baby…mmmmmph, shit!" she huffed as he began drilling hard and fast inside her gushing ocean.

"Get a condom for what?" he groaned, drilling in and out, in and out of her tight pussy while holding her huge ass cheeks apart. "This is what happens when you trespass on private property!" he said. He began smacking her ass cheeks, causing her to scream out joyously.

She got into his game and began gyrating her wide hips, forgetting all about the protection. She couldn't believe how his thickness slid inside her, and she hugged his pounding stiffness like a surgical glove.

"Now let this be a lesson to your fine ass," he said, pounding violently in and out of her until he exploded deep inside her gripping pussy.

"Aaaaaaah, Swol! Damn, that was good!" she moaned, climaxing seconds after him, now knowing how he got the nickname Swol.

After the sudden sexcapade, they went up to Carmelo's office for round two, which turned out to be an all-day fuck fest all around the club. Swol couldn't believe all the perks he was getting with his new job.

CHAPTER 73

After the little meeting with the rats, I followed Jay to a gas station that had a McDonald's right behind it. It looked like an all-in-one rest stop. After I got out, Jay told me to hurry up and fill up my tank and get out there.

"What's up, Slim?"

"This the Murder Mac, Nigga. Niggas be getting killed over here all the time, I guess 'cause it's right off the highway and right down the street from the mall. This bitch always stay packed. So when you see a nigga you beefin' with, niggas just come through blastin'. Shiid, three niggas just got smoked 'round here the other day." He put me on point as a slightly heavyset brown-skinned guy called out Jay's name.

"Whuddup, dough?" Jay greeted as the big guy came walking over.

"I see you got that new piano keys, huh?"

"Cut it out, Debo. You been knew I had this bitch, you just tryna be nosy as usual," I heard Jay tell the big guy, who looked me up and down blatantly as if to say, "Nigga, who the fuck is you?"

"Where you coming from?" he asked as a big-body silver Lexus pulled inside the gas station.

"Joe-D. I just took Gy and Red's money and shit. Them lames was faking as usual."

"Yeah, them hot niggas be having that money, though," Debo said, keeping his eyes on the Lexus and me at the same time.

"Ay, Slim, I'ma go get the gas real quick," I said wanting to get away so Jay could talk to his nosy friend. I decided to head inside the McDonald's and get a quick bite to eat. When I got inside, I heard Jay's chain jingling as he ran behind me. I turned to look out the door and saw Jay running towards the McDonald's while his fat, nosy friend argued with the driver of the Lexus.

"Yo, that's the nigga Lucky right there," Jay said, slightly winded after entering the fast food establishment.

"The Lucky I'm s'posed to meet with Red?" I asked, looking out at the two men going back and forth. "What they out there arguing for?"

"Naw, Debo just on his bullshit, trying to argue the nigga down about some shit. That's just how Debo is; don't mind him. But that ain't the Lucky you s'posed to meet though. His name is Victor Holmes. That nigga out dere is Damien 'Lucky' Hawkins."

"Fuck is up with all these Luckys?" I asked Jay, knowing that the rat's luck had just ran out.

"I don't know." Jay shrugged as I walked outside and went for my gun.

When I walked up on them, Debo was still arguing with the rat while he pumped gas into the pretty Lexus.

"Nigga, how the fuck you know" the rat asked Debo.

Debo looked at the rat like he lost his mind. "Nigga, I was right dere. Plus I know everything!" he said, pushing his Cartier frames up the bridge of his nose.

"Cut the bullshit De - " That was all the rat got out of his mouth before I shot him in the back of the head twice right in front of Debo.

When the rat's blood sprayed Debo's face, the big guy backed up a little and began vomiting. The two muffled shots didn't draw any attention as the rat fell to the ground, already dead. When I turned the gun on the big guy, Jay rushed from the McDonald's screaming for me to let the big guy live.

"He's cool! He's cool!" Jay said as I lowered the weapon and squatted down and began searching the rat's body.

He had a huge knot of money on him, a diamond chain, and a diamond Rolex. I took everything off him and gave the diamond chain to the big guy. He wiped his mouth and took the chain from me.

"Thanks, main man, but you should've checked the nigga's car. He might got that work up in there. He be having money, fo' real."

"Why don't you go ahead and do that, and whatever you find up in there, call up Jay and split it with him fitty-fitty. If I find out you ain't do it, I'll be back in town to see you," I told him and then walked to the rental car, jumped inside, and pulled off.

I see you looking with your looking ass, nigga, I thought while staring at Jay's nosy friend and remembering a line from the Rick Rozay song.

One down and three more to go, I told myself as I drove away from the Murder Mac. After helping the place hold up to its deadly reputation, I decided to drive a good distance from the Murder Mac and wait for Jay's phone call. While waiting on him, I began counting the money I took off the rat, which came out to a little over $15,000.

Nigga, getting that hank out here, I thought as my cell phone began ringing. I looked and saw Markita's number and I sent her to voicemail. I didn't need any distractions right now from what I came out here to do: eliminate $200,000 worth of human rats off the streets of Detroit.

CHAPTER 74

An hour after the killing at the Murder Mac, I sat inside a restaurant near the casino watching the news coverage of my work. Jay sat across from me, speaking clearly about what Debo discovered in the rat's Lexus.

"Yeah, that nigga must've been making a drop somewhere, 'cause ain't no nigga in they right mind just gon' be riding around in the D like that with twelve on 'em."

"You get your cut from Big Boy?"

"Yeah, but I told him he had to kick in some work, 'cause at the end of the day, he wouldn't have shit if it wasn't fo' you."

"You ain't satisfied with six bricks?" I asked, slightly irritated. "That's a come up that most niggas dream about and never get."

"See, that's the problem right dere. I ain't like most niggas. I never forget my blessings. So here's the deal. I took three birds, gave Debo three birds and brought you six of dem thangs. If a nigga can't bubble off three of dem thangs, den, he's just in the way, fo' real."

"You brought me six bricks? Fuck I'ma do with that shit?" I asked, staring directly into Jay's eyes. "I'm not a hustler no more, homes. I got a million niggas on lockdown all over the world depending on me to get their revenge and I'm trying to get this shit over with and get back to my city soon as possible. I can't be carrying around six bricks with me."

"Put it up in your room, I don't give a fuck. You deserve that shit; you put the work in for it. Look, there's a lotta money you can make off dat work just by selling it wholesale back in your town."

"Hustler's Ambition" suddenly filled my mind before the wheels of my cranium began turning. Before going to prison, I had never seen one kilo of cocaine up close and personal. During those hustling days, my goal had always been to reach a kilo status and take off from there. Now I had six bricks and didn't really need them. I had more money than I could count and a legitimate hustle with the nightclub and publishing company. I figured I could just dish off the work in my city and get paid handsomely by the middle of next month. Catching another view of Murder Mac on the television, I turned back to Jay and nodded. "A'ight I'ma take the work, but what I really want is you to show me where the rat's mother lives on Archdale."

"Fo' sho'!" He got up and began walking towards the elevators with the bookbag full of kilos slung over his left shoulder.

For the next three hours, I sat in the rental on Archdale Street watching the rat's mother's house, feeling hopeless until the break came that I'd been waiting on. A sleek platinum drop top Corvette ZR-1 pulled up and parked. When the driver jumped out of the convertible carrying a Louis Vuitton print tote bag, he turned out to be the same rat I'd seen earlier at the basketball court. As Gy rushed up on the house's front porch, I got out of the rental and eased up behind him. By the time the rat opened the front door, I had my gun out and aimed at his back. As the rat turned to take another cautious look before entering the house, he froze at the sight of me.

"Omerta!" I said with a smile before shooting him once in the forehead, which pushed his thought, brains, and blood all over the front door, making a crimson mess.

"Live by it, die by it!" I said before putting two more slugs in his face and two more slugs through his heart. I squatted down and took the luggage off his shoulders and walked calmly back to the rental.

Two down and two more to go, I told myself as I drove back the hotel/casino, geekin' to see the contents inside the Louis Vuitton tote bag that had a little weight on it.

CHAPTER 75

Little James sat in the grocery store's parking lot in Alexandria, Virginia. He looked down at his watch and read the time: 5:58 p.m. Suddenly his attention got grabbed by the joyful sounds of laughter. He looked up and smiled at the woman carrying a little boy on her hip and two plastic grocery bags in her right hand. He got a little excited like a kid playing hide and seek who was already aware of where everybody was hiding.

To actually be in position to make his uncle's murderer suffer felt like a dream come true. He foolishly thanked God for the Internet. The Internet gave him all the necessary information to get revenge on Carmelo Glover and his family. He watched attentively as the woman and baby walked closer and closer to her car.

Pure excitement filled Little James's eyes. His adrenaline rush reached an all-time high, watching the Glover family get ready to go home after doing a little grocery shopping. He got out of the new Buck Le'Sabre Turbo and approached Markita's car. He watched the woman and baby with disgust.

I wonder, will their deaths even make the news if I kill them right here? Will Carmelo suffer and hurt the same way my grandma does every day? He bumped into Markita lightly, just enough to get her to pause and look at him.

"Oh, excuse me." He smiled goofily. "I'm a little high and just wanted to know if you could give your man Carmelo Glover a message for me?"

The stranger's words scared Markita. She began trembling instantly while looking at him with pure fear in her eyes. Little James looked into her eyes and saw the frightened look on her face, which was a good enough message for now.

Little James gave Markita a wink and flashed his gun on her. "Hey, lil man, you look just like your daddy. Yes you do!" He laughed, making Ray-Nathan giggle. "Make sure you tell your daddy that lot of bad things happen to his family when he's not around to protect them." He laughed and walked back to his car.

Markita's heart skipped a beat as she held her son tightly, watching the stranger pull off and speed out of the parking lot. She couldn't believe what actually happened. What disturbed her the most was that the stranger could have easily abducted her and the child, or even worse, shot them to death. Markita inhaled deeply, trying to calm her nerves as she lowered her son to the ground. She pulled her phone from her purse and tried to call Carmelo. After several rings, she got his voicemail.

"Grrrr!" She growled in frustration before hanging up infuriated and disgusted. "Some motherfucker rolls up on me and your son, talking about hurting us over your ass, and you can't even answer the damn phone," she vented with heart pounding ferociously in her chest.

She was worried to death about the stranger approaching her and her son. More importantly, Markita felt helpless by not being able to reach Carmelo and tell him about what had just happened.

CHAPTER 76

I waited on Red inside L's Barbershop, a little spot on Grandville and Joy Road. I got the phone call at the hotel while counting the money in the Looey bag that I had taken from it. The rat also had four kilos of cocaine in the bag along with several stacks of money. I had reached the amount of $85,000 before the call came, disturbing me. I threw everything back in the bag and then left my suite to go meet up with the rat.

I sat around listening to all the guys in the barbershop debate about trivial matters, such as who had the flyest cars and money in the streets of Detroit all the way up to what women in the entertainment industry had butt cheek implants or had butt cheek injections and who were the top five dead or alive best rappers in Hip-Hop. After hearing most of them agree on 2-Pac, Biggie Smalls, Jay-Z, Eminem, and Nas, I got another phone call from Red. He told me to drive out to Fair Lane Mall like I was a flunky or something. I felt like if I did what he requested then it would easily make me look like a peon who was too eager and too pressed to follow orders.

"Look here, Slim, I ain't with all that driving around town shit. When you ready to fuck with me on some real shit, gimme a call," I said and hung up.

As I got up to leave the barbershop, one of the barbers asked for my input in the top five rappers.

"For real for real, I jive like that list, but I think y'all could have at least thrown Scarface and Jadakiss in there somewhere."

"See, I told y'all!" one man yelled, which sparked another heated debate.

I looked around and smiled before slipping out of the spot undetected. When I got back to the hotel/casino ten minutes later, I counted up the money, which totaled to $138,000 plus the four kilos. Now I had a total of ten kilos of cocaine and $183,000. Plus on top of that, I was guaranteed another $100,000 for eliminating these cheese chumps in Detroit.

Later on, I got a call from Markita and sent her to voicemail. I looked at the clock, which read ten minutes after 6 p.m. I decided to head down to the casino and do a little gambling to pass the time.

By 11 p.m., I had lost $80,000 and won back $95,000 and then loss $20,000 more. I decided to call it a night and take the $5,000 loss on the chin from the $80,000 I brought out of the suite to gamble with. As I began walking back towards the elevators, I got a phone call from Red the rat. I answered on the third ring.

"Yeah?"

"Whuddup, Dough? You ready to do business, nigga?"

"You mean right now? Sounds kind of funny to me, dog, to be making moves this late at night?"

"I ain't on no bullshit, nigga. I just got up with my nigga and I'm filling orders right now," he said, sounding a little drunk or high off something.

"I'm in the bed, homes," I lied.

"With all that fucking noise in the background? How you sleeping through that shit?" he asked.

"I jive went out with the TV on," I lied as I jumped on the elevator. When the doors closed, the noises of the casino died.

"Oh, a'ight den. Well look, if you still want that work, meet me at the French Quarter apartments tomorrow at noon."

"Listen, Slim, don't have me chasing a ghost like you did today."

"I won't, and I'ma get you to meet my guy Lucky too."

"I hope everything official so I can keep coming back to fuck with you."

"After tomorrow, you gon' see the benefits in fucking with some real niggas from the D."

Real niggas? Picture that! Yeah, some real cheese eaters! I thought. After thinking for a second, I called up Jay. I told him about the phone call and told him to take me to the French Quarters apartments that night.

"I'll be at you in about fifteen minutes, my nigga."

Thirty minutes later, Jay pulled up to the French Quarter apartments in the rental Volvo. After he pointed out the rat Lucky to me, I chambered a round in the .45 and switched my mind over into murder mode.

"You about to kill the nigga right now?'

"Yeah, why, what's up?"

"You should at least get both dem niggas together."

"Well, well, well….speak of the devil. I guess you just talked up the other rat," I said, catching Red exiting the duplex row houses.

The apartment complex reminded me of Sursum Quarters projects back in D.C. After making his way across the grassy front yard, Red walked up to Lucky and gave him a manly hug. They jumped in a charcoal-gray black Bentley Continental GT and pulled off.

"Wait a few minutes before you follow them niggas," I told Jay.

"I can't wait that long, them niggas in a Bentley. They might take off soon as they get out the parking lot," Jay replied.

"You right, go on and get on 'em."

Moments later, we ended up parking on Heyden Street. The quiet block was lined with big houses as far as my eyes could see. While tailing them, all I could think about was how much money these rats actually had. I mean, they had to be getting some change to be pushing a Bentley GT in the hood. I never seen no shit like that unless it was in a music video.

"Ay, I heard that's the Reload House them niggas going into. A few niggas who be jacking niggas been tryna find out about the location of this spot for years. All the work them niggas be moving round the D probably up in there," Jay said, invading my thoughts.

"You just keep the car running. I'll be back!" I said, sounding like The Terminator, drawing laughter from Jay.

"Nigga, you stupid!" He giggled. "I got you though."

As I got out of the car and moved towards the house, I looked back at the rental. I saw Jay waiting on me like a getaway driver does for his team who heading inside a bank to make an illegal withdrawal. Instead of planning on making a withdrawal, my mind was set on making a bloody deposit.

CHAPTER 77

I had been puzzling over how to raid the house without raising hell on the quiet street while Jay gave me the 411 on the spot being a stash house. The quiet neighborhood provided the perfect cover for the rats' hidden motives. I waited and watched. The civilian couple walking down the street holding hands looked like high school lovers. Their open show of affection made me think about Markita for a minute. I wondered about her and my son. I ended the thoughts as the couple disappeared into the shadows of the night.

I walked up to the house, allowing the killer inside me to return. I rang the doorbell and glanced around at the shadows of the night. Seconds later, I saw the peephole's flick of light eclipsed with darkness by whoever stood on the other side ready to answer the door.

"Whuddup, Dough?" I heard a male voice call out as I raised the .45 and fired through the peephole.

The bullet shattered the glass, tunneled through the door, and plunged into Victor "Lucky" Holmes's right eye. Red caught his crime partner in his arms as he fell dead. A second shot splintered the lock, the bullet passing right above Red's shoulder as he knelt, lowering Lucky to the floor.

"Oh shit! Oh shit!" Red said while flinching.

A third bullet penetrated the door and the lock shattered.

Red retreated to the kitchen to get the gun he had set down on the kitchen counter by the drugs they were about to whip up. As he grabbed the Sig Sauer, he heard the front door crash open.

The back door to freedom from the kitchen and whoever wanted to kill him was a heavy duty wooden door studded with glass panes, painted an off-blue to match the house. The back door could be seen from the front foyer. Red knew if he made a run for the door, he'd be putting himself in the line of fire for a few seconds.

Nigga stop over thinking the shit! Just run for your fucking life or stay here and die, he thought over the rattle of his panicked breathing.

Suddenly Red heard footsteps on the tile floor. He'd waited too long and let himself get concerned.

After stepping over the body, I put two more bullets in Lucky the rat's head as I moved inside the house. I put both hands on my .45 like you do at the shooting range while listening to the house. It seemed quieter than an empty church.

The noise of my own breathing seemed loud as a drum beat as I aimed the .45 at the kitchen's back door. I had no idea where the fourth and final target was hiding, but I figured he still had to be somewhere in the house. He couldn't have gotten out the back door that fast because it was still closed. I know if somebody was trying to kill me, I wouldn't take the time to close the door behind me. Would you? Hell no, you outta there, right?

As the thought passed through my mind, I saw a rush of movement over near the far corner of the kitchen and instinctively fired rapidly in that direction. I didn't anticipate hitting anything in the dark, but the sound of a body dropping made me rush further around the kitchen island's corner, extending the gun, running into the surprise of my life.

Red felt a tug in his flesh through the Pelle Pelle button-up shirt, then heat, and with horror, he realized he'd been hit in the arm. He hesitated and then raised the gun to fire as the man rounded the kitchen island's corner, clutching a chunky automatic with an attached silencer - the same man he'd seen earlier at the basketball court.

But how he know about the Reload House? Red wondered as he squeezed the trigger.

CHAPTER 78

After the rat missed me by a long shot and the bullet plowed into the ceiling, I kicked him in his wounded arm.

"Aww, fuck, man!" He gasped and I shoved the silencer barrel of the gun onto his forehead.

"Drop it now!"

He obeyed, letting the gun fall by his waist side. The rat closed his hand around his arm and blood pumped out the wound between the cracks of his finger and shirt.

"Anybody else in the house?"

"N-No." He shook his head.

"Don't lie to me."

"Nobody in here, I swear."

I yanked him to his feet. "The money and drugs, where's it at?"

"I d-don't…know…We…we just got rid of a gang of that shit."

"You lying!" I snapped before shoving the rat back with the gun, catching him off balance. "Gimme everything right now and you live."

"Man, I swear to God, it ain't nuffin' up in here." He collapsed against the granite counter and held his hands up.

I forced the rat at gunpoint over into a kitchen chair. I kept the gun aimed at him while opening the kitchen drawers. When I found the roll of duct tape, I grabbed it and moved towards him.

"Please, man, you ain't got to do this. I ain't got shit!" he said.

I watched his eyes widen as the strip of duct tape covered his lips. It took me a few seconds to restrain him to the chair, leaving him totally defenseless and at mercy. "Since nothing is up in here, that that means it don't even matter if I kill you then?"

"HHHMMMMMMMMMRRRGHHH! GRRMMPPPH!" I heard his muffled screaming.

I snatched the tape off his mouth and he winced. "I…I…I don't want to die, man, puhlleeasse. It's some work in that bag on the counter over there. It's about six guns upstairs and about three pounds of weed up there too."

"So it ain't no money?"

"No, man, I swear. I mean, I got about three stacks on me, but that's about it."

"Thanks for the help, you hot bitch!" I smiled and shot him in the knee cap.

"AAAAHHHHH!"

He screamed bloody murder as I reached for the plastic garbage bag by the back door. I emptied the heavy duty green plastic bag on the floor and moved toward the rat. I hurried to cover the rat's face with the plastic bag and tape it tightly around his neck, leaving him no room to breathe.

"Please, man, I can't breathe!" he yelled as I stepped back and looked at his covered head.

"You should have thought about breathing before you snitched and got a nigga a million years!"

His restrained body began jerking violently and hopping around in the chair, speeding up his death by asphyxiation. His breaths hurried, sucking the plastic bag in and out, in and out…in…out…in…out….and out for good. When his body became still and the bag stopped moving, I aimed the .45 at his heart and fired twice. Blood splashed out new holes in his chest, assuring me that he was a goner.

I took the bag off the countertop and moved out to search the rest of the house. I completed my first job as an official hitman.

Chin needed lawyer money and his rich associate wanted to eliminate some cheese-eating chumps who got him a rack of time in the

Feds. When Chin called on me to put in that work and help him get some bread, I played my part.

CHAPTER 79

After the terrifying experience at the grocery store, Markita made it home in a flash. She called Carmelo again and got his voicemail. She glanced out the windows, terrified as if she'd been suddenly thrown into a real life horror movie. Her entire body shook as she took her son up to his bedroom and locked him safely behind the door.

Markita still couldn't believe that a total stranger had approached her that way in broad daylight. What made it even worse was that it happened in the heart of a busy VA. shopping center in front of several throngs of people. The incident shook her up more than the time when she got the horrible news about her brother being murdered two and a half years ago. That shook her up to the core.

But today had been something incredibly worse. Words couldn't describe the terror and anger Markita had coursing through her veins. She sat back rocking her son in her arms with her head hanging down as she kissed him until he drifted off to sleep. Putting him under the covers, Markita kissed his forehead and left the bedroom. She went to take a bubble bath to calm her nerves. As she walked through the huge house, the slightest noise startled her, making her shake. After the incident today, she had become a nervous wreck.

"Fuck this shit," she mumbled, making a beeline straight for her bedroom.

As soon as she entered the bedroom, she rushed over to the nightstand to grab the telephone. She called April, who answered the phone on the third ring.

"Hello?"

"Hey, girl. I really need you to come over here right now."

"Why, what's going on? I'm in the middle of a good-ass movie right now, Kita."

"Just come over here. I'm scared, okay? Some man came up to me and the baby today talking all crazy and shit. I just don't want to be alone right now."

"Where's Carmelo?"

"Does it matter?" she snapped. "Look, I just need for you to come over here. Why you making this so hard?"

"I'm sorry. Don't worry. I'm on my way. Just sit tight, okay?" April said an ended the call.

April rushed inside her walk-in closet, threw on some Juicy Couture sweats and pink Nike Air Max trainer sneakers. She grabbed the chrome .380 automatic that Suede had taught her how to use before he died. After checking the magazine, April chambered a round and took the safety off the gun. She then grabbed her car keys and bolted out the front door to go see about her sister-in-law.

Back at Markita's house, Little James sat on a milk crate in the woods that faced the house, looking through a pair of high-powered binoculars. He zoomed in on every move Markita made. After he sped off, leaving her shaken up at the shopping center, he drove back to her house in an effort to catch up with Carmelo. Little James figured that after the stunt he just pulled, it would make Carmelo appear in a flash. After waiting for a little over an hour, he realized he'd been wrong.

What the fuck I gotta do to get this nigga to show his face to me? he thought. He decided to watch the house for a little while longer. Little James wanted to be there with his guns ready to do damage just in case Carmelo made an appearance.

CHAPTER 80

Early Monday morning, I boarded the Amtrak train bound for Union Station in D.C. After searching the stash house last night on Heyden Street, I found a bunch of weed, three kilos of cocaine, two semi-automatics, three Mac-11's and a street sweeper shotgun. I also got $7,658 total off both bodies. I kept a pound of weed and gave Jay the rest. I also gave him one kilo of coke and all guns, which made him ask me how much money I wanted for the gifts I had blessed him with.

"I don't want no money, Moe. Just do you and take me to the train station in the a.m. in my rental.

"I can do that. I'll just swing through in the morning and - "

"Naw, just hang out right here with me for the rest of the night and drop me off in the morning so I can get the fuck away from this joint."

After pulling up at the train station downtown, Jay assured me that he'd turn in the rental soon as my train left the dock. I found my seat just as the train began closing its doors. I waved to Jay. He gave me a military salute and walked off. I nodded as the train left the Motor City carrying me, twelve kilos of cocaine, and $262,835. I got Jay to spray down the kilos with Pine Sol and a few other chemicals to throw off the scent just in case any hot police boarded the train with some drug sniffing dogs and wanted to fuck with somebody.

Surprisingly, the 525 mile, seven hour trip from Detroit back to D.C went smoothly and I even got the chance to get in a few hours of sleep. When I made it home around 2 p.m., I opened the rear taxi door only to find Gamble the crooked detective waiting on me in the driveway with another cop.

"Carmelo Glover, I'm here to serve an outstanding warrant for your arrest in the District of Columbia," Gamble stated, making me more scared than a black man in the midst of an angry Ku Klux Klan lynch mob.

Markita saw the taxi pulling up at the house, and she walked towards the door to open it for her man. She wanted to give him a piece of her mind for not answering any of her phone calls. When she saw the two men walking towards Carmelo and pulling out handcuffs, Markita ran from the house and directly into Carmelo's arms, shielding him from the cops. She hugged him tightly around his neck and began crying.

"Ma'am! Ma'am! You have to move out of the way!" Gamble stated firmly, going for his gun. "You are interfering with us doing our job!"

"Please, ma'am, move out of the way," Newsome added, stealing a few looks at Markita's plump rumpshaker jiggling inside the tight red boy shorts she wore. He could see the curves of her butt cheeks shaking as she hugged their suspect.

Ignoring him, Markita kissed Carmelo close to thirty times all over the face. "Baby, I love you. I love you soooo much, please don't leave me no more. I need you, I'm scared. When you left, this ma - "

"Shh…shh…" he whispered, cutting her of as he leaned into her ear and began whispering. "Kita, Baby, listen to me and listen and carefully.

Don't ask no questions. Just go and get my bag out the cab and take it inside the house with you. Whatever you do, don't look inside the bag, okay?"

Yeah, right, she thought while nodding at him. She then turned on the police. "What the hell is going on here?"

Ignoring her question, Gamble slapped the handcuffs on Carmelo's wrist and Newsome frisked him quickly. Both detectives looked at Markita and then hustled Carmelo over to an unmarked crown Victoria.

Carmelo looked over his shoulder at Markita and nodded right before the detective shoved him in the back seat.

"I love you, Melo! I'ma get you out, okay, boo? I promise!" Markita yelled with tears falling down her face.

She stood there feeling helpless while looking at the two cops jump in the car and drive off, taking Carmelo out of her life as soon as he returned to it.

CHAPTER 81

I couldn't believe my luck. This crooked-ass bitch got me back in prison. These past few hours had been a whirlwind for me. I had gone from living a peaceful life in a quiet neighborhood in VA and traveling across the states to visit friends in prison to sitting in gloomy police precinct interview room, not knowing if I'd ever see my wife and son again.

This had to be fate, I told myself, looking at the four walls of the oatmeal-painted interview room. Considering the fact that I had just gotten away clean for killing six people in the Midwest over the weekend, maybe this was a sign from God, telling me to slow down.

I was sick and tired of all this craziness upending my life. Things hadn't been the same ever since I took N's phone call a few weeks ago and killed the final witness scheduled to testify against him at his appeal hearing. I could feel guilty about the past, apprehensive about the future, but only in the present could I act, which is what Gamble's crooked ass was forcing me to do.

Some years back I would have frozen in panic at the thought of killing a cop, let alone two of them. Now that Gamble seemed to be forcing my hand, that fear would become a tool of survival. I couldn't hesitate anymore or even second guess myself. I had to kill Gamble and his partner to keep them from messing with me and my life. Gamble's partner had to die just on the fact that he was associated with Gamble. I was quite sure Gamble gave him the 411 on me.

I mean, even if I killed for Gamble, he would never leave me alone to live happily ever after. Gamble was a bloodsucker – a creep who would use me up and then throw me to the wolves the first chance he got.

I just can't see myself going out like that, I thought, hearing the soft click of the interview room door opening.

I looked up and saw Gamble and his partner standing in the interview room. Gamble walked over and took a seat in the gunmetal gray chair directly in front of me on the other side of the matching metal table that they handcuffed me to.

"Mr. Glover, I'd like for you to meet my partner, Detective Newsome," Gamble said with a smirk as the pig nodded at me.

"Mr. Glover or Carmelo, which one do you prefer?"

Putting a bullet through your skull, you hot bitch, I thought with a smile before answering. "Mr. Glover is cool. It shows that you respect me."

"Yeah, right!" He laughed. "I respect the fact that you're a fucking flight risk, you murdering sack of shit," he said and his face changed into a mask of anger. "I respect the fact that you leave me no choice but to detain your ass in a halfway house right up the street, where I can keep my eyes on your sneaky ass until you carry out the little job we agreed on."

I ain't agree to shit! You blackmailing me into doing this shit!

At the same time in the Trinidad Northeast section of the city, Zetta sat on her mother's front porch with Domonique, Liz, D.C., Ugg, and D.C.'s little brother Pooh, enjoying the hot humid day. Zetta had been hanging around her mother's house a lot lately after catching Poobie and April kissing in Markita's house. She felt that it would be better just to leave Poobie alone altogether instead of playing mind games, like Markita had suggested.

Zetta decided to give Ugg the chance he always claimed he wanted far as being her man. They'd been getting close over the last two weeks, but Zetta didn't let him hit the pootie tang yet. Even though she tried to brush it to the side, she still had feelings for Poobie and didn't want Ugg to just be a rebound relationship.

"So what we going do tonight?" Ugg asked Zetta, who just shrugged her shoulder and gave him a sheepish smile that warmed his heart.

"Don't even trip. I got somewhere we can go that you gon' love," he said, giving her a wink.

"Ugg, quit being nasty. Don't nobody wanna go nowhere with your freak ass," Liz blurted, making everybody laugh.

"Yeah, you're probably talking about taking our girl to some cheap-ass hotel. She ain't no freak like these other bitches round here," Domonique added.

"You need to stop cock blocking," D.C. said, making Domonique shut up instantly and give him an evil look.

"All y'all need to quit." Zetta giggled as her cell phone began ringing. She answered it quickly after seeing Markita's number. Ever since the day they met and had a talk about Carmelo, they became friends and never went more than two days without calling and checking up on each other.

"Hey girl, what's up?" Zetta asked with a smile. After listening for a few seconds, Zetta's face took on a serious look, causing everybody to look at her in a funny way. "Don't cry, Kita. Look, I got my uncle right here with me. I'm pretty sure he knows somebody that can help him out. Hold on," Zetta said and gave D.C. a quick rundown about what had happened to Carmelo.

"You talking about the nigga who be selling books?"

"Yeah, boy, now do you know a lawyer who can help him?"

"Yeah, yeah, I was just about to take the nigga Brian McDaniels some money at his office. I can tell him to look out for Slim. Where he locked up at?"

"Hold on," Zetta said and then asked Markita where Carmelo was being held in custody. "Okay…okay… Look, just call around and find out where he's at and my uncle going to send somebody to get him out there. Okay, you do that. Don't thank me, that's what friends are for girl. I'll talk to you in a minute. Bye-bye."

After Zetta hung up, D.C. gave her a funny look. "That nigga better publish your book. You got me doing all this geekin'-ass shit for his ass."

"His wife is going to publish my book," Zetta said, sticking her tongue out at D.C., making everybody laugh.

"You put that part about Southwest in there"

"I don't know what you talking about."

"You hear that shit, Ugg? She don't know what we talking about."

"Shiid, why you think I'm tryna make you my wife? I need a go-hard chick."

"Kiss my ass!" Zetta giggled, trying to downplay their little secret in front of Pooh, Liz, and Domonique. After Zetta's giggling ceased, she stared off into space, zoning out like she had something on her mind.

I should have did that shit slick without them niggas knowing or seeing me, just like I did when I crushed that hot-ass nigga down Goodman League who told on my brother, she thought, remembering how close she had been to the last living snitch who told on her brother right before she shot him with her compact .380. After shooting him twice in the head, Zetta dove on the ground to make it look like she was trying to duck the bullets.

Nobody saw Zetta do the crime that day, but she wasn't as smooth as when she killed Sean Bullock down in Southwest. As Sean Bullock went to exit the car, Zetta eased her .380 out of her purse and shot him three times in the back of the head, annihilating his physical life. As she pulled Sean Bullock out of her car, Zetta caught D.C. and Ugg looking at her in awe as she drove past them like she didn't know them.

When Zetta's brother first went to jail over a few guys snitching on him, Zetta decided to take matters into her own hands. After getting a few details from her brother about where all the men hustled at in the city and what type of cars they drove, Zetta began hunting them down like they were fugitives from the law.

The first rat she caught, was Arthur Rice. Zetta saw him leaving the club after a Go-Go with a plus-sized woman. Zetta followed the rat's car for a few miles until she saw a perfect spot to get at him. When Zetta busted a U-turn on her motorcycle, she realized she had to make her move quickly before the target put the car in reverse and got out of Dodge. She managed to get up on the driver's side of the car and shoot the driver several times before speeding off into the night, away from the sounds of the screaming female passenger.

On her second kill, Zetta had caught the rat dead to rights outside the H2O nightclub. When she saw the actual target up close and personal, she hesitated for a second after seeing Kenneth Adams, a guy from K Street

Southwest and also one of her brother's best friends, the same person who used to spoil her to death every time he came over to the house.

As the betrayal for what he'd done to her brother outweighed her rationale, Zetta let her gun bust. When she saw him go down and start crawling toward his car, Zetta ran down on him in a skimpy mini dress and matching high heels and put three more bullets in his head before taking off into the night, thinking she only had one more snitch to kill for her brother.

After she heard D.C. joking today, Zetta regretted killing Sean Bullock in front of him and Ugg. Even though she felt in her heart they wouldn't ever say anything, Zetta hated the fact that they saw her in action as a killer.

"Fuck you think, Zetta?" D.C. asked, invading her thoughts after seeing the perplexed look on her face.

"Nothing," she said, adjusting her big Jackie-O shades over her mane. She wanted to keep the small talk to a minimum. Her mind was elsewhere.

CHAPTER 82

When the crooked detective told me that I would be detained at Hope Village, a halfway house located up the street on 2406 Langston Place, I concluded that I'd have to escape from the place soon as I got the chance. After all his threats and hours of pestering, the unexpected happened. When the knock came on the interview door, Gamble's partner Newsome opened the door and I couldn't believe my eyes. A conservatively-dressed black man rocking a blue pinstriped three piece suit and wielding a black leather briefcase and stern look entered the room.

"Good day, detectives. I'm Brian McDaniels, Mr. Glover's attorney. I've been called by his wife to find out why you guys have abducted my client and brought him all the way to the District without formally charging him of any crimes?"

"Ah," Gamble's crooked ass began stuttering.

Only then did I know Gamble couldn't touch me and that my baby Markita had my back to the fullest.

"Ah, we just wanted to question Mr. Glover on a string of unsolved homicides that date as far back as two years ago." I could tell by the look on Gamble's face that he was surprised just as much as me about this guy.

"Well, considering the way you guys went about doing this, I believe this is a very serious violation of departmental procedures and it could land you guys in some hot water with Police Chief Kathy Lanier, who is a very generous supporter of one of my charities, I might add," he said, arching his right eyebrow. I saw Gamble swallow hard. "So if you guys do not intend to charge my client with anything, I strongly suggest that you release him now."

It's your move now, you crooked ma'fucka, I thought, wondering where the hell Markita found this slick-talking fly-dressing superhero. He's definitely my type of guy. I mean, to burst in here and talk bad to the cops and be able to get away with it without catching a Rodney King beatdown was some fly shit to me.

"Turn him loose, Newsome." Gamble sighed, letting me know that the arrest warrant he claimed to have had to be bogus.

This hot pig think he got all the sense, I thought as Newsome walked over to me and uncuffed me without saying a word, but the look in Newsome's eyes told me the violent tale he'd like to show me. I rubbed my wrist, trying to make the red handcuff indentions disappear from my skin as I walked past Gamble. He gave me an evil look. If looks could kill, I don't think I would have made it out of that interview room.

Once we made it outside the precinct, the lawyer told me that one of his clients asked him to come and bail me out on short notice after Markita found out where I was.

"Who's your client? And how much do I owe you for this?" I asked, looking him up and down.

"Don't trip, I took care of everything, baby," Markita said, appearing out of nowhere. I looked at her and she had Zetta with her, which damn near gave me a heart attack.

"What you mean you took care of everything?" I said, trying not to look at Zetta, who just kept looking at me like she wanted to eat me alive. Damn, she's sexy as a ma'fucka!

"Well, your newest author here made a few calls to get you this guy, and I think we should put out her book ASAP for all that she has done for you." Markita smiled, throwing me completely off.

"What? You just went on me for trying to put her book out and did all that geekin'-ass moving out and shit and now you with it? What's really going on here?" I asked her, full of suspicion.

"Mr. Glover, here's my card," the lawyer interrupted. "Call me anytime," he said before walking away. I watched him get inside the back of a big Lincoln Towncar that already had a driver in front. Seconds later, the lawyer's driver pulled off, leaving me to face my wife and the woman who I'd been having fantasies about fucking.

"Now back to you, Kita. Fuck is up? You cool with her now?"

"Yeah, I'm cool with her. She's my buddy now." Markita smiled and Zetta waved at me.

"Hey," Zetta added before giggling.

"Anyway, I'm going to be working with Zetta to put her book out so you won't be tempted to do anything stupid or crazy enough that will get your dick cut clean off."

"Yeah, whatever. Do whatever, I don't care. I just want to go home and see my son," I said, walking towards Markita's car.

"Babe, when we get home, I need to talk to you about something very important that happened while you was outta town," she said as I reached the car and saw my son knocked out cold, sleeping peacefully in his car seat. It felt so good to see him again that I couldn't just let him sleep. I woke his ass up and made him cry.

"Whaaa-whaaaa-waaaa!" he shouted until I began kissing him on his forehead and tickling him. After he realized who I was, he began laughing and squeezing my nose.

"Da-da!" he called me in his excited baby tone.

"Yeah, lil nigga, Daddy's here. That's right. I'm right here and I ain't going nowhere no time soon," I said with confidence, knowing I had a slick attorney that could keep Gamble's crooked ass off my back. While I played with my son, I saw Zetta give me a look before hugging Markita and walking off to her car. I held my son in face to cover me from Markita so I could get a good look at Zetta's nasty strut all the way to her car.

"Babe, I know you heard me? And you bet' not be looking at the girl's ass neither! Markits said.

As I turned on her, I saw Gamble exiting the precinct with his partner.

"Yeah, I heard you and I wasn't looking at her ass," I lied with a smile. Just drooling like a ma'fucka over it, I thought before saying, "Now let's go." I took in Markita's pretty smile as she walked towards the car.

As Markita made her way over to me, Gamble gave me a mischievous smile, pointing his hand at me, making the shape of a gun symbol and shooting me. When he blew imaginary smoke from the tip of his index finger, I began to wonder how long my attorney could keep Gamble off my back before he came after me again.

At the same time, yards away, Little James sat in his car smoking on a Newport. He blew out smoke rings while watching Carmelo interact with his son and sexy girlfriend. He was furious when he couldn't kill Carmelo earlier because the cops got in his way. He had followed the cops into the District to see where they were taking his target. Now that he knew Carmelo wouldn't be in prison to hide from his wrath, Little James pulled off to put phase two of his plan in motion.

He sped back out to Carmelo's house and parked. After getting out of the car, Little James walked up to the front door like he belonged in the quiet suburban neighborhood. He looked at the "Protected by ADT" security sticker on the front window and laughed.

What a joke! I already been in this house a million times already and no cops ever showed up, he thought as he reached inside his pants pocket to get the little surprise that he wanted to leave for Carmelo.

CHAPTER 83

When Markita pulled up at our home fifteen minutes later, I jumped out of the car and went to take my son out of his car seat. I just ignored Gamble's unmarked police car. I figured that he only wanted to get me riled up by following me home.

I picked my little man up and walked towards the house. When I reached the door, I saw something that nearly made my heart stop. I snatched the picture of a smiling Twan off my front door and read the note attached to it.

I know what U did, bitch nigga and I'ma see U. Oh yeah, I'm gon' see U Everything you do in the dark always come to light. I know all about U and all your moves. Just ask your wife. Oh and by the way, your little police friends saved your ass from getting smoked earlier today. See U when I see U, bitch nigga!

Sincerely,

Your Ugly Past

I balled up the note and picture before Markita got up on me. I opened the front door and left it open for her. By the time she got in the house, I had already made it to my bat cave and armed myself. When I saw that I didn't have many fully automatic assault rifles, I made a mental note to call up my gun connect, Blade, the first chance I got. The note and picture really scared me. I knew I couldn't leave my family here in this house like sitting ducks if somebody out there wanted me dead for what I did to Twan.

"Go get Mommy, lil nigga," I told my son. He looked up at me and giggled and then took off running.

I followed him into the grand foyer and noticed Markita looking out the front windows like she was trying to see if somebody was following her.

"What's up, them Feds still out there?" I asked, making her turn around quickly.

"Mmm, yeah," she said, walking over to me. "Baby, I'm scared. While you was away, some man approached me and the baby when I came out from grocery shopping."

I don't think I heard the rest of her words. I had sunk into a deep abyss of fear and regret as soon as she told me that. Somebody really was playing for keeps and with a different set of rules. What made it even worse was that I didn't even know where to begin to look. I was at war with a ghost who really had the ups on me and my family and there wasn't a damn thing I could do about it but move far away as possible from the area.

"Go pack your things right now. You going to your mother's house until I can find us somewhere more safer to live."

"No, Melo, I'm not going anywhere. As long as you're here, we should be good, right?" she asked, looking at me for some reassurance that I could be her protector.

But how could I protect her from something I couldn't see coming? "Kita, this nigga stepped to you and my son. Who knows what he'll do next?" I said, not telling her what I had found on the front door.

"If you answered my calls, you would have known about this sooner. And why you got all that money in that bag and them drugs? Listen,

Melo, if you doing something to put us in danger…" She paused, giving me a nasty look. "That's why that man approached us, ain't it? You took something from him or something?" She went off.

"No…no…no. Baby, listen to me. I'm just holding that stuff for a friend. I'm not in that street shit no more," I lied quickly, remembering what she had told me when we first met. She said she would leave me if I ever got back in the street life again.

"Melo, you're scaring me. Why you got to be the one holding all that stuff? If he really was your friend, he wouldn't be putting you and us in jeopardy like this," she said as she began crying.

"Kita, listen to me. We're not in jeopardy of anything. I don't know who that guy was who approached you and the baby, but I'm going to find out. In the meantime, I'ma take you out back with me and teach you how to use a gun."

"Nope, uh uh! Why I have to use a gun if we're not in danger?"

"Just in case, Kita, so stop asking me a million fucking questions and being so difficult and just do what the fuck I tell you to do for a change!" I snapped, regretting it soon as the words rolled of my tongue.

"Mm-kay, I'm sorry," she said in a baby like voice. "You going to show me how to shoot right now or after we put the baby to sleep? Because you know the police are still right out front."

"You're right. We just gon' wait until nightfall, okay? Kita, I'm sorry for - "

"Don't trip, boo boo." She cut me off, picking up our son. "I know what I told you is a lot to take in right now and I'm sorry for being so difficult. It'll never happen again." I could hear the sarcasm oozing in her tone as she walked away from me, leaving me to bask in the misery of my past coming back to haunt me.

CHAPTER 84

My not-so-pleasant homecoming and conversation with Markita had driven me to head inside the sitting room and drink more than I should have. The reality of the past resurfacing to destroy my life was starting to sink in. I felt a cold chill shoot up in my spine and my entire body shuddered.

I stood up straight and quickly walked over to the wet bar to refill my thick glass tumbler. I loaded it with ice and filled it to the brim with Hennessey. After taking a large gulp of the cold, brown liquid, I walked over to the fireplace and noticed that it was stocked with wood and kindling. I set my drink down on the mantel and picked up a box of long matches that sat in a wicker basket next to the hearth. I grabbed one of the twelve-inch match sticks and struck it across the coarse strip on the side of the box. I watched the red tip spark and then burst into fiery flames, just like my life was doing right now. I waited until the wooden part of the match caught fire and then stuck the long match under the log, lighting the dry pieces of kindling.

The fire caught quickly and I pulled up a chair to watch the flames spread. Sliding off my 1500 New Balance track sneakers, I placed my feet up on the hearth and took a deep breath. The warmth of the fire helped me relax and momentarily forget the life-threatening elements hovering in the air outside the comfort zone of my home.

I stared into the fire and watched it burst into a full blaze as the white bark on the wooden logs crackled and curled from orange flames. The memory of the conversation with Markita finding the picture of Twan with a note attached to it and my run in with the crooked detectives began to surface again and I took another gulp of the Hennessey. But the drink still couldn't block out everything invading my life. I pulled the note and Twan's picture from my pocket, glanced at them again, and then tossed them into the fire. I sat back sipping my drink, watching the raging flames shoot out and consume two pieces of my violent past.

Drama came at me from everywhere. Markita wanted to know what was going with all the drugs in my possession. Gamble's crooked ass sat right outside my front door, waiting patiently for me to make my next move. And the phantom who been taking shots at me was slowly revealing their deadly hand to me, but still left me blind to the other cards up his sleeve.

I became a little unsteady and began shaking. I had to grab my drink with both hands to keep it from spilling. My lips and body trembled as I pulled the glass to my lips with both hands to take large gulps, finishing the rest of the Hennessey. I quickly stood to pour another drink. As I walked to the bar, the murders of Twan and the others I had erased from the face of the earth flashed sharply across my mind. For the first time, I realized just how cold and brutal I was.

The crystal tumbler slipped from my hand and shattered on the stone floor. I kept on stumbling over to the bar and found another tumbler. As I began pouring another drink, the glass neck of the Hennessey bottle clanged off the rim of the tumbler as my hands continued to shake uncontrollably.

CHAPTER 85

Everything after killing the whole 64 ounce bottle of Hennessey became a slight blur. I remembered heading upstairs, hugging the railing on the staircase, trying to cope with the head-splitting dizzy spells as I tried to get to my master suite.

For the life of me, I couldn't hear the soft music playing in the bedroom or see my girl walking up to me completely nude. I was wasted like a college kid hanging out at a frat party. The next thing I knew, I was being pinned against the wall, feeling Markita's ass pressed firmly against my groin.

I had a tumbler of Hennessey in my left hand. She had my right hand wrapped around her naked body and placed close to her right breast. From her position, she managed to extract my joystick from the confines of my jeans by gently tugging and pulling and giving it a hard squeeze to get the blood pumping down there. I dropped my drink on the carpet, not even caring about the damage it would do, and pushed her forward until she was bent forward. I pulled hard on her soft ass cheeks, parting them as I slid my boner inside and then stopped.

"Boy, you better stop playing and put it in me," she moaned, backing up, forcing her pussy to swallow me whole. Her pussy convulsed and her inner muscles rippled up and down my rock-hard shaft. She whimpered as each stroke stretched her vaginal walls to the limit.

"Ssss…I never knew make-up sex could be this good," she moaned in a throaty voice I had come to love. "Your drunk ass better make this count for making me wait this long to get some."

That's all I needed to hear. I had held back a little to give her pussy time to expand over my invading tool, but now I had to answer her challenge. I did so by driving my shaft to the hilt. As my pelvic bone collided with her soft butt cheeks, I felt the juices bursting from her tunnel of love. My dick expanded as I sped up my plunging in and out of her tight pussy. She jerked up straight on my pounding piston, and her back stiffened.

"Ahhh shit! "Oh my Gawd, boy! Ahhh!" she panted in a breathless voice as she collapsed on the floor.

When she made her descent, I followed her, ready to finish what she started and get my nut off. She rested her head against the carpet as I slid my hard beef pack up in her from behind. Each time I changed my stroking, she humped her ass against my middle leg and moaned over the long stroking I gave her. Suddenly she cocked her right leg up to her chest and cupped it with both arms while pushing her gaping slit onto my sawing girth.

"Fuck me, boo. Beat it up, boo. You better beat it up real good too!" She demanded that I stick it to her just like the first time we ever fucked.

I quickly took hold of her waist and pulled her down onto my up driving position. I went in and out, in and out like a giant javelin spearing an open hole in the earth.

"Ahhh…aaahhhh….yessss….baby…YESSS!" she shrieked and began throwing her silky, deep-red, tight pussy back on my mammoth pole, which seemed to fit perfectly in her sweet love box.

Sweet smells of sweat mixed with our lovemaking filled my nostrils. The moist sounds of our organs slapping and colliding overwhelmed me, making me go faster and faster. I looked down at her large ass cheeks spread and at the swollen pussy lips that looked like they were sucking my shaft inside her tight, wet love canal. As I leaned over my panting woman, digging my shaft in and out of her fleshy womb, I grasped her hips, pulling them back as I thrust my dick forward, sliding all of my love deep inside her.

"Ooooh, you big dick bastard…I'm…c-c-cuuuumminnnng, boy!" Her unrestrained howl of ecstasy sent a surge of primitive passion through my veins as I plowed my rod deeper into her contracting wet canyon of bliss.

"C-cum with me, boo!" she urged, bucking up and down, pressing her ass back against me, pushing my shaft even deeper inside her.

As her howls of joy echoed through the room of our love nest, neither of us made any pretense of restraint as I let the drink take over my fucking. I firmly held her hips and with each stroke, I slapped her ass hard as I could then withdrew my ramrod until only the head remained.

The juices of her orgasm flowed so freely down her thighs that my jeans were soaked, and the scent of it raised me to a new, even higher level of excitement. I paused for just a moment to enjoy the hot friction of our union.

As I relaxed my grip, she slid off my impaling dick in one quick, continuous movement. She rolled over onto her back, brought her knees up the her breasts, spread her legs far apart, and rhythmically raised and lowered her parted pussy lips in tune to my racing pulse.

"Mmm...." She licked her lips and ran her hands slowly down the insides of her widespread thighs to her drenched slit, which she spread open with her fingers.

Reacting instinctively off the Hennessey, I flung my frame on top of her and slammed my dick in to the base of her pussy. "Ahh, fuck," I groaned, slamming the dick in her harder and harder a few times before that oh-so-good feeling surged up through my balls. "You nasty...lil b-biiiiirrrgghhhh!" I groaned, feeling hot jets of semen surge from my dick as waves of orgasmic ecstasy hugged my body. With her legs wrapped around my waist and her arms around my neck, we fused into one as I emptied load after load into her hot, welcoming pussy.

"Ahh, baby...sssss...mmm, shit.... Gotdamn, you filling me up!" she huffed, shaking over my oozing and throbbing dick.

With each stroke, her legs clasped my waist even tighter and another load of hot semen exploded into her contracting love box. In my drunken daze, I pumped on, mostly from reflex, until I finally lay exhausted in her arms.

She rubbed the back of my head, kissing me tenderly all over my face as my flaccid dick drained dry in her horny hole. The last thing I felt before drifting off to La-La Land was Markita's tongue darting in and out of my mouth.

CHAPTER 86

The following day inside USP Terre Haute, Chin walked casually on five minute rec towards the gymnasium, where his Sahaba wanted to meet him. Chin had only come out the unit to meet him because he took the man to be a trustworthy guy - for an out of towner.

Chin passed through the metal detectors before entering the gym. After entering the gym, Chin saw the Detroit boss standing with another older-looking guy. Chin smiled as he walked over to the two men.

"As-Salaamu-Alaikum," Chin greeted the Detroit Boss with a smile and the Arabic greeting of "peace be upon you".

"Wa-Alaikum-As-Salaam-Rahman-Tuhallii-Wa Baraktu," He returned the greeting with one even better before giving Chin a manly hug.

"What's up, Ock?"

Even though nobody paid attention to the trio, the Detroit boss leaned in more out of the habit before speaking. "Ay, I got word on the wire about them rats. The obituaries flying in here to me any day now. Good work, my man…real good work. The money should touch down in a few minutes, but the reason I called you down here is 'cause I need another favor from you."

"Talk to me, Ock," Chin said, wondering why the older guy kept hanging around and looking at him funny.

The Detroit boss nodded his head towards the older guy. "This is my man Derrick Harper, one of the Harper Boys outta Riveria Beach, Florida. You know he wants to pay you fo' the same services you provided me with."

Chin nodded, his face tight and serious. "Sorry, Ock, I don't know what you talking about." Chin backed up and turned to leave the area.

The Detroit boss stopped Chin by grabbing his shoulder. "Listen, Ock, I would never put you out there like that."

"You already did, Big Boy," Chin said, turning to face him. "You better be glad you Muslim."

"C'mon, Ock, this a very good friend of mines, and I just thought you could use the money, you feel me?" he replied, trying not to dwell on the threat Chin had just thrown at him.

Chin looked the older guy up and down, taking in his laid-back, quiet demeanor. Chin figured the man had to be a stand-up guy to be hanging with his Sahaba, but Chin was still a little leery about the stranger. Still looking at the older guy, Chin said, "Yeah, I can always use the money. What you got in mind?"

"Give me a second and let me talk to him fo' you, a'ight," the Detroit boss said before stepping off and pulling the older guy to the side.

Once they were out of earshot of Chin, the Detroit boss explained to the Harper Boy that he would have to be the go-between on the murder for hire scheme.

"He wants fo' of 'em off the count. Here's all the info you need on them. He got a pot man and everything."

Chin looked at his Sahaba as he talked under his breath. When he finished, Chin locked eyes with him. "You know I did that for you on the strength. Now you got other Kafirs in my business?" Chin sighed, trying to contain his rage. "What the fuck is wrong with you, Ock?

"Chinchilla, c'mon, baby, I didn't know," the Detroit boss laughed nervously. "I'm sorry, baby."

"If I decide to do this, it's going to be very costly. I don't know if your man can pay - "

"Money ain't a thing, Ock," the Detroit boss said under his breath. "You'll see as soon as you return and check your account."

Chin nodded, his face creased into a smirk. "If things work out when I get back and check on that bread, I'll get in touch with my people, who hafta get in touch with they people. I'm not making any promises though, but if it's a go, I'm going to need half the cash up front, non-refundable. When the job's complete, get the other half to me on the wire transfer ASAP."

"I gotcha, Ock," he replied as Chin walked over to the handball court.

Chin waved the Detroit boss over. "Since you got me stuck down here fo' a whole hour, you might as well play some handball."

As Chin and the Detroit boss got sweaty during a game of handball, Derrick Harper looked on in disgust. He felt disrespected that the bin Laden-looking Muslim didn't acknowledge him for the boss he was in his town in Florida and all over the penal system. After giving it some thought, Derrick Harper realized that the man was only being cautious. He just hoped the man could deliver death from prison like the Detroit boss had been bragging about over the. last two days

CHAPTER 87

It was a little after noon by the time I woke up and looked at the clock. I worried that I should have risen earlier to stand guard and protect my family instead of leaving them on their own while I slept. I wouldn't have been the least bit surprised if the person who wanted to avenge Twan's death had stormed right inside my house and killed my girl and son.

I sat up in bed still fully clothed from last night, waiting for Markita to appear. I listened to silence and became acutely aware of the sounds of it. I heard the air streaming through the vents of the central air system, the faint clicking of the number rolling on the clock, and my own breathing.

I went through the routine of checking my cell phone messages, annoyed by hang-ups. There were a few of them, plus two calls from Swol's phone number and two from an unavailable number. I heard a car door shut outside my bedroom window and got my Glock 40 out of a drawer by the bed and rushed to the window to see the cause of the noise.

When I looked out the window, the little white kid who delivered the daily newspaper at this time every day was peddling away on his yellow and red mountain bike as Gambles' crooked ass picked up the newspaper and rang the doorbell. I couldn't stand the way this crooked cop invaded my privacy, but he did serve a purpose by keeping the phantom killer at bay who wanted my head on a silver platter.

I rushed from my room and down to the front door as Gamble hit the doorbell again. I got my Glock in my waistband and turned the doorknob as Markita appeared, holding my son.

"That's the same police guy?"

I nodded and opened the door for Gamble. Something about Gamble's devious smile had an effect me.

"The paper's late, Mr. Glover," he said. "Real late, just like you'll find yourself if you don't take care of our little arrangement."

"What the fuck is wrong with you, man? There's nothing else better for you to do then harass me?

"Ah…nope, there really isn't." He laughed as his eyes roamed curiously around the hallway and foyer of my home.

"Please just give me some time with my family."

"Did you give that guy in Barry Farms some time with his family when you roasted him on an open fire?" he hissed, bringing up the murder of a rat I had burned alive over two years ago. "Naw, buddy, I believe your time has run out, especially after you pulled your fancy slick-talking lawyer into what we had going on." His demeanor tightened a bit.

This crooked bastard reminded me of Hunter. It was the eyes, the pupils of fear that hid behind the power of his police badge. I stood in the foyer looking at Gamble like he had lost his mind.

"You are aware that you are on private property and a long way from your jurisdiction. By law, I could get away with murder right now," I whispered, and apparently my threat hit home.

Gamble cleared his throat and backed up a little. "I'm going to head back out to the car to wait on you, Mr. Glover. I have all the time in the world, Mr. Glover," he replied with an ironic smile. "Oh, and do yourself a favor. Just stay in the house if you don't want a police escort to shadow your every move." He winked at me and backpedaled to his car.

I slammed the front door as a sudden headache came on and began boxing with my brain.

"What gives him the right to keep messing with you?" Markita asked.

"Just be glad it was him and not that guy that approached you and the baby the other day."

"That's not funny, Melo."

"Do it look like I'm laughing? I'm just saying… I'ma go call the lawyer guy and ask him why they keep on harassing me," I said, already knowing the answer.

I walked into my office and sat down at my desk. I ignored Markita standing on the threshold hawking me. I decided the time had come to set up an escape from my own home. I pulled out my cell phone and sent Swol a text message.

Hold up Swol Up,

I'm in serious trouble. Need U in a major way! Remember where I live—meet me in the next block over at 3:30. Park on the back street facing the back of my house. I'll tell you everything in the car. If you can't make it call me. Otherwise, I'll see you then.

-Carmelo-

Then I made a fake call to my lawyer for Markita's ears only. "Hello? Yeah, this cop is at my fucking house. No…no, you don't understand. I'm the one being harassed here, not you. What am I paying you for?" I said and hung up on the computer-generated female that told the time and weather in a dramatic fashion to appease Markita. "That's a done deal." I said smiling at Markita. "That should get some results, huh? What you think?"

"I think your ass is hiding something, that's what I think. Hopefully whatever it is won't destroy our relationship and all the trust I have in you," she said. She shook her head and walked away carrying my son.

As soon as they disappeared from sight, I rushed upstairs to take a quick shower and prepare for my rendezvous with Swol.

CHAPTER 88

Swol met me on the cul-de-sac behind my house as planned, and I got in his monster Dodge Ram SRT pickup truck and looked back to see if he'd been followed. I had grabbed a few guns and the bag of kilos and snuck out the back door. I didn't want to take the chance that Gamble might return and want to arrest me again. It was cool and breezy out, but the sun beamed down on us, trying to warm the Metropolitan area.

When I got in the quad cab, Swol began backing up and I could smell the showroom floor smell inside the ride. Before I could ask him about the truck, he gave me a funny look. "Slim, where the fuck is my car at?"

Before I could answer him, I spotted Gamble's unmarked Crown Victoria turning wildly onto the quiet cul-de-sac.

Several minutes earlier, Detective Gamble had been taking a nap when his partner, Newsome, slapped his thigh, waking him. Gamble pulled out his service Glock, looking around wildly.

"Wha-what?"

"Our guy's on the move," Detective Newsome said, pointing at the computer monitor mounted on the dashboard.

Gamble adjusted his eyes and focused on the blinking red dot that told them the whereabouts of Carmelo Glover's cell phone. Both detectives' eyes followed the blinking red dot as it moved to the next street over, a quiet cul-de-sac in the area where upper middle class families lived and a place detectives didn't expect to find the red dot moving.

"Let's hit it. Go, go, go!" Gamble slapped the dashboard as Newsome started the car and sped off to catch the man who could erase all of their problems with one shot - one kill.

As the Crown Victoria sped towards us, I looked at Swol and said, "Go through dem bitch-ass niggas, Slim. Go, go, go, go!"

"Hold on!" Swol said, and he didn't hesitate to floor the pickup truck in a peal of rubber.

My back slammed into the bucket seat and got stuck there like a magnet as Swol pressed the accelerator against the floor, making the truck roar down the street. Gamble's police car headed straight for us, but Swol accelerated more, playing a deadly game of chicken.

"Slim, wha-what you doing?" I asked as we got closer and closer to final impact. My heart had dropped to the seat of my pants.

"I'm going through 'em like you said," Swol said, gritting his teeth and then hunkered over the steering wheel as he sped towards the white Crown Vic. "C'mon! C'mon!" he growled.

Through the windshield, I could see the white car speeding right for us. I paused to silently pray to God and brace myself for final impact.

10…9…8…7…6…

I counted down in my head, looking at Swol and then back at the speeding car directly in front us. I closed my eyes, hoping that I would survive the crash.

5…4…3…2…

CHAPTER 89

At the last second, I heard Swol yelling. I opened my eyes just in time to see Gamble's car veering away from Swol's speeding pickup.

"Aaaahhhh yeah!" I yelled triumphantly as we shot past the Crown Victoria.

Then the next thing I know, I heard the crack of rapid gunshot. I ducked instinctively as a few bullets dinged the Dodge Ram's metal armor. I stared in the rearview mirror on the passenger side and saw the white car making a dangerous U-turn.

"They coming for us, Slim," I alerted Swol as he sped down the street.

A stop sign stood at the end of the street, but Swol kept on speeding and took the turn hard, nearly crashing into a Alexandria police cruiser.

Somebody must have called the police on us, I thought as the police car honked at us and slammed on the brakes. I knew the development like the back of my hand. There were a lot of curving streets and cul-de-sacs and circles that would get you caught up with no place to go if you made the wrong turn.

"Take this street right here. Go, go, go!" I pointed down the long street, seeing the police car and Gamble's white car closing in on us.

I wanted to tell Swol to stop so I could explain everything to the Alexandria cop, but there we had enough drugs and guns in the truck to get a million year in ADX Federal Super Maximum Security penitentiary.

The police cruiser came close behind us. Swol swerved in front of the car as Gamble's car revved up behind the cop's car.

I can't believe this shit. How did Gamble get on me so fast? I wondered as Swol gunned the engine and arched away from the curb as Gamble's car revved and caught up to the police cruiser.

I saw Gamble's car swerve in front of the police cruiser. Then Gamble leaned out the window and pumped several shots at us.

"Motherfucker!" I yelled, hunkering down as low as possible as Swol accelerated the powerful engine.

"Turn here! Turn here!" I directed, looking back quickly as Swol slammed hard into a left turn and I saw the police cruiser car screech to a stop. The officer jumped out of the cruiser and aimed a camera at Gamble's car.

By the time he jumped back in his car, Swol had made another quick turn. Gamble stayed close on our tail. I knew we couldn't outrun him on these suburban streets. The road curved, dead ending, and Swol took the turn hard enough that I felt the pickup truck wheel lift up and crash back to the ground. We faced another cul-de-sac of new houses being built. One was finished, the other four in various stages of completion, one bricked, two more framed, and the other just a foundation waiting for wooden bones.

"Where to, my nig?" Swol asked just as more gunshots rang out in the back window.

He peeled past one of the houses being framed - a driveway had already been poured, circling back inside a side entry garage that was nothing but concrete and lumber. Swol drove off the driveway to flat dirt and veered hard past the skeletal houses.

Why is Gamble shooting at me if he wants me to kill for him? I wondered as Swol leaned into a hard turn.

As we drove through a minor smoke cloud, I prayed that the tires wouldn't puncture on a stray nail. A flat tire would definitely mean the end of the road. I saw Gamble's car drop back, unable to handle the ridges of dirt terrain at the same speed. Swol drove his ass off and roared onto the main road.

"That's right, Slim. Drive dis ma'fucka. Drive, nigga, drive!" I yelled excitedly, looking in the rearview mirror.

I saw Gamble's car rocketing onto the cleared land as we sped on and began to slope down. We were speeding towards a head-on collision with a fence of strung wires.

"Hang on, Champ!" Swol warned me as he floored the truck up to 95 mph and hit the fence hard.

CHAPTER 90

The Dodge pickup tore through the wire fence, pulling posts from the earth, and one of them rammed against the passenger door like a fist.

"Damn!" I flinched after the impact as wire scoured the paint off the hood.

A post clobbered the front windshield into a web of shattered glass. The pickup spun out and Swol floored it again, trying to regain speed. In the rearview mirror, I saw Gamble's Crown Victoria gliding through the gap Swol had just made in the fence.

"You's a driving ma'fucka, Slim!" I praised Swol as he sped up a gentle incline that led to a large heavily-trafficked road.

Two lanes were divided by a thick white construction cement barricade. Traffic looked to be humming at a fifty miles per hour clip. Swol began hitting the horn, trying to time the cut across the highway. He swerved a bit to the left, trying to give a champagne-hued Cadillac Escalade room to get ahead of us and open a small break in traffic.

Swol nearly made it.

The Dodge SRT exploded across the northbound lanes, aiming for the direction of D.C. just ahead of a minivan. Swol and I didn't see the blue pickup truck powering past the minivan on the outside lane. As soon as we made it across, the pickup clipped the back left bumper of our Dodge SRT.

The SRT began spinning and Swol fought hard for control to keep from spinning back onto the highway and back into the path of traffic. He wrenched the steering wheel with both hands. He managed to get the pickup back under control and barreled forward.

My heart jammed in my mouth as I looked back and saw the blue pickup complete its own spin, causing traffic to suddenly slow down, cars braking and horns blaring repeatedly. The driver of the pickup was an older white man who looked frightened when I saw his face - frightened but unhurt. I glanced back again and saw Gamble's Crown Vic dodging most of the traffic. I looked back as Gamble's car tried to close in on us.

"Push the ma'fucka, Slim! He's on us! He's on us!" I yelled, feeling the SRT rattle like it was shaking apart as Swol regained speed.

The rearview mirror showed that Gamble's car wasn't chasing us in a straight line. He drove along the highway's shoulder and then cut across at an angle, drawing closer. Half a mile shot by and then another mile. Swol wheeled towards the Pentagon City Mall exit on my right, zipping past three lanes of traffic.

"Fuck is you doing?" I asked, hearing the sounds of angry commuters honking their horns at us I looked back again. I could see Gamble's car moving like an express train, surging towards is.

"Not getting caught," Swol replied before veering over into the last lane before the exit, narrowly missing a sleek metallic-gray BMW with a silver-haired lady driving it.

She cut us a diamond-studded finger as Swol straightened the truck. I glanced back and saw Gamble's car swerving, looking for an opening, a few car lengths behind us.

"Go! Go! Go!" I yelled as Swol punched the accelerator. But the SRT responded with a grind and jerk like a runner hobbling from injuries.

As we sped toward the highway exit for the mall, I saw the Macy's department store on the horizon and the massive parking lot and four-story parking garage. Swol shoved his way onto the shoulder of the highway, honking a clear path to the right. I saw Gamble trying to cut over to nail us before we made the exit. Two seconds later, we collided and slid into each other.

I looked down, seeing the crooked detectives' faces. They seemed etched with fury, hatred, and determination as they tried to run us off the road. Swol wrenched left and then back to the right, sliding into the exit ramp, and made Gamble's car overshoot the exit. As I watched the white car crash into the huge round yellow water-filled rubber barricades near the exit ramp, Swol made the truck limp down the incline and jetted up a parked row of cars. Suddenly a front tire blew out and the rim started working toward the pavement. Swol pushed the crippled pickup another fifty feet or so.

After we jumped out of the truck, I began scanning the parking lot for any signs of Gamble's car. I tossed Swol the bag with the drugs inside and peeked over a parked car. I saw Gamble's car speeding around the same stop sign that Swol just ran through. His car came speeding into the parking lot, five rows over from where we hid. As he drove toward the mall entrance looking for me, I gave Swol a nod.

"We hafta split up, Moe. Just take the bag and get paid and I'll see you later or whenever!" I told Swol, figuring it would give us a better chance to lose Gamble and his crooked partner inside the mall.

Swol nodded and got low to the ground and ran. He bent close to the ground, hugging the bag like a football. As Swol made it safely inside the mall, I saw Gamble's Crown Vic come to a stop.

I stood up in plain view so Gamble and his partner could see me. I waited about ten seconds before taking off running for the side entrance. I did that to take the heat off Swol. I looked back and saw Gamble and his partner leaping out of their cars. I saw them walking fast, following me with purpose.

As my gaze locked in on Gamble, he smiled as if he was enjoying this cat and mouse chase. That's when I realized that I'd never be able to shake these crooked cops unless they were buried six feet deep.

CHAPTER 91

After entering the mall, I hurried through the thickening crowds. A pair of mimes with white-painted faces performed in one of the intersections. As people stopped to watch the juggling, which involved bowling pins, bowling balls, and shiny machetes, I veered toward the Macy's department store. I hoped that the store would be crowded enough with shoppers to help me hide from Gamble's hot pursuit.

"Hey! Watch it, why don't cha!" an older woman told me as I bumped into her. She carried Hecht's and Macy's shopping bags and gave me a funny look.

"Sorry, Miss, my bad. I'm kinda in a rush." I gave her a half smile and a nod as I rushed past her.

I glanced back and saw Gamble and his partner keeping their pace, not worrying about Swol's location.

I hope Swol got ghost, I told myself as I speed-walked, creating more distance between me and Gamble.

I went into Macy's, past a young Chinese woman handing out lipstick samples and past several glass display cases filled with the latest electronic gadgets, cell phones, and digital cameras. I dodged mothers pushing strollers, couples walking hand-in-hand, and a trio of homosexual men searching for the female underwear section.

Good move. I should be about to duck these ma'fuckas in here with all these people in here, I thought before jumping on the escalator.

I jogged past the standing riders. I turned and saw Gamble and his partner in casual pursuit like they'd find me wherever I chose to go. I jumped off the escalator and ran around, taking the next escalator to the third floor. Once I got up there, I took a hard right through housewares and furniture, which provided the perfect cover.

The merchandise hung on walls and stood close together like created bedrooms, living rooms, and dens. I figured the area provided enough cover to hide from Gamble and his partner Newsome. The only thing was that fewer customers hung in this section.

I lay down and began crawling behind a minimalist Asian sofa with red silk pillows and Chinese characters and temples sewn all over the couch in black and gold thread. Flowers sat in large jade vases on each end of the sofa. I lay behind the sofa motionless and waited.

When I saw Gamble and his partner run past, trying to locate me, I jumped up and rushed away from them in the opposite direction in a cab run, bent low behind the furniture and walls. I pulled out my compact suppressor .45 and prepared my great escape.I knew shooting off the gun in there would startle many people. I'd just to take my chances and fire two shots in the air and try to escape from the soon-to-be panicked room. As I rushed towards the escalator, I glanced back and saw Gamble turning suddenly.

"Hey!" he shouted as I aimed the gun at the ceiling and squeezed the trigger twice.

I took off bolting down the escalator as screaming and chaos ensued all around me. As soon as I made it out of the department store, I saw mall security running towards the store. I slipped off into the crowd, keeping my head low until I reached a door marked "Employees Only". I checked it, and surprisingly, it wasn't locked. As I went through, I heard a woman yelling behind me. I bolted down a long corridor leading off to an empty break room and a much larger back stock area. I found a freight elevator and hit the button.

The wait for the elevator seemed to take forever but it arrived in a matter of minutes. I got on the elevator and pressed myself against the wall. As the noisy elevator sluggishly made its distance, a million thoughts ran through my mind, but the main thought was finding an exit and getting away.

The elevator chimed its arrival. The cargo-wide doors slid open like a slowly drawn curtain. I hurried out the cargo bay exit and jumped down to the parking lot. I looked around and saw nobody following me. I ran fast; remaining free drove me like an engine. I reached a stretch of parking lot that had arrows directing me to the nearest Metro subway station.

I followed the arrows, keeping my head low. Hope filled me as I reached the coolness of the underground subway station. Seeing the train pulling into the dock gave me energy and fueled my desire to escape like long, dry tinder exploding into flame. When I hopped the electrical turnstile, I heard someone yelling for me to stop. I didn't stop at all out of nervousness and fear of getting caught. I took the downward escalator three steps at a time.

Thoughts of being caught up in Virginia for shooting up a man made me hurdle a little blond kid at the bottom of the escalator and tumble roll inside the subway a second before the doors close. Twenty seconds later, the subway pulled off, plunging the outside windows in darkness. After another minute or so, I breathed a sigh of relief. Escape was escape. As I road in silence, I imagined Gamble's face gaping in hot and fierce anger and disappointment.

The triumphant smile tattooed on my face felt good and made me really appreciate my great escape from the long arms of the crooked law, but now I was officially on the run.

The adrenaline had me angry and scared like shit by the time I made it to D.C., but I couldn't let that stop me from what I needed to do. I had to check something out, and it couldn't wait another minute.

I walked from U Street's Metro station to First Street where I grew up -my old stomping grounds. It took me roughly ten minutes to reach my destination on Flagler Street. The four-story house with manicured front lawn and chipped and cracking blue and white paint hadn't changed one bit since the last time I had been here with Twan.

I walked up to the front door and knocked. Ten seconds later, Twan's mother answered the door, wearing an all-white cooking apron with huge red letters that told the world: #1 Mom in the Kitchen Burning. She had on some worn, dingy white house slippers and a baggy pink sweat suit. Her sweet Big Mama aura and demeanor were just as I remembered her.

After she opened the screen door, recognition registered on her face. She smiled and gave me a warm, affectionate hug. "My, my, my…boy, look at you!" she said excitedly. "C'mon in here right now. I know you hungry. I got some taters, collard greens, and smothered pork chops in gravy about to come out the oven right now."

That's why I could never play the game like somebody was playing with my wife and kid. I felt that some lines shouldn't be allowed to be crossed under no circumstance when you beefing, but that's just me. I felt sick to my stomach even being there like this. I just stood there looking at her, feeling a little sad that I took her son away from her. I didn't feel bad about getting revenge on a rat who took away a large part of my life. I felt bad about robbing a mother of her chance to love her son

"Naw, I can't come in right now, Ms. Vernie. I'm sorta in a rush. Is your daughter home?"

"Baby, that chile has gon' on home to the Lord. She's been gone a little over six years now."

Damn, I ain't know that. So if it ain't her, then who would seek revenge on me? Twan ain't have no brothers. Could it be one of his men? I thought and quickly got my answer.

"Yep, all I have left of that chile are memories and her bad-ass son that I'm trying to keep outta the streets."

A son? Twan's nephew? Could he be the one? But how did he find out that I crushed Twan? Damn, that letter I wrote Ms. Vernie while I was in prison, he probably got his own conclusion from that, I told myself. I asked her, "How old is he?"

"Seventeen. He's just a baby that needs a little guidance."

Straight into a casket, I thought and quietly backed out of the foyer. "Well, it's been a pleasure, Ms. Vernie," I said before digging in my pocket. I pulled out my bankroll, peeled off a few hundred, and gave it to her. I felt like I owed it to her for some reason.

"What's all this for, baby?" Mama Vernie asked, making the money disappear under her cooking apron near her huge breasts. She probably stashed the cash away in her bra like many older women did back in the day when they came to buy crack from me.

"For remaining strong through all the pain and losses you've been through. Oh, and tell your nephew that I'd be willing to change his life around if he ever wants to talk to me face to face." From living to deceased, I thought while heading down the concrete steps.

"I will, baby…I sure will!" You be good now, you hear!" she called out and waved to me as I walked down the block.

I needed to find Twan's nephew quick, fast, and in a hurry so I could clean his ass up for the stunt he pulled on my family and the way he left the picture on my door. I overlooked the two attempts he made on my life, 'cause he was only doing what he felt he had to do, but bringing my family into the equation catapulted this into something far more deadly and totally uncalled for.

No more thinking needed to be done. Twan's nephew wanted me dead, I'm sure of that now. And even if he didn't mean no harm, he still got the beef. There would be no more looking over my shoulders or worrying about some creep like him ambushing me or approaching my family in a threatening manner. No more phantom stalker or ugly past bullshit. His hand had just been exposed.

By leaving him a message, I felt like that would give him a taste of his own medicine and hopefully intimidate him. Even though I'd never harm one strand on Twan's mother's head, the little creep didn't know that. I wanted him to experience the same fear and mixed emotions that I felt when I found out about how he came at my family.

I was still fucked up mentally about it all and I didn't think I'd ever be at peace with myself if I didn't send him to hang out with his dead mother and uncle.

CHAPTER 93

After leaving Mama Vernie's house, I walked down Flagler Street and then turned on First Street. The first thing that caught my eye when I got close to U Street was the sleek Lexus cruising up the street. I had been thinking about getting one of them before all this madness had upended my life. The car reminded me of happier times when I had a simple life.

Then the car suddenly threw me off - well, the driver did when he began mean mugging on me as I made the turn on U Street. I looked on the block and noticed a small crowd of guys gathered around a dark station wagon. I glanced back and saw the Lexus making a quick U-Turn.

I began speed-walking up U Street until I reached the crack house where I killed Twan over two years ago. I thought the paranoia had gotten the best of me until I saw the Lexus turning on U Street in a fast motion. I pulled out my .45 suppressor, eased it down by my leg, and turned on the Lexus ready, to Swiss cheese the sleek automobile. As I locked eyes with the driver again, he smiled. I relaxed, not taking the driver as a threat, but then he jumped out of the car and started shooting at me.

Blat-tat-tat-tat…blat-tat-tat-tat! The deadly sounds of his continuous shooting rang out. I was a sitting duck, but I refused to die this way.

"You tryna kill me for your hot-ass uncle, huh! Fuck that bitch-ass nigga! He deserved everything he got!" I yelled over the loud sounds of rapid gunfire and then I went to work.

Everything that'd been affecting my life and making me frustrated was unleashed in my actions. I wasn't thinking clearly and I let my emotions carry me into battle. I leaned around the side of the Bronco and let the cannon loose on Twan's nephew from about thirty yards away. I felt like a cowboy in the old West at a high noon deadly shoot-out.

Remembering the Teflon body armor I wore like a second skin, I raised up in plain view, getting some Superman heart. I spotted him ducking as I leaned over the hood of the Bronco and fired until the .45 emptied. As soon as it did, more shots came from his fully-automatic weapon.

I had to tread lightly because the gun battle wasn't in my favor. I had to make him come to me so I could eliminate him. His sudden move threw me off track, and honestly, he had me because he struck hard and fast. But he made the mistake of giving me the chance to recover, so I used my instincts to regain balance and an advantage in this deadly gunfight. I stuffed the warm .45 in my front pocket and pulled out the Glock 40 from my waist as I heard bullets chiming and dinging the metal armor of the Bronco that I hid behind.

Damn, this young nigga ain't bullshittin', I thought as more gunfire erupted from behind me. I really got low, thinking he had someone helping him to end my days of living. I flinched and looked back up the street through the back windows of the Bronco.

I saw Lil Wee Wee, his man Leo, and none other than big homie Titus in the flesh taking up positions on the block and firing non-stop at Twan's nephew. Seeing the back-up come to my rescue, I felt bold enough to run out into the street and fire down on the Lexus.

As he jumped back in the Lexus, he threw a few retreating shots my way, giving himself cover. As he backed the Lexus all the way down U Street, peeling rubber, I ran after him shooting in the middle of the street.

"Moe, I'm outta here!" I heard Leo saying before breaking into a wind sprint through the nearest alley.

I jogged back up the street to where Titus and Lil Wee Wee stood waiting on me. I looked around and saw nobody on the ground bleeding from the gun battle, so I figured that nobody got hit, which surprised the hell out of me. We just had a mini gun battle out here in broad daylight like we were working in the climax of the movie Heat.

"Moe, who the fuck was that?" Lil Wee Wee asked me.

"Somebody that ain't bullshittin', that's who!" Titus blurted, saving me from telling them.

I really didn't want to say a word because I didn't know how they'd react about Mama Vernie's grandson shooting up the block. Everybody loved her and she was considered family to all, but when guys violated, some guys went to the extreme to get revenge and I just didn't want Mama Verne to be in harm's way

"Man, I'm gone. I know them peoples on the way," Lil Wee Wee said as he jogged over to his SUV.

I saw Titus running over to his Cadillac DTS and I followed him. As soon as he jumped inside the car, he hit the automatic locks for me so I could get in the passenger seat.

"Fuck you doing over here bullshittin'?" Titus asked as he sped over to North Capitol Street before the cops could swarm the area.

As Titus made a right turn and sped to only God knows where, I began running the whole story down to him, starting from the night I smoked Twan. As I explained everything to him, I made it a point to leave out Mama Vernie and what I suspected to be the truth about Twan's nephew wanting to kill me.

Titus looked back and forth at the road and me as he drove and listened. I finished up the story to the point where he along with two of the younger homies had to save my ass from Twan's nephew.

CHAPTER 94

When Titus pulled up around Trinidad, he parked on the corner on Montello and Oaks Streets. After he parked, I stared ahead vacantly, worrying about Markita and my son. I pulled out my phone to call Markita and saw that I had an email from Chin. I ignored it, but made a mental note to check it out later as soon as I got Markita out of that house.

"You straight, young nigga?' Titus asked in a joking manner.

He always had an easy going joking demeanor that could change in the blink of an eye. Titus could kill at any given moment and laugh about it seconds later. To people unfamiliar with him, Titus appeared to be very mysterious and hard to figure out. To people cool with him, he'd go to war with them against the Devil in the pits of hell rocking gasoline underwear. He told me that he had only been out of prison a few days and he didn't hesitate to jump into a shoot-out to save my ass.

"Yeah, I'm cool."

"A'ight, well sit tight then while I go holla at my man right quick," he said as he got out of the car.

After he got out, I shifted into total concern mode. I called Markita, but got no answer. My heart began beating hard in my chest as I hung up and tried to call her again. She still didn't answer.

Where the fuck is she at? Please God, don't do this to me. She don't have nothing to do with nothing, I thought while trying to reach her again. This time she answered on the fourth ring.

"Hello."

Thank you, God…thank You, I thought, sighing with relief after hearing her voice. "Kita, listen to me. Baby, I need for you to stop whatever you're doing, pack up a few things, and go to your Mom's house right now."

"Why, what's wrong?"

"Don't ask no questions right now. Just go."

"No. No, Melo, not until you tell me why I have to wake up the baby and leave our home," she rebelled, making me mad.

"So you won't die with your stubborn ass! Now get ready and take your ass over there!" I yelled and hung up on her. Two seconds later, my phone rang. Already knowing the caller without looking at my phone, I answered on the third ring.

"Yeah, talk to me."

"Who the fuck do you think you are? Just for talking slick to me like that, I ain't going no-motherfuckin'-where. Kiss my ass!" she said and hung up on me.

I tried to contact Markita after that, but she wouldn't answer the phone. This bitch is lunchin' good when I'm tryna save her ass, I thought and called Kisha.

When she answered, I began talking fast. "Kisha, get in touch with Tiny real fast and get over to my house and check on Kita ASAP."

"Whoa, whoa, whoa… Slow down and tell me what's going on."

"Now is not the time. I really need your help here, Kisha. Please just do that for me. I gotta go," I said and hung up.

I closed my eyes and began asking God to protect my girlfriend and child from whatever evil plans Twan's nephew might have in store for them.

CHAPTER 95

Out on the corner of Montello and Oaks Street, Titus walked up on Jawbreaker and D.C. while they loitered outside, holding up a wall near the corner store. After giving both men manly hugs, D.C. asked Titus who he had riding with him in the car.

"That's my lil homie from down First. Slim was locked up with me out Marion a few years ago."

"Slim looks like that book nigga who be hustling down at the Goodman," D.C. said with a light chuckle. "You know, I had to get Brian to get Slim outta some shit the other day."

"Young nigga was official and ain't going for nothing. You know how we breed 'em down on First," Titus bragged, stamping Carmelo's pedigree to the two cold-hearted killers.

"How long you been home?" Jawbreaker asked.

"About a week and some change."

"And you just coming through to holla at a nigga?" Jawbreaker and D.C. exclaimed in unison.

"I had to get my daughter and work some shit out with her. You know how it go. Family first. But what's up though?"

"We 'bout to go check on this move," D.C. said.

"What's up?" Titus pressed, letting them know he was down for whatever.

"Shit might be sweet; just follow us," Jawbreaker said.

"What's up, Slim, fuck?" Titus snapped, not wanting to go in blind on the move.

"A'ight look...." Jawbreaker said and filled Titus in on the victim they wanted to rob, who turned out to be Vincent from Uptown.

As Jawbreaker talked, Titus learned that Vincent used to be getting money uptown with Fat Man up on Clifton Street.

"After Fat Man went to jail, rumorville got it that he snitched on Slim. The nigga went into hiding after the trial. He didn't turn on nobody's radar until I was over at this little broad's house in Landover one day chilling and seen the nigga. I just thought he was a Maryland bama until my bitch began hollering out the window at him and his girl. I just laid back and listened while she talked to Vincent and his girl. When I told D.C. about the move, he hipped me to the nigga being a rat. His real name is Safari Washington, but everybody in the city knows him as Vincent. I been laying on 'em ever since. It's been about two weeks now."

"Slim fucking with that cheese, huh?" Titus asked.

"Hell yeah, he loves it. You know I fucks with Fat Man, and he told me everything about that nigga," D.C. said.

"A'ight, let's go," Titus said.

"You taking the Librarian with you?" D.C. laughed at his own joke. "He should be down at Goodman, selling them weak-ass urban novels."

"You fucked up, Slim," Titus said while laughing at D.C's joke.

After the laughter died down, Jawbreaker told Titus to follow him.

"Where to?" Titus asked.

"I'ma take D.C. down his mother's joint so he can grab a few things and then we out."

"I'ma wait up here in the car, 'cause I hafta put young'in on point. After y'all handle y'all business, just come up here get me." Titus headed back to the car to put Carmelo on point about the move they were about to go on.

CHAPTER 96

When we got out to Landover, Maryland, I noticed a silver Maserati parked in the driveway of the huge house we planned on raiding. Titus explained to me all the intricacies of the move and I just went along for the ride to take my mind off Markita and the way she was acting.

I watched as Zetta's uncle D.C. climbed out the passenger side of a burgundy Nissan 350ZX and walked over to the driver's side to talk to his co-conspirator. All the huge houses lining the block looked like something you'd see on the front cover of a Home & Garden magazine. I even saw a red pull wagon and yellow and black painted motorized go-cart sitting in a neatly-trimmed front lawn.

"I hope this nigga got some cake, 'cause I really need a payday bad. I want to buy my lil grandson some shit and my lunchin'-ass daughter some shit too," Titus remarked, keeping his eyes on D.C. and the silver Maserati.

After hearing his statement, we waited for like twenty more minutes to peep out the area and see what was going on before heading to the side of the house. Several seconds later, the victim exited the house, styling in a custom gray suit and green apple-hued Gators. As he made the trek to his car, he began patting his pockets as if he forgot something. When he turned to head back inside his house, I spotted D.C. running down on him with his gun drawn.

As soon as Vincent reached his front door, D.C. got the jump on him. He jammed the gun in Vincent's ribs and walked him back inside the house without making a scene. After ushering the rat back inside, D.C. released an owl call. When Jawbreaker heard the signal, he bolted from the driver's cockpit of the 350ZX and rushed towards the house. Before he crossed the threshold, Jawbreaker looked back at Titus and nodded, signaling him to follow.

By the time Titus and I entered the house, D.C. had the vic's face on the floor turned away from us. He passed Jawbreaker a rusty chrome gun with an extended clip.

"I got dat up off him after laying him down," D.C. said, then he looked at me in a funny way.

At that moment, I realized that I had made a grave mistake underestimating Zetta's uncle. The older mild-mannered looking guy definitely had me fooled until today. Seeing him in action made me really believe in the saying: looks can be very deceiving!

"Somebody grab some telephone wires so we can tie dis nigga up." D.C. and I rushed off to find something to restrain him.

I looked around in the kitchen first and spotted two cooking mittens, the kind you wear to keep from getting burned while carrying a hot cooking pot or pan. I put them on immediately and began checking all the drawers and cabinets for some duct tape. When I found none, I settled for the telephone wire. It took me a good five minutes to gather up all the telephone wire and a pillowcase from the bedroom and to restrain the victim to a kitchen chair with the pillowcase covering his head. I stood behind him just in case he could see through the pillowcase covering his head. I didn't know if these guys were going to kill him or what and I just didn't want to take the chance of him recognizing me.

"Look, Slim, you ain't seen none of our faces, so just let us get that and you won't hafta worry about me killing you," Jawbreaker said, making me look at him and then throw a crazy look at Titus like he'd lost his mind.

I know these niggas ain't really gon' let this nigga live, I thought as Jawbreaker continued his spiel.

"Just give dat bread up and we gon' let you live to make some more. Money comes and goes, but you only get one life."

After several silent minutes passed, the victim spoke, "It's in the bedroom closet, under the carpet all the way in the back. It's a few bricks in there and $120,000."

"That's it?" Jawbreaker asked calmly.

"That's it, man, I swear," I heard the victim saying. Titus and I were already moving to check out the victim's confession.

CHAPTER 97

After finding everything in the closet, I found a silver aluminum baseball bat. I looked at Titus and smiled. He gave me a funny look as we emerged from the closet with the goods.

"What's up?"

"That nigga in here lying, T. He gave up his stash too quick. I know he got some more cake in here somewhere. This little shit might just be his throwaway stash."

"How you gon' get him to tell you about the other so-called stash?"

"Just watch my work." I winked and swung the bat so hard through the air that it began whistling while slicing through the airwaves.

"I'ma bag this shit up while you go do what you do," he said as I left the bedroom to indulge in a little practice.

"What's up, Slim? Everything cool?" Jawbreaker asked me as I entered the kitchen with an angry look on my face.

"Naw, this bitch-ass nigga lying," I stated. I touched the victim's left kneecap gently with the tip of the bat two times before reeling back. "Nigga, give dat shit up!" I said and swung the bat with all my might.

"Aaaaaaaaiiiiiiie !Aaaaaahhhhh!" He hollered bloody murder after the bat shattered his kneecap. "Man, I sw-swear to God…that's….that's everything…I swear!"

"Don't lie to me!" I yelled. "Don't you lie to me! You gave that shit up too quick! Ain't no nigger doing no shit like that unless he got a back-up plan or more shit to hide!"

"Man, I swear, I got so - "

I swung the bat again, cutting him off with a direct hit to his right knee.

"Aaaaaahhhhhh, you motherfucker! I'm telling the truth…I'm telling the truth! Okay, okay, I got some bread out in the streets that a few niggas owe me, but that's all man, I swear. You got everything. You got everything," Vincent cried and Jawbreaker believed him. He tapped D.C., signaling that the time had arrived for them to depart the house.

"Let 'em live, Slim, he ain't gon' hold back after that. Ain't no nigga gon' hold back no shit like that," Jawbreaker said as Titus appeared clutching two pillowcases.

Titus looked at Jawbreaker and gave him a nod. "He wasn't lying, Slim. Everything's in here," he said, holding up the red pillowcases.

"Your little Librarian be lunchin out like shit, Slim," D.C. joked as he headed to the front door with Jawbreaker.

As Titus followed them, I looked back at the injured victim and didn't want to leave him alive. Going against my gut instincts, I reluctantly followed the trio to the front door.

Before they left the house, D.C. turned and asked the victim, "Ay, don't you know Fat Man who be Uptown on Clifton?"

D.C's question chilled Vincent to the bone and he instantly knew that this wasn't an ordinary home invasion. He still tried to lie his way out of the situation, hoping for the best.

"Naw…naw, I don't, Slim."

"Stop lying, you hot-ass nigga!" D.C. said as he rushed back over to the rat. "Your hot ass knew him when you snitched on him, Safari Washington. Ricardo Epps my man, fuck you think, he wasn't going to hip me to your bitch ass? He told me to holla at you, but you disappeared before I could get the chance." He backed up two steps. "So go ahead and snitch on this!" D.C. said. He raised his gun and shot the rat several times in the head.

"That nigga was hot, huh?" I asked D.C. as we headed out of the house.

"Yeah, his bitch ass ate the cheese," Zetta's uncle replied before we separated.

Titus threw the pillowcases in the trunk of the DST and we got in and pulled off. After we turned on Brightseat Road, we waited until the Burgundy 350ZX got in front of us and sped up the road.

Titus followed the car to the Boulevard. The place we parked in used to be the old Capitol Center, but it got a make-over. Now the place had a lot of little stores, the twelve-screen Magic Johnson movie theaters, a Sports Authority, and Lavar Arrington's Sports Bar

After getting out of the car, Titus opened the trunk and waited. Second later, we were breaking down $120,000 evenly four ways. The other pillowcase had eight kilos inside. I didn't want to be greedy, so I gave the two kilos they offered me to Titus.

As we headed inside the sports bar, I saw the rat that snitched on Lance "Big Six" Applewhite, a good man I knew who had to do ten years because of this bitch ass heading my way.

CHAPTER 98

As I rushed back to Titus' car to get the baseball bat, my cell phone began ringing. I kept my eyes glued on the rat as he headed inside the sports bar. After he went inside the establishment, I looked at the screen and saw Markita's number. I contemplated whether or not I should answer her call, thinking that she wanted to be a drama queen and start some shit. Then I got to thinking about Twan's nephew and I wanted to know if she was safe.

"Yeah, what you want?"

"Boy, forget you. I'm on my way over my mother's house right now."

"Naw, go 'head and stay there with cho' smart ass. I got Tiny and Kisha on they way over there. They should have been there by now?"

"They came and I sent them on about they business. Don't be sending nobody over here to be checking up on me. What's wron - "

"You did what?" I snapped, cutting her off. "Fuck you do that for, Kita?"

"'Cause I wanted to. I'll call you later on when I get to my mother's house."

"You better…soon as you get there too, you hear me?"

"Yes, Father know-it-all," she replied, sucking her teeth.

"Stop acting all crazy and shit. I only told your ass to go over there for a reason."

"I know…I know…" She sighed. "I'm going already, dang."

"Okay. I love you; make sure you hit me back," I said and hung up.

I checked Chin's e-mail and saw that he wanted me to handle another job for him in the state of Florida.

You doing the shit for free anyway, you might as well get paid to do it. I might as well do it, since I'm officially on the run from the crooked cop and at war with Twan's nephew, I thought while pulling the baseball bat from under the passenger seat.

I got out of the Cadillac DTS, slammed the door, and went back inside the bar, directing all senses, thoughts, and feelings towards eliminating another rat.

It had been a few hours since Detective Gamble and Newsome had seen the streets. Things for them took a turn for the worse at the mall. When the Virginia police detained them without accepting that they were D.C. vice detectives, they realized they had no power in VA's jurisdiction. They also lost a tremendous amount of time in pursuing Carmelo Glover. Their number one problem solver could be halfway to Mexico, for all they knew.

Detectives Gamble and Newsome waited in a dark, dirty, and smelly security holding cell in the back of the mall somewhere discussing the crazy shit going down and how Carmelo Glover outsmarted them.

"I swear I thought we had him. I can't believe that little fuck got away from us!" Newsome complained, punching the graffiti-stained wall.

"As long as he keeps his cell phone on him, he's never going to get away from us," Gamble said, smiling and glad that he made the early move to get the warrant to track Carmelo Glover's cell phone.

"What good is that going to do us if he goes out of town again?" Newsome griped. "We can't keep waiting on this guy to clean up our mess. Sooner or later I.A.D. is going to come for us, so I think we need to start planning something else to get outta this mess."

"No, we stay the course and make Glover kill that ma'fucka. If all else fails, fuck it. We'll just have to do it ourselves. But if Glover does it, we can kill two birds with one stone. We use Glover as the fall guy and arrest him, which will make us look like heroes for taking down a cop killer and take any future heat off us."

"Fuck arresting him," Newsome said. "He knows too much. After he does the killing, we have to kill him, no way around it."

"That'll work too," Gamble agreed with a smile.

When Gamble and Newsome got released, several VA cops along with the mall's security guards apologized to them. They ignored the apologies and started jogging for the nearest exits to get to the car and continue their pursuit of Carmelo.

Once I entered the dimly-lit sports bar, I began my search for the rat. I felt eased by my decision to eliminate the rat before heading out of town to kill again for Chin. This was more like release therapy and a good chance to get revenge for a forgotten man.

I didn't expect to see all these people up in here today. Flat screen TV's all over the bar showed the Miami Heat and Boston Celtics players going through the pre-game warm-up rituals.

As I walked around looking for the rat, D.C., Jawbreaker, and Titus called me over to their table in the dark section. I went over and noticed two flat screen TV's hanging inside a glass wall for the occupants of the table. After taking a seat, I didn't put them on point about my plans to kill. I figured the less they knew, the better for me.

"Fuck you bring that bat up in here for?" Titus asked.

"I'm tryna get it autographed." I smiled all the time, thinking, …with that hot nigga's blood!

D.C. laughed and said, "It ain't no baseball players in here."

"Thanks for the heads up, big guy," I remarked and slid out of the booth. "I took a step back, looking the trio of killers up and down. "I'm gonna go over here by the bar and holla at this lil broad. I'll be back in a minute." I stepped off before they could respond.

While walking around with the baseball bat cuffed beside my thigh, I spotted the rat at the open bar. He laughed and turned a drink up to his lips. After he killed his drink, he gave the woman sitting next to him a peck on the cheek.

While he backed away from woman and the bar, I eased back in the shadows. When the cheers erupted all around the bar, the rat walked off, heading to the restroom. I followed right behind him to make sure he met the promises of death for his betrayal of the street code: NO SNITCHING UNDER ANY CIRCUMSTANCES!

CHAPTER 99

"I'll show you what beef is…
Have me runnin' through the back door of your mom's crib…
Knowin' it might be the same spot where yo' kids live…
Your baby moms known to play the card, so don't play big…"

Little James rapped along with Head's latest single off his Ain't Hard To Find mix tape as he sped out to Virginia to show Carmelo exactly what beef was. Little James felt heated and a little messed up in the head that he had missed his chance to kill Carmelo earlier. Little James figured that if Carmelo didn't get help from the other guys on the block during the shoot-out, he would have finished him right there on the same block where his uncle got killed.

"I got two fifths, four clips, niggas going 'round talkin hoe shit...
Ain't got no cuts who I war with...
You can bring yo' guns and yo' whole clique...
Long as y'all don't come throwing rocks atta whole brick..."

Little James allowed the song to get him pumped up for what he was about to do. He wanted to make Carmelo really suffer for getting away today. He only knew one way to do that, and that was to kill his wife and son.

"I Ain't hard To find. I'm Uptown always wit' a hammer...
Or catch me on that southside right off Alabama...
Where dat drama at...want work, you get over there...
I'm the breeze of death...you can feel it in the air..."

By the time the song reached the second verse, Little James had parked the Lexus right outside of Carmelo's huge house and pulled out his gun. After chambering a round he looked at house and smiled. Without waiting another second, Little James got out of the car with one thing in mind:

"I'll show you what beef is...
Have me runnin' through the back door of your mom's crib...
Knowin' it might be the same spot where yo' kids live...
Your baby moms known to play the card, so don't play big..."

CHAPTER 100

I slipped inside the restroom and looked around. Nobody lingered in the fancy bathroom, which had all the amenities except a service attendant (the people who passed out cologne and fresh hand towels in them fancy spots). I heard the rat whistling and figured that he and I were in here alone - just two men, one official and the other a bitch-made weakling.

Two men enter, one man leaves. That was the only thing running through my mind as the rat's whistling picked up, angering me more and more. As I moved in for the kill, I realized that at this very moment, a good man was going through the strenuous hassles of doing time in the Feds, enduring a bunch of bullshit with the racist C.O's and other prisoners, and just living fucked up all because of this creep just a few yards away taking a piss.

Man is only defined by the decisions he makes. This creep made a very bad decision that defined him as the worst weakling who ever walked the face of the planet. I braced the aluminum baseball bat with both hands while creeping up to the nearest black-painted sheet metal stall. There were six of them in all. I checked the diamond-shaped mirrors across the aisle that faced each stall, trying to zero in on the rat's position.

Checking the first stall, I found it empty. As I moved to the next stall, I spotted movement in the mirror as the whistling got louder. I picked up my pace and rushed towards the white porcelain urinals. I wanted to bring the element of surprise to where the rat stood taking a leak.

He probably never imagined that his life would end today. Nobody does, but to die like this inside a bathroom when you least expect it is fitting enough for someone like the cheese-eating rodent standing inches away from me, I thought while quietly stepping around the last stall. I saw the rat leaning his head back with his eyes closed, enjoying the liquid waste oozing from his body. I raised the bat high over my head and swung down hard. Right before the bat made contact, he opened his eyes one second too late.

Biiinnnng! The baseball bat connected with the crown of his head and echoed in the restroom. The impact of the blow knocked the rat to the ground instantly.

"Ahhhhh! Aaaah!" he screamed as I stepped around him, trying to get in a better position to whack his ass again.

"Shut the fuck up, you hot-ass nigga!" I said as I swung the bat again at his head.

Biiinnng!

"Snitch on this!" I said before bashing his skull in one more time.

When he began twitching and shaking on the ground like someone having a seizure, I knew I had nailed him good with three hard blows that would've sent any fast ball right out of the ballpark. I dragged him from the urinals by his yellow Polo shirt and kicked him in the face.

"You thought Lance wasn't gonna get no get-back on your hot ass, huh?"

When he didn't respond, I began stomping him brutally. Seeing him bleeding from the head and face made me feel a little better about being shot at earlier by Twan's nephew. I really wished this rat was Twan's nephew, but he wasn't. He was just another guy to take my pain and anger out on.

"Your bitch ass did the crime…"

I swung the baseball bat.

Biiiinng! The sound echoed again, and blood and some green slimy stuff shot out of the rat's head. That's when I knew the baseball bad had cracked open the rat's skull.

"You like talking, bitch nigga!

Say something now!" I snapped

I raised the baseball bat and prepared to give the blow of death. As I began my swing, the bathroom door burst open, startling me.

"PG police! Freeze! Drop the bat right now and step away from the man!" the caramel-complexioned plainclothes cop demanded.

Looking at the black man aiming his service Glock at my head, I felt the fear consuming me and pouring from my trembling hand. As my heart got caught in my throat, I realized I was through booking even before I made it to my first court appearance.

The way the cop locked his gun's aim, cornering me, I knew that I had finally reached the end of my road. The way he caught me red-handed in mid-swing would allow any jury in Upper Marlboro, Maryland to find me guilty of all charges.

All I could hope for now was that this rat didn't die on me. If he did, I was shit outta luck. I dropped the bat to raise my hands in surrender.

CHAPTER 101

With the .45 drawn and revenge embedded in his heart, Little James walked up to the huge house in the VA residential community. As the sun's rays beamed down on the area, Little James crept around the back of the house and eased next to a window leading to the kitchen. The cracked window seemed like a blessing in disguise and an open invitation.

After staring inside the empty kitchen for a moment, Little James raised the window and stepped back. He looked around the spacious backyard at the red-painted dog house and brown wooden kiddy play, waiting for someone to show up. He waited for a few minutes to make sure nobody entered the kitchen before going back over to the window.

Oh where, oh where have your little son and wifey gone? Oh where, oh where can they be Carmelo? Little James wondered before climbing through the window. He landed on the sink and countertop, pausing for a second to look around. Realizing the coast was clear, Little James eased quietly off the sink and countertop.

He raised the .45 up like one does at the shooting range before creeping down the hallway leading from the kitchen. The sun lit up the hallway as he rushed through the house. When he reached the spacious living room, Little James aimed the gun around the empty room cautiously.

Oh where, oh where has your little family gone? Oh where, oh where can they be? he wondered, hoping Carmelo's wifey and son were still inside the house so he could kill them as planned.

Markita looked at the clock hanging on the bathroom wall over the huge mirror. She couldn't believe so much time had passed since her last phone call with Carmelo. Going with Carmelo's decision to leave her home had really upset her because for one, she'd just moved back in, and secondly and most importantly, being submissive to a man had never really been her thing. Her last conversation with Carmelo made her come around a little bit and take the trip over to her mom's like he suggested after she handled her business. All she cared about at the moment was giving her child a nice hot bath so he'd be good and tired by the time she reached her mother's house.

From her spot in the sandy stone-hued octagon Jacuzzi bathtub, Markita looked at the clock again, knowing Carmelo wouldn't approve of her hanging around the house after he told her to leave. She decided to put her finishing touches on the bath so she could leave. As she applied a subtle amount of baby shampoo to her son's scalp, she could have sworn she heard a strange noise.

"Ma-ma!" Her son laughed as she got scared and began looking around the bathroom, wondering if she had enough time to grab something to defend her child and herself.

After checking every room downstairs, Little James still didn't find any sign of Carmelo's family. He decided to check upstairs. As he reached the top of the stairs and eased into the first bedroom, Little James heard water splashing in the nearby bedroom.

"Ma-ma." He heard a baby voice laughing and rushed towards the sounds, ready to crush something.

He opened the bathroom door and looked inside. She sat right there before him, butt naked and bathing her son in the Jacuzzi-style tub that looked like it could have been carved from a huge mountain boulder. Little James stared at Markita's succulent breasts and hard nipples that looked good enough to eat, which made him a little excited. He wanted to fuck her before the kill.

Markita glanced up and nearly had a heart attack. "Aaaahhhhhhhh!" she screamed, startling her son. He jumped and began crying.

"I'm really happy to see you too, sexy," Little James quipped, aiming the .45 at Markita's head while she cradled her son protectively, covering up her breasts.

Little James could tell the moment he looked into her eyes that fear had frozen her, making him feel very good and in control.

"Pl-please…D-don't hurt us," Markita begged and began crying.

"I hafta, sexy. You fucking the wrong nigga," he told her over the wailing sounds of the baby while fingering the trigger. "Outta here now! And shut his little bitch ass up before I do!"

Markita obeyed and moved quickly. She finally stood outside the bathtub holding her son, fully exposed and trying to get him to stop crying.

"Shh…shhh..shh… It's okay, baby, Mommy's got you, I'm here!" she whispered in his ear before kissing him on his cheeks and lips to calm him down.

Damn, this bitch phat as shit. I gots to sample that pussy before I smoke her ass, he thought as he moved closer to her, keeping his eyes on her pretty-shaped pussy lips, which had water dripping from them.

Little James looked in Markita's eyes while she trembled. He took the gun and used the barrel to trace the mouth of her vagina. After easing the gun from her wet slit, he eased the deadly weapon up her wet, shapely body. When the gun barrel reached the baby's body, Little James placed the gun against the baby's curly mane.

"Pleeasseee, no…please, God!" She flinched backwards, shaking like a leaf on a tree during a windstorm.

Markita tried to take a step back, and when she did, Little James gave her a vicious backhand slap across the mouth that drew blood. The powerful impact from the sudden blow knocked Markita down on the smooth, rocky-looking heated floors.

"Pleaasseee!" she cried, tasting the warm blood inside in her mouth while holding her baby in her arms. She looked up at him with sad, pleading eyes.

Looking around to the left and then to the right, Little James took a step back and aimed the .45 at Markita's head. He knew right then that he couldn't rape her and leave his DNA on the scene of a double homicide. He could just picture the police coming to arrest him immediately if he went that route. Another thing he envisioned which made him smile was Carmelo posted up at the funeral in mourning over the loss of his wife and precious child.

That would definitely be a sight to behold, he thought, looking at the woman crying and raising up a hand to shield her son's eyes. Little James caught her timid stare, and for a long moment, it seemed as if time stood still between then. Then he smirked, sending chills down her spine.

"W-wait! Wait! I ca-can - "

"Help me show Carmelo what beef is!" He cut her off and felt nothing but pure elation as he fondled the trigger.

Licking his lips, Little James looked Markita dead in the eyes, his smile disappearing as he lowered the gun. In his heart, he knew to kill them was wrong. But something about killing the woman and child to avenge his uncle's death compelled him to lift the .45 back up and take aim.

"Pl-please. No…please!" she cried.

"Sorry, sexy, but it's all Carmelo's fault. He did this to y'all." He pulled the trigger, letting destiny take its course.

About The Author

Nathan was born in Washington, DC and was found guilty in 1996 and sentenced to a lenghty prison sentence. Over the past decade, Nathan has been entertaining various inmates with his page-turning Urban Tales. He is tha author of Wrong Move, A Killer'z Ambition 1 and 2, and No Turnin. Nathan is hard at work and will be releasing several projects with DC Bookdiva Publications in the near future.

DC Bookdiva Publications
#245 4401-A Connecticut Avenue, NW
Washington, DC 20008

Name: ____________________

Inmate ID ____________________

Address: ____________________

City/State: ____________________ **Zip:** ______

QUANTITY	TITLES	PRICE	TOTAL
	Dynasty, Dutch	$15.00	
	Dynasty 2, Dutch	$15.00	
	Dynasty 3, Dutch	$15.00	
	Que, Dutch	$15.00	
	Secrets Never Die, Eyone Williams	$15.00	
	A Beautiful Satan, RJ Champ	$15.00	
	A Beautiful Satan 2, RJ Champ	$15.00	
	The Commission, Team DCB	$15.00	
	Tina, Darrell Debrew	$15.00	
	Trina, Darrell Debrew	$15.00	
	Smokin Mirrors	$15.00	
	The Hustler's Daughter	$15.00	
	The Hustle, Frazier Boy	$15.00	
	Lorton Legends, Eyone Williams	$15.00	

Shipping/Handling (Via US Media Mail) $3.95 1-2 Books, $7.95 1-3 Books, 4 or more titles-Free Shipping

Shipping $ __________

Total Enclosed $ __________

Certified or government issued checks and money orders, all mail in orders take 5-7 Business days to be delivered. Books can also be purchased on our website at dcbookdiva.com and by credit card at 1866-928-9990. Incarcerated readers receive 25% discount. Please pay $11.25 per book and apply the same shipping terms as stated above